DISASTER-IN-WAITING

Elle M Thomas

First published 2017

Cover design: QDesign
Editing: Bookfully Yours

This is an Elle M Thomas mature, contemporary romance.
Anyone who has read my work before will know what that
means, but if you're new to me then let me explain.
This book includes adult situations including, but not limited to:
adult characters that swear, a lot. A leading man who talks dirty,
really, really dirty. Sex, lots and lots of hot, steamy, sheet
gripping and toe curling sex. Due to the dark and explicit nature
of this book, it is recommended for mature audiences only.
If this is not what you want to read about then this might not be
the book for you, but if it is then sit back, buckle up and enjoy
the ride.

Other titles by Elle M Thomas:

One Night Or Forever
Revealing His Prize

Acknowledgements

For as long as I can remember I have threatened to write a book and that's quite a long time! But rather than write I chose to read, a lot. I found brilliant authors, characters and stories but then I found myself imagining new characters, different plots and the die was cast.

That was about four, maybe five years ago. I decided to put my money where my mouth was and write the story I wanted to read. So after many stories were written, some unfinished, Disaster-in-Waiting was born.

I truly love this story and its characters and can honestly say it has been a real labour of love. My dream is that you might enjoy reading my words as much as I have enjoyed writing them.

I could never have achieved any of this without the love and support of my family so my thanks and undying love go to them; my parents who never put a ceiling on what I could do or who I could become, to my nearest and dearest who have offered love and support and never once complained about the amount of time I spend on my computer and my wonderful children who quickly grew to understand and wait patiently for me to 'just finish this paragraph' when they needed my time.

Finally, love and thanks to my small group of writing friends who have encouraged and supported my decision to self-publish through all of the panic and bouts of serious self-doubt. Ladies, we will forever be #authorsontour

Chapter One

My friends, the ones I had at that point warned me that I was marrying my dad and I had no issue with that, none at all. Michael was older than me, by thirty years, but when I was twenty-three he seemed awfully exotic with his greater knowledge and experience of, well, everything. He represented all the positives of a good dad in my mind; he was caring, protective, and considerate of my needs and wants, and he offered me security and safety, although like an overindulgent father he did spoil me, showering me with gifts and material possessions. I smiled with a still disbelieving shake of my head as I remembered how he had once bought me a new car because my old car, which was less than a year old was dirty. But here I was almost six years later married to my dad, or at least a dad, a man who played golf, often, read, a lot and not even works of fiction, big books on real life, history, geography, architecture, things I had no interest in. That was fine though. He had no issues with my interests, not that I had many, so I reciprocated.

My issue was sex, or lack thereof. If memory served me right, which it did, it had been six months since he'd touched me intimately and another six months since we'd had sex, real sex and at twenty-eight I wanted sex. Needed it. Craved it. After a few health scares after hitting fifty-five Michael had lost confidence and stamina so he'd distanced himself from me physically and as much as I wanted my needs fulfilling I didn't feel able to complain. Especially not as I knew how guilty my husband felt about his inability to satisfy my most basic needs.

He had been my boss, not my immediate boss, but my

4

ultimate boss. He had owned the whole company I'd worked for, Stanton Industries, not that I understood what the business was, not really. I worked as a secretary for a middle manager in accounts on the seventh floor and Michael ran the whole shebang from his floor, the top floor, the twentieth where he occupied a corner office that looked out across the whole city. I didn't really know that when I was plain old Eloise Ross, although I was still Eloise Ross at work, having resisted the temptation to become Mrs Stanton in all areas of my life. Today I was to return there as P.A. to the new CEO having left my post there after marrying five years ago. I had been desperate to gain promotions and recognition in my own right, not for being married to the boss, which I'd done. Michael was no longer the boss, not since the downturn in his health when he'd made the decision to sell the company to a bigger conglomerate, Miller Industries.

"Darling, I've made you some tea. We don't want you to be late on your first day, do we?"

I smiled at my husband's kindness as I gave myself a final once over, dressed professionally in a black pencil skirt and a white silk blouse. I had opted for tights so I wouldn't be worrying all day that I was flashing stocking tops at my new boss, Denton Miller Snr who I had yet to meet in person. Along with commendations from my husband and a few webcam and Skype conversations I had decided that he was a boss I would enjoy working for.

Denton was of a similar age to Michael, but unlike my husband he had been married for thirty odd years to his teenage sweetheart and was living the American dream with his main home in California but numerous other residences around the world, seemingly in the cities that housed the offices of his vast business empire. Michael, by contrast had been married three times before me and I was the only wife not to have given him a child. Although sex would be required for a baby meaning that I was only a stepmother to four; two girls from wife number one, both older than me by a year and two years. His sons were aged twenty and fourteen with wives two and three respectively. God, I was like his middle child I realised with a smile, a smile that evaporated as I remembered I was also a step-nanny to three children under five and then he called me again.

"El, come on, Denton is a stickler for punctuality," he reminded me for the hundredth time causing me to bristle slightly.

"Yes, I know. I'm coming!" I screeched slipping black heeled shoes onto my feet but Michael laughed, annoying me further.

"If I was a jealous man those claims might offend me Mrs Stanton," he added as I appeared before him in the kitchen where my tea was waiting for me.

"What?" I asked impatiently, confused by his words.

"You shouted, *I'm coming.*"

Unsure how to react and thinking that if I did I might say something to open the can of worms that represented our lack of a sex life, I simply accepted the cup of tea and killed another ten minutes or so before dropping a kiss to Michael's head as I left the house.

****

Upon entering my former place of employment that was now my current place of employment I noted that very little appeared to have changed, except for the new signage.

"Hey there stranger," called the receptionist as I arrived on my new floor, my husband's old floor.

I spun to find a former colleague and friend, Maya, looking back at me with a grin spread across her face.

"What the bloody hell are you doing here?" I asked as I hugged the other woman, glad to find a friendly face. "Michael never mentioned you were back here."

"First day, babe. You remember I went to Provence with Aaron?"

I nodded, remembering her leaving a couple of years before with her boyfriend who had also worked for Michael but after his divorce was finalised decided to travel.

"Yeah, well that was great for a while, right up to the point where I found Aaron was indulging in some serious online shenanigans."

"No way!"

"Way babe. So, I packed up, after paying the astronomical internet bill. My oldest sister still works here, in H.R. so she offered to put my C.V. forward and here I am, receptionist for the exec floor and I believe you are Mr Miller's P.A.?"

"Yes, first day too."

"So, you and Mr Stanton…"

I could see that what Maya really wanted to ask was, 'are you still married to the old man?'

"Michael is at home."

"Ah," she replied dropping her glance to my narrow gold wedding ring. "I heard he'd been unwell."

"Yes," I confirmed. "He had some heart trouble that required surgery, but he's on the mend," I added with a smile that not even I was convinced by. "Look, I should go, apparently my new boss doesn't like lateness."

"Okay, later, we'll catch up."

At ten o'clock I wondered if Mr Miller was one of those, 'do as I say, not as I do' bosses because he was a no show and I was over an hour and a half into my day. I considered calling Michael to ask him if I should be concerned, but decided against it. Another hour and then I would attempt to contact Denton Miller.

Another hour came and went, however as I was engrossed in a stationery delivery I was unaware of anything that wasn't made of paper until it was almost one o'clock when Maya appeared in my doorway.

"Do you want to grab lunch?" she asked as I stood up and faced her, still flushed from my exertion unpacking new paperwork.

"You'd have thought that such a forward thinking company would rely on electronic copies of this shit," I observed, opening yet another box of compliment slips.

"Lunch?" Maya repeated causing me to check out the clock on the wall behind my desk.

"No way, is that the time already? Where the hell is the boss? I should call him, he could be ill or have had an accident." I panicked, grabbed the phone on my desk and hit the speed dial that had already been pre-programmed to my boss' mobile first, or cell as my directory had it listed as. Well, he was American I supposed as I heard the tone that seemed to ring forever before connecting to what I had anticipated being an answer phone.

"You've reached Denton Miller's den of debauchery and iniquity. Unfortunately Mr Miller is unable to come to the phone right now as he is busy between my thighs, can I take a message?" the voice asked, the voice of a woman I was fairly certain wouldn't belong to Mrs Miller, so who was she, with her soft and subtle American accent that sang with amusement?

"I erm, sorry, I'm, my name is P.A., well not, I, erm," I stammered while Maya watched on with a horrified expression that was in stark contrast to her grin. With a deep breath and a wipe of my free sweaty palm down my thigh I composed myself and tried again. "This is Eloise, Eloise Ross, Mr Miller's P.A. He was expected in his office this morning..." I allowed my voice to trail off so that my words might register when I heard another voice on the end of the line, a man's voice.

"Tia, what are you doing? How many times have I told you, do not answer my phone? That's not your place."

I glared down at the receiver in my hand wondering how my husband had got his views on my new boss so wrong. Arrogant prick I thought, except when I heard Tia giggle down the line and Maya stifle a laugh with a gulp, I realised that I had said it, out loud.

"It's your office, your P.A.," Tia explained. "Checking up on the boss."

This woman was also a pain in the arse, her and my new boss, maybe they were meant for each other.

"No, no," I stammered before I heard Mr Miller's reply.

"I don't need checking up on. I'm going in now, as per the email I sent to my P.A. Could this day get any worse?" he asked as I flushed crimson despite him being unable to see me.

"Did you get that, honey?" Tia asked still laughing.

"Yeah, got it, thank you, sorry, sorry to have interrupted your erm, sorry," I cried and hung up. "Oh bollocks, his day has nothing on mine!" I told Maya slumping into my chair.

"And you kind of hung up on him at the end there." She smiled with an accompanying cringe.

"Oh God! Why am I even doing this? He was so sweet on webcam," I said, thinking aloud.

"With Mr Stanton?"

I buried my face in my hands. "Shit, yeah. He was with a woman, maybe not his wife and like with her with her I think." My whispered realisation made Maya laugh loudly.

"So, to sum up, you have inarticulately interrupted a secret shag, somehow made it sound like he was a naughty boy by being late and then hung up on him?"

My horrified expression must have conveyed how awful I felt because Maya appeared before me on her haunches.

"It wasn't that bad babe. He'll be fine, I'm sure. Come on, lunch." Getting to her feet she pulled me to mine. "Come on, no arguments, we'll go to the pub over the road, no alcohol, just food."

Nodding, I grabbed my things and then quickly checked my emails, only to find an earlier email from my boss.

Morning Ms Ross,

I was hoping to be in before you this morning, but I had to change plans.

Will be very late afternoon so may not get to meet you until tomorrow as I have a busy day planned.

Regards,

Denton Miller
CEO Miller Industries (Europe)

"Oh," I whispered almost undetected as a second email hit my inbox.

Ms Ross,

Thank you for the nurse maid duties, however

unnecessary they were. I am able to tell the time and arrive at the office without assistance!

After further changes to my first day I may not make it into the office at all today.

I shall expect to see you in the morning no later than 8 a.m.

Oh, and Ms Ross, don't ever fucking hang up on me!

Denton Miller
CEO Miller Industries (Europe)

"He's really got to be kidding me, hasn't he?" I asked pulling Maya to see my second email, but she literally just squealed with some kind of delight.

"I think I am going to enjoy working here, a boss that emails with swearing and a bollocking! Come on, lunch, I only have cover on reception for one hour, meaning we now have exactly forty seven minutes to be back here."

****

Every mouthful of my linguini that tasted like shoe laces rather than pasta got stuck where I imagined my gullet might be, even with the assistance of two glasses of a non-alcoholic beverage.

"Do you think he'll sack me?" I asked Maya who had no problems digesting her food that was a steak and ale pie with seasonal vegetables and seriously chunky chips.

"No, I wouldn't have thought the interruption of a mid coital rendezvous with his mistress would be classed as a sackable offence."

"Thanks," I replied, wondering what else I could say to that and decided there was no more to say.

I returned to my office, which was actually a working space within Mr Miller's office space. I suppose it could be seen that I occupied his vestibule or an atrium, the space between his inner sanctum and the world beyond, although as this space happened to be at the furthest point of the building everywhere else was the world beyond. I liked that a small amount of reworking had been done up here so I didn't mistake the office as Michael's, it was Mr Miller's and I couldn't, wouldn't forget my place. As well as my work space, this area also housed his reception area, the place where I'd be responsible for entertaining any visitors who were waiting for my boss. Maybe if he was finishing off Tia, or whoever.

With I sigh I observed the boxes of stationery that still littered my floor and decided to tackle them, get to the bottom of it all, just not yet. After a cup of coffee, if I could find where the coffee machine was housed. Yes, that was a plan. Coffee, and just in case my wayward boss turned up I'd take my photocopying down the hall with me and make myself look busy.

It was another forty-five minutes before I found myself back at my desk, with coffee and the photocopied proposals that Mr Miller would need later in the week. The mess on my floor was worse than I had remembered. Could this day get any worse I wondered once more as another email hit my inbox?

Ms Ross,

You appear to have littered the floor with semi-unpacked boxes of stationery, please resolve this issue. Also, why do we have such a ridiculous amount of compliment slips and headed paper? We live in an age of electronic communication. I think you may have overstocked somewhat. Again, resolve before tomorrow morning.

I am out for the day. In the event of an emergency, I repeat, EMERGENCY you may call me!

I take my tea with just a dash of milk, no sugar, and coffee no milk, one sugar. I drink tea until 10 a.m. and coffee thereafter, unless I instruct you otherwise.

Regards,

11

Denton Miller
CEO Miller Industries (Europe)

"Fucking numb nuts," I told him even though I was alone. The cheek of this man. "I have semi-unpacked the stationery that was ordered by someone else, not me, and I know we live in an age of electronic communications, so I have not overstocked anything and yet I am expected to sort it. I will call you when hell freezes over after my initial attempt at contact and on top of that I am now your tea girl!"

The sound of my phone's ring brought me back to the here and now, Michael.

"Hi, you okay?" I answered.

"Yes, just checking in. How's your day going?" he asked and as much as I wanted to vent I knew he wouldn't get it. He'd turn everything on its head and blame me. Not me personally, but my position, so I replied accordingly.

"The new boss had a change of plan. He appears to have popped in, a visit I missed and now he's not in until tomorrow, but things are fine."

"You don't sound sure? Maybe you should think about scaling back, love."

Oh my God! I actually wanted to scream at him because he was the retired one, not me, I wasn't even half way there. Why the hell would I want to scale back, but as usual he continued to speak.

"There's a group, at the hospital, a support group for families. You could help them out, or Johnny at the golf club was saying they're looking to take on a part timer to help with memberships…"

I cut him off, abruptly. "Michael, I don't want to scale back, nor work at the golf club, nor listen to people discuss how hard it is to, well, whatever. Denton Miller may prove to be more of a challenge than I had first imagined, but it's fine. What do you fancy doing this evening?" I asked hoping he'd say something exciting, different to the norm, maybe even dinner, alcohol, a bath and an early night.

"I'm easy, whatever you want darling, although there is a documentary on the demise of the bee on at half-past eight so I'd like to be done by then."

"And an early night?" I suggested, hating myself a little for pleading for his time, attention and his penis. This day really was turning to shit.

"El, I don't know, we'll see," he said, the dismissal obvious in his tone.

"I might be going out straight from work," I lied. "Maya is back here, she's the exec's receptionist now, so I thought we might catch up, in the pub, or a bar or something."

I was slightly disgusted with myself for lying so blatantly to my husband. Something I'd never done, about plans that didn't exist, but the mere thought of sitting and listening to a blow by blow account of why bees were disappearing made me want to cry. Almost as much as the idea of drinking cocoa before finding myself sitting up in bed reading stories of passion and romance while my husband slept next to me, snoring, having managed to fall asleep in the time it took me to wash my face and brush my teeth.

"Oh, okay, well let me know when you've decided what you're doing, and remember me to Maya."

"Okay," I whispered before guiltily but honestly adding, "I love you, Michael."

"I know darling, and I love you too."

Throwing my phone into my bag I felt shittier than I might have ever felt, but more than that I felt discontent, sad and restless, and possibly a little reckless.

Chapter Two

My lies were in vain it seemed when Maya informed me that she was unable to catch up further in the pub as it was her dad's birthday and she was expected to visit. When faced with the prospect of going home to Michael I decided that a drink alone might not be the worst thing in the world and if one drink turned into two, or three or more, then I knew my car was safe in the company's secure car park and I could call a taxi. So, with that in mind I made the choice to go out alone, not back to the pub across the road but to a bar a few blocks away where I'd been a few times in the past with friends from my old firm.

****

The bar was always a cross between a rowdy pub and a club, and it hadn't changed, with its well-stocked bar and a small dance floor that had a resident DJ who was doing a fine line in dance tracks.

I ordered myself a beer and sat at the bar, still dressed in my work clothes. A couple of men attempted to chat me up and buy me a drink, but I wasn't interested. I simply told them I was married and able to buy my own drinks.

I was on my second beer when I recognised the song starting and virtually ran to the dance floor where there were only two girls of around nineteen dancing together. I smiled thinking they were only missing the handbags on the floor to really look like they belonged at a school disco.

As I began to move all thoughts of anyone else disappeared. It was just me and Jason Derulo telling me all about how he wants to want me. I have never had any inhibitions on the dance floor so threw myself into the rhythm and beat, letting it vibrate through me, thrumming through my veins, making me come to life. As the song merged into a high energy remix of David Guetta and Akon singing about a Sexy Bitch I remembered dancing to it before I married Michael and suddenly I morphed into that woman. The woman I was and although I was sure nobody else was really aware of me I couldn't help but feel that somebody was watching me and then a body came up behind me. A solid body that smelled beyond divine; woody, citrusy and masculine.

An arm snaked around my middle and pulled me back firmly against solid planes of muscle. His mouth found my ear to sing the lyrics to me; something about being a diva, like a girl never seen before and being a sexy bitch. I had no clue who this man was, but the fact that he was singing to me while we danced was a major turn on for me. I had a vague recollection of Michael singing to me when we were first married, but it was a song I had never heard of. My dance companion's second hand had wrapped around me, but this one sat on my hip, slowly smoothing its way down to my thigh, possibly testing the waters as I recognised Sweat, another David Guetta number and pushed all thoughts of my husband from my head.

I don't know that anyone, any man had ever made me feel that way before. My whole body had an awareness of the one behind me. I was reacting to his every movement, each and every breath arousing me into something of a frenzy. The fine hairs across my body were standing on end, I was flushed from my cheeks to my neck and down across my chest and I was hot. Burning, everywhere. My nipples were pebbling into hard points and as much as I wanted to dismiss it all, I just couldn't, because the dampness between my thighs would bear testament to the fact that I was seriously turned on, in the middle of a dancefloor with a stranger. The feel of the hands on my body were making me sweat and then some, however I didn't want it to end so I reached behind me to find my companion's hip and pulled him closer until the song ended, when he whispered against my ear.

"Do you have any idea how close you are to getting fucked right here, right now?" There was a gruffness to his voice that suggested arousal and then as if reading my mind he pulled me back against an obvious erection. "But I think you know that. You like the idea of that, having that effect on me and every other man in this place."

I made no attempt to put any distance between us, nor did I dispute his accusation about liking the idea of my effect on him, but I did look around for the first time and realised that I must have been putting on something of a show judging by how many sets of eyes were watching me.

"Come on." My dance partner grabbed my hand, his back suddenly in front of me as he led us away. Down a corridor, up a short flight of steps, not stopping until we passed through a couple of staff only doors and then into an office with a large window overlooking the bar, including the dance floor.

I quickly found myself being pushed against it, looking down at the hustle and bustle of the Monday night revellers drinking and dancing and experienced a brief moment of panic that they could all see me.

"One way glass, baby. We look out, they can't look in."

"Ah."

The effects of my two beers and the music were wearing off and I had begun to return to my sensible, safe and married self. A state my *friend* sensed and disapproved of if the speed with which he moved was anything to go by. Suddenly, the music was back, all around me, us. The beat hit me instantly, causing my body to relax and then he was behind me once more. His hands explored me over my clothes, his fingers skimming across my behind, hips, thighs and then back up, covering my spine, sides and shoulders before curving around the front of my body.

"Can I see you?" I asked as one hand skated over my breast, pausing to skim my fully clothed, eager nipple with his thumb.

"See me?" He laughed against the back of my neck and for the first time I noticed an accent, Canadian maybe.

"Yes, let me look at you, first," I clarified and allowed the meaning of those words to sink in.

"First? Sure." He released me briefly so that he could spin me to face him.

"Wow," I stammered as I took in the sheer beauty of the

man before me and he really was beautiful, too beautiful.

He towered over me, a good foot taller, putting him at around six feet two, and broad, muscular, a 'works out at the gym' rather than body builder shape. His eyes were big and brown, rich chocolate you could dive into, and happily drown in. Then there was his hair. Dark, dark brown, almost black hair that curled into his neck slightly but styled so that it was a glorious mess of product and good DNA. It didn't occur to me at the time to question how we came to be here, in the office, and neither did it occur to me to question his mode of dress, a three-piece dark grey suit, a startling white shirt and a red tie with matching hankie in his pocket.

"Wow yourself baby, but enough seeing and looking." He grinned, revealing a perfect set of straight, white teeth, and oh my God, he was even more beautiful than before, if that was even possible. Surely that degree of beauty should have been made illegal at some point.

Before another thought could enter my head, I was being spun back to the window.

"Hands on the window baby," he demanded and immediately I complied as he put a foot between mine and kicked my feet apart, spreading my legs a little.

"I, erm," I muttered thinking that I should probably explain that I was married and how out of character this behaviour was for me.

"Ssh, no more talking," he told me with a nip against my ear. "Now, let's just rearrange a little."

I felt my skirt being lifted until it was bunched around my middle and as I heard his *tut* in my ear I remembered I was wearing tights, making me a little cross with myself. Tights were never an attractive thing.

"Shame, I was hoping for thigh highs, stockings, but…" He hummed, dropping behind me to slide my tights down my behind and legs revealing the tight, lace, Brazilian brief I'd chosen to wear. "Very nice."

With a smile at his compliment I allowed him to slip my feet from my shoes, my tights from my feet and then he replaced my shoes to remove my pants, leaving me bare. Feeling him rise he pressed against my back as he reached round to undo my blouse.

"In other circumstances I would rip this open, popping your buttons until they're flying across the room, but I can't send you home with your tits out, can I?"

I offered no answer, I just willed him to hurry before I backed out or exploded. Who was I kidding? There was no way I was backing out of this. The sensation of hands everywhere was unexpected. Fingers tracing down my body again until they settled on my behind. Another kick to my foot suggested I should open them a little wider.

"Spread, those sexy fucking legs!" he hissed making me swallow hard as I realised I was not going to back out of this. I was about to commit adultery and I felt no guilt, only excitement. More excitement than I could ever remember feeling, so much that it had my legs trembling, my nipples stiffening further and liquid arousal running down my thighs.

I gasped as the sensation of being filled hit me. With no preamble I was pulsing around two thick fingers. My fingers grasped in front of me, but with only a sheet of glass I found nothing to cling to.

"You fucking like that, don't you?" His fingers pumped in and out of me, leaving me panting. "You are so wet baby. So fucking desperate for this."

Michael had never done this, the talking. Not like this. My husband, in the days when we had sex would tell me how beautiful I was from time to time or that he loved me. Never how wet and desperate I was.

By contrast, I remained silent. Although there was no denying just how much I was enjoying the dialogue, not that I could ever do the same and I hoped he wouldn't expect me to. I'd be horrified to be that open and exposed.

"You're so fucking close already. I can feel all of these muscles hugging me, pulling me in closer, begging to be stretched and worked until you're coming all around me. God, you're fucking tight, let's see if you can take more," he tormented, withdrawing slightly and then added another finger before pushing his way back in.

The stretch of my flesh burned, causing me to fidget in an

attempt to what, get away? But the almost painful burn had me panting and pushing into his hand, desperate for more and he delivered.

"Oh you are a dirty girl, aren't you? I bet there's nothing you wouldn't do right now to make me fuck you, is there?"

He bit into the flesh of my neck making me cry out in ecstasy and pain. It quickly became clear that I was expected to reply.

I didn't know what to say or do and somehow ended up asking, "Do you kiss your mother with that mouth?"

I was relieved when he laughed and then shocked by his response. "I do, just not when I have the taste of a woman's pussy on my breath."

With that he removed his fingers from me, spun me to face him so I could see his fingers disappearing into his mouth. My eyes must have been like saucers as I watched him suck my juices of arousal from his fingers, three of them. His fingers dropped to his belt after leaving his mouth and before I could process it his trousers and boxers were being pushed down his thighs and then his hands were rolling a condom down his length. His considerable length that had my eyebrows raising and my breathing erratic. His hands suddenly grabbed at my thighs, lifting me up the window before lowering me so that I hovering above him.

"I am going to fuck your brains out baby, and if you're a good girl I'll make you come until you scream and then I might just do it again. Would you like that?" he asked and still I struggled to find my voice. "Answer me or that will go against you being the good girl who comes," he chastened with a clear threat.

"Yes, I'd like it," was my awfully tame response but he just smiled at me as he dropped me onto him, forcing me to take his whole length quickly. I sucked in air as I absorbed the sting as I was stretched again.

My companion was moving, slow and steady as he gripped my behind, digging his fingers into the flesh of my ample bottom making me think that I might end up with bruises. Even that didn't make me reconsider what I was doing, nor did it make me think of Michael who was most likely absorbed by the documentary telling him all about the demise of bees.

"Touch yourself," he demanded as I felt the stirrings of climax coiling low in my belly.

"What?" I was flustered by confusion as much as arousal.

"Baby, I think we can safely say you're not a sweet and innocent virgin, so stop playing coy." He slammed into me harshly but if he'd intended to cause me some discomfort he was going to be disappointed because his harsh words and rough movements only excited me further.

I was confused and embarrassed as I felt my internal muscles squeezing around him.

"I rest my case," he almost sneered as he felt my body react to him. "Touch yourself, play with yourself, your tits, pinch and pull them baby, show me."

The flush across my face, neck and chest burned intensely and yet still I found my fingers stroking across my nipples through my lacy bra.

"You have fantastic tits, keep doing that, tease them, and tease yourself."

I said nothing, but as instructed I continued. I skimmed a finger beneath the lace cup, allowing the briefest contact of skin on skin. The pad of my forefinger touched my nipple making me groan and arch into my new friend.

"Dirty, dirty girl, but not yet. Not unless you want me to bend you over and smack your ass, hard!"

The threat of that was less scary than I would have expected as my body reacted to the words and began to quicken further as I became slicker by the second.

"Oh yes, you'd fucking like that, wouldn't you? I hope you're not going to present me with a bill when we're done," he laughed.

He had just called me a whore, a prostitute? Even that was an aphrodisiac.

"Right then baby, get those tits out, let's see what you can do with them."

I used both hands to lift my breasts from my bra and allowed them to sit on the wires, forcing them up, making them appear perky.

"Pinch your nipples, pull them, hard."

His demands were unexpected and alien at the same time, and yet again, as I had at every turn tonight, I did exactly as instructed. At that moment I realised that I had no name for the man currently buried inside me and it didn't seem to matter, not beyond the fact that I would have really liked to use his name to encourage him to move faster.

I could feel how close I was and I think he sensed it too as he answered my unspoken request to move with hard strokes that had him virtually pulling free of me before pushing back in fully, hard and brutal.

"Come on, come on," he spat through gritted teeth. "Give it to me, come all over my dick, baby," he demanded as a finger and thumb found my clit and pinched it. And just like that, I fell apart, splintered before his deep and questioning eyes, screaming, crying out inaudible words and sentiments.

I felt spent as I realised his mouth was slanting across mine, taking it, possessing it, possessing me as his tongue invaded my mouth, duelling for the win. I didn't doubt he would be the victor, especially when he bit down into my bottom lip making me whimper until I tasted blood that had me digging my nails into his shoulders, nails I hadn't realised had made their way beneath his jacket and waistcoat so that only his shirt separated my fingers from his skin.

"Oh yeah, you deserve another orgasm, with me."

I wasn't convinced that after the last one I'd be capable of another. I wasn't really a multiple orgasm kind of girl and the first one had been pretty outstanding, so much so that I was still struggling to see straight, never mind think straight. I really had never felt anything quite like that. The pressure of fingers squeezing my bottom was increased and a set of lips found their way to my neck, nipping and kissing my skin as his strokes shortened. Stoking the orgasmic aftershocks I was still experiencing, pushing me back to the precipice I'd already fallen off. I was close, I just needed the final nudge and what a nudge I received in the form of lips dropping to my left nipple that became encompassed in wet heat and then the gentle scrape of teeth before a hard bite and finally my world exploded and imploded simultaneously.

I had no clue how long I remained wrapped around the guy who really had fucked my brains out if my inability to think, focus or see was anything to go by, but suddenly I was sitting on a sofa, still semi-dressed.

"Beer?" he asked, appearing before me carrying two bottles of beer.

"Thanks," I replied, suddenly uncomfortable as I returned my breasts to the confines of my bra, breathing deeply at the ache I found when I touched myself. I refastened my blouse before ensuring my skirt was straight and down which is when I realised that I was minus pants. Surreptitiously, I looked around hoping to find my missing clothes, but to no avail, so I pretended I was fully clothed as I took a drink of my beer.

"Why beer?" he asked, startling me with his question.

"Erm, I guess because I like it, the taste."

"I would have put money on you being a wine girl, *a rosé girl*, you know the sort, *I don't like red wine, nor white, but ooh, it's pink, I like that!*" he told me making me laugh at his words and his attempt at what I believed was an Essex accent.

"Wine is not my thing. I can tolerate it when I have to, but I like beer," I explained. "Are you Canadian?" I asked, thinking I was usually a bit shitty with accents, having once asked a South African business associate of Michael's which part of Australia he was from. Like that, Michael was in my mind and weighing heavily, very heavily on my conscience.

"Jeez, I really need to haul my ass back home if I'm sounding Canadian!" He winced with his perfect grin that made me melt all over again. I knew I needed to go before I did anything I might regret, well, anything else. "I'm American, Californian to be precise," he expanded as I leapt to my feet, suddenly in need of air and distance between us. "Should we introduce ourselves?" He leaned forward from his position on the seat opposite the sofa where I'd been.

Introduce ourselves. This from the man who had just fucked me against a window and made me come, twice, hard, and now he thought we needed an introduction. Not me. What I needed was to get my arse, my naked arse out of there and back home, to my husband who had never once made me feel like this stranger had.

"I'm married," I blurted out with my ring finger held aloft as if to confirm my words.

"What? Married? But…" he began as he pushed a hand through his hair and then dragged it over his face that once revealed had changed into a flat, blank expression. "Don't let me keep you then," he snapped venomously as he stalked to the door and pulled it open for me to leave. "I'm sure you have other places to be, other dicks to be riding."

I took a step on wobbly legs, unsure whether that was due to the disgust and anger being aimed at me or the after-effects of what I'd done with the angry man before me. I hadn't anticipated anything beyond what we'd done so his reaction to my marital status was totally unexpected and had me reeling, but not as much as his final words to me.

"Come on, chop-chop. I'm sure your husband must be wondering where you are and those kids won't get themselves off to school in the morning."

I wanted to say something, but words wouldn't come out, not that I could protest or deny that I was married nor that I had committed adultery. My mouth opened and closed several times when a woman appeared in the doorway.

"Cy, you're still here. I thought you'd bailed," she said in a slightly stronger American accent than his. "Hey," she smiled at me.

I returned her smile as I took in the effortless beauty of the woman standing in front of me; she was tall, taller than me, but at five feet two most people were. She must have been edging towards five ten and willowy in stature, standing there in a white dress that clung to her boy like frame, finishing mid-thigh revealing never ending legs. Her bright blue eyes bore into me questioningly and then she flicked her long, dark blonde hair back and transferred her gaze to him, Cy.

"You okay?" she asked him with a concerned frown, presumably as she saw his face that resembled thunder.

"Yup. Just escorting the *lady* out," he replied, but the way he said lady was anything but complimentary. It was an accusation, an insult.

Chapter Three

"Darling, let me make you some breakfast," Michael offered across the kitchen the following morning.

"I'm fine, really. I need to go," I extended a weak smile as the dog, Balder, a huge, but seriously soppy Great Dane pushed his head into my hip. "Hey Baldy. I know, but I've gotta go." My words were apologetic knowing that the dog was desperate for a little love and attention. My guilt for my inability to provide that for the dog was greater than my need to give my husband the same.

"Let me drop you at work. I could even come and see what they've done to my building," Michael suggested.

"No thank you, and no again." I grabbed my bag and dashed to the door where the dog blocked my path. "Don't do this, Balder, not today, please. I will take you for a run at the weekend, a long, muddy one," I promised sincerely and was glad when Michael appeared with the dog's lead.

"Come on matey, Mummy has to go to work so you'll have to make do with me for a dash around the block."

"I am not his Mummy. I'm sure she was hairier than me," I told Michael with a smile.

"And taller."

"Below the belt." I laughed, feeling a familiar and genuine warmth for the man before me. "Take it easy, don't push yourself on your dash around the block," I warned with a combination of concern and worry that turned into resentment that if he did I'd be nursing him through the whole weekend.

When did I become such a bitch? And I was a bitch, had to

be after what I'd done last night to the man I'd promised to love, cherish and be faithful to. Never to obey though, that was a step too far even for me at a naïve twenty-three.

"Mmm, speaking of which, I'm sorry about last night, breaking the moment with my medication alarm..."

I cut him off with a wave of my hand. "Michael, it's fine. There's more to life than sex. More to us, right?" I was desperate to believe the words leaving my mouth, but not quite succeeding.

"Of course, but you're young. You have needs that I might not be able to fulfil..."

"Michael," I snapped as the sound of the taxi beeping outside made me rethink my mood. "This is not the time. I don't have time for this right now. I have a ball breaker boss who is likely to sack me if his tea, just a dash of milk, no sugar isn't waiting for him, and besides that, what is the solution to this, us? Viagra, a cabana boy, a time machine? I have to go," I cried, stepping over the dog to open the door just enough to squeeze through.

"Well done, absolutely fucking marvellous Eloise!" I shouted at myself as I slammed the taxi door startling the poor driver who confirmed my destination and then didn't speak again until he told me my fare, almost apologetic for disturbing my bitch of a mood.

I needed to sort out my head and frame of mind before I landed in the office, so I used the time in the lift to think.

When I'd returned home Michael was sitting in front of the TV watching some interactive 'extra' show about the bees which was almost enough for me to forgive myself for shagging a nameless man behind my husband's back, almost. After nearly falling over the dog I ran upstairs and showered. All evidence of any wrong doing washed away, physical evidence anyway. I threw on a pair of cotton shorts and vest before returning downstairs where my husband was lounging on the sofa with his legs stretched out reading the paper.

"You okay?" he asked looking at me over the top of his reading glasses as he placed his paper down on the coffee table.

"Mmm. I love you," I declared and almost made a full

confession when he took my hand in his and pulled me down into his lap.

"I know that El, and I hope you know that I love you too."

"Are you happy?" I asked him as I turned so that I straddled his groin.

"Of course, and you, are you happy?" he asked making me think how stupid I must be not to have anticipated him throwing that right back at me.

"I am," I began causing something to flicker in my husband's eyes. "I miss how things were," I added and immediately he nodded. He got what I was saying.

"I wasn't fair to you when I married you, I was being selfish..."

"No." I attempted to stop him, to prevent him continuing, from saying something neither of us could go back from.

"Yes. You were, you are beautiful, funny, clever and sexy, but I didn't think it through, that when I was approaching sixty you wouldn't even be thirty, that our needs and capabilities would be poles apart, always were really. I want you to be happy darling. I want to make you happy, but I can't be the man I was five, ten or more years ago, or the man you probably ever needed."

I didn't know what to say or do, so said and did nothing. Relief washed over me as Michael reached up and pulled me to him and kissed me. Not the usual peck on the cheek, but a kiss of passion and desire. Whilst it wasn't the battle I'd engaged in with Cy, that was what that blonde woman had called him, it was wonderfully different. I adjusted my position so that my sex was positioned over his burgeoning erection.

"You are so beautiful, so sweet and beautiful," Michael told me as he pulled back from our kiss and gently cupped my breast, the one that had been bitten earlier in the evening.

A low, loud groan echoed around us as the earlier, sweet pain was reignited by my husband's gentler caress. I wanted to ask him to be firmer, like earlier, but didn't know how.

"Let's go to bed," Michael suggested but with thoughts of this and my earlier encounter mingling in my mind it meant I didn't want this moment breaking.

I hadn't had sex with my husband for a year or more and I wanted this, needed it, if only to prove that earlier had been a mistake and this was real.

"Here, do it here," I pleaded as I undid the buttons on Michael's shirt revealing the scar that ran down his chest.

"We'll be more comfortable in bed, love." He prepared to evict me from his lap.

How did I tell him that I didn't want comfortable and I didn't want to be beautiful, sweet or his love? I wanted to be a dirty girl, his baby and I needed to feel desperate.

"No!" I protested becoming a little bratty before hastily reaching beneath me for the belt on his trousers. "Michael, please, here, please, now," I begged.

He seemed to take pity on me and relaxed against the sofa, allowing me to free his semi-erect penis as his hand made its way into my shorts via the leg where he found me naked. I continued to stroke along his length, attempting to further arouse him and myself with limited success, but that was okay, we could do this. Unlike earlier I wasn't wet enough meaning that Michael withdrew his fingers and resorted to sucking them to add some moisture before returning them to my sex as horror filled my head at the idea that a complete stranger had turned me on in a way my husband wasn't able to. Had never been able to.

"That's better," he told me as his finger found my clit and his spit allowed it to move freely.

I stared at his hand moving beneath my clothes and closed my eyes, trying to conjure images in my head that would block out the actual one I was part of.

"Michael, wait. I want to feel you," I told him as I began to free myself from my husband's hold, lowering myself down the sofa until I was faced with Michael's groin, intent on making his penis a full erection, to let us move on from this awkwardness.

Slowly, I licked along his length from his sac to the tip of his penis that I circled with my tongue and immediately he stiffened a little more allowing me to cover him with my mouth that I began to move up and down. His hands dropped to my head inspiring me to continue while his hands carefully and tenderly stroked my hair which was less comforting than it used to be. The sound of a loud shrill startled me into an upright position.

"Sorry, love, time for my meds." Michael reached across to turn his phone alarm off.

"Now, where was I?" I prepared to return to my previous position.

"El, let me go and take my tablets and then we'll take this upstairs to bed," he told me, already moving me into a sitting position on the sofa, breaking the moment.

"Michael." I frowned, but quickly found myself feeling ridiculous and selfish when he reminded me about the importance of his medication.

"Eloise, I am not taking multi-vitamins. These are my heart meds, the ones that help to keep me alive," he told me with a stern frown, admonishing me with his use of my full name and in that second something died. Something other than my desire to have sex with my husband, even if my 'desire' was really a means to absolve the guilt of my infidelity.

"Sorry." I was already on my feet. "Maybe that third beer was a bad idea," I added with a weak smile thinking that all of my beers may have been bad ideas considering where they'd led me.

"Beer?" Michael queried with a disapproving frown. "Beer is not a drink for a lady." I'd heard those words a million times before. "You know my feelings on beer."

With a sense of failure and resignation pouring over me I resisted the temptation to point out that I was not a lady. "You should take your tablets. I'm going to turn in, early start tomorrow."

****

Stepping off the lift the reception desk was unmanned, but why wouldn't it be, it was barely half-past seven. I hung my jacket up revealing my fitted black and white striped, button through blouse that today was teamed with a black trouser suit, consisting of a contemporary black blazer with a single button fastening and high-waist cigar trousers. At least I hadn't had the debate on stockings and tights today with bare feet that were nestled in black leather, heeled shoes.

Once my computer was logged on I checked my emails whilst congratulating myself on the lack of stationery filling the floor. One email jumped out with its subject of **'Flowers.'**

Ms Ross,

I need flowers ordering for delivery, an arrangement. Simple, elegant, nothing fussy. Charge to my personal credit card and the delivery address is listed in my directory under Tia Mamodo.

The card should simply say:

Tia,

I'm an ass, sorry.

X

Denton Miller
CEO Miller Industries (Europe)

"Major arsehole maybe," I told his email through gritted teeth, but his order is fulfilled before ten to eight. "Right, 'Mein Fuhrer' will require his tea." I take myself and my bad mood into the small but well-equipped kitchen up here.

Once back I knew with certainty that my boss had arrived. He was in his office, the door to which was shut. With a deep breath I braced myself and knocked on his door with one hand while the other held firmly onto the cup of tea I'd prepared.

"Come in," called a softer, friendlier voice than the one I remembered from the previous day.

Another deep breath and I virtually threw the door open to find the smiling friendly face of Denton Miller. The one I recalled from our webcam chats looking up at me with a warm friendliness I hadn't expected.

"Lovely to finally meet you properly El. Sorry about yesterday. It all went a little pear shaped," he explained with another smile.

Pear shaped was not how I would have expected anyone to describe being caught with their head between their mistress' legs, but there it was. I really wished I hadn't thought of that. I couldn't remember the last time I had been on the receiving end of a head between my thighs, er, never, not properly anyway.

In an instant I thought of Cy; his touch, how intensely I'd felt it, how intensely I'd come, both times. Foolishly I allowed myself to wonder what his tongue would feel like, running along my whole length, although I understood that not everyone was into that. Michael had told me on more than one occasion that it was something some men did out of obligation, but most disliked it. I supposed it really was a matter of taste. Why had I even gone out last night? My boss' fucking and my own were now fucking with my whole life, so much so that I didn't even giggle at my own unintentional *taste* joke.

"Your tea," I managed to say when my mind returned to the room my body occupied.

"Tea?" Mr Miller asked with first a frown and then a smile that threw me, causing me to stumble into the middle of the room. "Sorry, I think there's been some confusion, I don't drink tea. My wife is the tea drinker. She's English you know," he told me, positively beaming as he mentioned her and made it even more impossible to reconcile this image, this man with the wayward, cheating, cunnilingus giving man of yesterday. "I'm a coffee guy, through and through." He laughed.

Maybe I'd got it wrong, but he had said tea yesterday. Tea up until ten o'clock, unless I was going completely, clinically insane and was imagining details.

"Oh, sorry. I'll get you some coffee." I'd already turned to exit the room, only to find myself crashing into a solid wall of muscle, muscle whose pristine white shirt was now covered in tea.

My world was turning into a tragic farce, if such a thing could co-exist. Apologetically I looked up to actually apologise only to find two big, familiar pools of melted chocolate staring down at me. Cy, my nameless, adulterous encounter. This had to be a nightmare that I was about to wake up from, but seemingly not.

"Jeez, what the fuc…"

"Denton Miller Junior, do not finish off that sentence to a lady," my boss behind the desk bellowed, causing me to spill the final drops of tea onto the chest before me.

"Lady," he cursed beneath his breath before I realised that my boss was Denton Miller Senior and he had just called my dance partner from last night Denton Miller Junior.

I was beyond fucked here; the father knew my husband and my husband's old friend's son had shagged his wife. Definitely more farce than tragedy right now.

"El, are you okay?" Senior asked as he appeared at my side. "Go and gather your thoughts and maybe bring back some coffee for us all," he suggested with another warm smile.

"And some cleaning cloths," snapped Junior. "And tea, I have tea. I emailed you," he added as something resembling a stone settled in the pit of my stomach.

"I think you've had your tea," Senior laughed as I actually ran from the room and doubted I could ever return.

****

This couldn't be happening, and yet it was. What the hell was fate playing at now? I sat in the corner of the tea room, on the floor and pressed my head between my knees, taking deep breaths, trying to stop myself from hyperventilating before deciding that I needed to put my big girl pants on and put up or sod off home.

With a tray of coffee and tea for one, dash of milk, no sugar I re-entered the office of my earlier mortification to find Senior sitting behind the desk and Junior emerging from the en-suite bathroom, naked from the chest up. This was not going to be as simple as pulling on big girl pants, especially not when all I could think about was him removing them for me.

"Ooh, I, erm," I stammered, allowing myself an ogle of the firm chest, torso, muscular shoulders and upper arms that were adorned with tattoos.

"You should maybe turn around if the sight of me is likely to result in a whole tray of drinks falling," he sneered at me, but still I stared with my drying mouth hanging open.

"Cy, cover up and stop being an ass!" Senior told Junior reminding me of his presence. "El, please, come and sit down so we can cover the changes that occurred yesterday."

Finally, I turned away and followed my boss' orders, taking one of the seats across from his. Junior took the other seat, next to me, making me question whether this was judgement, or punishment for my sins the night before, being forced together, in front of his dad. My boss. My husband's old associate, and friend. Especially when he kept drinking in the shape of my legs, his eyes roving up and down.

"Buckle up, Ms Ross, I think we're in for a bumpy ride," Junior told me without expression but his pronunciation of Ms seemed loaded.

"So, let me introduce you formally. Miss Ross, Eloise, my son, Denton Miller Junior, Cy to his friends."

I turned to smile only to find a tight and curt expression staring back at me. "You should call me Mr Miller," he added with acidity, making it clear that I was not a friend.

"As of yesterday things changed with our company. There were some personal reasons in me taking over here, at the UK end of things, but those things have changed meaning that I will be returning to The States in a couple of weeks to run things from there. That leaves Cy to take over here at the European end."

"I see," I muttered the words, wondering where that left me. "Will you be bringing your own PA on board?" I felt unsure how long I could help out with charities and the golf club I despised if I lost my job so soon.

"My last PA is currently in the Eastern European office, so no. My father insists that your credentials are second to none, so we'll see," Junior sneered again, earning another reproachful glare from his father.

"El, your job here is safe," Senior assured me with a smile. "Your role hasn't changed, ours have and as I say only because of changes to a personal situation."

"Dad, I am sure Ms Ross has no need or desire to know our personal situation."

"Cy!" his father chastened again. "El, I apologise for my

son's rudeness. I have no idea what has gotten into him today, although he is never the easiest person to work for," he mumbled without expansion. "He certainly wasn't raised this way."

I nodded for no reason other than not knowing what else to do and was relieved when Senior ran through my role again, which as he'd said hadn't changed.

Somehow we got onto the subject of travel and The States which is when he genuinely said, "You should come out and visit when you get the chance. We'd love to have you over."

Whilst the offer was generous, I had in no way been expecting it, an invite to visit Senior and his wife, but I knew the offer was to me and Michael together, unlike Junior. For the second time that day he ended up wearing tea down his shirt, this time as a result of him choking on a mouthful that now covered his chest.

"For fuck's sake!"

His shout made me jump in my position next to him.

"Cy," his dad began but found himself cut off.

"No, Dad, no. What is going on here? She is my PA, you do not invite staff home to visit, not unless you are having a mid-life crisis and plan on getting me a new mommy, and I don't think Ms Ross would suit your needs. Not to mention the fact that Mom would kick your ass! Especially after that friend of yours did it, the one you bought this place off, Stanton," Junior laughed, completely missing his father's horrified expression. Mine not so much so, I knew what people had most likely thought about me when I had got together with Michael. "You know that although Mom says live and let live she has no time for young, pretty girls on the make, taking advantage of, and I quote, 'old, stupid, rich guys,' so Ms Ross don't start packing or sorting a visa anytime soon."

"Hey, are you lot slacking already?" came the call behind us.

"Definitely a farce. I hate farce," I whispered to myself earning a puzzled frown from Junior while Senior was leaping to his feet a little too enthusiastically to greet our visitor, my husband.

"Hey, look at you," Senior shouted, again

overenthusiastically making Junior frown quizzically in his direction, whereas I just wanted to wake up, or fall into a coma, or die, whatever would get me away quickest.

"I should go," I muttered, getting up on shaky legs that struggled to move me.

"What's the hurry?" Junior asked, reaching for my elbow to slow my retreat.

"Don't rush off on my account, love," Michael said when I eventually reached him. "Sorry, you're cross with me, aren't you? For turning up here?"

Yes, I was. Furious, but if I hadn't shagged my new, new boss the night before would I have been quite so cross at my husband's presence?

"Sorry," he offered with a childish pout that normally melted my resolve, but today it just made me want to punch him, as did his arm scooting around my waist. "Forgive me. I couldn't resist sneaking a peak at the old place," was his next excuse before seeing Junior on my other side, but no longer cupping my elbow.

He had released me and was staring between his father and Michael, but more so between Michael and me.

"Michael Stanton, and you are, Cy? Bloody hell, it must be fifteen, twenty years since I last saw you," my husband said, offering his free hand in greeting.

"Mr Stanton," Junior replied, still staring at Michael's arm around my middle with a look I couldn't fathom, but it wasn't positive.

"You seem to have already made my wife's acquaintance."

I now decided that death was the only way out of this unscathed upon hearing my husband's choice of words, *made my wife's acquaintance*. Who the fuck speaks that way outside of a Jane Austen novel? Michael Edgar Stanton, that's who.

"And then some!" I heard Junior say as he somehow managed to lean in towards me without appearing suspicious.

"Michael, I need to get on," I said, finally finding my voice, shaking my husband off.

"Yes, you do. Thank you, Ms Ross, Mrs Stanton," Junior said with a snarl for my married name. "We will catch up in a while," he added.

Yes, I officially wanted to die I decided in that moment, until I realised that Junior, Cy, Denton Miller Junior was watching me leave, eyes raking my body from my hair that was up in a messy bun right down to the soles of my shoes. Maybe I didn't want to die, not yet.

****

I ensured that I closed the door behind me. I needed a barrier between me and, all of them really. Once settled behind my desk I made preparations for the next few day's work and sent some emails before going back to the kitchen to wash-up, including both tea cups whose contents had decorated my boss' shirt, again. I giggled at the memory of him doused in his own tea, twice. I laughed, to myself, but still out loud.

"I had no idea you were his wife when I made the comment about him."

Turning on my heels I found myself face to face with Junior again, although once I'd looked up at him I decided that Junior was not an appropriate name for my boss.

"I know. Your face said as much when he introduced himself." I hoped we'd be able find some neutral ground to build on.

"Why were you trying to hide it?" he asked with a more accusatory tone suddenly. Maybe he didn't do neutral. Maybe his two settings were shagging you or giving you a hard time.

Another laugh escaped me as I thought that my summing up was a hard time either way.

"You think this is funny? That one of your extra marital hook-ups is now in my fucking office? That I was the hook-up and your stupidly grateful husband is an old friend of my father's? You are un-fucking-believable Mrs Stanton," he barked, full of fury that I reciprocated with a sharp slap across his cheek.

"How dare you!" I snarled back. "I don't do extra marital anything, didn't and I had no clue who you were last night, or this morning and do I look amused, do I?" I asked him shaking with anger. "And lose the judgemental Mrs Stanton or you might find yesterday morning's hors d'oeuvre getting another bunch of flowers telling her that you might be an arsehole, but you're actually a cheating arsehole."

"What? You're threatening to tell Tia about last night? And it's asshole," he replied looking incredulous with a slightly smarmy smirk that only annoyed me more. "Is this where you tell me that your husband doesn't understand you?"

"I'm not telling you anything about my husband and you heard exactly what I said." My breathing echoed around the small room we shared. "And it's arse-hole," I corrected, emphasising each part of the word.

"Yes, I heard what you said but you should be aware Ms Ross that you are pissing me off, have been since you revealed your marital status, post coitus. I am not known for my tolerance, so consider yourself warned."

"Darling," Michael's voice acted as an interruption, again. "I know you're angry…"

"Michael, please go home. I'm at work. I have things to do and you're not helping by being here, quite the opposite is true, so please, go home, walk the dog," I begged, almost crying with frustration.

"Okay, okay. I didn't mean to make you so uncomfortable." Guilt covered Michael's face, making me soften in response to his sincerity and my own guilt.

Cy remained with us, having moved behind my husband, watching us, but when Michael pulled me in for a gentle hug Cy's expression became conflicted making him impossible to read, if he was ever anything else. As quickly as he pulled me to him Michael released me with a smile.

"Nice to see you again Cy, and as you're new in town make a date for dinner with El," Michael told him causing us both to stare wildly. "At our house. El's a dab hand in the kitchen. Nobody cooks up a storm like she does"

"I can imagine," is how Cy replied with an arched brow making me want to slap him again, harder. "I'll see if I'm available and let Mrs Stanton know."

Yeah a much, much harder slap I decided as Michael added, "It's her birthday soon, well, in a few months. Maybe we could have a pre-birthday and new job dinner?"

Chapter Four

Maya called for me for lunch, but I opted out since she was solely focused on discussing the boss, Mr Miller Jnr and he was the last thing I wanted to talk about, even if he was all I could think about. I couldn't risk slipping up and revealing my detailed knowledge of the man.

Fortunately, Mr Miller left me alone. He didn't attempt to make conversation about anything, even his business talk was delivered in the form of emails and for that I was grateful as one more uncomfortable conversation might have been enough to send me running for the hills.

I sat at my desk collating and binding proposals for the Friday afternoon meeting that was now scheduled to take place in the conference room down the corridor when another email landed with a ping.

Ms Ross,

Coffee, no milk, one sugar, when it's convenient and a copy of your electronic diary before the end of the week, the diary, not the coffee.

Regards,

Denton Miller
CEO Miller Industries (Europe)

"Twelfth of never," I muttered to myself having stifled a

small smile of amusement before I realised that his office door was open, which apparently was how he liked it.

"You really are an awkward bitch, aren't you?" he called through to me making me want to slap myself rather than him now.

When did I develop such violent tendencies?

"Takes one to know one," I whispered with a self-satisfied grin, but the man with better hearing than a bat responded.

"Keep pushing Ms Ross, see how that pans out."

I took the warning and got up to make the coffee that I secretly hoped my boss would choke on.

****

We, my boss and I, managed to avoid real conversation until Thursday afternoon and then it was via email, after another cup of coffee had been delivered with a reminder that I still hadn't sent my diary. I returned to my desk where I opened the compose box on my email and attached my diary, my near empty diary.

Mr Miller,

My diary is attached, there's not much on it other than the meeting tomorrow, assuming you want me to accompany you. My previous boss preferred me to attend and take minutes etc. and I have no leave planned.

Regards,

Eloise Ross
P.A. to CEO Miller Industries (Europe)

Ms Ross,

Thank you.

I shall enter your commitments to me and return your diary forthwith. I prefer at least a month's notice of holiday

requirements and I do expect you to attend tomorrow's meeting with me, to minute etc. Was your husband your previous boss that had you escort him?

Regards,

**Denton Miller
CEO Miller Industries (Europe)**

I was stunned by his question about my boss, my husband. Confused as to whether he was making chit chat or if there would be future inferences.

Ms Ross,

Don't overthink it, reply.

Regards,

**Denton Miller
CEO Miller Industries (Europe)**

My mind raced as I considered his most recent email; How did this happen? How did he figure me out? How could he know this, know me? I overthought everything, almost. When I got married, I was unsure that I thought about that at all.

"Answer me!" bellowed Cy making me jump.

Mr Miller,

My previous boss that I was referring to was my last employer at Stark Insurance, not Michael. I never worked as his P.A. I was a secretary here in accounts when I met my husband.

Regards,

Eloise Ross,
P.A. to CEO Miller Industries (Europe)

He didn't speak to me again that day using any means until I was ready to leave for the day when he appeared in his doorway.

"You off?" he asked, and had the good grace to look embarrassed by his unnecessary question.

"Looks that way."

"Your husband has invited me to dinner again, via my father this time."

"Why won't he leave this alone?" I asked with a shake of my head.

"I think he wants us to be friends." Mr Miller grinned, lighting up his whole face, beauty radiating from every pore, looking like the man I had met in the bar.

"I don't think he'd want that if he knew just how friendly we have already been, do you?" I sighed, wanting to push that one night from my mind, kind of.

"No, obviously. I'll extend my apologies and offer an excuse if you'd rather."

"Thank you."

"I'll see you in the morning then," he stated more than asked.

"Unless you're planning on sacking me."

"What? Why would you say that?"

"It was a joke," I explained, unsure why I'd said that. "Sorry, I just feel awkward still, after, well you know."

"After we fucked?" he asked bluntly, making me blanch with embarrassment and shame that he viewed it, viewed me that way.

"Goodnight," I replied before running for the lift, unsure how I really felt about anything anymore.

****

My silence all evening once I'd finally arrived home didn't go unnoticed by Michael who even resorted to turning the TV off during a documentary on Vikings in an attempt to prompt conversation. He tried talking about safe topics, like his grandchildren, the dog, his golf handicap and then finally addressed the elephant in the room, Denton Miller, Cy. I wondered where Cy came from but resisted the temptation to ask my husband, fearful that he might just see that my interest was something beyond platonic.

"How are things going with Cy? You seem a little distracted, El."

There it was, the gauntlet had been thrown down, but what could I say? 'Oh, it's okay. It'll just take a while to get my head round things and settle in, especially since I unwittingly cheated on you with him in the office of a bar,' so I did what any wife new to adultery would have done, I lied.

"It's fine, or it will be I'm sure. He's not the boss I was expecting, that's all. It might be better if you stopped inviting him for dinner though. It makes things a bit odd, for us both."

"I was hoping dinner would make things better for you both," Michael sighed as though he was trying to smooth over a sibling squabble. "I won't invite him again if that helps."

"Thank you."

"There seems a lot of tension between you, even Denny commented on it on the golf course this afternoon," he said, revealing that he'd seen Cy's dad that afternoon, moreover that they had discussed us, again like parents. Except the man in front of me was not my parent, he was my husband and surely he should be acting a little differently, like a husband might, like I imagined Cy might if someone suggested that there was heavy tension between his wife and another man. Pushing that thought from my mind I continued to discuss things.

"Michael, really, this is unnecessary. You do not need to intervene in my relationship with my boss, and certainly not with his dad on the golf course. You've never done this with any of my bosses. Why now, why this boss?"

"El, I have never seen you like this, like you've been the last week, preoccupied, restless, moody, tempestuous, it's not you," he told me with absolute conviction.

I wanted to cry, again, possibly vindicating his accusation.

"Maybe it is, maybe this is me," I suggested without adding the words, 'since I met Cy.'

"I don't believe that darling. You are sweet, focused, even

tempered, calm and quite possibly the loveliest girl I have ever met. Denny told me that Cy is difficult to work for. He's single minded to the point of bloody mindedness, he is a man of extreme moods and struggles to hold onto a PA because his standards are impossibly high to reach and maintain. He gets through staff like other men change socks and I don't want you to be brought down by being his PA. Maybe you should consider looking for a new direction…"

"No. No! I can't join the support group or process memberships at the golf course Michael, that would be soul destroying for me. I'm trying to build a career, not find a hobby to fill a few hours. Just give it some time. I'm sure I'll soon get my head round things," I desperately promised and pleaded.

"Love, calm down," Michael reassured, pulling me closer to him on the sofa we were sharing. "I didn't mean that, I meant, well what I was saying was that we should refocus and find a new direction, together."

My expression must have morphed into horror if not sheer terror at the suggestion I felt was on the table. That he was about to say that we could run a small business together or move abroad, both. The thought horrified me, the idea of being stuck together, just the two of us, twenty-four hours a day when I was currently, that week currently, struggling to spend more than an hour at a time with the husband I'd pledged to be with until one of us died.

"El, darling," he interrupted, breaking the racing of my mind, "What I am suggesting is that we should regroup, you and I, that you could take a break, not give up or retire, but take a break to start a family together. I think that's what we're missing," he said calmly while my blood pressure soared until I was convinced that my brain was going to explode.

I really should have taken longer to speak again I realised as soon as the words exploded from my mouth. "We don't have sex anymore."

"I know, and clearly we'd need to in order to conceive, and I know things aren't ideal in that department but we could always look at IVF…"

"Michael, this is a lot to take in. We've never really

discussed having children and IVF."

I couldn't believe that my week had deteriorated even further since leaving the office, but it had and now I was confused in the extreme. I hadn't expected this turn of events and the idea that we still might not have sex to conceive a child. A child I was unsure it was wise to bring into the world. The whole idea scared me. Not that I didn't want children, I did, but with two fit and healthy parents…

"I know it's a lot to consider, El, and I realise we haven't discussed it properly, but this is the next step. We can try to conceive naturally. I wasn't saying we had to have IVF from the get go, just that if we struggled, if I struggled."

Guilt descended as I nodded. His conciliatory tone was intended to soothe me, but it didn't. It made me cry guilty tears and not just guilt over Cy.

"Hey, I know this is down to me," Michael insisted, continuing, "I told you that I can't be the man I was, this is who and what I am darling. I want you to be happy and I will do anything I can, including having a baby with you. At least I know you won't be alone when something happens…"

"God, Michael! I know you can't turn the clock back, I have never asked you to, not ever and if something was to happen to you I don't know that a baby or child would be the best person to be here for me, with me. You know how I struggle without my dad." And that was me done for as I became a sobbing heap.

****

The following morning Michael handled me with kid gloves, keeping conversation to a minimum. We shared a breakfast of croissants and tea for me and a high bran cereal and orange juice for him, his usual 'good for my heart' start to the day that usually lasted until about half-past ten when he tucked into a full English 'not so good for your heart' breakfast at the golf club. I returned his smile as I recalled him holding me the night before, gently rocking me as I cried before putting me to bed where I slept soundly until the alarm went off an hour ago.

"Think about things, El, what we talked about. I'll abide by your decision," he finally said.

"Okay," I agreed, hoping the conversation was over, it

wasn't.

"I can give you anything you need other than a more physical relationship…"

"Michael!"

"No, Eloise, please let me finish. You are beautiful and I do still find you desirable in my own way, but," and there it was, *but*. "But while my mind is willing, my body is almost sixty years old, not under thirty like yours. I probably shouldn't have entertained a relationship with you, and I certainly shouldn't have married you, not if in doing so I selfishly took away your youth and saddled you with an old man incapable of being the husband you need. So, no hurry, but I repeat, think about things. Decide what you want and I will abide by your decision."

"I have to go," was my stammered response. "I might be late, there's a big meeting this afternoon."

"Let me know when you're done, and El, you look lovely."

I offered a final smile and a quick fuss for Balder before I headed off to work thinking how different I felt this Friday compared to last.

****

At least with Mr Miller's tendency towards consistent, ordered and habitual routines, it kept my mind off my night, morning, and ultimately my life. His tea was delivered to his desk before he arrived, just, as he was running late. The only man I knew who was late at ten to eight in the morning.

"Thank you," he said after almost colliding with me in the doorway as I exited his office.

I offered a half-smile in response and returned to my own desk to finalise the people attending the afternoon's meeting and to arrange the following week's diary. A ping meaning I had an email startled me.

Ms Ross,

You seem distracted, are you ok? Is this about last night?

Regards,

Denton Miller
CEO Miller Industries (Europe)

I really could have done without this, this discussion and the cross over between our usual frosty and awkward encounters to this, what, concern?

"Overthinking it, answer," he called impatiently from his chair. I knew this because I could hear the wheels rolling across the wooden floor beneath his desk.

"I'll stop overthinking when you start shutting the door," was my muttered whisper, but old bat ears was on form.

"That's a stalemate then. Now answer or I'll insist on elevenses, together."

"No way," I replied in a still hushed tone, not hushed enough.

"Thought not."

In spite of myself I allowed a small smile to curve my lips.

Mr Miller,

I can assure you that I am not distracted by or from my work.

What about last night?

Regards,

Eloise Ross
P.A. to CEO Miller Industries (Europe)

Ms Ross,

I'm calling bullshit! I asked if you were ok. Are you ok?

Last night when I raised the subject of dinner, or not, of our situation, your employment.

Regards,

Denton Miller
CEO Miller Industries (Europe)

Mr Miller,

How very American, calling bullshit! Have you heard the phrase, 'when in Rome?'

I don't know what to say to you. I could lie and say I am fine, but you are likely to call bullshit again. I have things on my mind, but it won't impact on my work.

Regards,

Eloise Ross
P.A. to CEO Miller Industries (Europe)

Ms Ross,

Chiamo cazzate, however, I was under the impression we were in England not Italy.

Again, you misunderstand, I didn't ask about your work, I was asking about you.

Coffee in half an hour. Email me final details for this afternoon.

We'll talk later.

Regards,

Denton Miller
CEO Miller Industries (Europe)

"Can't wait," I said at the prospect of us talking later and was unsure if I bothered to whisper as Bruce Wayne seemed to hear everything anyway. I smiled a genuinely amused smile as I thought of my boss as Batman and at the same time I realised that he had made me happy and taken my mind off my life, my other life.

"I do believe that was sarcasm Ms Ross. The lowest form of wit and all that, or would you like that in Italian too?"

"Smart arse," I retorted, grinning rather than just smiling.

"And then some," he called before ending our exchange with, "and it's ass!"

****

The conference room was where the old one always was but with the addition of the former stationery cupboard and a single office that neighboured it there was now storage space and a private area, although privacy and glass walls seemed contradictory to me. I set up the empty room, as per Mr Miller's instructions with a named copy of the proposal in front of each required seat. I had been instructed to put the boss at the head of the table, surprise, surprise, and me opposite him at the far end of the room. I'd set up the ICT and checked it, twice, before allocating note pads and two pens/pencils per attendee, just in case. Tea, coffee and soft drinks had been ordered from the catering people along with biscuits, cake and a fruit basket.

A quick dash back to the kitchen that served my office allowed me to grab a couple of jugs of water in case the catering didn't arrive until mid-afternoon and it was as I was carrying them back to the conference room that I happened upon Mr Miller and Maya at reception. I heard him asking if she was familiar with the names of today's visitors. She confirmed that I'd already provided that information which seemed to please him, which in turn pleased me until I heard him ask Maya about her weekend plans. Why did he even need to know that? And then he made me want to slap him again, really, really hard when he asked her if she was familiar with Bazooka, the bar where we'd met, me and him. I was ready to slap them both when Maya shook her head coyly and began to flirt. How dare she, not when he was my...my what? He's my boss I told myself and rushed past them without saying a word.

"Are we all set?" he asked causing me to spin around to see him entering the conference room behind me.

"Yes," I replied a little shortly, still holding two jugs of water in front of my chest.

"Nice jugs," he quipped making me blush a little before he added, "Déjà vu," which made me blush a lot at the memory of his commendation for my boobs in that damned office.

He saw my reaction. I knew he had and then he stepped closer, and closer and then closer still until he was almost toe to toe with me causing my body to react in its typical, default way to this man; I felt hot, breathless, fidgeting from one foot to the other, hoping to somehow disguise my hardening nipples and the slickness between my thighs. I really needed to get a grip on this, rein it in.

"Sorry, they're fantastic tits, not nice jugs."

His grin was the best way of him conveying that he knew exactly what he did to me.

"I like your outfit," he told me, undressing me with his eyes from my tightly fitted, black blouse with its short sleeves, the three buttoned down top and frilled detail, down to my even tighter fitting, knee length, dark grey skirt, but rather than the usual split to the back this one had a pleated vent over the front of my leg. Then there was my almost customary black heeled shoes, today's were a mock croc design and stockings rather than tights, smoky grey ones complete with a seam up the back, almost inviting looks at my behind. Why had I opted for stockings? Was it because of the turmoil in my mind, my husband's lack of interest in the bedroom, or maybe it was because of my boss and his blatant interest in me, if not my tights on Monday night.

"I'd love to know what you're thinking," Cy told me as he reached forward and pushed a wayward strand of hair behind my ear.

I wanted to soften into his touch, but resisted, just.

"My husband wants us to have a baby," were the words that formed my response shocking us both, him so much that he jumped back from me as if he'd been burnt by my words.

"This way gents," I heard Maya coo and like that we both morphed back into our professional personas.

Mr Miller was a sight to behold in full CEO, 'kicking your arse when you piss him off, laughing at your ridiculous requests and taking no prisoners in order to get the deal he wanted' mode. I was in awe of his knowledge about everything, the insight he demonstrated about the proposal, the company and future projections. His business kudos was second to none, knowing exactly when to speak, when to shut up and when to laugh.

I minuted the meeting, making any follow-up notes he directed and added a few to do notes for myself.

For most of the time in the room I was able to focus on my work, not my home life, nor my confused feelings towards the man sitting directly opposite me. Then I glanced up and found his eyes fixed on me causing me to drop my glance quickly, hoping to avoid my body's default mode, aroused, with little to no success. Crossing my legs, which I used as a self-distraction technique, giving myself something to focus on, like the invisible thread on my clothes that I pretended to brush off did nothing to divert my focus or his as his eyes fixed on my crossing legs through the glass table top.

Providence was clearly watching out for me when the meeting ended and the head honcho from the telecommunications company that was being 'absorbed' by Miller Industries needed to speak to Mr Miller on the way out.

Alone, I tidied and packed everything away and I was able to get back to my own office, albeit well after five o'clock, almost six. I was just washing-up my cup when my boss reappeared triggering yet more flushing, heat and strange breathing in me.

"Ms Ross, thank you, for this afternoon, I was impressed," he said with a stolid expression.

"No problem, it's what you pay me for," I replied, picking up a tea towel to dry my hands.

"You can't help yourself, can you? You have to make a smart ass comment, remind me that you're here on the payroll and for no other reason. I think bitch must be your middle name."

His face had suddenly changed from an impassive one to one contorted with emotion, just none I could name beyond anger. If my default mode around him was aroused, his around me was angry. I wanted to say something, offer some words to dispute his summing up of me and yet I couldn't because when I spoke to him beyond snide one liners the lines between us, the black and white ones, they blurred into a big pool of grey. With little risk of an interruption now that greyness might lead me to a place I shouldn't revisit, up against a window, door, spread across a desk or splayed on the floor.

"Goodnight Mr Miller," I offered and his face changed again to one of uneasiness, as if he could sense my own perturbation.

"We didn't talk," he called as I attempted to pass him.

"No," I agreed. He caught my arm and pulled me back, scrambling my thoughts and determination to leave.

"I could ask if you're okay, but we both know you're not."

"No, I'm not. I'm in a perpetual state of confusion, meaning I am struggling to sleep, eat or just function leaving me irritable, anxious and more confused than ever," I replied, undoubtedly with too much honesty but it didn't stop me carrying on. "And the worst thing about that is that I don't know how to deal with how I feel, I don't even recognise myself, neither does Michael…"

"And you think now would be a good time to have his child?"

There was no judgement in his voice when he asked this which allowed me to answer without breaking the moment even with Michael metaphorically joining us.

"I don't know that there is ever going to be a good time for us to have a child. He, Michael suggested it as a way for us to regroup, as an alternative to me working here and being brought down by your exacting standards." I laughed but was far from amused.

"He wants you to quit? Why? Did you tell him about us?" Cy placed his hands on my hips. "You do look fucking fantastic today."

I swallowed hard as the grey descended replacing all black

and white in my life.

"He wants to make me happy, make me the woman I was, before Monday and no, I didn't tell him about us."

"This is my fault then, your confusion?" he asked with the ghost of a smile crossing his beautiful face as if he was happy with my conflicting emotional state now that it was because of him.

"It could be a coincidence," I suggested with a coy half-smile of my own.

Confusion clouded his eyes now. "I do not sleep with staff and more than that I abso-fucking-lutely do not ever sleep with married women."

"We're not sleeping together."

"Such a fucking bitch," he accused before spinning me round and placing my hands flat on the counter top.

My breathing hitched and if it was possible the sound of it was deafening, or maybe that was my heart thudding in my chest, or even the blood pounding through my veins. I felt the fabric of my skirt being dragged up my legs revealing inch after inch of seamed stocking until I heard a gasp from behind me and then a mouth on my ear.

"I do love it when people take my recommendations on board. I have wanted to kiss my way up these seams all day, not stopping until I could taste you," he told me gruffly making me gasp. "Oh yeah, you are so on board here, baby. You should never wear pantyhose, thigh highs or stockings and a garter should be the only things that cover these great little legs," he told me, pressing into me so that I was trapped between the cupboard front and his hard body. "And I really approve of these little panties," he added teasing the tiny lace back of my black thong that he quickly infiltrated, slipping a finger beneath until he was skimming through my obvious arousal. "Open up, baby," he said licking against the shell of my ear.

I didn't know how this had happened. How I found myself in this position, again. We were talking and now his finger was buried inside me without protest. Rather than protesting I opened my legs a little more, encouraging him to give me more, which he did when his thumb reached up and found my clit that he manipulated to arousal quickly.

"Oh God," I cried, having forgotten where I was, who I was, but not who I was with.

"You like this baby? You wanna come?" he asked, pausing his fingers until I responded.

"Yes, don't stop, please."

His fingers began to move again, but still not quickly enough. "Not yet," he told me as I moaned in protest.

"Yes, now," I demanded making him laugh.

"Still a little bitch, but a little desperate now. Have you heard of delayed gratification?" He slowed his movements again.

"Yes, but I like instant gratification. Except it's not really quick enough for me."

Laughing he told me, "I really need to tame you baby, but not now."

With what I thought were two fingers thrusting inside me and a thumb caressing my clit I began to tense all around him with a warm burn spreading from low in my belly, travelling down into my pelvis and up along my spine until I was splintering into a million pieces, calling, crying and fighting for every breath over the sound of a vacuum cleaner fast approaching.

"Come on," he said freeing himself from my underwear before pulling my skirt back down. "We should take this elsewhere, somewhere we won't get busted," he expanded, spinning me back to face him, grinning as he took my hand in his.

"Ooh!" squealed the cleaner who suddenly appeared in the doorway. "I thought I was all alone up here." She smiled whilst clutching her chest as if having a heart attack, although I think I may have been more at risk of a cardiac arrest than her.

"Sorry," Cy and I both said in stereo.

"We're just leaving," he told the friendly looking woman of fifty or so standing in front of us.

Leading me back to my desk we stood, staring at each other, knowing that potentially this was going to be a turning point for us both, certainly for me, or maybe a point we wouldn't ever be able to turn back from.

Rooted to our own spots another interruption arrived in the form of Tia.

"Hey, my favourite ass! You'll need to send more flowers if I have to wait around much longer, maybe flowers, a movie and dinner."

She, Tia was the woman from the club, the one that came into the office, after we…this just kept getting better. He was calling me a bitch when all along he'd made plans with his girlfriend or another whatever she was.

"Tia, Ms Ross and I aren't done." His words sounded firm, but still warm as he addressed the other woman who looked more his sort than I might ever be.

"I was done, am done. I'm going home and I will see you on Monday," I said with more conviction than I felt at that moment as I shook my hand free of Cy's hold.

"Is that English reserve or is she always so prickly?" Tia asked as I left.

I didn't wait to hear his response.

I went home with a renewed certainty that I should make a concerted effort to get along with Michael over the weekend. To get over my Monday night madness and get the old me back.

Chapter Five

My husband's love of history paid dividends when I arrived home to find him engrossed in a docudrama retelling the last days of Pompeii. This meant I was able to shower, removing Cy's touch and my arousal from my flesh, again, before rummaging around the kitchen and finding something to throw together for dinner. By the time we were eating I felt calmer and was happy with my decision to forget Cy. Well, not forget him, but relabel him as just my boss and find the wife I was before I met him. Dinner was easy, with me and Michael chatting amiably. Neither of us made reference to having children, my work or anything likely to turn the mood sour and when we went to bed he followed his usual routine of falling asleep while I was in the bathroom leaving me more relieved than I thought I probably should be.

****

I woke alone and was shocked to find it was a little after ten, a very long lie-in for me. Without going downstairs I washed and dressed for a run, the run I'd promised Balder earlier in the week. I used to hate exercise until I moved here with the huge garden and wooded area beyond. Somehow I'd learned to love it, the solitude of it, although I walked for the first year, then moved onto a slow jog before building up to the actual running I planned on doing this morning.

My running gear wasn't anything special, but was highly functional; form fitting black leggings with a purple flash up the legs and a matching crop top with a zip fastening to the front and a built in bra. I fastened my favourite running shoes and dashed

55

down the stairs expecting to find Michael milling around with Balder waiting expectantly, but what I discovered as I was half way down was the sound of voices. Michael's was doing most of the talking, to one of his golf cronies I assumed and then I turned into the kitchen to hear his friend's voice at the same time that I saw him, Denton Miller Junior, in my kitchen, with my husband. What the hell was the matter with this man? More to the point, what was the matter with me? I was reacting again, getting all hot, breathless and giddy while my breasts tingled. My whole body tingled, everywhere, inside and out.

"Ah, here she is, sleepy head this morning, aren't we?" Michael asked, already handing me a drink of tea. "I think you wore her out yesterday, Cy."

Accepting the cup with shaking hands I had no clue how to behave or what to say.

"Cy brought your scarf back," Michael told me handing me a beautiful Hermes scarf with cascading shades of black and grey and a faint line of purple running through it, the same shade as on my running clothes.

"That's not mi…" I began realising that this scarf didn't belong to me. Shit, it was a ruse and I knew it, my boss knew it, but did my husband?

"I think you must have left it at the office, it was a late finish though." He smiled and sounded like the most wonderfully reasonable boss in the world.

"Have you had breakfast?" Michael asked.

I stared across the kitchen at my husband who I knew was on the verge of inviting my boss for breakfast.

"No, but I was going to hit the gym on my way home and grab a late breakfast or early lunch."

I noticed for the first time that Cy was dressed in his own workout gear of black track bottoms, a tight fitting t-shirt and similar running shoes to my own and he looked pretty awesome, like he belonged on the cover of a magazine.

"If you want a good run, I am sure El would be happy of the company this morning."

Cy's eyes lit up at the offer being extended while my stomach seemed to flip in a good way and churn in a bad one at the same time.

"Farce," I whispered reaching down to pet the dog who seemed to be viewing Cy with mistrust, clever dog.

"I was thinking more rom-com," Cy whispered back as Michael began prattling on about having never understood the desire to run.

"Screw you," I retorted.

"That's a whole new genre, although I'm game," he joked making me smirk against my better judgement when he continued in a slightly louder voice, "but won't he mind?" I should have seen that comment and the grin coming but I didn't.

"I don't mind at all. I know you'll take care of her," Michael replied having turned and heard, completely misunderstanding Cy's meaning.

Arched brows were my invitation to punch him this time, but I didn't have time before I found him pulling me to my feet. "Come on then, Ms Ross. Let's see if you can keep up!"

Michael laughed at that, making me want to punch him too. I really needed to get to grips with my anger management. I grabbed my iPod and plugged myself in.

"Balder," I called but my boy was already waiting for me at the door to begin my run leaving my boss making up ground as I attempted to get lost in my music.

Unable to trust myself to speak to Cy, never mind ending up in a compromising position, which was another default setting of mine if the club and the kitchen last night were anything to go by, I ran. After about a mile and a half I decided it might be safe to at least make eye contact with him.

Balder and I had an established routine, he ran slightly ahead for the first half a mile, which is where we leave home turf, then he settled in alongside me, guarding me almost. He doesn't have a vicious bone in his body, he just liked to be there in case I need protecting. There was a very good chance that I might, not from runaway dogs, as I once was, a yappy little thing that savaged my ankles, nor from potential serial killers posing as joggers I usually managed to imagine, but from Denton Miller.

Presumably, having had enough of my avoidance Cy

grabbed my arm, pulling me back with a start making me squeal. Alarmed by my shriek Balder came to my rescue, placing himself between me and who he perceived to be my attacker. I laughed to near hysteria when I realised that Cy was backed against a tree with Balder's teeth at his groin. I removed the buds from my ears as my fellow runner did the same.

"This is not funny."

"I beg to differ," I disagreed laughing louder.

"Ms Ross, please call her off," he pleaded, yet despite his precarious position still sounded pissed off with me, like this was my fault.

"Her? Balder?"

"Yes, I assume you and she trade in bitch tactics!" he snapped making the dog growl with his slightly threatening tone.

"Balder." I smiled at the light sweat causing a sheen on his face, his encounter with the dog having caused more of a sweat than the run had triggered.

With the dog obediently sat at my feet I explained, "He is a boy, Balder, named after the son of Odin and the God of light and purity, a gentle giant, just like the big boy here."

"We might have to disagree there, he wasn't very gentle with me," he complained making me query his presence as I petted my dog in reassurance.

"Why are you here?" I asked on a sigh of confused exasperation.

"In the country? My dad explained; family shit hitting the fan, forcing a change of roles, blah, blah."

I shot him a withering glance and chose my words carefully to achieve the desired effect. "He did, but you also explained that I had no need or desire to know your personal situations. So, why are you here? In my home, drinking tea with my husband, returning scarves that don't belong to me?"

"Ah, I getcha." He grinned. "I have no fucking clue. You like the scarf though don't you?"

"It's beautiful, but I don't wear scarves," I told him unsure how or why we'd managed to make this conversation about the scarf.

"That's not what Michael said. He told me that you're

singled minded and often forget things. He was in no way surprised that you had a scarf that you'd forgotten, so either you're lying or he doesn't know his wife as well as he thinks he does."

Shit! This innocent and safe conversation had just turned very dangerous and far from safe with my husband's lack of knowledge of me hanging between us.

"I don't wear scarves," I confirmed. "Why are you here?" I repeated, adding, "What are we doing?"

"No fucking clue on either front. This thing between us, the tension, the energy, I don't understand it and don't fucking like it. I don't like you. You are an uptight, argumentative, little bitch and yet I can't get you out my head. I want to touch you, kiss you, fuck you, it's all I can do not to rip your panties off, bend you over and fuck you senseless whenever you walk into the room, and that pisses me off. It makes me pissed off with you and myself, so that just leaves why I'm here."

He ran a hand through his hair, mussing it into a tantalising mess that I had a desperate urge to add my own fingers to while I kissed him, hard, as my tongue licked against his until there was nothing and no one except us, me and him and the sensation of us.

"And again, I wish I knew what you were thinking right now, although, no I don't. In fact, you really need to stop thinking whatever has your breathing picking up, your sexy as fuck tits heaving like they're about to burst from your little running top and your pupils dilating like you've just taken a serious hit or I am going to be forgetting any respect for your husband and whatever good intentions I might have and end up fucking you right here."

"I, erm, sorry."

"No. Don't be sorry, just stop, okay? Right, why the fuck am I here? Let's see if I can explain any of this to me as much as you. Last night, you ran off and I wanted to chase you, to explain, but I didn't because this, you and me is a disaster-in-waiting and we both know it."

"And yet you're here," I stated rather obviously as I dropped to sit on the ground while Balder settled next to me.

"And yet I'm here," he agreed sitting in front of me, his legs crossed too, mirroring my own position. "I regretted not coming after you last night, so much, but by the time I realised just how much, it was late, too late to turn up here. Plus, I hadn't bought the scarf as my shoe in."

"And your girlfriend might have become suspicious?" There, I'd done it, raised the subject of Tia, the girlfriend he had cheated on with me.

"Girlfriend? Tia, you mean Tia?"

"Yes, the one who claims your arse as her favourite, ringing any bells now?" I snapped, wanting to sound anything other than the hypocrite that I was.

"She's not a girlfriend and I am her favourite ass, my ass is not her favourite anything." He grinned, incurring more of my increasing wrath. "Oh, come on baby, you're the married one, not me," he retorted with his own wrath aimed at me.

"I don't know what to do here," I admitted, feeling defeated suddenly. "I wish I'd never met you. My life was so simple before Monday."

"Because meeting me has messed your life up?" he asked enquiringly with a flat expression that still demanded a reply, which I understood. I only wished I had answers for us both.

"If it were only that simple. No. It's more a case that meeting you has made me see how messed up my life is."

My words couldn't be considered sexy or romantic but before I knew what was happening, I was being pulled into the lap opposite. Without any conscious thought I found myself nestled in Cy's lap, my legs wrapped around his hips, my fingers laced through his hair and our lips and tongues tangled together. Balder appeared in our faces with a loud growl for Cy, breaking yet another moment.

"We shouldn't make out in front of your dog when he seems so intent on eating my balls."

I laughed as I moved back and called the dog off, again. "He is Michael's best friend, they spend a lot of time together. Maybe he perceives you as a threat."

"Why? Because I'm doing stuff with his mistress that he only ever sees his master doing?"

It was such an innocent question and a simple yes, or maybe would have been an acceptable response, so why the hell did I open my mouth and spill more details? Because I couldn't help myself where this man was concerned.

"I think he perceives you as a threat to his happy home, and he has never seen anybody do that to me."

The weight of the stare I was under made me wary of looking up or speaking further. So I focused on petting the dog.

"That is a fucking crime baby," were the words that had me looking up to find an intent set of eyes watching me. "I can't imagine living with someone like you and not permanently planning on fucking you, actually fucking you or recovering from it, especially if you could tone down that whole bitch fest thing you have going on."

"You are such an insufferable..." I paused, not really knowing where to go with that sentence.

"Numb nuts? I seem to remember hearing that one before you hung up on me. Your dog would approve of that I'm sure, or maybe smart arse, although it's still ass."

"You really are an arsehole and it is ARSEHOLE," I retorted before he could correct me.

"Okay then, from a bitch to an arsehole, tell me what we do, how does this work, how has it worked in the past?" he asked and like that, the whole thing detonated around us.

He thought this was a regular thing for me, that I picked up men and began what, affairs with them, casually fucked them, like I'd fucked him? Well no more because I was done, well and truly over whatever the hell this was, had been, could have been.

"You are disgusting," I screeched, causing the dog to leap up with me, growling. "I have never, ever, entertained this before and this is over, done, so what we do is nothing. You go home or wherever, and I will see you in the office, on Monday. Goodbye, Mr Miller," I said coldly although I didn't feel cold, anything but and then I ran, like my life depended on it with a cry of 'Ms Ross' ringing in my ears.

****

I was pushing the confounded scarf that was taunting me every time I looked at it into a drawer on Sunday morning when

61

Michael appeared behind me.

"Did you hear the phone?" he asked and continued without waiting for a reply. "It was Denny. He and Elizabeth have invited us for dinner."

My farce life was going to turn into a blood and gore fest, I could almost see the spray and splatter of it up the walls of my chaotic world.

"When?" I sighed already thinking up a short list of good excuses not to go.

"Tonight, and I've accepted." Michael responded with a smile and a determined tone. "It will be fun to catch up. We'll leave here about half five," and then he turned away and left me with my thoughts and a horrified expression.

The house we pulled up in front of was a large, detached property with sprawling grounds in a gated community.

"I thought they lived in L.A." I queried.

"They do predominantly, but as Elizabeth is English and still has a few relatives over here, they keep a house here. Plus, I think she wanted to make sure as the children grew up they shared some of her English nationality."

"I suppose that makes sense," I agreed as Michael removed the arm from around me to ring the doorbell.

"Have you thought about having a baby?" His question left me agog that he would ask me that, here and now. I began opening my mouth without any words forming as the now open door revealed Denny.

"Hi there, I'm so glad you called Mikey."

Mikey? I had never heard anyone call Michael anything that wasn't Michael or Mr Stanton.

My face was agog before and now it had surpassed that at this revelation that Michael had called the Millers and presumably facilitated this shindig. I wondered just what his game was before I disappeared beneath the other man's enveloping arms.

Forty minutes passed in a strange blur as I sat in a plush yet elegant lounge in the middle of conversations about a life and time before I was born making me a spectator here. The last time I'd felt like this was when I was a little girl during holidays like Christmas and all the grown-ups would be talking, laughing and joking, whilst we, the children sat around playing together unsure what most of the talk was about. I was the child here, silently waiting, but for what? There were no other children here, nobody to play with. It was going to be a very long night, especially as I felt Elizabeth was judging me with every look and glance. All of them made me think back to Cy's comment that first day about his mother's feelings towards young, pretty women bagging older, rich guys.

"Hey there, anyone home?" came an all too familiar female voice.

"Tia?" replied Elizabeth sprinting to the doorway where Tia now stood, her gaze landing on me curiously.

The older woman giggled courtesy of the third glass of wine she was on, unlike me. I was still on my first, because I really didn't like wine, unfortunately my husband always disagreed and insisted that I loved a glass of a good rosé, which is what I sat nursing.

If my life was a movie it would have been a very short one. The heroine, me, would have just put herself out of her misery and killed herself right here, right now, in the middle of this actual scene, overdramatically, while they all looked on; the husband, the old friend and his wife, oh and the male love interest's girlfriend or fuck buddy or whatever Tia represented.

"Come and meet everyone sweetheart. This is Michael, who I doubt you'll remember, his wife Eloise, El, and me you know, and of course, Daddy."

"Daddy?" I shrilled startling myself as well as everyone else.

"Yes, Daddy," came Cy's voice from behind us all. "Ms Ross, I'm sure you remember my sister. You met her at the office, briefly."

We were definitely back to farce again. All that was missing was the vicar turning up and ending up minus his trousers.

"Mr Miller," I replied, making everyone except Cy laugh.

"Are you two always this formal?" asked Elizabeth with a strange expression crossing her face. An expression I couldn't quite name or recognise.

"Yes," we answered in stereo realising that we had never addressed each other as anything else beyond unpleasant names such as bitch or arsehole, although I'd had baby bestowed upon me a couple of times.

"What a pair, uh?" asked Denny causing Michael to laugh with him.

"You'll both stay for dinner, won't you?" Elizabeth asked flicking her glance between her children.

"Sure," grinned Cy. "Can I get drinks for everyone?" He nodded as he was told who wanted what and then turned to me. "Any chance of a hand, Ms Ross?"

Two choices; first, point out that I was his P.A. during business hours only, or, second, go with him, for drinks, and everything else I knew would follow. So, what did I do? I went with the only choice I could. "Of course."

Entering the traditional English country kitchen my senses shifted into overload, each one being encumbered as a previous one began to buckle under the weight of the sensory overabundance.

"Did you know I'd be here?" I whispered as I felt backed into a corner, metaphorically and then physically as I felt the counter top bump my behind while Cy stood a few inches ahead of me.

"We, Tia and I weren't planning on popping in on our way back from a trip to the movies, but when we called Mom about an hour ago and she mentioned that Michael had called and suggested you getting together…"

"You decided to join us?"

"Yeah. See what I meant yesterday, a disaster-in-waiting. Yet neither of us can keep away, can we?"

"No," I whispered with a shake of my head. "I had no idea she was your sister, Tia, and after I called you that first day and she answered…" I allowed my voice to trail off, unsure what else to say.

"But then, you didn't ask, did you? You just went ahead and thought the worst of me, me and Tia."

"I suppose," I reluctantly agreed.

"What did she say on the phone, Tia?"

"You didn't hear her?"

"No, or I'd have no need to ask, but I could guess."

"She said things about you being between her thighs and a den of debauchery and iniquity," I recalled with a shudder, but Cy just laughed, a loud and genuine laugh.

"Okay, I could have guessed some of it. Tia likes to play pranks, she enjoys a joke, we all do," he revealed making me let out a disbelieving huff. "You doubt my love of laughter and a sense of humour?" He sounded offended somehow, and yet more pissed off than anything.

"I suppose, maybe, or it could just be that I have yet to see any evidence of a light hearted, playful, joker in Denton Miller, CEO Miller Industries (Europe)," I replied using his closing address from his email, making him smile a little.

"Maybe you just bring out the serious, sombre monkey wrench you perceive me to be. Had you considered that?" There was clear accusation in his voice.

"Perhaps we should forget this..." I replied with minimal conviction despite wondering whether we were going to prove to be completely destructive and ruinous to each other and our lives long term.

"Whoa!" Cy called as he closed the distance between us briefly. "I don't think we can forget, do you?" he asked seriously.

"No." My voice was barely a whisper as I shook my head.

"Good, although there is one thing that might just blow us out of the water. So, I need to ask, do you plan on having a baby with him? If you are, I'm out. I'll find a way to work in another city or I can get you a transfer."

"I have no plans to have a baby and if I was, well I wouldn't be doing whatever we're doing here."

"You've never done this, have you?"

"What? What we've embarked on, what was it you called it, 'a disaster-in-waiting?' No. Up until Monday I had been a faithful wife which is why I was so angry with your suggestion yesterday. Although I could see why you might think that based on Monday."

"I got the anger." He smiled. "So, no babies?"

"No," I confirmed. "Sex would be necessary for a baby anyway," I revealed and then remembered the IVF suggestion.

"You mean you and he don't have sex at all?"

"No, not really, not for a while."

I needed Cy to believe what I was saying, to believe that I didn't have a track record and to know that he was different, he made me different and what we had was special.

"Okay. Then we need to let this thing run its course, get it out of our system."

"Agreed," I muttered, thinking that my life might never be the same after this, whatever this was.

"Here may not be the best place."

"No. I think your mother might have some kind of meltdown or seizure if she walked in on us."

"Yeah, I can see walking in on your son and an old friend's wife might prove to be a shock," Cy smirked.

"I was thinking more from the point of view that I don't think she likes me very much."

"Why wouldn't my mother like you? She doesn't actually know you, does she?" he asked with a seriously confused expression.

"No, but I think she thinks she does."

"Do you have any idea how inarticulate that sentence sounded?"

I shrugged, thinking that my meaning was pretty clear, but apparently not. "I thought I was quite clear, but to explain; your mother, she thinks she knows me, as in the type of person I am if not me personally. She thinks I am a young and pretty girl who has succeeded in bagging herself a rich, older and most probably stupidly flattered man and it was you that said…"

"Ah, I get what you mean and I can't say that she doesn't think badly of you, but the only time her opinion would matter is if I was about to get down on one knee and I'm not. I think one husband is quite enough, don't you?"

His question, statement, whatever it was made me pull up short with feelings of acknowledgement that he was right, anger that he had somehow insulted me by insinuating that I was not likely to be on the receiving end of a Denton Miller proposal, which even I acknowledged, at least to myself was ridiculous, not that my brain seemed to realise as it conjured images of Cy as a groom, a husband, my husband. I also recognised the hurt that his inference that I already had one husband had caused, which I did, but somehow him pointing that out to me, again, was like a sucker punch to the guts because it made me feel dirty and guilty. My facial expression or something must have registered in Cy's mind because I suddenly found my head being tilted up by his hand cupping my chin whilst he took a step back in order to observe me more clearly.

"You're overthinking again Ms Ross," he accused correctly. "Don't, there's really no need."

I nodded, knowing he was right. I just needed to get my mind to accept and understand that.

"I had no idea Michael called, he kind of told me that they'd called him," I seemed to blurt out in an attempt to change the subject.

"And why would he do that? Unless he thought that it would show you that this is where you fit, with him. That you'll decide babies are the way forward for you both. Babies and sex."

I shrugged, clueless as to what to say or do next, but again I needn't have worried because I didn't need to think or do, he did it for me. He threaded one hand along my neck until his fingers had laced through my hair, cupping the back of my head, pulling me close enough that I could feel his breath on my lips and then he slanted his mouth across mine. He consumed me with every touch, caress and stroke of his tongue, kissing me as if he had known me the whole of my life, like nobody else had kissed me, ever. Instinctively, my arms wrapped around his neck, tugging at his hair, urging him to give me more, but somehow I managed to resist the temptation to wrap my legs around him, just.

"Fuck! This is going to be harder than I thought, not touching you, here, tonight." A loud exhaled breath sounded around us.

"Sorry," I replied, equally as breathless.

"Why do you do that, apologise, for this?" He flicked his finger between the two of us.

I shrugged nervously, unsure why I apologised as I questioned whether I actually did.

"Yeah, well don't. It makes it sound like you regret kissing me, being kissed by me. Do you regret it?" He took a step closer, intent on a little torment.

"No, never." I panted for different reasons to my earlier breathlessness.

"Good. I would really like to kiss you again." His expression was dark and his eyes twinkled with mischief. "And maybe touch you, you know, run my hand across your abdomen, cup your fantastic tits until your nipples are between my finger and thumb. And then pull them, pinch them before sucking them into my mouth where I could gently nibble on them, then bite down making them hurt in a really, really good way."

A low moan was my response to his suggestion making him smile as he took another step closer again, his hips resting against my belly as he looked down into my eyes intently.

"We're on the same page then?" He grinned wolfishly, pressing an erection into me. "Then I'd head south a little until my hand was at the back of your knee and then I would lift it, opening you up for me baby…and then, real slowly I would trace my fingers up your thigh until I could feel your heat and your wet panties that you get all in a tangle and then…"

"What? What then? Please…" I begged knowing what next. Hoping, almost feeling it already. I was a big bag of sensation and need and we both knew it.

With a single chuckle, Cy backed off. "Tomorrow we'll talk, iron out the details."

"You are a complete arsehole. I fucking hate you!" My words and tone wiped the smile off his face, but I found myself unceremoniously spun around and bent over the back of a nearby stool.

"And you are a spoilt little bitch, overindulged and too demanding of your own wants and desires. I am not like your sugar daddy in there, believe me. While he gives in to your every whim, except in the sack, I will not. I am not loving and gentle. I will not shake my head in disapproval when you push, I will push right back, bending you over and spanking your sexy ass red," he warned as a single strike landed on my behind making me cry out a muffled groan, desperate for nobody to burst in and find us like this. "And rest assured if I wanted to start a family with you, we'd be fucking twenty-four seven with no protection. We will pick this up tomorrow."

Standing, I stared at him as he prepared the drinks orders with his back to me, leaving me confused and a little scared of what picking it up would entail. My bottom stung and felt hot, yet it also felt tingly, in a good way, a really good way which only added another layer of bewilderment to my confused state. So confused that I blocked out some of his words, most notably the ones relating to me, him and starting a family.

"Here," he said, handing me a bottle of beer. "Why were you drinking wine?" He reached out to brush my slightly untamed hair behind my ear.

"Michael insists that I like wine, rosé no less. I don't. But he refuses to accept that and tells me that beer is not the drink of a lady."

Shaking his head, Cy smirked. "And you think I'm the asshole?"

"Arsehole," I corrected.

"You pushing?" he asked, referring to his threat to push back.

I rubbed a hand over my throbbing rear and resisted the temptation to nod, shaking my head instead.

"Good, now stop being such a snarky bitch and grab the other beer for me."

I followed him towards the door and then stopped in my tracks as I eyed the beers I was carrying, his and my own.

"What now?" With a sad and sympathetic expression, he turned to find me several paces behind.

"Michael won't like me taking a beer back in there. He'll expect me to have wine," I replied nervously, more nervous about Michael's reaction than anything else.

"Oh Eliza, Henry Higgins has certainly done a job on you," he sighed as I frowned. "I want to tell you to bring the beer, to drink it and enjoy it, but I don't want you to feel pressured by me and him. Take another mouthful and then leave it in here, bring mine out and I will make you something pink and ladylike, with no wine."

I smiled, wondering how this man who had spanked me, made my bottom hurt, and claimed that he was not loving and gentle, had made me this offer that was precisely that, possibly one of the most loving things anyone had ever done for me.

Chapter Six

The journey home seemed long and strained, but fortunately it was late so I could legitimately go in and go straight to bed, or so I thought.

"That was a surprise, Tia and Cy turning up like that." I was unsure whether it was a question or a statement, but Michael didn't wait for any input as he continued. "You didn't say you'd met Tia. I was a bit surprised to find that out in front of people." He sounded irritated that there was something about me he didn't know, a trait I'd never noticed in him before.

"I hadn't realised she was his sister," I admitted truthfully. "She came in as I was leaving."

"I see," mused Michael. "Have you met anyone else I should be aware of?" he asked curtly meaning he was definitely annoyed.

"Not that I'm aware of. Where is this going Michael?" I sounded like the bitch Cy usually accused me of being; short, terse and a little hostile, however this was Michael I was talking to, not my boss, but I was finding this whole conversation tiresome.

"Nowhere that I'm aware of. Why didn't you have wine at dinner?"

I was going to be dizzy at this rate if he kept switching from topic to topic like he was currently, although it felt as though this was a quiz and there were certainly right and wrong answers.

"I've told you before, I'm not overly keen on wine and you don't like me to drink beer, so…"

"So you thought you'd come to the table drinking pop,

through a straw no less, looking every inch the young girl others perceive you to be rather than the grown woman you are?"

Suddenly it all made sense. He had arranged dinner to make me see where I fitted in, like Cy had suggested. Maybe to force my hand where having a baby was concerned and by drinking an alcohol free, pink lemonade with strawberries and lime floating in it I had clearly pointed out that I didn't fit as his young, but sophisticated wife.

"Michael, please, I don't think what I drink at dinner needs to be an issue, unless it's beer, clearly." We pulled up in front of our home as I took up my bitch mantle again. I chose not to point out that embarking on some kind of affair with my boss, who happened to be the person who'd made me the juvenile drink we were discussing could be an issue. "You told me you can't change what you are, that you can't be the man you were, five, ten or more years ago. Well neither can I, so can we please drop this before we end up rowing?"

"Sorry, of course." It felt that he had conceded before we entered the house, but once the front door had closed behind us, he spoke again. "Have you thought about a baby? You could stop your pill and see what happens."

I didn't know what to say because I thought we were done for the night but tried to soften my tone and facial expression with a small smile. "You said you'd abide by my decision and if you need a decision now then I say no, no baby."

"I did and I meant it, but I don't have time on my side," he pointed out, sounding sad and peeved at the same time.

"I know, but I do." I sounded like the bitch again but I didn't mean to, that was my attempt at honesty.

Balder was now running towards us, excited to see us and desperate to go outside.

"I'll let him out, maybe take him for a walk." I nodded. "I'm going to bed."

For the first time I could remember in my married life with Michael in the house I went to bed alone, fell asleep alone and woke up alone.

****

I arrived at work just after seven the following morning

having been awake since the early hours, meaning I was tired, agitated and emotional. As I sat at my desk typing up the minutes of Friday's meeting I kept hearing Cy's words from the previous evening, where he referred to me as being Eliza Dolittle to Michael's Henry Higgins. I wondered what he'd meant, although I could hazard a guess that it would relate to him being the emotionally inept, controlling, opinionated man moulding me into what he perceived as a lady with all the required attributes and me as the less intelligent, naïve and easy to manipulate young woman. My thoughts scrambled at the sound of Maya's laughter and then he appeared, Cy.

"Good morning, Ms Ross," he said placing his iPod on my desk. "Yours."

"No, mine is at home," I corrected.

"No. This is yours. We must have got them mixed up on Saturday. I didn't realise until I got to Time of My Life from Dirty Dancing, up until then it could have been mine with Jimi Hendrix, Led Zeppelin and The Who interspersed with Calvin Harris, Jason Derulo and my personal favourite David Guetta."

"You don't like Dirty Dancing?" I asked, a little outraged at the thought of anyone not loving Dirty Dancing. I had loved it from the first time I'd seen it. When I first realised that I wanted a Johnny when I grew up. A man that made me feel like no other woman existed for him. A man that made me feel special. A man that made me tingle all over like, oh God, like Cy.

"No man ever admits to liking Dirty Dancing unless he's trying to get laid."

I had no clue what to say, mostly because I was still picturing my boss as Johnny to my baby which prompted me to say, "We could watch it."

"Mmm, but would we be watching it because I'm trying to get laid?" He smirked before changing topic slightly. "Tea, Ms Ross?" he enquired looking over his shoulder to where his desk was, minus a cup of tea.

"Of course, right away," I stammered leaping to my feet clumsily as he grabbed my arm to pull me closer.

"Bring enough for us both."

His eyes scrutinized me carefully, suddenly turning from

their usual rich brown to a much darker shade of brown, almost black as his gaze bored into me, as if seeing into my very soul making me nervous and needy in equal parts.

"And close the door when you come in."

Okay, maybe I was just needy rather than nervous now.

With a tray of rattling cups I entered the office, nervously putting one foot in front of the other hoping not to douse him in tea again.

"For fuck's sake," he muttered, meeting me half way across the floor. "Do I make you that nervous?" Cy placed the tray down on his desk before gesturing for me to sit opposite him.

"Honestly, yes."

"And yet when I touch you I don't feel nervousness. I feel excitement, anticipation, desire, but no nervousness. Why is that?"

"Is this us picking things up from yesterday?" I asked a little sharply. Impolite to my own ears as I seemed to snap and accuse at the same time, but I was nervous.

"If it is, I predict a sore ass for the churlish attitude alone," he cautioned with a cold stare. "Now, stop being a bitch and answer me. Why don't I feel your nervousness when I touch you?" His voice softened in an attempt to encourage me to speak, and I did, with honesty.

"I don't know. I don't feel the same nervousness when you touch me, it's different."

"How? You're doing really well," he said and although I was unsure whether he was mocking me or showing actual support and encouragement, I went with the latter.

"This, now, is scary because I am never certain if I am about to put a foot wrong or step out of line and you are scary, shouty and an all-round arsehole. Not that I'm scared of you as such, just nervous, you're my boss. But when you touch me, it makes sense. Everything makes sense. My mind and body work together with yours and it's right all of a sudden, like we are somehow meant to be. It doesn't matter that we don't really like each other, nor that we irritate one another and somehow just manage to antagonise the other with our very being."

"Maybe I need you to be nervous when I'm your boss. To

keep some distance and control on things, but I couldn't have put it any better than you about when we're together. I would add to that the fact that I find the having sex with you far more compliant and agreeable than my bitchy assistant, but then you want what I have at that moment so maybe that's why you have two very different sides to your personality."

"Possibly, and you are less of an arsehole when all the blood in your body is rushing to your dick."

I was sure I saw a small smile tugging at Cy's lips, but as quickly as it appeared it disappeared again.

"So, how do you plan on keeping that distance and control, Mr Miller?"

"Not a fucking clue, Ms Ross, which means you might never know which me you're speaking to, the one with blood pumping around his whole body or the one with it only in his dick."

"So, do we keep it purely business in the office?" I began to wonder how I'd be able to manage an affair with a retired and increasingly inquisitive husband at home.

"How would that fit in with your home life? Can I demand your evenings and weekends?"

"Maybe this is a bad idea," I replied, grasping that this situation was going to become more complicated as we ventured further into it.

"Maybe it is, but I think the decision has been made," Cy said with confidence oozing from every pore. "By fate, our bodies or some sort of destiny. I've told you baby, a disaster-in-waiting. Now, what about Michael?"

"What about him?" Suddenly I was unsure if I could truly answer any question about my husband with anything resembling conviction or certainty.

"Are you sure you wouldn't rather revert back to being a faithful wife? You could do it and write off our night last week as nothing more than a mistake. He would never know and you and he could have your two point four children and live happily ever after."

I was unsure whether he was being an arsehole again or genuine so stopped trying to decipher him in that moment.

"I'm not sure I could write it off or return to my former self. He wasn't best pleased with your pink lemonade yesterday. Apparently it made me look like a child rather than the young woman I am. The straw really tipped him over the edge, as did me not mentioning that I'd met your sister and the bitchy me pointing out that I did have time on my side to put off having children after he suggested me coming off the pill and seeing what happened. It really did make for the perfect end to a perfect weekend."

"You're still on birth control though?" he asked seeming to ignore anything other than that.

"Yes. Which is why I went to bed alone, slept alone and woke alone and finally got up at half-past five this morning, and don't forget the key factor that we don't have sex."

A stare across the desk was all I got in reply. A strange shadow across his face that seemed to be a mixture of a dozen different feelings and emotions.

"I'll have coffee at ten and the details on the acquisition of Faulkner Telecomm. Leave the door open," he told me in his usual business-like mode, dismissing me, confusing me a little more, but I did as I was told and left.

My morning passed off uneventfully with no emails, shouting from his desk or anything at all from Cy. It was a comfortable way to work though. I got on with my things and he got on with his. Whilst photocopying, Michael text me to check what time I would be home and if I had any late nights scheduled for the coming week.

I replied quickly and concisely:

<Should be home on time as far as I know, unsure what is happening the rest of week>

<Don't forget that we're attending the hospital fundraiser on Friday>

With a sigh, I considered his reply because I had forgotten the fundraiser.

"Problem?" Cy asked, sidling up behind me trapping me

again, but this time between his body and the photocopier.

"No, not really," I replied as his hands came to rest on my hips.

"That sounds like a yes," he countered as one hand pulled my blouse free of my skirt and his hand began to caress my abdomen making me hiss at the burn of his touch. "Problem?" he repeated.

"Michael has just reminded me that we've got some fundraiser on Friday for the hospital where he had his heart surgeries. Where they saved his life meaning we owe it to them." I was shocked at the contempt I detected in my tone. I hadn't meant my words to sound that way. To be so hard and callous. I really was grateful they'd saved him.

"He has no clue what to do with you like this, does he? Had he met the bitch in you before last week? I like this blouse." His hand skimmed up my body until it was cupping my lace covered breast. "Oh nice baby," he told me brushing my nipple a little too softly as he nipped my ear.

"I think he's confused by me," I admitted as I pushed my breast more firmly into the hand that was tormenting me. I was confused by me so there wasn't much hope for Michael.

"I bet he is. I'd be happy to offer a few pointers," he teased, or at least I hoped he teased. "I'm going to fuck you today, fuck you and send you home wet and sore."

"Oh God," I moaned pressing my behind into his groin that was hard and ready.

"Not yet though. You finish what you're doing here and then go to the bathroom and remove your panties so that when I want you, you're ready, do you hear?"

"I can't, what if? I don't know what if, but I can't wander round naked," I whispered, not wanting to be overheard, although we were unlikely to be as this copier was for executives only and so far Cy was the only one in-situ.

His reply came in the form of me being pushed forward over the photocopier at my shoulders and spanked three times, fortunately through my straight and tight pencil skirt because his strikes were really quite hard.

"If I find your panties still on I am going to spank you red and then fuck you, but I won't make you come. You'll be going home wet, sore and frustrated."

And like that he was gone. I knew I would comply with his wishes, although as it was lunch time and I was meeting Maya I decided to wait until I returned to make my bathroom stop.

****

It was in the bathroom that my phone began to ring insistently, my sister, Susan. Even her ring sounded irritated and impatient, almost as irritated as her voice when I answered as I adjusted my clothes.

"I have been trying to contact you for the last two hours," she huffed.

I resisted the temptation to inform her that I was probably being inappropriately touched up by my boss. Possibly being spanked and then having lunch with one of my few friends, possibly my only current friend, Maya.

"Sorry," I compliantly replied with a diffident tone I knew she'd appreciate.

"Mmm, not as sorry as poor Michael. He is beside himself, Eloise, with worry about you and your strange moods."

"I'm not discussing this Susan," I insisted, determined not to get drawn into this because apart from anything else this was not her business and Michael had no right to involve her in this meaning I was going to go home with another strange mood and my bitch persona in full swing.

"What do you mean you are not discussing this?" She screeched as I left the bathroom and headed back to my desk.

"Like I say, not discussing it, not with you."

"Don't you dare take this out on poor Michael," she shouted now, beginning to lose any semblance of control.

"Susan, this really is none of your business—"

She cut me off with a bitter and acidic cry, "After all I've done for you, I even stepped aside for you El. I gave Michael to you on a plate…"

"Oh for fuck's sake Susan, grow up! He was never yours to give and maybe your act of generosity had ulterior motives. I have to go," I snapped as I hung up and slumped back into my chair before realising that Cy was standing before me, filling the doorway between his office and mine.

"Come through, now." He was already turning his back on me.

I followed him and found myself directed to the sofa in his office where he joined me.

"Who is Susan?" he asked making me shrug. Not because I didn't know who she was but because I was unsure why he wanted to know and whether I wanted to tell him.

"My sister." Clearly I wanted him to know.

"Problems? With you and Susan?" he asked but we both knew that he'd overheard enough to know that, yes, we had problems.

"Mmm, problems with me, Susan and Michael actually." I immediately saw his confusion. With a sigh I felt compelled to explain. "Susan worked here, a long time before me. She and Michael had, well I'm not sure what, but I do know that she loved him and would have given anything to be with him."

"He didn't want that? He wanted the other sister?" Cy frowned, making me laugh, confusing him again.

"Sorry, no, not at that stage. I was about twelve at the time though, so probably for the best. I'm the baby of the family. A very late in life baby meaning my siblings are considerably older. Susan was probably thirty by then."

"Ah, so even if Michael didn't have you in his sights, he didn't have your sister in them either?"

"No. He liked her, admired her even, still does and somehow they remained friends and she worked here for years. Anyway, when I came to work here, via Susan I was twenty-one. I met Michael one day, in the lift of all places. I didn't know who he was and we chatted, had a laugh and then I met him again when I had inadvertently covered reception downstairs in the day's post on my way home."

I looked up and found Cy smiling at me. Not a panty melting smile, but more of a slightly dampening of the panties smile. A kind smile with the promise of something more. I wondered what he was thinking. Maybe he thought I was genuinely a clumsy cow with my admission of yet more dropping of things.

"You were the post girl?" He wore a strange expression that I soon realised was some kind of questioning of how the post girl had risen through the ranks.

"I started my career here working as a secretary in the pool and I would take the late post on my way home. Then I went to work in accounts in a very junior position before eventually getting the post of secretary to one of the middle managers there which is whose post I threw across reception. That was when I started dating Michael, in case you were wondering," I explained with a degree of hurt and a greater amount of snarky, bitchiness at the inference I detected.

"The bitch is back then." There was a dark expression in his eyes and a tightening of his lips.

"Along with the arsehole," I bit back only to find myself pressed flat against the sofa with Cy's full weight holding me down as his lips found mine, open and eager.

With his lips firmly pressed on my own, his tongue brushing against mine, he was forcing me to submit to his will. His body was almost crushing me, every inch of him pushed me into the upholstery beneath us.

"Oh God," I cried as I registered a hand beneath my skirt, heading toward my stocking top.

"Fucking hell, baby, you smell so good," he told me as he buried his face into my neck, inhaling my scent before I felt his teeth as they grazed the soft, tender flesh above my collar bone.

I could feel my nipples as they pebbled inside the confines of my lacy bra that was abrading my breasts in the most uncomfortably frustrating way I could imagine or had ever known.

"Please, please," I pleaded, unsure what I was begging for beyond release.

"I don't think I'll ever tire of your begging," he whispered against my skin, causing vibrations to push me closer to the despondency of my unresolved pent up sexual desire. "What do you want? Where do you want me?" he asked and although I knew for sure he was taunting me I didn't care one iota.

"I want you to touch me," I replied weakly.

"Already there baby, can you feel me?" he asked with his

lips still littering tiny, exciting nips lower, towards my breasts. The hand beneath my skirt had finally come to rest on my stocking top, a finger tracing below the elasticated fabric making me pant until I sounded like I was about to hyperventilate.

"I mean, more," I whined loudly making Cy laugh against the upper swell of the breast his mouth was currently kissing, licking, mouthing against. Somehow my blouse had opened more, a couple of buttons having popped, or been popped.

"More?" he whispered, causing his breath to heat and then cool against my skin, bringing every single inch of skin on my chest to prickle to life.

"Fuck!" I squealed when his tongue darted out and licked lower to the exposed skin that lay between the two heaving mounds of sensation and desire that were my breasts.

"No fucking yet," he told me. "Not unless..." his voice trailed off and I realised that the hand beneath my skirt had reached my very hot and wet core that wasn't as naked as it should have been. "Oh dear," he admonished, although he sounded less than disappointed to find my pants in his way. Clearly he had wanted me to defy him, which in turn meant he wanted me red, sore and frustrated, the latter being the last thing I wanted.

"Sorry," I spluttered when he roughly pulled at my sodden, lacy pants and slowly dragged a finger along my length, through my arousal that was only increasing with each passing second.

"One instruction," he reminded me at the same time a finger filled me while his body moved up to cover mine again until my ear was in his mouth and I was unable to avoid or miss his words. "Somebody is going home with a very red and hot ass."

"Please," I offered but that was insufficient I realised when a second finger joined the first making me gag, gasp and clench simultaneously.

"And," he continued with a sharp nip of my earlobe. "That same somebody is going to be fucked."

"Yes, yes," I cried, attempting to buck against his hand, but to no avail as I was pinned in place by his greater weight.

"No, no," he replied with a laugh at his use of the negative to my affirmative call. "So, you're going to have the red, hot ass while you're fucked, but what else did I say?"

"No!" I sobbed as his thumb brushed my clit just once before his whole hand stilled while my body began to quake gently, in preparation for what was to follow, or not. At that specific point there probably wasn't a single thing I wouldn't have done to get what I needed.

"Answer me, now," Cy demanded with his eyes fixed on mine.

"Frustrated," I cried, with actual tears brimming my eyes. God, just how pathetic could I actually be?

"Yes, frustrated, really, really frustrated. I can feel just how close you are. How badly you want this. But not today, not for you," he gloated. Freeing himself from inside me he stood in a single, fluid movement until he stood over me, his hand extended to help me up.

With my hand safely enclosed in his he led me towards his desk, reminding me of the fact that we were at work, in an unlocked office, with the potential for discovery. Strangely, I felt a little less apprehensive as he came behind me, as though his mere presence next to me was all I needed. He unzipped my skirt and allowed it to drop, pooling at my feet.

"You are so fucking sexy." He ran a hand from the tops of my stockings, along my suspenders that matched my bra and pants that he finally reached with a finger from each hand settling where they finished at my hips. "How could anyone leave you barren and dry?" he asked and although I didn't need or want the reminder of my husband or his inability or unwillingness to make love to me, somehow the reminder was timely and welcome. It reminded me of what I was doing. How this made me feel. How Cy made me feel.

I felt the lace skimming down my hips, behind, thighs, and then they were gone. If only I had removed them for myself he might be buried inside me, driving me towards climax, maybe a second or even a third one by now. But no. I had forgotten because of Susan calling and that was another reason to be pissed off with my sister.

"You're going to leave me barren and dry too," I cried, hoping to appeal to Cy on some competitive, alpha male level.

If he was right and I was sexy and he thought my husband was a fool not to touch me, pleasure me and satisfy me then surely, he was about to tar himself with the same brush if he followed through with his earlier threat.

"Oh baby, you are as far removed from dry right now as anyone has ever been." I felt shamed by his accurate summation, backed up perfectly by a finger slipping and sliding along my length. "And barren...well there is nothing here to suggest anything inhospitable, nor sterile or desolate. So, no, you will not be left barren by me."

"But you said," I moaned, struggling to keep my tears at bay, a fight I wasn't sure I could possibly win.

"That you wouldn't come?" he asked leaning round to look at me. "You won't baby, so if you want to end this, you should put your clothes back on and go back to your desk."

He was giving me a get out, one word and I could end this. In fact, no words, just simply going back to work and this would be over, but that was the last thing I wanted, to end things.

"And if I stay?"

"I will spank your ass and fuck you."

"I don't want to end this," I admitted, tears already overflowing slightly.

"Good," he replied and with that single word he placed a hand between my shoulder blades and pushed me forward until my upper body was flat against his desktop leaving my arse bare and primed, like a beacon in a storm, calling to him, asking to be smacked.

I hissed at the feel of his hand roaming across one cheek, then the other and then it was gone. I braced myself, waiting for the feel of his hand returning, but he spoke first. "If you want me to stop you say and I will."

"Like a safe word?" I asked, thinking the only adult women I had ever heard of being spanked were the submissive types who had dominant men to keep them as slaves; I'd read a few low key erotic fiction titles and had seen a documentary once.

"No, not like a safe word," he snapped angrily. "You are safe. If you want me to stop, you say so and I stop, no questions. I just stop."

His final word had barely registered when I heard a loud noise, not quite a bang and then a sensation, a burning that was spreading through one cheek before a second strike landed on the other side. I lost count of how many times his hand landed. I just felt the warmth increasing until I was convinced he'd set fire to me and then I heard the sobs and cries that emanated from me. The tears I had been battling all day, all weekend, maybe all week wouldn't be held at bay any longer. They ran down my face as I gasped and sniffed. No more smacks landed, presumably meaning it was over, a thought that was confirmed when I felt hands running up my body; along my hips, skating across my torso before settling on my still dressed breasts.

"So, so sexy baby," he crooned as his body covered mine and his mouth settled against my neck. "Are you okay?" he asked me quietly, calmly.

"Yes," I whispered, because I was. I felt calm and centred.

The feel of his trousers brushing my behind had me wincing and moaning, but then with the sound of his zipper lowering I felt skin on skin; his legs against mine, his erection brushing my behind, the room silent except for the sound of our breathing. I thought I should probably say something just in case the silence between us was uncomfortable. I really needed to sort out my ideas on polite behaviour and etiquette. Apparently it was okay to be bent over his desk and spanked, but perish the thought that our silence should make him uncomfortable.

The sudden sound of foil being ripped alerted me to the fact that Cy was opening a condom and then he gently tapped my foot. An indicator, I assumed that I needed to spread my feet, which in turn meant, spread my legs. The feel of a hand in the middle of my back pushing me down and his other hand on my hip, pulling me up preceded the nudge of his sheathed length pressing against my core.

"Ready baby? This is going to be hard and fast," he seemed to warn as he entered me slowly, stretching me, causing my whole centre to burn until he was buried in me fully. "Okay?"

"Mmm, can we just hold still, for a moment?" I needed to become accustomed to him filling me before he moved.

"Say when." He pushed my blouse up, exposing my flesh,

making me shudder as the air hit my skin. "You have beautiful skin," he mused. He ran both hands up to my shoulders and beyond to my neck before he brought them back down again.

"Okay. When." I thought he might start slow, literally break me in gently, but he didn't, he pounded at me from the first thrust. "Oh God!" I gasped as my whole body began to glide up and down against his desk with the force of him sliding in and out of me.

"You better fucking believe it. Squeeze me, work those muscles baby, come on," he encouraged.

I followed his instructions and began to tense my internal muscles, but kind of regretted it when I immediately began to feel the pulsing burn in my clit that signalled I would be going off like a firework on the fifth of November if he carried on like this.

"Don't stop!" he hissed from between what I knew would be gritted teeth.

I squeezed again and immediately felt the first stirrings of a real orgasm.

"I can't," I whimpered, "I'm going to come," I hissed myself now, suddenly aware that I was wringing wet with sweat.

"Don't you fucking dare!" he threatened gruffly as he dug his thumbs and fingers into my hot and sore behind.

"Please," I pleaded, "Don't make me," I added, unsure what the hell I meant by my pleas.

"Oh yes, fuck, you are so tight, pulling me in," he told me as his grip on my arse increased making me forget coming for a split second as the burn turned into a very real pain.

With his thrusts increasing in speed and force I thought he may knock me off my feet, but he gripped me more firmly and that was when I could feel the burn and sting in my behind spreading through my sex making me hotter and wetter than I had ever been in my life.

"Please, I can't," I bleated and with that he thrust one last time before he was discharging his seed into the condom and then everything stilled under a mist of grey. That place where my whole world ended up spinning on its axis leaving me unable to fathom anything. Where everything was confused and blurred.

Our loud and laboured breaths were almost deafening until my desk phone began to ring in the distance, threatening to break the moment we were sharing. His arms were wrapped around my middle, his front blanketed my back, and lips caressed my neck and upper spine as he softened inside me. I attempted to straighten, but clearly Cy wasn't on board with that idea.

"My phone," I whispered, unsure what to say or do now that the sex was over. My mind began to question if this was normal extra marital affair behaviour. I'd almost expected him to shoot, eat and leave, but minus the eat, and in fairness it would be me that would have needed to leave as we were in his office.

"They can leave a message or call back," he replied straightening himself now.

He withdrew from me and without embarrassment or discomfort removed the condom, tied it securely, wrapped it up in a tissue and then passed me my clothes before redressing.

Leaning towards me he brushed my rather unruly hair behind my ear before asking, "Are you okay?"

"Yes," I whispered nervously.

"Sure?" He sounded almost as nervous as me.

A nod confirmed my earlier claim as I pushed my own hair back in an attempt not to look freshly shagged only to find his hand covering mine. The sunlight streamed through the large window behind Cy's desk and put me in its spotlight. As the rays hit my hand that was toying with my hair the gold band on my wedding ring finger seemed to sparkle and glitter, almost blinding us both. It was as though the symbol of my marriage burnt Cy judging by the way he recoiled, shaking me off him.

"Mmm, I might just pop to the ladies and then I'll be at my desk," I prattled on with fresh awkwardness and discomfort.

"Of course. Coffee in an hour please." His suddenly reinstated game face prompted me to rush back to my own work space. "And Ms Ross," he called after me causing me to spin back to face him. "Close the door."

"Fuck! Fuck! Fuck!" I cursed once the door closed behind me. "You stupid cow."

At that moment I felt a complete and utter fool, a fool who

had just experienced some seriously hot sex, even without an orgasm, but with a red, sore arse. I'd compromised my professional position by agreeing to have an affair with my boss who now appeared to be having second thoughts with his business as usual face and tone along with the unusually closed office door.

Chapter Seven

I visited the bathroom and cleaned myself up a little before returning to my desk. Upon my return I call screened to avoid speaking to my sister or my husband as I attempted to try and order my thoughts in silence, right up to the point where the silence was broken by an email arriving.

Ms Ross,

How are you?

Regards,

Denton Miller
CEO Miller Industries (Europe)

Mr Miller,

I am unsure what you're asking me

Regards,

Eloise Ross
P.A. to CEO Miller Industries (Europe)

I hit send and waited for some clarification on exactly what he was asking me.

Ms Ross,

The bitch is back then! I was asking how you are, simple!

Regards,

**Denton Miller
CEO Miller Industries (Europe)**

I regretted not being clearer in my confusion because now the arsehole version of Denton Miller was waiting on a response and I'd have to deal with him for the remainder of my day. With renewed thoughts of a pissed off sister and a suspicious twit telling husband in my mind I wasn't entirely sure I'd survive it.

Mr Miller,

I feel confused in addition to sore and frustrated.

Regards,

**Eloise Ross
P.A. to CEO Miller Industries (Europe)**

Ms Ross,

Confused how, why?

Regards,

**Denton Miller
CEO Miller Industries (Europe)**

Mr Miller,

Confused at what happened between us, it was intense, but more about afterwards.

Sorry, I am probably not making sense.

Faulkner Telecomm have emailed, they'd like to discuss things with you in person.

Regards,

Eloise Ross
P.A. to CEO Miller Industries (Europe)

Ms Ross,

I understand the intensity, I felt it too, and the confusion, hence the door remaining closed.

This thing between us is likely to remain that way I think. We need to deal with it, accept it.

Schedule a meet with Faulkner Telecomm that fits in with both of our schedules.

When you bring my coffee in you should leave the door open.

Regards,

Denton Miller
CEO Miller Industries (Europe)

"Numb nuts," I muttered with a smirk at his final line yet felt more settled knowing that he felt it too, the intensity and it appeared that the confusion was something else we shared. But most of all it was the knowledge that he wanted to remove the physical barrier between us, the closed door that made me happiest.

Another email landed in my inbox and I couldn't help but laugh out loud.

Ms Ross,

The bitch really is back if you're reverting to numb nuts, unless, unless you're pushing…

Regards,

Denton Miller
CEO Miller Industries (Europe)

Mr Miller,

Definitely not pushing, arse is too sore to push, so it must be the bitch, which probably makes you the arsehole.

Thank you for easing my confusion.

Regards,

Eloise Ross
P.A. to CEO Miller Industries (Europe)

Ms Ross,

Glad to be of service. Coffee??

Regards,

Denton Miller
CEO Miller Industries (Europe)

I smiled at his message and then felt the doubts creeping in. Service. Was that in relation to easing my nerves and confusion or was he acknowledging what had happened in his office? If I didn't have a meltdown before home time it would be some kind of miracle I decided as I got up to make the coffee.

Cy had remained fairly up beat throughout the afternoon, seeming to understand my need for stability and calm in order to avoid my impending nervous breakdown. He left for the day shortly before me, pausing several times in my office space as if he was going to say something.

Eventually he left with a simple, "Good night, have a good evening."

I wondered how this would work for us. Could we text or call during our evenings and weekends apart, or would that be overstepping the mark? The mark of what I had no clue but decided we were not casual texters. Just the thought of sitting in front of the TV with Michael whilst texting my lover was wrong, even for me, the unfaithful wife.

****

The drive home passed far too quickly meaning that once I got there I was confined for the night and Michael was in an odd mood from the second I walked through the door.

In my mind I had planned on storming in and telling my husband that if he called my sister to discuss me again I would return the favour with his daughters but when I saw him I felt tired and resigned so quickly changed into my running stuff. With my iPod plugged in and Balder at my side I ran until eight miles later I returned to find my dinner on the table, fish. I hated fish and to top my day off completely there was a large glass of rosé next to it.

"I might just eat the veg'," I said, returning from my shower that had only served to leave me tingling all over, from my slightly pink, but no longer red arse to my aching sex that had been well used, but was still desperate for some kind of release.

"You love seabass," Michael argued.

"I don't, not really. Fish is not my thing," I countered.

"Since when?" He looked genuinely surprised.

With a sigh and a shake of my head I replied, "Always Michael. You and Susan are the only people that insist I like fish and that it's good for me."

"It is." He bristled before me but ignored my sister's name. "So what would you have prepared for yourself?"

"Pizza and beer," I told him, because, firstly it would have been nice. I liked pizza and beer, but secondly because my husband disapproved of me drinking beer and fast food, including pizza, and I had a strong, almost overpowering urge to gain his disapproval.

"Don't be ridiculous," he snapped. "Now eat the bloody fish and drink your wine, unless you want another childish attempt at a mocktail."

I stared at him with his face reddening in annoyance at the memory of my pink lemonade drink and began to pick at the seabass on my plate. Eating in near silence was a relief in some way, at least I was absolved of making polite small talk and soon enough Michael would retire to the lounge to watch whatever documentary was earmarked for tonight.

With half of my dinner eaten and my wine drunk I finally broached the topic of Susan. My time at the table had allowed me to calm my nerves and remember that potentially the only changes Michael was demonstrating were on the back of the changes in me. The changes that had occurred since I'd met Cy. When I'd danced with him, my mysterious stranger, and then had permitted him to shag me in the office of the club before agreeing to an affair or whatever the fuck it was we were now embroiled in. The same thing that had allowed me to be spread across a desk and spanked before being fucked. With those details freshly established in my mind I was determined to stop being a bitch with Michael, at least until bedtime I hoped.

"Why do you think Susan called today?"

I had been aiming for a flat tone to my voice. Non-accusatory was my aim and I think I achieved it, just.

"Because, like me, she cares about you. She loves you and wants the best for you," he replied, with a speed that shocked me.

Maybe he had been waiting for this conversation, expecting it and therefore had planned for it.

"Michael, I know you want the best for me, you and Susan,

but…" I floundered. "I want to be in charge of my own destiny, make my own choices, my own mistakes. I do understand why Susan does what she does, why she feels so responsible, but she is not my mother and you are not my father."

Michael stared at me for long minutes before responding with a short and blunt response. "No, and yet it has never bothered you before, El."

I didn't even know what to say to that and still felt obliged to say something. "Sorry," was my effort, although I was unsure exactly what I was apologising for.

"Me too," Michael replied, but was clearer in the reason for his regret. "For involving Susan again. I just didn't know what to do with your current mood swings."

"Okay," is what I came up with in answer to that statement and was surprised and relieved when he allowed the conversation to die a natural death.

"There's a docudrama about life in the trenches during world one on in a moment, if you don't mind," he said brightly, possibly relieved to be moving on from our earlier topic of conversation.

"No, of course not." I smiled weakly. "I'll load the dishwasher and come through," I added, already scraping the remnants of my dinner into the food waste bin.

"This is all quite grim, isn't it?" Michael asked, infiltrating my private thoughts.

I came back to my living room with a start as I wondered what he was referring to and then looking up at the screen could see the desolate images of darkness and despair. Young men who looked middle aged, dirty, lonely, scared and sad.

"Unimaginable, isn't it?" he asked and assuming he meant life in the trenches rather than feelings of loneliness and sadness in a dark place of unhappiness, much like my life, I agreed with him.

"Yes, it is. Although this gives you a good sense of how it must have felt," I declared a little sadly. "It's a bit gruesome for me, I might head up to bed."

"I'll be up when it's finished." He smiled up at me as I leaned down and placed a gentle, friendly kiss on his cheek, almost daughterly.

Returning from the bathroom I climbed into bed and tried to organise, no, quash my feelings of guilt over Cy. After the evening I'd spent with my husband part of me wondered if I should try to get my marriage back on track and write Cy off as a moment of madness, several moments. Realistically I knew that I couldn't just forget it and move on. Move back, because now I knew what I was missing. Not just the sex I told myself, although, I didn't know that I could go back to a predominantly sexless marriage when a single look from my boss was capable of leaving me on the verge of ecstasy.

Remembering the early days of my marriage I recalled how Michael would make love to me with some frequency. There would be periods of satisfying foreplay before he'd take his own pleasure. Not that I would now describe it as passionate as I once would have. Not since I'd experienced real passion with Cy. What I had once thought of as passionate and satisfying was now very different in my mind. Michael and I had been sexually tame and almost perfunctory which was only made odder by the fact that I was my husband's fourth wife. Unless that was why his marriages had broken down. No, I knew that wasn't true, not in that singular entirety.

What had happened to us, besides the decline in Michael's health? For the first time since our sex life had reduced I wondered why he had chosen to just stop all intimacy. Maybe I was being selfish in thinking he could have still brought me pleasure and satisfaction without penetrative sex. When did all of my thoughts lead back to sex? Since I'd met Cy. With all roads coming back to him, I had to ask myself, where did that leave me?

I reached for the bedside lamp, hoping the darkness would swallow me up and give me a solid eight hours sleep just as a text message sounded from my phone. If this was Susan I knew my eight hours would be restless, sleepless and pointless. Nervously, I unplugged my phone as I grabbed it and felt the familiar rush of excitement when I saw the name on my screen.

Arsehole Boss

I opened the message with a shaking hand and a huge grin on my face at the one word text.

<Hey>

Well what could I say to that? I was unsure so took my lead from him.

<Hey yourself>

<How you doing? Can you talk?>

I wondered if he was asking about my confusion, thoughts and feelings after our encounter earlier that day, or maybe it was his own thoughts that had prompted him to make contact.

<Am good thanks. Yeah, I can talk. Michael is watching the TV downstairs, I'm in bed.>

<Ok. Hope you've had a good evening, that this afternoon hasn't made things weird at home.>

Maybe he felt guilty, guilty for me and Michael.

<No. We had dinner and chatted a little and then watched some TV, well he did, I was thinking while the TV was on. Hope you've had a good evening.>

What the hell was I doing here? Making polite chit chat with the man I was having an affair with in spite of the fact that we didn't like each other. Damn, we barely tolerated each other when we weren't kissing, touching, shagging.

<Did you have wine with dinner, Eliza? What were you thinking of? My evening was good, pizza and beer always makes for a winning night.>

"Bastard!" I muttered with jealousy at his pizza and beer over my seabass and rosé.

<What was on your pizza?>

Even I couldn't believe I had sent that as my sole response to his last message. When my phone rang in my hand, I physically jumped meaning him actually calling me was a bigger surprise to me than my text message.

"Really? I make a reference to you being Eliza and I provocatively ask what you were thinking about while you were sitting in front of the TV with your husband and you only want to know what topping I had on my pizza."

I laughed at his observation because it was ridiculous that it was the pizza that had truly engaged me.

"So, what did you have on the pizza? Tell me it was meat, not a veggie or fishy one," I pleaded and was rewarded with a warm and throaty laugh.

"Meat feast all the way, baby, complete with stuffed crust, garlic bread and chicken wings, all washed down with beer." He seemed to gloat, making me huff in response, feeling genuine envy at his description of dinner.

"I don't think I have ever been so jealous of someone else's dinner before," I admitted.

"Really? What did you have then?"

"Fucking seabass," I hissed with genuine disgust that again had a rich laugh coming back down the line, one that warmed me from the inside out. Melted me judging by the damp feeling between my thighs.

"Clearly not good seabass."

"I don't really like fish," I admitted awkwardly, knowing that an Eliza was coming my way.

"And wine? You had wine with it, didn't you?"

"Yes," I conceded with a burn in my throat that suggested tears might follow.

"Oh my, what am I going to do with my Eliza?" Cy asked, but it sounded rhetorical so I remained silent although his use of *my* sounded like the greatest compliment I might ever have been paid. "You never did tell me what you were thinking of while watching your husband watching something scintillating on the TV."

I realised that every time Cy spoke of my husband he somehow said it with distaste. Like just uttering it offended him, almost as much as my wedding ring burnt him when he touched it.

"You. I was thinking of you, and us, and me. Of how much my life has changed since we met. How much I've changed."

It felt as though the weight of the world had been lifted from my shoulders with that cathartic confession.

"I like that you think of me, and us, but I don't believe your life or you have changed since we met. It's just that since that first night you have allowed yourself to be you and in turn that means you no longer fit in."

"Maybe," I muttered.

"When did you last have pizza?" he asked causing me to pull up short as we shifted back to dinner.

"A while, a long while. My birthday, my twenty-third birthday," I recalled in shock.

With tears brimming my eyes that I had been that, what? Subservient, malleable, compliant, stupid, pick any adjective that meant I had simply been directed what to do in every aspect of my life and never once thought to question it and that would describe me just fine.

"Fucking hell!" I heard Cy say in the distance as my awareness of my plight, my upset and tears began to take over everything else. "Don't cry, please," he pleaded as I realised I was failing in my attempts not to cry.

The sound of Michael pottering downstairs made me aware of the need to calm down.

"Sorry," I whispered to Cy. "I told you I'd never been jealous of someone else's dinner before, didn't I?" I hoped to lighten the mood because despite my tears I wasn't actually sad. A little overwhelmed with, well everything, but not sad.

"Don't apologise for feeling," he insisted, sounding irritated by my apology.

"I should go. I can hear Michael, he'll be coming to bed

soon," I said and immediately regretted it when the atmosphere between us became heavy and tense.

"Goodnight, Ms Ross," he replied curtly, but I had nothing to offer in response so replied in kind.

"Goodnight, Mr Miller."

I was still staring down at my phone in my hand when Michael appeared in the doorway, allowing Balder to come in and nudge my hand for a fuss.

"You alright?" He nodded towards my phone.

"Mmm, fine. It was Mr Miller. I appear to have double booked him in meetings, but it's sorted now," I lied with a smile.

"He phoned you for that? Has he upset you? He has no right, he is a menace. I'm going to speak to his father."

"No!" I insisted crossly. "You do not interfere in my work, ever. You are not an irate parent contacting your child's school. It is bad enough that you think it is acceptable to phone my sister to discuss me and our marriage. Now, unless you'd like me to return the favour and call your cronies from the golf club or maybe your daughters and discuss why we are not communicating or having sex, you will not be calling anyone about me again."

The conviction with which I spoke shocked me, maybe as much as my husband, although, maybe not as he looked ready to keel over.

"Are we agreed, Michael?"

"Yes of course, but it's not that we're not communicating or having sex," he stammered to a halt as I levelled a cold stare in his direction.

"So, you're saying we are communicating and having sex? Are you? Because if we are then I appear to be missing it, so feel free to point out the next time we're having an in- depth discussion or I'm about to come!"

I was definitely being what Cy would describe as a bitch now. However, he wouldn't bat an eyelid at me speaking of coming, unlike Michael, but right now I was past caring how I came across. My head was swimming with a million thoughts again and I just needed to go to sleep and find some peace, but it didn't look likely.

"Don't be so crude," Michael chastened with a raised voice I rarely heard.

"Crude? That wasn't crude," I told him, already out of bed and preparing to go to the spare room. "I can do fucking crude if you really want me to."

Heading for the door he pulled me back roughly by my wrist, spinning me to face him where he stared down at me like a disapproving father.

"Enough Eloise. I will not have you behaving like a cheap and loud commoner from the local council estate. I have taught you better than that."

How had I never seen this before? That my husband was a snob. But worse than that he really was Higgins to my Eliza.

I laughed an ironic, pained cackle at his words. "I am a commoner from the local council estate or did you forget that? And maybe I would have, should have been cheap and loud, but life, Susan and you wore me down. Oh, and if I was being crude I wouldn't have said come, I would have said that you should point out to me when you were fucking me."

A loud slap, followed by a warm sting to my cheek sounded out around us before Balder wedged himself between us, his back to me while his teeth were bared at Michael as he growled.

"El, darling," he began but I waved it away.

"No, no, it's fine. I deserved it," I acknowledged with my hand rubbing across my smarting cheek, not that I really knew what I thought I deserved it for; for being a bitch in general, fucking my boss or going out of my way to destroy the life Michael and I had shared. "I think it would be better if I slept in a guest room and maybe we should both do some serious thinking about what we want from our life together."

"Please stay." He reached forward to touch me, making Balder growl louder as he repositioned himself in case he needed to defend me. "I'll sleep next door."

****

The following morning I arrived at work very early having managed to avoid any conversation with Michael beyond agreeing that I'd see him at home later and that he would take Balder for a good walk. His need to build bridges with the dog seemed stronger than his desire to build them with me. He had rightfully defended the dog's protection of me, but offered no further apologies to me, not even acknowledging the faint red mark on my face that I'd all but covered with make-up.

I hadn't even considered Cy's tea when he appeared behind me in the stationary cupboard.

"Hey," he muttered as he closed the door and turned off the light, plunging us into darkness.

"Hey," I replied as I felt his body pressing into mine, one hand wrapping around my waist, pulling me back into him.

A soft kiss landed on my neck that was exposed courtesy of my hair being clipped up in a messy bun.

"Are we having a competition for who gets to the office first?" he asked with a gentle laugh against my skin that was prickling with anticipation.

"I'm not." I sounded terse rather than expectant.

"Could you be a bigger bitch?" He stroked a hand down my fitted dress until his fingers were skimming around the hem.

"Depends, could you be a bigger arsehole?" My reply received a sharp nip of his teeth in response.

"You have no idea and it's asshole! But just to be sure, is this you pushing me?"

"No, no pushing, not today," I replied a little sadly. I didn't think I had it in me to argue for real.

"What's wrong?" he asked with only concern in his voice as he released me and prepared to turn me to face him before Maya's voice called from the corridor beyond the cupboard we were in.

"El, El," she called. "I have chocolate croissants," she seemed to chirrup.

I smiled before I laughed at Cy. "What is she, the child catcher? Sweeties," he called doing an impression of the character from Chitty Chitty Bang Bang.

Stifling a louder laugh I called to my friend, "Yeah, coming."

"You could have been," Cy teased as I flicked on the light and with a pack of envelopes left my boss alone in the cupboard.

When Cy next found me, I was making tea for three; him,

me and Maya who was returning to reception with her own chocolate and pastry breakfast already eaten.

"Mr Miller." She smiled tightly before leaving us alone again.

"Your tea," I seemed to announce thrusting the cup towards him.

"Thank you. You know that's not the healthiest of breakfasts don't you?" he asked pointing at my croissant.

With a shrug and a bite into the chocolatey goo I asked, "You want some?"

"Only if it's spread across your naked form," he replied quickly, maybe too quickly as he and I both stared at his suggestion, although I in no way objected. It was just a shock for him to be so candid and, I don't know, unguarded, open. Whatever it was he looked as disconcerted as I felt. "I'll take my tea through. Join me to go over this week's diary, after you've eaten."

Just like that he was gone and was more closed again leaving me wondering what had happened between us that I was unaware of.

Chapter Eight

We went through the week's diary and although it was all business and professional I felt under serious scrutiny from Cy's intense gaze that seemed to be permanently on me every time I looked up.

"What?" I finally asked.

"I dunno, there's something different about you."

"No, same as yesterday," I insisted thinking that was the truth.

"You're wearing make-up. More make-up than usual," he detected with triumph. "Is it for my benefit? Because if it is, there is no need. I like your natural look." He smiled and I think attempted to pay me a compliment.

"Not for you, arsehole." I suddenly felt irritated that he'd think it was for him. I remembered how much he liked my natural look on that first night when I was probably down to mascara and a little lipstick at best.

"And there she is. You should definitely have stayed shtum in the cupboard. Assuming you didn't convince your husband to do you the grand service of fucking you last night you must be burning for it baby," he taunted and I was. I was desperate to be touched until I found the release I so desperately wanted, needed maybe. "I could have made you come in there, let my fingers bring you right to the edge and then fucked you, or not. I may have just buried myself between your legs and licked you until you were screaming for it and then, when you finally came all over my tongue, then I could have fucked you."

I was already on my feet and ready to storm out, but where

to? My own desk where he could follow me? Or worse still not follow me. He could leave me there, all day, all week, desperate for him and only choose to tease and taunt me. I had never been much of crier. That was the benefit of a shitty and sad earlier life, you learnt to only cry for the really tragic things, and yet here I was, standing by the door, facing it, too scared to leave and yet somehow more scared to return to the seat I'd been in and I was ready to cry. My highly emotional state was just ready to spill over with little to no further input.

"Where the fuck do you think you're going?" Cy sounded angry, but concerned too.

If I didn't get sacked or have a nervous breakdown within the next month it would be an absolute miracle. I warily did a quarter turn so I was in profile to Cy.

"What the fuck?" he asked with anger as he got to his feet and approached me.

My frown clearly conveyed my confusion regarding his question, but as he reached me and turned me to face him I understood. With a finger stroking across my cheek, the one he'd seen in profile he spoke again.

"He hit you. The bastard hit you and you've tried to cover it up," he stated more than asked. "Oh baby," he whispered as he cupped my face gently in his hands. "My poor Eliza Dolittle," he said and I thought those words might serve as the further input my tears were waiting for until I realised his lips were lowering towards mine.

My mouth immediately softened as he deepened the kiss, incorporating the use of his tongue that aroused me, tears now a distant memory. I began making soft mewling cries that were captured in Cy's mouth. My hands were in his hair, pulling him closer, pleading with him not to stop, silently, with the exception of my moans and whines. His hands were everywhere and nowhere at the same time; my back, neck, behind, then my legs, pulling and pushing at my clothes before making their way back up my body until they skimmed across my belly and breasts. Then finally they were back on my face, cupping it again with just a thumb brushing across the bruise I thought I'd hidden. As his lips left mine I panicked, thinking he might stop and let me go.

"Please," I begged.

"We don't have to do this, do anything," he offered causing me further bewilderment that what we were doing, this disaster-in-waiting was sex and now he was telling me we didn't have to do it, but if we didn't do that, then what did that leave?

"I want to." I pushed my own questions and probable answers away.

With my dress already pushed up to my thighs I wrapped my legs around Cy's as if offering further confirmation that I was on board with this.

"You want to stop, you say. Whenever you want."

"Okay." I had no doubt in my mind that I wouldn't be calling time on what we were about to do.

The sound of the door locking behind me confirmed it and then with me wrapped around Cy, his lips back on mine and my hands back in his hair he carried me over to the sofa and gently lay me down.

"You are fucking killing my work ethic," he told me pulling his red, geometrical patterned tie from his pure white shirt.

"Sorry," I anxiously replied and immediately regretted it when Cy lowered his face to mine.

"Let's just clarify, again. You do not apologise for this." He wagged his finger between us. "Maybe I needed my work ethic killing a little. We, both of us, are in this together and whatever happens is on both of us, so, do not apologise, ever."

"Sor—" I began with another apology before laughing at the realisation and changed it for a simple, "Okay."

"That wasn't so hard, was it? You are going to be a quick study, I can see. Now," he grinned, throwing his tie behind him before unbuttoning the V-neck, dark grey, wool waistcoat that was the third part to today's suit. The jacket already on the back of his chair.

I licked my lips as his sculpted chest and torso became apparent through his shirt.

"I think I know what you're thinking right now," he laughed with an arched brow.

"If you're thinking that I am imagining us undressing each

other and spending an indeterminate amount of time exploring each other's bodies, before…" I gasped exciting myself with the sound of my thoughts being expressed out loud.

"Before what baby? What then, because I am totally on board up to your *before*."

"Before we fuck in every conceivable position leaving us both exhausted, barely able to breathe and totally incapable of walking. I'd feel everything you'd done and everywhere you'd been with even the tiniest of movements as my sore and tender flesh struggled to recover…"

Any further words were lost as Cy's shirt was pulled over his head, still partially fastened and then his body was crushing mine again, kissing me as if his life depended on it.

There were hands delving beneath my dress until it was as high as my waist while my neck and throat were being devoured.

"I need inside of you baby," he gruffly announced pulling back into a sitting position between my splayed legs. "Lose some clothes."

With a pull forward Cy found the zip at the back of my navy, wool blend dress that I hoped wouldn't look as though I'd slept in it when I needed to put it back on. I thought it looked fairly dishevelled as it flew past me leaving me in just my midnight blue lace bra that was currently struggling to contain my heaving breasts, and the matching tanga brief that was actually stuck to me due to the arousal seeping from me. I was preparing to toe off my navy heeled court shoes that were still on my feet when Cy got to his feet to shed his trousers and boxers in one, leaving him absolutely, gloriously naked.

"Oh." I felt that my one word response was seriously insufficient as my eyes roamed over him, up and down; from his handsome face, the warmth of his deep, warm eyes, down to his mouth that I already knew so well; soft and hard at the same time, then his shoulders; broad, bronzed and tattooed. His chest seemingly adorned by the brown discs of his nipples. I was almost salivating as my eyes roved past his narrow waist only to find the trail of dark hair that led to a thatch of darker hair that housed the most glorious statement of male virility I had ever seen, not that I had seen that many penises, but still. This one was a prime specimen, pretty long, but thick, explaining why I had the sensation of being stretched whenever he entered me and his own arousal was clearly evident, leaking from him.

"Still overdressed." He grinned down, having caught me ogling him, the same ogling that distracted me from his hands making their way into the sides of my tiny pants, preparing to remove them.

I should have been mortified at the effort required to prise them from me and yet I was anything but when I saw his obvious pleasure at seeing me so ready for him, hot, wet and opening before his very eyes. So pleased was he at the lewd image I must have presented that his erection seemed to lurch toward me. With my pants flying in the same direction as my dress that was unlikely not to be creased beyond recognition now, all £149 worth of it, his body blanketed mine again, his mouth against my neck as I wrapped my legs around his back, only too happy to feel his naked erection rubbing against my belly as we both moved together. His hands lifted my back off the sofa enough for my bra to be unfastened and then with a little space between us that went too.

"My shoes," I whined as he pulled one leg higher, teasing my core with the very tip of him.

"How simple would this be?" he asked, confusing me with his seemingly random question. "I could just slide into you, right now, no delay, whenever, wherever," he growled against my ear and then seemed to think better of it. Reaching for his discarded trousers he found his wallet and retrieved a condom that he rolled down his length hastily. Still dressed in only my shoes I reached down to cast aside a shoe.

"No, keep them on, they're hot." He was already moving my foot away from my hand. "Unlike a guy in just socks," he added making me giggle as I looked him up and then all the way down to his feet complete with corporate looking black socks.

All laughter dissipated when he returned to the space between my spread thighs that he was guiding his dick towards and then in a single thrust I was gasping with an arched back as I tried to acclimatise to the invasion of my body.

"Ssh," he soothed as I lowered my back for a second until

he withdrew and slammed into me a second time, this time it was accompanied by my nipples being pincered and rolled by unforgiving fingers, intent on literally squeezing every ounce of pleasure from my body. "You like that, huh? What did I do to deserve you? I only wish I'd done it sooner. So tight baby, squeeze me, real tight, don't fucking stop," he cursed as the sweat began to appear in a sheen that covered his face, chest and torso.

"Oh God, oh God." I panted as my internal muscles had me pulsating and quivering everywhere, inside and out.

"That's it, like that, fuck that's so good. Do you come like this?" he asked me still torturing my nipples that were really beginning to throb in contorted versions of pleasure and pain.

"I don't know," I confessed, unsure of his question or my response.

"Do you come from penetration or do you always need your clit playing with too?" he clarified making me question whether I should be so clueless.

"I never have, with just this," I admitted with an embarrassed flush that made me question why that was the awkward thing here.

"We'll work on it because you seem pretty fucking close to me and I haven't even begun to suck those amazing tits." He gave each of my nipples another squeeze that seemed to have a twist thrown in for good measure.

"Oh yes, shit, I am so close," I told him with a purr that I didn't recognise as belonging to me.

"You and me both baby, so let's take this home, together."

He thrust again and again. I was near delirious when his strokes became shorter but fast and then he leaned forward to take one cherry red nipple into his mouth while the other had to make do with his hand. He sucked and sucked before releasing it enough to lick and lap before finally slipping a hand between our bodies to stroke my clit, slick with arousal, mine and his, driving me to the edge. With incoherent cries echoing around us, my insides trembled, his hips pumped against me and his teeth sank into my sensitive peak causing me to crash into the most intense physical sensation I had ever known, made all the sweeter as I took him there with me.

Lying together seemed to be the most natural thing in the world until I raised my hand to rub my fingers across Cy's lips that seemed swollen and red. He moved my hand from his face and with a disgusted glare for my wedding ring he pulled away from me, disposed of the condom and passed me my clothes.

"The bathroom is over there," he said almost coldly, pointing to the closed door, as if I needed directions.

I headed for what I perceived as being the safety of the bathroom, stopping only to hand him his trousers.

"Thanks, I'll give you ten minutes," he explained with a nod of his head.

"I'll get you some more tea."

He shook his head. "Coffee." He gestured to the clock that told us we had been shut in here for a couple of hours.

"Of course," I managed with a tight smile.

****

I worked without interruption until lunchtime when Cy appeared in the doorway between his office and mine.

"Can I shout you lunch?" He startled me with such a simple question.

"I erm, I don't, erm…" I stammered like some kind of idiot making the most handsome face I knew smile. Making him a little more handsome if that was possible.

"Hey there El, are you ready?" came Maya's voice from the other door to my office.

"Ready?" I was still in a state of confusion.

"Lunch? We agreed to do lunch today. We arranged it last week," she reminded me.

"Oh, yeah, course, sorry," I said, but was unsure who I was addressing, Cy or Maya.

"I'll see you when you get back then." Cy returned to his own office closing the door behind him.

Lunch was strained, at least for me, with my head full of a million things; Michael, Cy, my sister, my marriage, my future, Cy's tenderness when he'd discovered the bruise on my face and then his distaste for my wedding ring, his invitation to lunch and of course the fact that my husband who until last night had rarely raised his voice let alone raised his hand, not that I could honestly say I hadn't deserved it. Maya made up for my lack of conversation but somehow seemed more interested in talking about me, my new boss and even Michael than anything else.

To say I was relieved to be returning to the office was very much an understatement, but even as we entered the lift together Maya was still asking questions.

"Do you think Michael, Mr Stanton, will remain retired or venture into something to keep him busy?" she asked and although it seemed a little odd that she should be so interested in my husband's retirement plans I answered honestly.

"I don't really know. He seems to be enjoying the extra rounds of golf and he gets to see his children and grandchildren more, but who knows if he'll get itchy feet in the future."

The lift thankfully arrived at our floor and I was able to leave Maya at reception where her lunch cover seemed to be having a problem on the phone.

"Hey," said Cy, appearing behind me in the kitchen where I was hanging my jacket up. "Good lunch?"

"I suppose, Maya was in a weird mood and I was preoccupied," I freely admitted.

"You and she are old friends, no?" he asked, making my laugh with his strange way of wording the question. "What?" he queried.

"You're very American," I smiled making him arch a brow at me.

"You think? A lot of my American friends find me to be very anglicised. And what of you, are you very English?"

I shrugged, suddenly unsure what the hell I was and how I perceived myself. "I don't know, although I am English so I suppose I must be, like your mum, she's English too."

"Yes she is, but I think you and she are very different," he said and immediately the friendly banter, inane chatter I thought we were sharing had gone. It was replaced with tension and angst because presumably she was not a married slapper that shagged her boss behind her much older, rich husband's back.

"I'm sure we are," I snapped and pushed past Cy before coming to a dead standstill as the sound of laughter filtered through my office from reception. "You have got to be kidding me," I muttered, marching towards Maya's desk but came up short as she was almost at mine, complete with my husband, whose arm she had linked hers through causing me to arch a brow as I stared at it, but without anything resembling jealousy.

"Look who's popped in to say hello, Mich—I mean Mr Stanton," Maya announced, reverting to his professional title but was still holding onto his arm.

"Mmm," muttered Cy from behind me, causing me to jump. "Michael," he addressed my husband curtly. "Ms Ross, ten minutes and then I'll need you to join me for a conference call that I'd like minuting," he said with a small curl of his lips for me that somehow managed to look more like a snarl than a smile, then he turned to Maya and Michael. "And Maya, if you'd like to put Mr Stanton down I am sure you're needed at reception." His sneer shocked me because although I had only seen a few exchanges between my boss and my friend they had been amiable, flirtatious at times, until now.

Suddenly alone, I looked at Michael as if I was seeing him for the first time and honestly, I had no clue exactly what or who was before me.

"Is everything okay?" I asked, unsure why he had turned up at the office.

"Yes, yes, never been better." He smirked making me wonder if he had forgotten the last twenty-four hours of our life. "I won't be at home for dinner. I have a meeting, business," he informed me tapping the side of his nose to imply a secret.

Previously I would have laughed, maybe even tried to discover what his big secret was, but today I was just relieved that I wouldn't be enduring another strained dinner, boring documentary or a row before bed.

"Any idea what time you'll be back, it's my late night," I reminded him.

"Of course, love. It could run over. If it gets too late I might stay in town."

I waited for him to suggest that I could stay in town with him, but he didn't, for which I was relieved, grateful. He leaned forward to kiss me on the cheek, the bruised cheek, making me flinch as his lips brushed against the sore skin, but rather than showing any sorrow, guilt or even empathy, he simply shook his head at me.

"Don't be melodramatic, Eloise. It really isn't becoming." He gave a soft chuckle before brushing his thumb across the contusion that must have been virtually make-up free after all these thumbs had brushed across it.

"Ms Ross, if you're ready," said Cy, interrupting what I thought, feared could have appeared to be a moment of tenderness to my boss', no my lover's eyes judging by his 'face like thunder' expression.

"Of course," I replied grabbing my laptop, already heading into Cy's office.

I sat at his desk before I realised I hadn't even said goodbye to my husband and was sure I could hear a muffled conversation between the two men I'd left behind before Cy appeared and promptly slammed the door behind him.

We worked for the next two hours, Cy on a conference call across three continents and throughout he remained agitated and annoyed with everyone involved. I minuted proceedings and made several notes-to-self relating to work before the guy in Finland suggested a fifteen minute recess, something Cy eventually agreed to.

"I could get you some coffee," I suggested nervously, seeing his irritation still present.

"In a minute, in fact we could get it together," he stated more than suggested already heading for the door and then the kitchen.

Dutifully, I followed and found him filling a kettle and adding instant coffee to two cups after seeing the fresh coffee jug was empty.

"Milk, sugar?"

"Milk, no sugar," I replied still shocked that he was making the coffee, although I got that it was a fairly simple process.

"I didn't mean that you were a different person to my mother in a bad way," he began, addressing my earlier crossness with him. "But you'd have known that if you hadn't gone super bitch on me."

"I thought you meant she wouldn't do this, what we're doing. And because I am, that made me less than her, although I probably am." I felt true shame for possibly the first time.

"She wouldn't, well not in my mind. She's my mother and married to my father and what they do, have done or may do in the future, I don't want to consider," he told me with a shudder that made me smile. "Was he begging for forgiveness, telling you it would never happen again?" he asked making me frown in confusion. "Your husband," he spat.

"No, the opposite I suppose. He touched my face and I flinched, it hurt and he thought I was being dramatic."

"He is some piece of fucking work! Why do you put up with it?" he asked and now he was the confused one.

"He has never done that before, hit me, until last night and it was kind of my fault."

Cy stared at me with a million questions and before I knew it I had retold him my whole evening from the second I'd left work until arriving back there that morning.

"You didn't deserve it, and don't ever think you did. What we're doing, although inevitable for us is right, for us both. I know it is. I know you feel it too," he insisted as I nodded my agreement. "I get that if he knew he would be the injured party to some extent, but he must have known that this was a possibility, when he married someone beautiful, vibrant, young and sexy as fuck."

I blushed, I knew I had as the heat spread across my face, neck and chest.

"Hey, you own a mirror. You are all of those things and you are such a sensual and sexual being, how did he think he would ever keep up with you? Is he your first older, considerably older man?"

If I thought I'd coloured up when he was paying me compliments, I was ill prepared for just how red and hot I could physically become with embarrassment before I answered his question.

"Yes, in fact before Michael I only had a couple of boyfriends, but not long term. Not once my sister introduced herself and scared them off."

"What is her deal? She wanted him, but he didn't want her so she what, passed on her sister instead? Jeez, you'll be telling me next…" his voice trailed off while I shifted from one foot to the other with increasing discomfort as I figured where this was going. "No fucking way! You were a virgin when you started seeing him? She procured him a sweet and innocent virgin. What the fuck have they done to you?" he asked but rather than reply I simply shook my head and battled tears at hearing his summing up of me and my life.

"We should get back with the coffee, and finish the conference call," I said with a little composure regained as I remembered how shitty things had been in my life before Michael and reasoned in my head that giving him my virginity had been something I had wanted to do at the time and until Cy had turned up, I had been happy, hadn't I?

"This conversation is not over baby, but let's wrap this up first," he agreed before leaning across the space before us to land the gentlest, most tender kiss I had ever known on my temple.

It was past home time by the time we wrapped up and Maya had already left making me feel relieved that I wouldn't have to endure any more probing questions about my husband or my life.

"If you're at a loose end this evening we could have dinner," Cy suggested as I picked up my bag from the drawer of my desk, already wearing my coat.

"I can't," I replied, regretting him asking on a Tuesday.

"Pizza and beer, how can you say no to that? I am willing to suffer it on two consecutive nights for you," he smiled wryly.

"Sorry. I'd really like to, but I can't, I have plans," I explained looking at the time on the clock on the wall.

"What plans?" Cy asked with increasing irritation which I took to mean he thought I was making excuses. I wasn't. Tuesday was my busy night.

"I'm sorry, but I don't have time for this, I need to go," I insisted, already trying to push past Cy.

"I don't get this," he sighed. "Every time I think we're making some headway, that the bitch within is not your natural persona, that the woman I catch glimpses of is the real you, you do this."

I stared at him, his face conflicted with feelings of anger and sadness, but I knew that if I didn't leave now I would be late, too late.

"What about you? Are you really the arsehole?"

With a shrug, Cy corrected me, "Asshole."

"Sorry," I repeated like some kind of pre-programmed drone, unable to think of anything else to say, hastily heading for the lift and probably pissing him off a little more with yet another apology.

Chapter Nine

My Tuesday night routine was essentially the same, week after week, had been for months, years even. I left work, as close to on time as possible and after an average fifty minute drive I got there, the place that I hated going to and yet, I had to. It was expected. I wanted to. It was my duty and tonight was no different, except tonight my mind was awash with thoughts of my relationship with Cy, if that's what it was. There were times when I thought I'd glimpsed some emotion behind the passion, tenderness, but then as quickly as I detected it, it vanished. It was as if it'd never been there, maybe it hadn't, maybe it was my imagination, or worse, wishful thinking. This was a mess, a really big mess and I could see no way of it ever being anything else, in fact it could actually be a total bloody disaster. I smiled with irony as I realised that Cy's original description of us was spot on, a disaster-in-waiting, but the real question was, waiting for what?

The sound of the nurse's voice on the other end of the intercom brought me back to real life with a start.

"Hi, sorry, it's Eloise Ross, for Jeremy Ross," I called, wondering for the first time why I had always been so reluctant to use my married name in all areas. Work was one thing, but here?

"Come through," was the chirpy response before I was buzzed in.

The short walk to the nurse's station always made me feel like I was walking the green mile. God, I loved that film, even if it did always make me cry. I could see that the nurse on the desk was one of my favourites, Angela; a woman of around fifty, very warm, caring and compassionate. She was a similar height to me but with a figure a little fuller than my own and a sprinkling of grey hair that was visible, even with her perfectly highlighted hair.

"El," she grinned when she looked up and saw me approaching her. "You okay? You seem a little, erm, preoccupied." She smiled kindly, a smile that started on her lips and sparkled in her blue eyes.

"Yeah, fine, work and things," I explained, resenting my own vague lies. "How is he?" I asked, saying a silent prayer that her response would be positive.

"Today has been a good day. He was a bit disorientated this morning and then after his afternoon snooze he seemed more with it. He was quite lucid, he even chatted about you and your siblings. He's had dinner and complained that the mash was lumpy and had no salt in, so he must be feeling with it." She laughed, laughter I joined in with before heading towards the day room.

I entered the room that always made me a little uncomfortable, the day room. Although, in reality it was the anytime of the day and night room. It had a feel of institutionalised living; generic furnishings, carpets only ever found in these rooms made of a material I could never name or describe beyond being flat. The walls were smoothly plastered and painted in two colours, a dark red, maroon almost beneath the handrail that sat on all the perimeter walls and above it a very unimaginative cream or magnolia shade broken up by framed pictures of flowers, all screwed to the walls. The smell in here was a mixture of heating, cooked dinners and people, old and or sick people. Even though I truly believed this place to be a place of care and compassion it made me sad, sad for everyone in it, especially me and the man who was sitting in his usual seat, near the hatch to the kitchen, with a slightly open window behind him and the piano to his side, all things he complained about. I approached him, hoping he would still be lucid, or at least with it enough to speak to me. To recognise me, Eloise Ross, his daughter.

"Hello," I said as I prepared to take the seat in front of him. "How are you?"

"Are you talking to me?" he asked, already looking around for anybody else I might be addressing.

"Yes," I replied tearfully. Clearly him recognising me was too much to ask for today. I had missed his lucid moment, again.

"Do you work here?" He sounded genuinely interested.

I felt overwhelmed. I wanted my dad. I needed him. For him to reassure me, advise me and love me. Unable to risk replying, I simply shook my head.

"Oh. Well you can stay if you want, for a while, with me, until my wife and kids are ready to be picked up."

"Thanks," I managed to say without crying because these moments, when he thought he was married with dependent children could be truly beautiful to me. He would find himself in a place in his brain where he was well and would chat for hours about his family, my family. He would usually rehash old stories from twenty or more years ago I found entertaining, like I was a little girl sitting on a grandparent's knee asking what it was like in the 'olden days'.

"What's your name love?" He smiled.

"Eloise, El," I told him, wondering why his brain wouldn't allow him to remember me.

"I have an El, an Eloise." He grinned, making me grin in response. "My baby girl, she is. Bit of a happy accident, but the best thing she ever got wrong," he beamed with pride. "She's five now, absolute light of my life. Don't tell anyone, but even though I've got three boys and two other girls, my little Eloise is something special. My favourite, even though I know you shouldn't have favourites. She lights up a room with her happy face. A mouth full of teeth that look too big for her face and eyes that beam with hope and happiness in spite of it all."

Although some of his words didn't make sense to me, I could feel that my face was wet with tears, happy ones for the love my father had for me. A love I didn't really remember and sad tears for no longer having him in my life and a few for the mess my life was becoming.

He looked up and clearly saw my tears, yet chose to ignore

them, simply continuing to chat before suddenly frowning. "Your turn now, tell me what a beautiful woman with sad eyes is doing here?"

I considered fobbing him off with a made-up tale of my presence, or maybe I could have told him that I was his El. I sometimes did that when he was in one of these moods, but I didn't, I told him the other truth; I told him about my husband, my marriage, my dog who seemed to be the only one in the world who truly loved me and had my back, and then I told him about Cy, about our affair and the confused and conflicted feelings we both battled with. By the time I came up for a very deep and relieved breath he was staring at me a little wildly. Maybe he hadn't expected such a full and frank explanation from me, the stranger before him. It was his turn to take a deep breath as he scratched his head, as if in thought, something he used to do when I was a little girl, something I'd forgotten about until that very moment.

"Right! Phew, that's quite a list you've got going on there, Muffin," he said and yet again I was allowing endless, silent tears to run down my face with his use of my childhood pet name.

I used to love that I was Muffin. Everyone in my family called me Muffin, until life got tough. Until my mum got sick and then my dad became forgetful and sad. When everyone grew up, then only he called me Muffin and when he seemed to stop remembering, well nobody called me Muffin. I knew, logically, intellectually, that the man before me had an uncooperative brain that played tricks on him and that the Muffin he had just called me was just another cruel trick of a dysfunctional and failing mind. Yet the other side of me, the one that was desperate for the love of a caring and nurturing father, fooled herself into thinking that maybe, for that one second I was his Muffin. Even if he didn't recognise me as her.

"Come on," he smiled trying to chivvy me along with a hand reaching for mine. "It'll all come out in the wash, one way or another."

We sat like that, in silence for ten, possibly fifteen minutes before my dad spoke again.

"Right, this is how I see it; your sister is living the life she wanted through you, that's not her right. Your husband is an idiot and even though I don't approve of adultery." He whispered the last word so nobody around us could hear. "I'm a bit old fashioned, but look where that got me. I understand why you would do that. You should never have married him, he wasn't right for you. This new bloke, I'm not sure he's right either, but he seems a better fit than the husband," he said as if discussing a plotline in a film or TV programme making me smile even though he was telling me just how fucked up my life was. "You just promise me that you will do what is right for you, just you, not for anybody else, for once."

I nodded my agreement, feeling that this moment, this exchange was profound and somehow going to be a major turning point in my life. As if he knew he was addressing his daughter and that the advice and opinions he was expressing were full of paternal guidance and love.

"Good girl," he yawned. "I've had a busy day," he suddenly told me. "I'm on earlies this week so I'd better turn in. Bye El." He smiled getting to his feet and began to exit the room while I remained seated watching him head to the door which is where he stopped and turned back to face me, this time with tears running down his cheeks. "You know what, if you want to drink beer and eat pizza you do it," he told me fiercely. "Don't ever, never let anybody tell you what you do and don't like when you know best. That's not right, not for you, not for my Muffin. You're perfect as you are and if people want to change you then you tell them," he stammered, choking on his tears as Angela appeared behind him. "You tell them, all of them, to fuck off. You are Eloise Ross. From the day she gave you to me, you became my beautiful little Muffin and you are perfect, just as you are."

Angela smiled around my dad's shoulder and nodded. "Told you he was lucid today, didn't I?" Then turning her attention to him she brushed the tears from his face and shook her head. "Well that told them all Jezza, now let's get you settled," she told him before giving me a final wink.

I was still sitting in the same position in the same chair

twenty minutes later when I was finally composed enough to stand, to go back to my car and leave. I had actually had a conversation with my dad, my actual dad, and although I would never have confessed the shit heap my life was to him if I'd thought he would have understood and reacted as my father, I was kind of glad we'd had tonight. That he'd had a moment of lucidity and I had been there, not only to share, but to somehow inspire it, and I would not let him down, nor myself.

****

When I arrived home Balder was pleased to see me, as he always was, but seemed extra pleased with the smells wafting from my pizza box. I delivered my pizza and beer to the kitchen and while Balder had a run around the back garden I ran upstairs to change into some comfy yoga pants and a t-shirt. Opening the pizza, I felt rebellious and decadent, but loved those feelings, even though I knew Michael would disapprove. I possibly loved those feelings because Michael would disapprove, but my dad wouldn't, nor would Cy. With my boss now on my mind I took the top off my bottle of beer before grabbing my phone and very immaturely took a selfie of myself with the pizza and beer. A message was waiting from Michael, informing me that he was indeed staying in town. Happy with my juvenile rebellion and the knowledge that it was just me and Balder I composed a message to Cy.

<Really wasn't trying to be a bitch, although I realise it's a gift I have. I have dinner.>

With the photo attached I sent it and waited for a response.

<Nor I an asshole, even though that is my gift. You do indeed have dinner and a sexy as fuck smile. You actually look happy.>

I laughed at the idea of looking happy and wondered whether that meant I was normally a miserable looking cow, but risking another look at my photo I agreed with Cy. I did look happy, genuinely happy which begged the question, why? Was it because of my choice of dinner, my husband's absence, my visit with my father or the reinstated friendliness between me and Cy?

<Thank you>

<Are you alone? You, your pizza and beer?>

I wondered if Cy's real question was, 'where is your husband?' Or maybe 'where did you have to go tonight?' Hopefully he wouldn't ask about my desperate need to leave the office that night because I didn't want to talk about it. My dad was private, and something I didn't share with other people, not even Michael, not really.

<Me, Balder, pizza and beer. Michael is staying in town tonight>

<Lucky Balder. Enjoy your dinner Ms Ross, until tomorrow>

****

The rest of the week at work was busy, lots of meetings for Cy, in the office and out, meaning I didn't really see much of him and before I knew it I was packing up for the weekend.

"You off?" Cy asked as I grabbed my bag.

"Yeah. I have that charity thing for the hospital to go to tonight," I reminded him, although I was unsure why I felt the need.

With a laugh at my grimace, he moved closer which only served to make me take a deep and obvious breath at his close proximity.

"We haven't had much time have we, to talk?" His hand was already moving up to gently caress my cheek.

"Talk?" I softened into his touch, like a cat turning into his owner's loving attention.

"Mmm. Talk. You know, like I speak, you listen and then you have a turn to speak while I listen. Oh, and kiss, we really haven't had much time to kiss, or touch," he seemed to whisper as my breath caught in my throat. "I've fucking missed you baby," he told me bluntly as his thumb skimmed down my face until it was pressed against the hammering pulse in my neck. "Maybe I should reorder the words in that sentence. I've missed fucking you baby," he told me darkly, his lips heading straight for mine.

My mobile phone rang in my bag, breaking the moment. Predictably my caller ID revealed Michael. As tempted as I was to reject the call and pursue this with Cy I knew I needed to deal with my husband, to presumably reassure him that I had left the office and was on my way home to get ready for the fundraiser, as I'd promised I would be by now.

"Hello," I answered, hoping I didn't sound as aroused and breathless as I felt.

"El, where are you? Tell me you've left the office," he demanded with impatience.

"Of course. I've stopped off for some new tights." I lied easily and with conviction.

Cy watched me with a raised eyebrow from his position still before me.

"Oh, well if you could hurry. I don't want us to be late."

Cy was already nuzzling my free ear now, seemingly unbothered by my husband's presence at the other end of the phone. Maybe it was because of Michael that he was continuing with his assault on all of my senses, especially my libido, assuming libido was a sense. It felt as though it should be, well mine had been since I first met Cy.

"I won't be long. I'll be as quick as I can," I assured Michael and was shocked when Cy whispered in my ear.

"Not as quick as I could be, baby."

As his words registered, I felt a hand beneath my skirt, pushing it up until a finger was teasing the leg of my tiny satin thong before skimming along my length, sliding in the wetness of my arousal, the arousal that a few words and the threat of a kiss had prompted.

"Shit!" I cursed straight down the phone line as a finger gently stroked across my clit.

"Eloise, are you okay?" Michael asked with concern.

"Sorry," I gasped as what I thought was a thumb sunk into my core while the finger continued to stroke. "They don't have my size," I added, throwing in yet another easy lie.

"Buy the stockings instead." Cy continued to whisper. "Far sexier. Even better with no panties."

"I don't think we need cursing over tights," Michael muttered with a short laugh. "Look, I will wait for you until seven, but if you're not here and ready for then I might head off without you. You'll need to come to me, get a taxi."

"I should be back. See you soon," I stammered quickly, desperate to come off the phone, or maybe just come.

Hanging up I was preparing to chastise Cy for doing the things he'd done as I'd tried to talk to my husband. However, when I looked up and found his eyes smouldering as they watched me what I actually did was grab his head, possibly pulling his hair as I dragged his face to mine where I proceeded to devour him, drinking him in as if I was dying of thirst and he was my only chance of survival.

"Cy, Cy, are you here?" called Tia, startling us both sufficiently that we each released the other, not that his sister could have been left in any doubt what she'd been about to discover had she not called out before entering. "Clearly," she muttered with a smirk that only served to embarrass me more than being discovered had.

"Tia," Cy replied, guiding his sister towards his office. "Give me a minute."

She shrugged with another grin before striding as far as her brother's door then turned to face me. "We really should meet up for lunch, just us girls."

Cy closed the door behind her and returned his attention to me. "Sorry, I hadn't really planned on that and when it happened I kind of forgot Tia was coming over."

"She won't say anything, will she? To your parents?" I was suddenly concerned about repercussions from my lack of self-control.

"Or your husband?" snapped Cy, annoyed with me, presumably for what he perceived to be the dishonesty of my question.

"I have to go," I barked back, slipping back into a slightly bitchy version of myself but that was mainly because I had no idea if my question had been honest. Did I really want Michael to remain in the dark about me and Cy?

"True to form Ms Ross." He was already opening his office door, leaving me alone.

****

As I made my way downstairs the hospital fundraiser didn't seem like such a bad idea. Although Michael and I had been getting along better after his night in town, even if that was only three nights before, I knew I would need to keep my mind occupied, tonight and the whole weekend, but with my body still thrumming from my earlier encounter with Cy, getting through tonight was my priority.

"El, thank goodness, come on then," Michael said as I came to a standstill beside him.

"Will I do?" I asked with a fond smile, remembering that this was something he had said to me many times when we were first together. I would ask if I looked okay and he would respond with the words, *you'll do*. I had never needed words of praise and flowery compliments from Michael, and yet, tonight I craved them as I hoped he would tell me I was beautiful, or something equally as complimentary.

"Of course. You're always well turned out, love," he told me, words that left me distinctly cold. Michael didn't notice, or just didn't care and was already heading for the front door with an impatient call to me of, "El."

We entered the large function room at the hotel where the fundraiser was being held and I was still questioning whether my choice of outfit had been the right one. I had thought I looked both elegant and sophisticated and just the right side of sexy. That was something I had learnt early on in my relationship with Michael, that as the much younger girlfriend or wife of a successful man you trod a fine line when on public display between dressing appropriately for your age and not appearing as though you had dressed for prom night. More than once I'd heard other wives, older wives, many who had been under the plastic surgeon's knife and still looked like mutton dressed as lamb refer to husbands like my own as looking like a sexual predator simply by being with an inappropriately dressed younger wife. I didn't doubt Michael and I had been described in this way, although I think I usually managed to gauge it right, like tonight. I was wearing an old dress, old as in I had worn it before, once, to a business function I had attended with Michael and had received several compliments on it, although with hindsight I realised not from my husband.

We were being greeted warmly by some of the fundraising team. One of them was a woman about ten or twelve years older than me, of a similar height but considerably wider than me, not that I had an issue with that, but she was wearing an identical dress to mine.

There were times when I had considered a boob job, just a small lift, sculpt and enhance, and whilst I believed myself to be curvaceous, I knew my behind was no Kim Kardashian, unlike the woman now hugging my husband. She had an arse that would have Kim K, Beyoncé and J-Lo saying, 'look at that ass' and her chest, well I had serious concerns that Michael might just suffocate if she pulled him in any closer to her bosom.

I smiled at my own musings, especially the 'ass' as I looked down at my own body, then back to the other woman's before returning my eyes to my own form adorned in black in the shape of an A-line, off the shoulder, three-quarter sleeved, woven satin dress. The satin skirt was fitted from my chest with a slightly ruched detail before falling into a slightly looser, full length skirt that covered the silver, strappy stilettos on my feet. With the exception of my wedding ring I wore no jewellery which seemed to draw more attention to my exposed neck, throat and chest courtesy of the scalloped neckline of the fitted top of the dress that was a stretchy lace fabric that covered the strapless satin over my chest, the edge of my shoulders and arms. I began teasing the loose tendrils of hair I had left down around my ears that I thought softened the overall look of my messy up do. The mark that had been on my face from Michael's slap had all but disappeared, but rather than risk it being noticed I'd made my face up with a natural foundation, smoky grey eyes and a clear shimmer of gloss.

My dress doppelgänger appeared to notice me now, or at least my dress judging by the sneer on her face, but that was nothing compared to mine when I heard my husband speak to her.

"Wow, Ness, you look absolutely resplendent. If I was your husband I would insist that you only ever wore that dress, but never outside of the house."

She, Ness, giggled like a school girl, and yet I was the one who had needed to ensure that I looked like a grown up tonight. I wasn't sure who I wanted to punch more at that precise moment, her or Michael.

It really was a close call, especially when he added, "And I think it takes a certain womanly figure to carry it off."

I heard the words fuck off sounding and hoped to God they had remained in my head. Michael was still spouting crap to his fundraising team fan girls and not slumping to the ground clutching his chest, so I felt assured I hadn't allowed those two words to leave my head. I really needed a drink.

There were clearly new, or potential supporters judging by the number of people present and the presentation we were subjected to. I had seen it before, the statistics on heart disease, the success rate the unit boasted and the astronomical costs involved. They did a great job and it was dreadful that they needed to fundraise in order to finance their work, but honestly; I felt as much like a fish out of water as I had ever done. I didn't belong here. I didn't fit.

My dad's words suddenly sprang into my mind *never let anybody tell you what you do and don't like when you know best.* Loud applause began around me, presumably I had missed something important and profound and yet all I could think about as I fidgeted, crossing my legs for the umpteenth time, feeling my stockings rubbing against each other was Cy. He was the only thing on my mind. It was going to be a very long weekend.

"You okay, love?" Michael whispered.

"Mmm."

"Then keep still, you're squirming like you're afflicted in some way," he told me and because it amused me, his words and the way he said it, I laughed, out loud, very loudly, just as the person presenting announced that one in every one hundred babies born has a congenital heart defect and that it was the leading cause of infant death.

Michael glared at me angrily, as if I had done it on purpose. As if I really was laughing at infant mortality. I'd been looking forward to this evening a little earlier but it was fast turning into a disaster, or maybe more of the farce my life was evolving into.

We both averted our eyes from the other and turned back to the person speaking who was none other than Ness. I had never believed I would be bothered to be at a function in the same dress as someone else, but as I struggled to get past that fact, I realised I'd been wrong. Unless it was the fact that my husband had managed to bring himself to pay the other woman a compliment. I realised how ridiculous I was being, particularly as I was shagging my boss, but it bothered me.

I was actually the most attentive person in the room for the remainder of the talk. Once it was over I was relieved that I could now move around, maybe even dance a little. I knew it wouldn't be quite the same if I wasn't dancing with Cy. Jeez, could that man move.

"Michael," called a soft American voice, Tia. I knew it was her before I turned to face her. "El," she added warmly, acting as though she hadn't earlier caught me kissing her brother like my life depended on it whilst his hand was wedged in my pants.

"Tia." I smiled as Michael pulled her in for a hug before we noticed the man behind her, an older man, much older. Maybe we, Tia and I had more in common than Cy.

"Michael," her companion said, clearly familiar with my husband.

"Edward." He looked slightly uncomfortable, shocked and taken aback by the other man's presence, hyperaware almost.

"And you must be the little wifey," Edward said, turning his attention to me, patronisingly.

"Eloise," I offered with an outstretched hand, a gesture he ignored.

"This is Uncle Edward. He insisted on being my plus one tonight," Tia explained with a tighter smile now.

"Not like you had anyone else to bring is it?" he sniped cattily.

"I could have brought Cy," she countered making my heart race as my skin heated. I just hoped there wasn't an obvious flush creeping up my body, revealing my interest and arousal at the mere mention of my lover's name.

"Well, he's here anyway," Edward revealed.

That information made my knees weaken so much that I thought I might actually pass out. I had it real bad and needed to get it under control before I outed myself as Cy's bit on the side, although, as I was the married one not him he may actually have been my bit on the side. Either way I didn't want to reveal either of us as that, especially not to my husband, his uncle or his sister, although she knew exactly what was going on.

"And he has his own plus one," Edward revealed at the exact second a waiter appeared with a tray of champagne. The tray was two glasses lighter by the time he'd actually moved past me.

Chapter Ten

I was doing a really shit job of playing it cool with my eyes scanning the room and a glass of champagne in each hand, one of them now empty.

"Excuse us," Michael said with a polite curtness I didn't miss, nor Edward, judging by the scrutinising glance he shot us both.

With a hand firmly gripping my upper arm, a little too firmly, he guided me towards a quiet corner of the room where we were unlikely to be overheard.

"Eloise, what the bloody hell is the matter with you? I swear to God if you embarrass me this evening, I will not be happy," he told me from his position, squatted and staring directly in my face. "I barely recognise you anymore since, since," he hesitated. "Since you went to work for Cy and although I know he is brash, tactless and American, I will not tolerate it in my wife, do you understand?"

It was like he was speaking to a misbehaving child who'd just been put on the naughty step. I nodded mutely as I raised the second glass to my lips which only fuelled his annoyance.

"No more alcohol," he snapped coldly. "This is about me tonight. I have some opportunities to network too, so you need to stay sober and act like my wife or I will not be responsible for my actions."

I stared at him, absorbing his words that carried a clear threat, but unbothered by his irresponsibility for his future actions I stupidly spoke.

"Why did you marry me?" The randomness of my question

seemed to throw him off balance, but only for a split second.

"Why do you think? Because I loved you." There was tenderness in his use of the past tense. "In my own way. I'm unsure why I ever did at the moment," he added with no trace of anything resembling love.

I knew I was the one cheating and the one in the wrong in our marriage. I also accepted that of late I had questioned everything that there was, that had ever been between us. Now I was ready to cry at his poorly masked admission that he didn't love me anymore, never had, except in his own way or maybe it was just the realisation that I had wasted our years together on this. That I had been manipulated into a marriage of convenience by my sister, even if the convenience was hers and Michael's rather than my own and now my life was in free fall and shit was the only thing likely to break my fall. I was ready to suggest that I should go home. That I had no clue what had come over me and I should go to bed and wake up in a better mood tomorrow. Still the errant child, even in my own mind.

"Are we okay here?" Edward asked, stealing my moment.

"Of course," Michael replied as he straightened and faced the other man who must have been a similar age to my husband, but bigger, taller, broader with a strong face. Handsome in a stern way, a face I didn't really think I cared for. It scared me a little which was strange considering the fact I'd never met him before.

"Good," he shrilled with a smile that never seemed to reach his eyes, somehow forcing me to lower my own gaze. "And here they are Prince Charming and his Cinderella."

I lifted my eyes only to find myself looking up at Cy and his plus one. His date. A woman as tall as him in heels and wearing a very low cut, bright red dress with a split right up to her thigh.

Clearly she hadn't gone for sophisticated glamour. No, she'd gone straight to whorish slut and that wasn't simple jealousy talking, well, maybe it was I conceded as I took in the rest of her appearance; bright red nails were on the fingers that were flicking her long, loose blonde hair back revealing earrings like chandeliers. I now had a Pat Butcher to add to my Kim K. What an evening this was proving to be. The earrings seemed to be part of a heavy, chunky set because the necklace and bracelet she wore matched. Gold, but not real gold I assumed looking at the thick links with a large clear stone detail to the centre. All conversation was passing me by as I continued to look at this woman with her arm laced through Cy's, like she had some kind of ownership over him. Maybe she did. I sure as hell didn't.

Her make-up was heavy and obvious, red lips, black eyes and an overpowering sweet fragrance from her perfume wafted towards my nostrils. She laughed at something someone else said, more of a cackle really. Fuck, I really was a bitch. Then she spoke and I heard her American accent saying something about holiday plans. Plans I feared were going to feature Cy. I had a heavy feeling of nausea now to go with my weak knees.

"This is my wife, Eloise," Michael told the woman.

"Hi, I love your dress." She smiled. "A little conservative for me I guess, but cute for you, and a timeless classic." She smiled again and although the curve of her lips seemed genuine, I refused to see that. Who precisely was she? Dona-fucking-tella Versace.

I was unsure how I didn't swear or hit her, but I didn't. I simply turned my attention to my boss.

"Mr Miller, I didn't see a function on your planner."

"No, well my planner is for work and this is purely pleasure, Ms Ross," he replied quite obviously raking his eyes over every inch of my body.

Maybe my dress wasn't quite so conservative. One to me, none to the fashion police.

"I need a drink," I blurted out earning another pissed off look from my husband. "Water, a drink of water," I clarified. "I'm hot, too hot."

"Allow me, there's something I need to discuss with you anyway," Cy said and without another word he had detached his friend from his arm and was taking my elbow to lead me away, gently, towards the bar.

"What the fuck are you doing here?" I fumed as I turned and fully appreciated his appearance. He really was the most attractive man I had ever seen; and in a black tuxedo he was sublime.

"Maybe if Tia hadn't interrupted us earlier your inner bitch would still be under control."

"Oh, just fuck off, you arsehole!" I snapped angrily.

I didn't think I could feel any angrier at that point, but Cy's laughter proved that theory wrong as I felt the small grip I currently had on self-control and reality slipping.

"You look fucking amazing baby," he whispered and my annoyance dissipated.

"Don't say nice things to me." I pouted, making him laugh.

"Absolutely awesome, the sexiest thing I have ever seen. All I have thought about since I saw that asshole with his hands on you was kissing you, holding you, and fucking you."

It was my turn to laugh now. "That was all going so well until the last two words."

"I dunno, I kind of liked the last two words, but at least you don't look pissed with me anymore." He smirked.

I nodded at his observation and remembered the reason for my angst with him.

"So, what are you doing here and who the hell is the vamp you had attached to your arm?"

"Vamp?" he asked with a grin in place of the smirk.

"Mmm, vamp or whatever she is, girlfriend, friend with benefits, whore, you choose." I was full of venom again.

"You really need to calm down. If Henry Higgins hadn't forbidden alcohol I would buy you a beer, but he has, so let's get you a grown up glass of water and then we'll try again."

With a glass of water for me and a bottle of beer I was in serious envy of for him, Cy began to speak as he led me towards an unoccupied table. "She, Rhonda is a friend, an old friend who is new in town, no more," he scowled. "I'm single baby. Remember, you're the married one here. Tia and I were coming tonight, because I knew you'd be here, but then fucking Edward appeared and suggested tagging along and I knew Rhonda was in town."

"You don't like your uncle?"

"No, I don't not like him as such. I don't trust his reappearance, although I trust him. He's not my uncle. He's an old friend, business associate of my dad's and some kind of distant cousin of my mother's five times removed or something, but we don't see too much of him."

"He seems scary."

"Yeah. He can be a dick, but he won't hassle you. He has no need to," Cy reassured.

The band was starting up and with a smile Cy stood, offering me his hand. "It's not really our usual soundtrack, but shall we?"

"I'd like that." I accepted his outstretched hand.

"Is he likely to give you shit for it?" He inclined his head towards Michael.

"I don't know, probably not, maybe," I said uncertainly. "But I'd still like to."

"Atta girl." He grinned, already leading me onto the dance floor.

Before that moment I had always been uncomfortable with *proper* dancing. I was unsure what Cy and I were doing, but I thought of it as being a waltz of sorts. He held me close, one hand in the small of my back while his other held my hand. His fingers linked with mine in a slightly bent and shortened hold. I loved the way our fingers felt. Interlocked. Connected. My other hand was gently pressed against his back, somewhere near his shoulder blades. This felt like the most intimate experience I had ever known, even with the number of other people in the room, many of them on the dance floor with us.

As well as *proper* dancing I hadn't really been a fan of the slow dance either. It evoked too many memories of uncomfortable encounters at school discos with boys I didn't think of in that way or later in clubs at the end of the night with a boy who'd bought me a drink and thought that entitled him to a grope with his tongue in my mouth. Possibly worse than that was getting to the end of the night with no would be suitor then being subjected to the last ditch attempt at the aforementioned grope and tongue in the mouth, without the benefit of a free drink. Now, after this experience of the slow dance it might just be my favourite thing to do, but probably only with Cy as my partner.

I shuddered as I remembered the first dance after my

wedding to Michael. We'd danced, at least he had. I had simply been dragged around the floor to The Blue Danube, a piece I wasn't overly keen on. I had suggested Everything by Michael Bublé, but Michael and Susan, who had been very hands on had vetoed that because it was too fast and too modern. I really had been very compliant and malleable from day one. I doubted they would approve of the music tonight, something that sounded familiar, but I couldn't identify as another shudder shook me slightly.

"Hey, you okay? Cold?" Cy pulled me closer still which never left me feeling anything other than hot.

"No. I was thinking, about dancing. I kind of like it, with you, like this."

"Yeah. Well it works for me too baby, and I don't think I will ever dance with anyone else without thinking about you or Frank," he told me as we came to a standstill with the end of the music.

"Frank?" I queried.

"Yes, Frank Sinatra, the band are playing The Way You Look Tonight. I couldn't have chosen a better song for us right now."

We were still stood in the hold we'd made for ourselves, me gazing up at him and him staring down at me with his discomfort at his own words only making my grin a little broader.

"I think we're back to you saying nice things," I teased with my top teeth biting down into my bottom lip.

"Yeah, and yet all I want to say are really nasty things involving us getting naked and sweaty with lots and lots of bodily fluids and orifices involved," he told me seriously.

His choice of words had me laughing, really laughing, proper belly laughs that in turn made Cy laugh too.

"And now I would really like to kiss you until we're both breathless—"

"I think I might just need to whisk my wife away before I get jealous of you monopolising her," interrupted Michael as he appeared out of nowhere making me wonder, briefly, how long he had been there and exactly what he'd heard. More surprising was the fact that I almost hoped he'd heard everything.

"Of course," replied Cy with a tight smile before reluctantly releasing me.

****

I dutifully fulfilled my role as the attentive and supportive wife for the next hour. I spotted Cy a couple of times, albeit fleetingly before Michael commented on my change in demeanour and mood.

"Your dance with Cy seems to have improved your mood."

I was unsure whether he expected me to disagree but I actually couldn't because my change in mood was courtesy of Cy. Most of my mood changes, positive and negative of late were down to him.

"You're getting on a little better I assume." He seemed to tell me rather than ask and he was right, kind of, but I couldn't really tell him that I was a bitch to his arsehole for about fifty percent of the time, twenty five percent of the time we had a little friendly banter that allowed us to develop an understanding of one another and the other twenty five percent was spent shagging so I just agreed.

"Yes. I think we're getting used to how the other works now. What makes us tick."

"Good, I'm pleased." His voice seemed to sound with true sincerity. "If you're okay, I might try and catch up with a few people. I think I saw Tia around."

"I'll be fine, you carry on." I questioned when I had last been genuine or honest with Michael. When there had been no deception or dishonesty between us and felt a small pang of guilt, right up until the point where I received a text message.

<Did you know there's a fat lady wearing the same dress as you? I saw the sexy black lace pass by! Thank fuck I wasn't close enough to say any nice things to her, or nasty>

<She's not fat, but I did notice her earlier. I hope you were able to tell us apart, so no risk of you saying anything to her by mistake>

I could detect the bristle in my tone at the idea of him saying the things he said to me to anyone else. I was certain he'd pick up on it too.

<No risk of me ever mistaking anyone else for you nor saying things to them. Did I detect jealousy, just and earlier with Rhonda?>

Yeah, he'd got it.

<Nice things, nasty things! I think I was jealous, not too sure, never been jealous before>

<Where are you? Where's Michael?>

<Just off for a wander. I might take a look at the raffle, I noticed a designer handbag earlier. Michael has gone to mingle and network>

No reply came back so I did as I'd said I would and checked out the raffle where the designer bag seemed to be calling to me to buy some tickets and at a fiver apiece I settled on four. Tucking them safely into my bag I felt breath on my neck.

"Fancy meeting you here," Cy whispered with a smile I could sense.

"Mmm, who knew?" I replied with a grin as I turned to face him.

"Five minutes, go to reception and ask for The Rossdale. They'll be expecting you."

I didn't even have time to ask what the hell The Rossdale was or who *they* were, the ones expecting me before Cy left me alone, still at the raffle display causing something of an obstruction.

****

The Rossdale was a room, a room on the ground floor and part of the spa facility. The receptionist had called it the private therapy room as she guided me to it and unlocked the door for me before leaving me alone with the key. Looking around, it was a very soothing and sedate room and as I imagined lying face down on the massage couch I also wondered what it would be like here with Cy, officially, in the hotel and to use the couple's massage tables. The thought of a relaxing massage and a naked Cy had my whole body coming to life in a combination of goose bumps and deep breaths with my mind unable to think of anything beyond the most basic and primal functions. The soft, sweet and intimate notions that had filled my head when he'd held me tenderly to dance were replaced with dark, rough and crude urges.

His timing was impeccable as he entered behind me at the exact moment I began to stretch my arms, neck and back in an attempt to ease the building tension within me. With no relief apparent I allowed my hands to brush over, to caress my own curves before ending up in an obscure position where I appeared to be almost hugging myself.

"Hey," he whispered as the lock on the door turned followed by the lights being put out. "You seem a little strung out," he whispered when he reached me, his body pressing against mine, his front to my back.

"Mmm," I admitted. "Why are we here?" I hoped the obvious answer was correct.

"Because dancing with you gave me all kinds of ideas. I love that you didn't wear anything on your neck. I like all of this skin just begging to be kissed and licked."

"Yes." I groaned as his lips gently caressed the back of my exposed neck. "Please, touch me," I pleaded.

"Maybe we should always meet in the dark. It's making you needy and confident enough to tell me what you want." He laughed against my spine that he was kissing his way down.

"Please," I repeated.

"Where baby, how do you want to do this?" he asked flatly as I felt him fingering the zip of my dress.

"Take my dress off and then touch me. Anywhere. Everywhere."

Clearly my response was somehow the right one because the next sound I heard was the zipper of my dress lowering, slowly. I could feel the air around us, thick and heavy, cold as it shocked the increasing amount of my skin that was on show. The whole of my back was exposed as Cy pushed the sides of the fabric away revealing my braless upper body. Pausing briefly he kissed my shoulders, first one and then the other as he slid the lacy fabric off my shoulders, down my arms until the material bunched at my elbows, almost trapping me.

"Yeah, we should always meet in the dark and you should never wear a bra," he told me before pushing the sleeves off my arms completely, allowing the top of my dress to fall to my waist, leaving me bare from the middle up. "Such beautiful skin," he whispered as his hands began to explore the expanse of flesh before him; down my shoulders, back, spine, waist, and then back up my sides until his hands were on my shoulders, skimming down my arms, slowly, too slowly.

"Please," I seemed to whisper on an exhale while his hands continued their journey without pause until they were holding mine. His fingers laced through my own digits, joining us together, like on the dance floor.

"This is crazy, isn't it, you and me?" His lips traced a line from my neck to my shoulder and then my ear.

"I don't know what I'm doing," I admitted and whilst it was a moment of total honesty I wasn't entirely sure exactly what I meant myself. "I don't recognise myself with you."

"I think you know what you're doing baby, and this person you don't recognise? I think she might just be the real you," he told me confidently before somehow managing to twist me to face him. "Fuck, you're beautiful." He growled as his eyes roamed my naked upper torso and chest. "I wish we could take this slower, but not tonight." He sighed with regret as his hands reached for my face, gently cupping my cheeks and chin, drawing me closer until his lips were on mine, over them, parting them, his tongue gaining access to my mouth. The sudden taste of beer in my mouth from his tongue only spurred me on to suck him in deeper, devouring him in every way.

All around us were the sounds of our passion and desire; gasps, sighs and moans, skin against skin, rubbing and abrading, broken words, intimate, crude words. The feel of a hand cupping one of my breasts, then the second repeating the action on my other breast filled me with relief at finally being touched. He gently held them before his touch became firmer, more assured in his circling movements. Ever decreasing circles were traced across and around my breasts, from the full undersides, the areolas that were puckering and pulling tighter and tighter to form the painful peaks of my nipples.

"I thought we couldn't take this slowly," I managed to say when Cy briefly released my mouth.

He said nothing in response. He just laughed and then skimmed his thumbs across my over-sensitised nipples. His next move was to roll each of my nipples between a finger and thumb making me throw my head back in sheer ecstasy at the bolts of electricity that were searing through my whole body, from my nipples down through my body. It settled in my belly before spiralling out to my sex that was wet, aching and now clenching in anticipation while my clit continued to throb which was almost enough to send me soaring.

"I think I could spend a whole night just touching your tits baby."

"No, no." I panicked making Cy laugh again.

"No, not tonight," he agreed. He released my breasts to rest his hands on my dress at my hips that he began to push down until it dropped in a pool around my feet.

"Oh fucking hell! If I had known what was under this dress, or not, I would have fucked you the second I first saw you tonight. You do know that you appear to have forgotten your underwear." He grinned, his teeth somehow glowing in the dark.

"Yeah. But somebody once told me that stockings worked far better with no panties," I replied using his own line from earlier.

"Sounds like a very wise man."

"Maybe. He also told me that the only things that should cover these great little legs were thigh highs or stockings and a garter, although I went for lace topped hold-ups."

"I can only dream that you might one day pay this much attention to all of the things I say."

It was my turn to laugh now. "Maybe I will."

"When hell freezes over baby. The only time you do as

you're told is when we're fucking and then you become super compliant, but aside from that…you are a giant pain in the ass."

I shrugged, unable to disagree and also not wanting to for fear of making this situation between us disappear. That seemed unlikely as I reached for Cy's belt that I was already undoing and preparing to release him.

"You choose, how we gonna do this?" His question startled me slightly as I had simply expected him to handle me into whichever position he wanted.

I lifted myself up onto the massage couch until I was balanced on the edge of it. With one hand still holding his belt and the other grabbing the flaps of his open trousers I pulled him closer to me, between my open thighs.

He grinned with a raised brow. "Like this, face to face?"

"I want to see you," I admitted, still glad that the lighting was almost non-existent.

"As you wish." The incline of his head seemed to suggest that he was surprised by my desire to see him as we coupled.

With impatience and a desperate desire to feel him inside me, I was already pushing his trousers and tight shorts down to reveal his erection that I palmed greedily. "Then hurry up."

"I might permanently keep us in the dark, Ms Ross. I kind of like this feisty, needy little minx."

He reached into his jacket giving me a sense of relief to see a condom held aloft, but increasingly impatient for the condom to be on Cy and for Cy to be inside me.

"Well done Mr Miller, but if you're waiting for a round of applause; I am going to need a little more motivation."

"How many glasses of champagne did you have?"

"One. It would have been two but I had the second one confiscated," I replied, inadvertently bringing my husband into this moment, a move we both picked up on but chose to ignore.

"You really need to stop speaking now baby, unless it's to tell me just how good it feels to have me fuck you, or when you come. I love to hear you then," he told me cockily, already sheathed in latex and pressing himself into my core.

He was as impatient now as I had been from the second I saw him. Not giving me time to grow accustomed to his invasion he was pushing into me, even with the wetness I could feel coating him I still felt the burn of his flesh stretching mine. With a few deep breaths I was fully impaled.

"Jeez, how can you be so wet and still so tight?" he asked, although I didn't think he required a response. His hips began to move, his thrusts seemed desperate and hurried. "I want those tits baby. Give them to me."

I leaned back so that I was in a slightly more reclined position, leaning back on my elbows. I used my hands to cup my breasts in order to offer them to Cy who was leaning over me, almost blanketing my body with his. The sight of his tongue appearing from between his lips as he prepared to lick my swollen globes made me moan and tighten around him in anticipation.

"Monday, we need a conversation. About this. Us. About making some time," he told me as he drew a nipple between his lips, sucking on it until I was bucking off the table. He transferred the attention to my other nipple as I began to call out in garbled, almost incoherent moans.

"No, yes, God, like that, please, now, bite me!"

The final request, demand was a serious shock for me, but as if following my instructions Cy bit down into my left nipple and that was it for me. Stars, lights, darkness and delirium followed as my whole body came apart beneath this beautiful man who was also finding his release within my quaking body that he was stroking in the most intimate of fashions, finding every nerve ending no matter how deep inside me. Suddenly he was frozen in the moment with an expression that suggested ecstasy and agony embroiled, and yet with his gritted teeth, heavy breathing and eyes that seemed to stare through to my soul he was undoubtedly the most beautiful human being I had ever seen.

It was probably only a few minutes that we remained that way, although it felt longer before we each reassembled our clothing and demeanour.

"Let me," he said as I struggled with the zip of my dress.

With the feel of his hands on my body, albeit in the innocent gesture of fastening my dress I could feel my arousal reigniting.

"In answer to your question before, about penetrative sex." I flushed. "I guess I can get there without other things," I garbled, wondering why I had decided to open up this topic post-coitus when I sometimes struggled to discuss sex.

Cy was grinning at me with a wide, white show of teeth and God if he wasn't stoking the embers within me with that alone.

"Hmm, although I think my teeth and your nipple might qualify as other things, unless you meant having your clit played with when you said *other things*."

He was teasing me and we both knew it.

"Arsehole," I accused, but was still wearing a smile and a post orgasmic glow.

"Says the bitch, and it's ass." He turned me to face him. His hands remained on my hips. "I wish we had longer," he whispered with a serious expression.

"Me too. It's always so rushed, isn't it?"

"Monday, we'll talk." He seemed to pledge. "There's a bathroom through there," he said, releasing me to point towards a door on the opposite side of the room. "You might need to sort your hair, and your lipstick," he explained with a smirk.

"Thanks." Then I did that thing that pissed him off. With one move, a simple gesture, I reached up and rubbed my thumb across his lips, removing my lip gloss from his recently kissed lips. Unfortunately I used my left hand, the one adorned with my wedding ring.

"Hurry," he said with a surly tone and quality to his voice and stature as he drew away from me, physically and emotionally. "Use the bathroom and then you go back out. I'll go and find Rhonda and Tia."

I wanted to say or do something to make this moment less tense. More, well more of whatever we'd had before. What we'd shared in this room. But I had no clue what I could do so I did nothing beyond doing as I'd been told and went straight to the bathroom to freshen up.

Chapter Eleven

My Friday night escapade with Cy certainly made the prospect of the remainder of the weekend a little more bearable, even with the post-mortem of my behaviour the following morning.

"I am just saying El. You are different, whether you care to admit it or not and I can't say that the new you is a good thing, take last night."

I could hear the disapproval and judgemental air to my husband's tone. As much as I wanted to repeat Cy's like of the new me, or maybe the real me, I didn't allow myself to mention my lover's name, for fear of somehow revealing the fact that I was shagging him.

"I don't know that I have changed. Not really. Maybe I am just gaining confidence and revealing the real me," I countered as I grabbed a carton of juice from the fridge.

Michael laughed, startling me enough that I swung to face him, unsure if it was a genuinely amused laugh or an ironic one.

"That, darling, was not the real you. If it was, I would never have married you. Last night you were beyond prickly, erratic and even without the alcohol you were as near to openly hostile and rude as I have ever seen you. Poor Ness didn't know where to put herself," he cried, referring to the woman who had worn an identical dress to my own.

I laughed now. "Where Ness should have been put was probably not poured into that dress," I snapped bitchily.

"That was unfair and unnecessary." Michael frowned reproachfully.

"I thought what was more unfair and unnecessary was the moment you decided to tell that woman how fantastic she looked." I watched as he recalled his words from the night before. "Yet you couldn't even bring yourself to compliment me in it."

I hadn't raised my voice, I had remained calm, and now we were staring at each other silently.

"I'm going for a run with Balder," I finally said.

"El, I was being nice to Ness and I hadn't realised you needed compliments," he said in his own defence.

"Michael, I know you were being nice and although I don't need compliments hearing one occasionally is never a bad thing." I sighed. "Look, we are struggling here, you and I, and I have no clue what to say or do anymore. Then consider the fact that you were attentive, complimentary and fawned over another woman it grates when the truth is that you have no interest or desire in anything beyond words, unless that's just with me." I felt a pang of something uncomfortable at the sight of my husband's own guilty and sad expression. "Sorry. I'm not saying this to be a bitch, really, I'm not, but it's the truth. Even with your health difficulties there could have been more than this, if you'd wanted to explore alternatives."

I really wanted to laugh at Michael's horrified expression at my reference to a conversation we'd once had after watching a documentary on sex, real people, and some odd couples, like us and how they overcame their differences. I smiled at the memory of a couple similar to us, an older husband, although disabled in ways Michael wasn't but with the same problem that he struggled to satisfy his wife's needs physically. They discussed, quite openly that they had considered several options including the idea of her taking a lover, with his knowledge and consent. An idea they had both dismissed because they loved each other and valued fidelity, unlike me it seemed. This couple had then bought a number of sex toys that allowed the husband to participate and pleasure his wife in ways his body no longer could. I had thought, and expressed those ideas to Michael, that it was wonderful that he would do that for her. That he would use artificial substitutes with no resentment or selfishness. That her desires and satisfaction meant more to him than his own feelings of inadequacy.

My husband, who had still been able and willing to have sex with me at the time had ridiculed the whole situation and had assured me that he would never allow sex aids in our marriage, an assurance that he had stood by, even when I had clumsily attempted, and failed to suggest it a few months ago.

He was still staring at me and I knew he was aware that I was recalling that TV show, the same show he had turned off before the end to take me to bed where he had made love to me, a little too gently, carefully. Suddenly, I realised that the sex between us, even from the first time had always been gentle, loving, but lacking in passion and had never made me feel the way Cy did. I really should never have married Michael and as I watched him watching me, I wondered why I had.

"You know my feelings on alternatives, Eloise," he told me and with his use of my full name I knew I was in trouble, like an errant child once more. "I do not see why any woman would want a plastic phallus thrusting inside her by her husband. It's crude, vulgar and undoubtedly unhygienic."

I did laugh at his final comment but bore him no sulky petulance.

"I think we're coming at this, if you'll pardon the pun, from very different perspectives Michael. It can't be crude and vulgar for everyone, unless they make it that way, if that's their thing. Oh, and I believe there are alternatives to plastic." I had no clue why I added that final part, as if the material used was the issue my husband had.

"Eloise, love, please. I don't want us to argue," he said with a resigned sigh that made me feel guilty.

"Nor do I and it wasn't my intention to broker an argument with you," I informed him, but stopped short of discussing sex because apart from anything else I realised that I no longer wanted him to rediscover his lost libido, not with me anyway. The idea of sex with anybody other than Cy suddenly scared and saddened me, as did the thought of Michael attempting any kind of seduction.

"I don't know what to say," he began.

"Then say nothing Michael and hopefully things will come out in the wash." I was totally unsure what I saw as the *right* outcome anymore. Balder's bark interrupted us and gave me my get out. "I might take a longer run today. I could be a couple of hours."

"I have some calls and a few business things to do," he replied with a change in his expression I couldn't identify. He seemed somehow content, as if our conversation had given him some resolution and now he had refocussed on something else, something that made him more controlled and slightly sinister.

I shook that final idea from my mind and with a small smile grabbed my iPod, pushed the buds in my ears and headed out.

I was just setting about heading home after an hour or so when my phone that was tucked into the little media pocket of my running trousers began to ring.

"Hey," Cy said with his almost customary opening line.

"Hey," I replied, slowing my pace to continue with our conversation.

"You okay? You sound weird."

"I'm running. I'm on my way home," I explained as Balder began to bark in the distance.

"Ah, I could have met you had I known. I wanted to apologise, for last night," Cy told me when I reached Balder who was barking at a herd of rabbits on the other side of the fence to where we were.

I threw his ball in the opposite direction to distract him while I turned my attention and angst at Cy's apology on the man himself.

"Sorry, you're sorry? For what? For turning up at the dinner, dancing with me or fucking me in the spa?" I shouted loud enough that Balder stopped to turn and look at me, wanting to check on me. Seeing me alone with no obvious threat he gave me one of those confused cocks of the head that dogs do before looking back at the rabbits I was sure he was viewing as lunch.

"I really am going to keep you in the fucking dark! Jeez, the bitch is certainly back this morning." He didn't raise his voice, yet was clearly as irritated as I was, not that I considered his to be in any way justified. "I was actually apologising for cutting

147

out early. For leaving within minutes of us both leaving that room. Within minutes of me fucking you in the spa, as you phrased it."

"Ah," I almost whispered and decided that his annoyance with me was indeed justified, whereas my own had been judgemental and completely misplaced. Although he had made no effort to offer an explanation for his decision to leave early.

"Yes, fucking ah!"

"Sorry."

"Shall we start again?" he asked but didn't wait for an answer. "So, I am sorry for running out on you last night after the best time I've ever had at a spa." He still offered no explanation for his sudden exit the night before.

"Mmm, me too," I agreed.

"Were things okay? With you and Michael, last night, this morning?"

"Mmm," I confirmed and then laughed as I remembered his stern expression when I somehow broached the subject of sex toys up.

"Well clearly things are going well between you," Cy snapped, ending my laughter as I realised he thought my laughter signalled something more than amusement. Something intimate between me and Michael maybe.

"No, no! Looks like the arsehole is out and about too."

"What the fuck was the schoolgirl giggling about? And it's asshole."

"Well, arsehole, I was giggling because this morning Michael and I were talking and I managed to infer that I was thinking of sex toys," I explained, whispering the final two words. "Michael disapproves of such things, not that I'd want to pursue that with him.

"Does he? Why? Why wouldn't he want to bring you pleasure in any way he can and as he can't himself?" he mused. "I would love nothing more than to fuck you every which way using a variety of instruments. Maybe I would tie you up and tie you down while I fucked you, over and over until you begged me to stop, but I wouldn't stop baby, not until you knew exactly who you belonged to."

"Oh God," I moaned, already sliding down a tree to the ground and instinctively pressed a hand against my sex through my tight fitting trousers.

"What are you doing?" He seemed to sense my highly aroused state.

"I'm sitting under a tree." I had no intention of expanding on the location of my hand, but with the silence thickening between us I knew he was waiting for me to continue. "The things you say and do to me. You make me want things, to do things," I admitted, rubbing my hand against the seam of my pants. "I want to touch myself."

"As much as I'd like to let that play out right now, I have to go, and you should probably take your crazy dog home, but soon baby," Cy said with a hoarseness to his voice that I now recognised as arousal. "Don't be late in on Monday," he added returning to his boss persona.

****

My weekend actually turned out to be relaxing, cathartic almost, and as much as I wanted to put that down to a combination of sex with Cy and my visit with my father, his words, I knew that the biggest contributor to my frame of mind was the absence of Michael from the house for most of it. He told me over dinner on Saturday and again at lunch on Sunday that he had plans afoot, business, but that was as much as he said. If I was honest, I had no reason to question him further because his business had never been my concern, not beyond being a brief topic of conversation between us.

I realised, as I lounged in the bath on Sunday afternoon that I had never really been alone, never lived alone and for the first time I thought I might have missed out on something I would have enjoyed.

When I was born our house was already pretty full, with older siblings and parents. The place was never empty and certainly never quiet. By the time I was thirteen there were less siblings in the house, with just me, Susan, my brother, my nearest sibling at ten years older, Gary and my dad living there. My mother had died six months before. With hindsight there were already signs that my dad was unwell. That his early onset dementia had begun, but I didn't recognise it. I just thought it was grief from losing his wife, it wasn't.

Gary only stayed for another six months and poor Susan drew the short straw of staying at home, to take care of me and Dad whilst working for Michael. Whilst being his mistress, I thought with more hindsight. It had never really occurred to me before that my husband had been unfaithful to his previous wives, but I was fairly certain he had cheated with Susan at least.

Very briefly I questioned if he had ever been unfaithful to me and decided he hadn't, probably, and even if he had I wasn't even sure I cared. Susan had loved Michael, adored him, still did. After I finished college and with university being a no go I had done a variety of shop work and temping before she got me a role in the company. I knew who Michael was by reputation but she never introduced me to him. She talked about him often, built him up to be the holy grail of men before I threw the post across the floor in front of him. At that point I was seeing a lad who worked in legal, but once Susan got wind of it she somehow scared him off.

Maybe Cy had been right when he'd suggested that Susan had procured me, her younger, innocent, virgin sister for the man she wanted, but knew she could never have, not really. Was I the nearest she could ever come to having him herself on a deeper level, beyond sex. I laughed with that thought, she wanted him for more than the sex, and me? Lately I had wanted him for the sex, until recently. Not that I knew what I had wanted from him or marriage when I'd entered into it.

A sadness washed over me along with my bubbles as I questioned how easily I had been manipulated and ended up in a marriage of what, convenience? Michael's convenience and possibly Susan's. A marriage for me that was now very inconvenient. My sister must have been so upset, heartbroken to hand me over to him, when it was all she wanted, a happy ever after with him. Even after he sent her away, to a friend, a business associate, under the guise of being poached for a promotion with a huge company, when really, he wanted her out of the way, maybe for me. In case I found out who and what she'd been to him or to protect her feelings, allowing her to avoid having to see me, her baby sister living the life she'd wanted.

Suddenly, the water was cold and so was I.

****

I arrived for work and was just entering the lift when I received a text message from Cy.

<Am already in the office. Have had a ridiculous meeting sprung on me. Don't worry about tea…hoping to be done too soon to require refreshments>

Clearly it was going to be a long day if his meeting dragged on, a meeting he didn't seem too happy to be involved with.

I scurried past my own desk, ignoring the raised voices from Cy's closed office. With my coat hung up I returned to my own work space where I threw my bag into my desk drawer and dropped into my seat to turn my computer on. An email was waiting for me from Cy.

Morning Ms Ross,

Thought it was about time that I returned the favour. Enjoy the tea. I assume you drink tea?

Regards,

Denton Miller
CEO Miller Industries (Europe)

With a smile I found my cup of tea that Cy had made for me, presumably before his meeting had begun. I had never really been a big tea drinker, until I began to work for Cy, with his tea before ten and coffee thereafter rule. I was unsure if I should email a response considering the increase in volume from the other side of the closed door in front of me, but assuming he wasn't going to reply I composed a quick reply as I drank my tea.

Morning Mr Miller,

Thank you, for the tea. Yes, I drink tea, mainly before ten! You make a surprisingly good cup of tea. Do you need anything?

Regards,

Eloise Ross
P.A. to CEO Miller Industries (Europe)

It barely seemed that enough time had passed for Cy to have read my email never mind reply when a new message hit my inbox.

Ms Ross,

You're welcome, glad my tea meets your exacting 'English' standards. We have so much in common, don't we? Even our tea schedules. I need lots of things from you Ms Ross, but nothing I want to share in this idiotic and pointless meeting, but afterwards.

Regards,

Denton Miller
CEO Miller Industries (Europe)

I was hot and breathless with anticipation at what would happen once his meeting ended. What precisely would he need from me once we were alone? My nipples were already beading beneath my black blouse that was hiding a half-cup, black lace bra I'd selected with Cy in mind as I had the matching thong that was providing little in the way of a barrier from my aching and slick sex. With a start I realised the voices that were previously raised were now shouting, or at least one was, Cy's.

"Are you fucking kidding me? No way! If he's bored, tell him to find a hobby. Unfulfilled? Find a purpose. But not here and not with me."

There was a brief pause, presumably for someone else to speak, which they did. Another voice I recognised. Edward, the uncle, second cousin, five times removed or whatever he was from the other night.

"He made a mistake, selling up. He wasn't thinking straight. He wasn't bloody thinking at all. He hasn't had a real thought for years."

"Not my problem," Cy replied coldly.

"Maybe it's a mid-life crisis," Edward continued and by the sounds of it he had moved closer to the door, maybe directly behind it.

Cy simply huffed at the suggestion Edward was making about whoever they were discussing.

"Look at his life Cy; he always had business even when he had little else and now he has no business, but he does have golf and a young and demanding wife, wouldn't you want more?"

The penny was beginning to drop for me now and as my face transformed into an expression of pure horrification the door began to open and Cy began to speak.

"Get out. I don't give a shit what he has in his life and if his young and demanding wife is such a fucking chore maybe he should divorce her," he barked as I glanced up to see Edward in the doorway, clearly surprised to find me sitting at my desk.

"Mrs Stanton, what an early starter you are." He coughed awkwardly.

"Ms Ross," Cy countered. "She's Ms Ross, and this meeting is over and will not be reconvened ever again."

I noticed Mr Miller, Denton Snr standing next to Cy looking at me apologetically before placing a hand on Edward's shoulder, leading him away as he spoke, "I did warn you that this was a non-starter here."

I was struggling to breathe normally, yet now it was a genuine physical difficulty I was experiencing for reasons of pain and humiliation rather than my previous arousal that had been completely doused by the fact that my husband had been conspiring behind my back with Edward. Edward, who until two days ago had been a stranger to me, if not my husband. But to what end? To get a job? A business partnership? Here, with me. With my boss, my lover? The solace of my weekend was a distant memory now as I staggered to my feet, embarrassed and uncomfortable, struggling not to cry in discomfiture.

"Come into my office," Cy said stepping towards me, gripping my arm gently.

"Leave me alone," I replied gruffly, shaking myself free of his hold, needing someone to blame for this situation and my position within it.

"No," he told me firmly. Determined to the point of arrogance.

"You are un-fucking-believable! Fuck me on Friday, phone me and fuck with my head and body on Saturday and then top it off with fucking me over on Monday," I accused with what I knew would be a very unattractive red hue of anger.

"Don't be ridiculous," he chastened as if this was my fault somehow and that my claims were inaccurate, which they weren't from where I was sitting.

"Ridiculous?" I screeched as Mr Miller Snr returned with an apology already leaving his lips.

"El, I am sorry if we made you feel uneasy in any way. That wasn't the intention and in Cy's defence he had no idea that Edward was coming here as an advocate for Michael."

"No?" I asked doubtfully.

"No." Cy replied with a dark expression clouding his eyes and spreading across his whole face.

"No," confirmed Mr Miller Snr. "This was something Michael has been considering, then running into Edward, well, he verbalised his ideas, and Edward in turn brought them to me. I called Cy last night, late, to ask for this, although I knew he would be opposed. He said as much on the phone, not that he had all the information then. Sorry again." He smiled before turning to Cy again. "I need to go son, and I have reiterated your feelings to Edward, and supported them. I'll call you later, or maybe come for dinner before we go home."

"Maybe," Cy agreed with a softer expression for his father,

if not for me.

"Okay, bye son, bye El," his father said with a warm smile followed by a concerned frown at us both.

Chapter Twelve

I was still standing, staring across at Cy when Maya appeared beside us carrying an envelope. With a deep breath and a sigh she nervously interrupted the tension hanging between us.

"Sorry, erm, internal mail," she seemed to gasp.

We both turned and saw she had clearly just arrived for work and was still wearing her coat.

I took the bundle she offered me, thinking the mail room was efficient with deliveries this early.

"It came up late on Friday and I forgot to send it through," Maya explained. "Ms Ross, PA to Denton Miller," she smiled offering me a second bundle.

"Thanks," I offered with the nearest I had to a warm smile, my body still shaking in confused annoyance.

Maya smiled back and turned to leave when Cy called to her, "Maya, Ms Ross is going to be unavailable for a couple of hours so her calls will be on divert to you."

"I can field my own calls," I protested with a snarl and a pout as I interrupted.

Maya looked awkwardly between Cy and me as she seemed to be trying to weigh up who she should be listening to.

"Yes, Mr Miller," she replied, having clearly decided where her loyalties lay, or at least who the boss was.

"Thank you." He smiled at her with a warmth I hadn't yet won back.

I was well and truly stuffed if I was so desperate to regain his favour so soon. Maya seemed to give me a sideways smile of apology as she left.

"My office, now!" Cy snapped.

"Fuck you," I retorted, still angry, although maybe not with him anymore. After all, he had done nothing wrong, had he?

"Maybe later. Now get your ass in my office before I carry you in there," he threatened, not that the idea of being carried and manhandled by Cy didn't appeal to my most basic desires.

"You can't make me go in or stay in there," I told him with immature defiance.

"Wanna bet on that? I've told you I'll carry you in there, and I will. I'll tie you up if I need to in order to keep you there long enough to shut the fuck up and listen. So, Ms Ross, anyway you want it, but you and I have a couple of hours to talk and listen, up to you, walk or carry."

"I fucking hate you, you arsehole," I barked, already stropping through his doorway.

A loud smack rang out as his hand made contact with my behind as it passed him, infuriating me a little more. Worse than that was the realisation that not only was my arse on fire but so was my whole body, heating me from the inside out, centred on my sex, again.

"It's fucking asshole, and your hatred? I can live with it better than your bitchiness, now sit the fuck down."

Compliantly I did just as I was told, maybe I hated myself as much as I hated him, maybe more. He joined me on the sofa, fortunately at the opposite end to me and pushed a sealed bottle of water towards my hand as he stared at me, studied me with an expression of wariness and a seriousness that seemed more intense than ever before.

"Am I really that much of an asshole that you truly believe I would have fucked you on Friday, fucked with you on Saturday and then fucked you over today?" he asked me, reusing my own words with a disappointed tone to his voice.

I heard a loud, confused sigh before I realised it belonged to me. I didn't know I had a sigh inside me, but now that it was out there, I needed to explain, to answer his question.

"You are an arsehole, like I am a bitch, but I just assumed, when I got the gist of that this morning, with Edward and your father. I jumped to conclusions, wrong ones. Maybe it's this whole situation that's getting out of hand and making my mind spin."

"Explain," he seemed to demand. "What is this whole situation, how do you see it?"

"I don't even know if I understand it," I began but plodded on with my explanation. "This is an affair. It's sex, no more and yet there are times when it seems more, but then it can seem a hell of a lot less. This is the craziest thing I have ever done, maybe the only crazy thing I've ever done. I am risking my job, my career, my home and my marriage. If Michael finds out and leaves me I will have no home, no marriage and in turn prospective employers, or at least their wives will view me with suspicion, like your mother does and they'd have good cause to, wouldn't they? And Michael, he doesn't deserve this, the unfaithful wife, does he?" I asked, yet he offered no reply, he simply threw back a question of his own.

"Why don't you end it then, if you have so much at risk?"

It was a simple question, there was no challenge in his question. I could almost hear the unspoken words, that this was my decision, that I could call time now and there would be no repercussions and I could avoid the disastrous fallout that I'd described. My reply was automatic, honest and immediate.

"Because I don't want to end it. I'm not exactly what you'd call experienced," I said with a warm flush creeping up my cheeks. "I thought everything I had with Michael was an ideal life until that night, when I met you and something switched inside me. A realisation that it was as far from ideal as anything ever could be. I don't think I'm being clear here, sorry. I am not trying to pin my happiness or the consequences of this on you. God, I don't even call you by your first name so to expect anything of you is not realistic, I know that." I laughed wryly at the realisation that I had only ever called Cy, Mr Miller. Never Denton. Never Cy. Never anything other than his formal name.

"I'm very glad that you don't want to end things, assuming I would have allowed you to," he grinned. "Look, I don't call you by your name, it means nothing. You can call me what the hell you want, baby. How did you come to get involved with Michael, never mind married to him? I know you said your sister knew him…"

I was still absorbing his words, that names meant nothing and that he had no issue with me calling him whatever I wanted before I could process his desire to want more information about my relationship with Michael and how it came to be.

"Why does anyone get married?" I asked, rhetorically I thought until Cy actually answered me.

"Because you can't bear to be without the other person. Because you can think of nothing else, day or night but them and the idea of them ever being with anyone else drives you to the verge of insanity. That you need to make them totally and utterly yours. Without them at your side for the rest of your life would mean your life would be less fulfilling and more painful than anything you can imagine, and as a man I personally love the idea of that someone taking everything I am, especially my name. Or am I wrong?"

"Shit." I had just heard the most heartfelt declaration of how it must feel to be in love. Real, true love. "If you should propose and there is any chance of her saying no, you should open with that," I said, hoping to lighten the thick atmosphere descending between us, yet somehow, I only managed to intensify it further as his words moved me, emotionally. I suddenly regretted not waiting to find the man who could make me feel all of the things he'd described. I regretted not waiting for Cy. The thing about the name resonated on a deeper level as I considered my own reluctance to be known as Mrs Stanton or the way it made me feel awkward when I was referred to in that way.

"I'll be sure to remember that. Go on, tell me about you and Michael."

I sensed that his outpouring of profound words that were spoken in earnest were over, that now he wanted me to continue. To fill in some gaps and although I wanted to share more, for us both to do so, I was also a little afraid because this might just be enough to move us from a purely sexual affair to, to what? Shit, I was fucked either way here.

"Susan worked for Michael, as his P.A. by the time I began work here. I had been here almost eighteen months before I met Michael personally. I saw him a couple of times around the building, without really realising who he was. I knew about him, from Susan, but nothing too specific, just general stuff about how great he was, a real gent, and I saw the gifts he'd buy for her at Christmas or her birthday. I never really gave much thought to their relationship until recently and I now realise she was totally in love with him, but he was still married. He'd left his wife when I met him properly with the post all over the floor." I smiled thinking how innocent and naïve I'd been at that point in my life. "He made the connection between me and Susan and told her we'd met and how charming he'd found me, I believe. By all accounts he had no knowledge of me before then, but no more came of it until after his divorce a few months later. Susan introduced us formally and Michael invited me out to dinner. I kind of wanted to say no because it seemed a bit weird," I admitted to myself and to a wide-eyed Cy.

"So why didn't you?" he asked flatly and expressionless, without any judgement.

I shrugged before offering an explanation. "Susan had already scared my boyfriend off by then and I was uncomfortable asking what his intentions were or why he was asking me out so I settled for agreeing in principle thinking it would be rude to refuse and with the assurance that I would check when I was free."

"You were that popular?" Cy smirked. "That you needed to check?"

"No, not really. I guess I just bought myself some time to get my head round what was going on. Susan told me what an honour it was, to be courted by Michael. Fuck I was gullible, wasn't I?" I asked before I continued. "We were having a really tough time at home and the bulk of the pressure fell on Susan's shoulders, including financially. I won't bore you with the details, but I think she could see that Michael could ease those burdens, not just the cash ones, all of them. She pushed me towards him and he was very, very charming." I smiled recalling his full-on charm offensive, however with hindsight I realised it was not the same as things had been with my boss. Michael's charm was old fashioned and traditional, polite and respectful, like I imagined old fashioned courting to be. "It was probably only a matter of three months before Michael proposed and we were married quite quickly I suppose. Maybe before I had time to rethink it or to come to my senses. He did give my whole family financial security, including a promotion for Susan with an old friend and business associate which meant she moved away. None of it was ever a calculated move on my part, to marry the rich older man. I cared for him, he's a nice man and I could imagine a long marriage. Not that I knew what a marriage was, not really. I had no real point of reference and the life we made together was good, although, possibly for the first time I can see that it might not have looked like that to people from the outside."

With another deep breath and a long sigh I hoped I hadn't just painted myself into the woman Cy's mother despised.

"I can see how you could be manipulated into the relationship and I can see that you entered it as a totally willing partner, if ill informed, but you never once mentioned love and your future sounded very much in the past tense."

I gave another, more juvenile shrug as my discomfort and unease increased under the close scrutiny my marriage and life was suddenly under.

"I have no clue about anything anymore. I still care for Michael, I do love him, always have, but probably not as a wife is supposed to love her husband. Maybe because I was inexperienced in so many ways what we had together was enough. Even the sex, it was okay at the start, as I thought it should be. When it became more intermittent through to non-existent, I didn't know that wasn't how it was supposed to be. I thought what we had was what everyone else had. I am a caring person by nature, but I had never been in love, never felt passion and had no clue how things should be or how I should feel. My marriage is floundering currently. The fact that I seem to be in a permanent state of annoyance with my husband and him with me, and frustrated, both of us, with each other and the fact that I take every opportunity to take my pants off and have sex in strange places with you, well I think that confirms that my marriage is on shaky ground, don't you? Although, I have no bloody clue how to make things right. I don't even know if I want to and simply walking away is complicated."

"How? How is it complicated, baby?" Cy asked, already moving closer to me where he rubbed a thumb over my cheek bone, down my jaw until his thumb was rubbing across my lips coated in pink gloss that he was now smearing over his thumb and my mouth.

"It just is," I gasped. "Family things," I stammered, not wanting to share the intimate details of my family's problems; my dead mother, my father's ailing mental health, the wonderful care home he lived in, paid for by Michael, not to mention all the crap he cleaned up before we married, stuff with my brothers. I really should be more grateful, and yet I could feel my nipples stiffening to hard, painful points and my sex becoming sleek with awareness and arousal as Cy's body edged ever closer. His chest came down towards me as my thigh was pressed firmly by his leg and still his thumb was playing havoc with my lip gloss and swelling lips.

"Okay," he smiled then turned more serious as he reinstated the distance between us. "My dad called me last night, to set up this meeting. A business idea he wanted to suggest with Edward. That's what that was this morning and the business idea was to employ some private consultants. For them to look at viable takeovers and opportunities, those consultants possibly being Edward and definitely Michael."

"I had no idea. He has spoken about business he was seeing people about, but he never mentioned you, Edward or this company, your company."

"I get that. He's old school, I think. He wouldn't dream of discussing his business plans with you, even if the plans would have had a direct impact on you, him being here, but it won't be happening baby," Cy said sincerely. "I don't want private consultants, don't need them. I employ people who work hard and know exactly what I want from them and I pay them well in return, and I don't believe that Michael nor he together with Edward would fit in with me."

"I am sorry for jumping to conclusions," I acknowledged.

"You need to trust me, me and my motives, like I trust you and yours."

"Really?" I questioned, on the verge of tears again that he trusted not only me, but my motives in this chaos we were creating together.

"What? Do I really trust you and your motives?"

I nodded.

"You fucking bet. I told you before, I do not fuck employees or married women and whilst I had no clue you were either when we met, I know both with certainty now, and yet..."

"And yet?" I gasped, praying that he was about to pull me to him, kiss me, strip me, bend me over or pull me into his lap, in fact I was hoping for all of those and more.

"And yet here we are, just you, my married P.A. and me, and I think we both know that I will be buried inside you long before you leave this room."

"Yes," I agreed and encouraged in a single word before I found my mouth possessed and owned.

Chapter Thirteen

After a very hot and sweaty round of sex on the sofa I actually fell asleep, only to wake again for round two. I had no idea that sex could be like that, so, well fucking awesome. I had returned to my desk, eventually, and worked for the afternoon, between bouts of yawning. My boss had been in a very happy mood for the remainder of the day. Clearly sex twice a morning was the way to his heart, or at least his smile.

I was still really angry with Michael. Not for deciding that he needed something more in his life than golf and walking Balder, but for attempting to find a place here. Moreover, for trying to circumvent his way around me, manipulating me again. I realised at that moment I had been manipulated all of my life, one way or another and I had had enough. At twenty-eight, almost twenty-nine, enough really was enough. How was I going to deal with this situation, Michael's failed attempt to gain work with, for Cy? My dilemma was made all the worse because I had no idea how I felt after my morning shag-fest had taken the edge off my mood. I knew Michael would be aware that I knew what he'd tried so I couldn't simply pretend it hadn't happened.

It was almost home time when Cy spoke to me. "You should get off, you look tired." He smiled from his position filling our shared doorway, the connection between our spaces. "Even after your nap." He grinned now.

"Thanks," I replied with a small smile in return. "For the early finish and the nap."

His grin broadened until I felt breathless all over again, like when he kissed me, or when I thought he might. Jeez, he was truly beautiful...this would be so much easier if he wasn't such a handsome arsehole.

"You're welcome, for the early finish, the nap and the absolutely mind blowing sex, both times." His expression was smug now with his grin of Cheshire cat proportions still in place.

"Are you familiar with the phrase, *less is more*?" I asked with a grin of my own.

"Are we still talking about the mind-blowing sex?" he asked cockily.

"I'm going home," I laughed. "Goodnight, Mr Miller."

With my jacket in one hand and my bag in the other I circled my desk and had passed him when I found myself pulled right back to the space immediately in front of my boss who was lowering his head, his lips towards my face. I was struggling to breathe again. His lips missed mine until they were landing a delicate closed kiss to my cheek, and although I was sure that should have resolved my breathing difficulties it only exacerbated them.

"Goodnight, El," he whispered and then released me.

I stared for several long, long seconds before I felt composed enough to move. I say move, but in the end it was more of a badly co-ordinated shuffle that eventually got me to the *safety* of the lift where I first let out a loud and desperate breath before turning into something resembling a teenage girl with a crush on a teacher who had just bestowed a compliment upon her. I giggled, hopped and jumped in the lift before reaching the car park and it was there that I pulled my phone out and sent a very brief message back to the twentieth floor.

<Goodnight Cy X>

A reply was almost instant, but it was a message from Michael rather than Cy, which was unusual as Michael generally preferred to call rather than text.

<Out of town tonight, hopefully back tomorrow, if not, Wednesday. We can talk then. Mx>

I stared down at his words and wondered what the fuck he was up to now, other than avoiding me, which if I was honest suited me just fine. I resisted another text to Cy, maybe to tell him that I was likely to be home alone. That was a sure-fire way to complicate things further, if that was indeed possible. Instead I replied to Michael with a simple *ok* and drove home via the supermarket to the consistent man in my life who was always pleased to see me, Balder.

When I arrived home, I let the dog out before running upstairs for a shower and some clean pyjamas. I returned to the kitchen and gave Balder his dinner before making some pate on crusty toast and with a bottle of beer I retired to the lounge where I settled down to watch reality TV. I wondered whether it was another selfie moment as I checked my phone where there was a message from Cy waiting.

<Told you names were not an issue baby, although I might need to work on El. Goodnight X>

I was back to juvenile with a crush again as I bounced in my seat while Balder viewed me with suspicion and if it was possible, he frowned at me before collapsing in a heap at my feet.

<*You don't like my name, Cy? X*>

<It's not that, but when I hear other people call you El, it kinda grates...you are at risk of overdosing on the Cy thing I think. See you in the morning X>
****

Having never been alone also meant I had never lived alone. I was that girl that never went away to university or even flat shared with friends. I never lived with a boyfriend. I went from my family home to my marital home. In fact, I had only ever had two homes, but as I got up and prepared for the day ahead I decided that was now a regret, that I would have liked living in my own space.

The drawback of lone living with a dog was leaving him alone all day, something he wasn't used to. Michael had been on a wind down over his last couple of working years, more or less since I'd known him and he'd had Balder just before me so the dog was rarely left for the whole day. Today I had no choice, unless our lord and master decided to come home. I'd text him, later.

Work was easy, Cy was in a pleasant enough mood, but busy meaning we didn't really speak about anything other than work until I was glancing at the clock on the wall that showed me it was almost home time.

"Am I holding you up? Somewhere better to be?" He grinned, looking bloody gorgeous in a navy blue suit so dark it was almost black. Today's shirt was white minus a tie and the top two buttons were open revealing his neck and a little chest that I had a near overpowering urge to kiss, lick and nibble.

"No. Well, I do have to get off on time, Balder is home alone and I wanted to dash home and let him out before I go... out. Before I go out. I go out on a Tuesday night," I flailed, digging a hole for myself.

"Where's Michael?" He frowned, ignoring my garbled explanation about my night.

"He didn't come home last night. He text when I left here to say he was out of town. Convenient after his party trick yesterday. He said he might be back today or tomorrow. I text him earlier, but I haven't heard back. Sorry, I'm sure you don't want to hear this."

"Stop apologising," he sighed. "I want to hear anything you have to say, baby." He smiled a little awkwardly. "Okay, how about this? We leave now, I'll follow you back in your car, you let that beast of a dog out and do whatever you need to and then we'll go out again, together, wherever."

I stared up at him and thought that he might have just made me the offer of my life, the kindest, most thoughtful gesture I'd ever been on the receiving end of. Sadly, not one I was in a position to accept.

"I..." I began as my phone chirped into a text message alert. "Just a minute."

<Sorry it's late. I have been home so Balder is fine. Out of town again tonight, will be back soon. Mx>

"What the fuck?" I asked staring down at the phone in my hand before glancing up to see Cy's look of confusion.

Passing him my phone he read the words on the screen with a shake of his head.

"I don't want to be an ass here."

"Arse," I corrected.

"You pushing?" he asked a little too seriously for comfort.

"No. Maybe a little," I conceded, causing an arch of Cy's eyebrows.

"Mmm. I wasn't being an ass, but do you think he's having an affair, Michael?"

I shrugged with a feeling of, well, nothing. "I don't know, I think we both know it wouldn't be his first. Sorry, I still need to go, it's Tuesday," I repeated.

"We can both go, together." He frowned as I decided that my nice calm day was about to implode when I disagreed and protested.

It was another twenty minutes of arguing before I left the office alone. Not that Cy knew I was leaving alone; he had refused to accept that we couldn't spend some time together and as I refused to explain where I was going and why he became even more determined for us to do something. I appeared to agree, allowing him to go back into his office to gather his things while I strolled out of my own office to the lift under the guise of *rearranging my plans*, which actually translated to giving Cy the slip. I think I probably only got the time it took the lift to travel down to the car park and back up again, but clearly that was adequate.

****

I arrived at my dad's nursing home a little later than I normally did but was pleased to see Angela at the nurse's station after I was buzzed in. She was talking to another patient's family so I hung back slightly until I caught her eye.

"Excuse me." She smiled at the couple in front of me. "El,

go through, he's in his usual spot and has had another good day, hasn't shut up and has been very lucid."

I could feel the beam of my smile pulling my face into a tight ache at the idea that I might just get some time with my real dad, again, although I understood all too well that when he slumped back into mental and emotional obscurity it would hit me hard, but it was worth it for the good moments, like last week.

"Thanks," I sniffed with happy tears burning my eyes.

I entered the day room to find my dad's usual seat empty. Scanning the room in something of a panic I was relieved to see another patient waving at me.

"Bathroom, love. He's just gone, so give him a minute."

"Thanks," I called to the older lady who for all intents and purposes looked totally out of place in our current location, but then so did my dad when he was lucid.

I turned back towards my father's seat of choice, not wanting to make conversation with any other patient. I was here to see just one person and honestly, I was shit scared that by the time he returned from the bathroom his switched-on brain may have gone back to standby. Immediately I felt a little pissy with Cy, if only in my head because his arguments had delayed me. I was still studying the picture, print, whatever it was of a lilac flower, maybe a lupin. Who wanted to look at a bloody lupin I wondered when I felt a presence behind me and without looking around I knew he was there, and it wasn't my dad.

"You need to leave," I snapped without moving my eyes from the flower before me.

"You need to tell me what the hell is going on and why we're here?" he asked in a whisper that I could feel against my ear.

He was so close that my whole body reacted in its usual way to his close proximity and the promise of what that might mean. I was slightly relieved that he had reined in his language with his *what the hell* rather than his usual *what the fuck* with other people, older people around us.

"Maybe, although maybe not," I hissed.

"You pushing, baby?" he asked and that was it for me. My

breaking point. I spun with absolute fury rushing through my veins.

"Pushing? Fucking pushing?" I asked, seemingly not so bothered about other people, older people hearing me swear.

"Watch your mouth." he warned. "Show a little respect."

"Respect!" I spat, verbally and physically I thought noticing a speck of my saliva flying towards Cy's chest. "Like the respect you have shown me by coming here, following me, invading my privacy?" I asked beyond annoyed.

"Cuts both ways, Ms Ross, and you, you lied to me, to my face, so…"

"Here he is," shrilled the older lady from only a few feet away.

"Fucking kill me now," I sighed, turning to see my dad walking towards me, us.

"Don't tempt me," Cy muttered as my dad arrived before us.

"Hey Muffin." He smiled at me. "When you gotta go," he laughed, referring to his trip to the bathroom, brushing past me to take his seat.

"Muffin," Cy mouthed. I ignored him.

"Sorry," called Angela from behind me, bustling into the room. "You okay Jezza?" she asked my dad who grinned at her in response. She was his favourite member of staff too.

"Sorry El," she apologised again addressing me directly. "This gentleman, he assured me you knew him, that you were friends."

"Mmm. I know him, but friends," I said shooting my boss a withering glance. "Jury's out."

"Do you want me to, well I'm not sure what, but?" she whispered and I assumed she meant something like asking Cy to leave or ejecting him and I didn't think that would be in anyone's interests, to create a circus here.

"I can hear you, both of you," Cy interjected.

"Bloody marvellous. Now you hear me, but before, when I was trying to tell you that tonight wasn't a good night for me, you wouldn't hear that," I accused.

"Language, please." Cy frowned before my dad was back on his feet.

"That's enough. You bloody kids, always somebody falling out," he frowned, shaking his head at us.

My heart sank when I thought that my dad was seeing me and Cy as bickering children, possibly his children and his lucid *Muffin* had disappeared. I was still standing toe to toe with Cy when my dad spoke again.

"Eloise, Muffin, come on, don't be like this," he cried as I turned towards him and took a seat next to his as he settled back in his own chair. "And you," he called to Cy who followed suit and sat next to me.

Angela looked relieved that we were all sitting down and not arguing as she turned to leave. "You know where the kitchen is," she called and then was gone.

"Who's your friend?" my dad asked with a flick of his head in Cy's direction. "I know he's not your idiot husband," he sighed. "Still don't know why you married him…yes, I do, me and the boys…Susan. She should never have allowed it. She more than anyone should have intervened."

"Daddy," I began and realised that up until that point my lover had no clue who the man before us was, not for certain.

"Daddy?" I heard him whisper from beside me.

"This is Cy, he's my boss," I explained.

"Nice to meet you, Sir, sorry for intruding," Cy said to my father, offering him an open hand to shake.

"American," he said as he accepted the hand offered. "Ah, American, oh Muffin," he sighed, and I hoped he'd just decided that he didn't like Americans, rather than having remembered anything from my confession the week before when I assumed he had no real clue who I was. "He's the American, the one you're, you know, having an affair with," my dad whispered with his head inclined towards mine.

"You told him?" Cy hissed beside me.

"Don't judge me," I hissed right back.

"Mr Ross," Cy began, getting to his feet.

"Sit down son. Jeremy, please," my dad told him with a wave of his hand. "I know you married him because of me, for this place, the boys and everything, but Muffin, I don't want you to be unhappy."

With my hand being pulled into my dad's I was unsure what to say.

"We discussed this last week. I'm sure we did. Did we?" he asked, his grip on reality slipping already, so soon.

"Yes, we did," I confirmed with a glance to my side where Cy looked confused and bewildered.

"Good, then we're agreed, you're Eloise Ross and you're perfect as you are and if anyone wants to change you, what do you need to tell them?" he asked.

"To fuck off," I whispered, repeating his words from the week before.

"Yes, but maybe not here, Muffin," my dad said with a nervous look around.

"Why Muffin?" Cy suddenly asked.

"Ah," my dad smiled. "I never wanted her called Eloise for one, stupid name, no offence," he offered. I simply shrugged, having wondered most of my life where Eloise had come from as my siblings all had such simple, normal names, Susan, Mary, Gary, Wayne and Neil. "So, I tried every other name and variation I could get away with, but she wouldn't have it. Always had ideas above her station, bloody snob, even the way she said it El-o-ese," he sneered drawing out my name making me laugh despite my confusion at his words about my mum. She was many things from what I remembered but not a snob and she only called me Eloise, or El-o-ese if I was in trouble. But for the most part I was El and she didn't really draw my name out as he described I didn't think. "But she was so stubborn, even as a baby. So determined and bloody minded, stubborn as a mule, Muffin the Mule," he laughed. "It could drive you crazy, but I wished she'd remained stubborn enough to avoid other people's manipulation," he added sadly.

"So, what did you call her other than Muffin?" Cy asked with a warm grin and no hint of sympathy or pity for my dad or me. He simply listened to his ramblings attentively.

"She hated it, her mother," he sneered again. "Elsa, like the lion in that film, Born Free, 'cause she was a real lioness, even then." He smiled proudly causing tears to burn the back of my eyes right down into my jaw that was tingling with emotion too.

My father's recollections of who and what I was were strange. It seemed obscure that he described the child I was as stubborn and fierce, a lioness and a mule, yet here I was as an adult the complete opposite; compliant, obedient and so easily manipulated, a doormat.

"Elsa," Cy smiled with a cock of his head. "I like it," he told my dad who was smiling back.

"No," I warned.

"What?" Cy asked, feigning innocence.

"You don't like it either," laughed my dad with a real belly laugh that he was pulling up from his boots, well, slippers as he took in Cy's expression of distaste.

"No," I repeated.

"Why not?" Cy was clearly not expecting an answer as he laughed along with my dad who he was now addressing. "No, I struggle with El and Eloise, especially when I hear other people say it, but Elsa, I like that for my lioness, grrr," he roared as I stared between him and my father.

I gave them both a shake of my head. "You like it that much I'll give it to you for your first-born daughter," I snipped with a tight expression.

"Jeez baby, at least let me decide what I'm calling you before we name our first born," he taunted, making my dad laugh even louder.

"No, what the hell is the matter with you? I meant your child, not mine, not together, that could be problematic, with me already having a husband," I pointed out and immediately regretted it when I saw his face drop and then darken before his steely expression kicked in.

"Elsa, I need to go to bed, I'm tired Muffin," my dad said, staggering suddenly as he attempted to get to his feet. "But you remember what I said, and that I like him, so be nice," he said seriously, grabbing for Cy's hand that he was shaking vigorously.

"I'll find someone." I was already up and leaving the room but still able to hear my dad telling Cy that I deserved to be happy, to have the best of everything.

Returning with Angela I found they were already at the

door, my dad ready to turn in for the evening and suddenly he looked old and tired.

Seeing me coming towards them, Cy lowered his voice, unlike my dad. "So remember, you promised, you can't back out now. I trust your word."

"Hey," I heard Cy say as I stopped before them. "I won't back out. I promise."

"Come on then Jezza, if you're ready," Angela said, taking my dad's arm from its position on Cy's.

"Nearly," he almost sobbed breathlessly. "Let me say bye to Elsa, to my little Muffin."

He turned to face me and he was crying, like last week when he left. Maybe this was the thing with not having a lucid mind and accurate thought processing at all times. When it was there you realised how out of it you were the rest of the time, and yet, it seemed more than that tonight. He seemed genuinely distressed, like he was saying goodbye to me, properly goodbye, like he might never see me again rather than next week. I found myself pulled towards him until I could barely breathe. He kissed me on the top of my head while stroking my hair, like when I was a little girl and upset, comforting me. However, I felt many things, but none of them were comfort.

"Always remember that no matter what happens, what anyone says, whatever you might discover, me and my Stella loved you, more than anyone ever could and we did what we thought was best for you, always."

I could feel my face becoming drenched with my own tears that I couldn't have stopped even if I'd wanted to and as the tears from my father's bowed head began to drip into my hair he continued to speak in broken gasps.

"You have done enough, suffered enough and when you're ready you should do what you want, with whoever you want. Promise me, Muffin. Or all of this will have been a waste if you ruin the rest of your life because of the choices we all made."

Again, I had no real idea what he was talking about, but again I got the gist of it. He wanted me to be happy, to be myself and not manipulated and taken advantage of anymore. If he'd asked me to make a pledge of this just a few weeks ago I wouldn't have been able to do it because I had truly believed that my life was happy and fulfilled, but now it was easy, so I repeated the words Cy had earlier, although clearly what we were pledging was very different.

"I promise, Daddy," I gasped as we both straightened.

"Good girl, never doubt how proud you made us, me and Stella," he said passing my hands to Cy who was already preparing to hold me, take me and then he turned away with Angela leaving me ready to completely fall apart in Cy's arms, where my father had put me.

Chapter Fourteen

The next thing I recalled was arriving home, with Cy who had driven me. I had no idea where my car was or what had happened after collapsing into the safety of Cy's arms.

Walking me to my door he took my key from my bag and let us in where Balder was waiting to greet us. Me with warmth and excitement, Cy, not so much so.

"I need to let him out the back," I said hoarsely. I'd been crying for a while judging by the feel of my throat and sound of my voice.

"Let me, maybe he'll like me a little more then. You go and sit down or whatever," he suggested with a weak smile. Looking down at me as a finger lifted my chin we made eye contact.

"Okay," I conceded freely. "I might go and get changed. Just call if he takes exception to you," I whispered with a half-smile.

"I think you mean if he tries to rip my balls off."

I let out a single, short laugh and turned for the stairs.

"Hey," Cy called, pulling me back a little, looking as though he was about to say something else, but came up short, simply stroking a thumb across one cheek.

I returned, dressed in my comfy uniform of yoga pants and vest to find Cy outside with Balder, throwing his ball for him. The dog, who at this time of the night was only used to being let out and badgered to hurry up was in his element with an attentive new friend who was intent on winning favour. Seeing me appear beside him Cy paused before picking up the recently retrieved ball causing the dog to bark impatiently.

"Hey, isn't it enough that your mistress busts my balls and pushes without you starting?" he asked the dog who did his half cock of the head thing which I always took to be his way of asking, *what the hell are you on about?* "Last one buddy," Cy told the dog who almost appeared to nod his concurrence.

With a final hurl of the ball I made my way back into the kitchen where I found some wine in the fridge, but no beer. I had drunk the one bottle I'd bought the night before.

"Tea, coffee, juice, pop, wine?" I offered.

"Beer?" Cy asked, but I think he knew the answer to that. "Or not. You really need to take control of what's in your fridge, baby," he told me as Balder bounded in and sat at my feet, waiting for his dinner.

An hour later I was sitting on my sofa, with Cy at my side and Balder fast asleep and snoring in front of the fire while the plates from our makeshift dinner of beans on toast sat on the coffee table in front of us.

"Do you want me to apologise for coming after you tonight?" he suddenly asked as the music around us faded, one song ending as another began.

"Do you?"

"No. You lied to me, and to the best of my knowledge that's not something you make a habit of, so it was a serious red flag for me. I was certain you would have told me if you were meeting Michael, a friend or a family member. The only cause for you to lie was if..." he trailed off with a guilty expression.

"Really? You thought I was off for some kind of fucking hook up? You really are an arsehole," I accused, feeling insulted, unsure if that was something I was entitled to feel. Not when I was having an affair with my boss whilst lying to my husband. Maybe Cy wasn't the unbelievable one after all.

"Yes, no, I don't know! Look, I just knew you were lying and keeping things from me and that bothered me and then you fucking tricked me, so no, I do not want to apologise for following you."

I nodded my understanding.

"You could have told me about your dad. I would have understood. I don't understand why you would want to keep it to yourself, he's great. I like him, he's a straight shooter and doesn't take shit, not from Susan and not even from you, Elsa." He grinned. I didn't grin as his words resonated.

"You think I'm ashamed of him?" I asked incredulously. "You are way off the mark there."

"Ah. When you said about it being complicated if your marriage ended, you meant your dad, Jezza."

I laughed at his Jezza because before dementia and Angela my dad was the least likely Jezza the world had ever known.

"He's one of those things, the main thing. What am I even doing with my life?"

"You tell me," Cy suggested, turning slightly so that he could slip an arm around my shoulders to pull me closer. A move I offered absolutely no resistance to and quickly found my head was resting back against his chest while his hand was stroking the naked skin of my chest and neck.

"I'm sorry if my lying hurt you, pissed you off," I corrected, thinking that hurt implied feelings and although I knew I was beginning to feel things, I refused to humiliate myself by assigning the same ones to him.

"I'm sorry you felt you had to lie and I'm sorry I implied or inferred that you might be off on some hook up mission," he said flatly as his thumb traced the hammering pulse in my neck.

"I wouldn't, never have, before you. I didn't even hook up with Michael, not really," I sighed, further realisation dawning on me with every breath I took and word I uttered.

"I get that baby, really," he whispered, landing the sweetest, gentlest kiss to my head.

"I love my dad and seeing him…today was a good day, and last week he was quite with it, but those occasions are usually few and far between. Most times he's friendly and chatty at best, but has no clue who we are. Sometimes he remembers his family, from years ago and other times he just sits there, clueless. You got to meet the real man tonight I think."

"Then I'm honoured," he replied with a total genuineness I couldn't help but believe. "This house, is it yours?" he asked randomly.

"Mine? Mine as in belongs to me, or that I live here, or

chose it, what?"

Turning so that I was beginning to lie across his chest I waited for him to expand on his question.

"Chose it, or do you simply live here?"

"This really is a fact-finding mission tonight, isn't it? Michael bought this place after he and his last wife divorced. He lived here and when we married, I moved in."

"Have you made many changes since you've been here?"

"No, not really. It's pretty much as it was I suppose."

Further realisation dawned that this house had no real stamp of me beyond personal belongings, not that there were many down here. What did that say about me, my marriage and my life?

"Do you think my balls are safe if I kiss you?" he asked with a mercurial turn.

"He seems to be unconscious." I smiled up with a point in the direction of Balder's snoring. "Assuming you mean from him," I added, allowing my smile to become a grin.

"Oh, Ms Ross," Cy replied with an arch of his eyebrows and a grin of his own before his lips slowly came down to meet mine, too slowly I realised when my hands reached up to pull him to me.

I became lost in the moment, the kiss, and the reverence I felt passing from his lips to mine. God could this man kiss. I pushed from my mind the thoughts of just how he'd honed his craft and who with, how many who withes. His lips were soft against mine, moulding against their counterpart, fitting together perfectly, worshipping me. Then came his tongue that showed no such softness, pushing against my tongue and gums, daring me to take him on, a dare I grabbed without a second thought, duelling with him, stroke for stroke.

The feel of a hand lacing through my hair, pulling and tugging was a further challenge from Cy. Provoking me to make my move for dominance, a move we both knew I wouldn't truly take. With a final, half-hearted attempt to take charge, I pulled on Cy's hair as I nipped his lip. That was it for the man at my side, who soon became the man above me as I found myself sprawled beneath him. His tongue overpowering mine, his teeth grazing and scraping against my lips and his hands everywhere. I was moaning and writhing, becoming almost disorientated when Cy pulled back so that he was kneeling between my thighs looking as breathless and aroused as I felt.

"Baby, I am loving making out with you, but I don't think this is the place for it. So, another night and another place, okay?"

I nodded, knowing exactly where he was coming from.

"I should probably go anyway. Bathroom, where's the bathroom?"

"Upstairs, third door on the left." I panted, moving into a sitting position.

I watched Cy climb the stairs and then looked over to the dog who was still sprawled on the rug snoring. Maybe some ice had melted between the two of them as a few of the barriers between us had dropped. For no reason at all I followed Cy upstairs and found my bedroom door open, and Cy filling the space.

"Sorry," he whispered, without turning to look at me. "I just, I dunno. I just wanted to see where you sleep." He pointed to my side of the bed. "How fucking creepy do I sound?" he asked with a grimace that made me smile before he expanded, "I can see you here, on that side of the room at least." He gestured to my area of the room that was littered with belongings; books, tissues, a framed photo of me, Balder and my niece who was only a couple of years younger than me, phone charger, iPod and docking station, my contraceptive pill and a tiny plastic Disney princess figure, Belle from Beauty and the Beast. "You're only missing a bottle of beer and a slice of pizza," he teased, making me laugh.

"It's late, you're welcome to stay," I offered and immediately saw the misunderstanding on Cy's contorted face making me laugh, although this situation was becoming less and less funny. "I meant in a guest room. Not in my bed. Not here."

"Ah, I see. I'll go. I really, really do not want to make love to you in this bed or this house, but I know that I don't have enough self-restraint to be with you all night without coming to you and doing precisely that."

I had no answer. No words. No nothing, not least because he had just said the words make love, not fuck, not even sex, but make love.

"We need to do more of this I think," Cy said gesturing to the space between us. "The talking."

I nodded although the making out appealed to me as much as the talking.

"Come on. I wanted to see this room and now it kind of makes me feel uneasy, like I can see you and him together." He shuddered and turned away.

Following him as far as the top of the stairs I pulled back, "I understand what you meant about the bedroom, but there really is no me and Michael in there."

"No, you said, but things change," he told me, sounding as close to nervous as I had ever heard him.

"You think if Michael rediscovers any interest in me that I will, what? Jump at it, literally bend over backwards to accommodate him, huh?" I felt decidedly prickly.

"He's your husband," Cy pointed out but without any hint of recrimination in his voice, just something that sounded like reluctant acceptance.

"I know what he is, but even with what we're doing I don't think I was made to cheat and I can't imagine having sex with anyone that isn't you," I admitted with a crimson hue. I waited for a reaction from Cy, half expecting panic or horror to cross his face, but it didn't come.

"I really do need to go because my self-restraint is shot to fuck right now with that thought alone. We definitely need to do more of this, talking." He grinned, looking happy, really happy, ecstatic almost.

"Talking," I repeated, "And making out?" I teased my sore and swollen bottom lip with my teeth.

"You bet, but I really have to go or there won't be an inch of your marital home untarnished by our fucking."

With a final kiss at the front door Cy dashed to his car, past my own car that had miraculously appeared.

I was still resting against the back of the closed front door when there was a knock on it. I wondered, maybe even hoped

Cy and his self-restraint had decided that respect for my marital home was seriously overrated and I was about to get nailed to the back of the door in every sense. I opened the door to find him standing with his self-restraint still intact, unfortunately. He had a large paper bag in his hand, the name of a top designer emblazoned across it.

"For you," he simply said.

"Me?" I queried, already accepting the gift.

"Mmm, you, from me. Just because you liked it and I wanted to buy you something." He rambled slightly.

"Thank you," I smiled as I began to open the bag. "Oh wow, it's beautiful, thank you." I gasped as I pulled out a handbag from the confines of the paper, exactly the same as the one from the raffle at the charity fundraiser. "You really shouldn't have," I told him, already knowing just how much the dark red leather handbag with matching calf skin lining that I couldn't help but stroke had cost.

I actually found I was holding it before me and then putting it up on my shoulder, modelling over a thousand pounds worth of Prada handbag whilst wearing yoga pants and a vest.

"You really shouldn't have," I half protested.

"Sure, I should. You liked it. It makes you happy. I want to make you happy," he admitted with a horrified expression that made me smile a little more.

"But it's very expensive," I replied, thinking that although Michael had always paid the bills, never kept me short and never ever questioned how I spent money I would never have spent so much on a bag. Maybe that was my upbringing.

"Tia guided me on what that bag was the other night, although she was going for a Birkin…"

"No!" I protested at that name alone making Cy smirk and shrug.

"I know," he conceded, I thought. "There's a waiting list or something," he added, suggesting he had looked into shelling out probably ten thousand pounds at least, on a handbag.

"You are mad," I accused.

"I can return it if it offends you," he suggested with an outstretched hand towards my beautiful bag.

"No, no, never," I cried, tightening my grip on the handles.

"You're welcome. I really need to go."

"I wish you didn't." My whisper sounded sappy and needy to my own ears.

This moment was deepening and becoming emotional and I wasn't sure that was in anybody's interests.

"But I'm going to, before I kiss you or touch you."

****

The next several days passed by in a blur; work was easy, Cy was easy and for all that I loved my time at the office I dreaded home time and weekends, more and more as days passed and became weeks.

Michael had returned home on the Wednesday night. When I tried to discuss the events that had led up to him disappearing for two days he shut me down, refusing to discuss *his business* as it had nothing to do with me. With each argument I offered against that logic he laughed and told me that I was no more than admin. I was unsure if whether he meant at home or work. By the end of that week I gave up discussing it at all, choosing to let it die a natural death as it had come to nothing. There was something on the horizon for Michael, as he had phrased it, but that was all I knew. He spoke of Edward a couple of times which was surprising as he had never mentioned him before he'd shown up at the fundraiser.

My dad had remained physically well, but his mental state seemed to have deteriorated to the point that on my most recent visit he hadn't uttered a single word. We'd sat in neighbouring chairs watching a crappy quiz that had rules that were impossible to follow. Cy asked me every Tuesday night if I was okay to go alone and then he'd text me to ask how Jezza was before asking me in person each Wednesday morning when I arrived for work. I really did fall a little harder each and every time he showed such consideration.

During private moments he had settled into calling me baby or El, with a very occasional Elsa thrown in as a wind up if nothing else. Professionally, he stuck to Ms Ross, which I found reassuring. The clear division between our personal and private moments. Although, they did blur whenever we had sex on office time, which was fairly frequent.

****

It was a Saturday afternoon when Michael appeared in the kitchen to tell me that we had been invited to dinner with Denny and Elizabeth, as a goodbye before they left for The States for a few months. Inevitably Cy would be there and I was unsure how to feel about that. Partly because I knew as time went on I was finding it harder and harder to mask my feelings for him, even Maya had begun to notice, with a few questioning glances and comments, but it was more than that. I worried that he would view me as more married than I felt if he saw me with Michael and then there were all the rules relating to my behaviour that Michael favoured, no beer being a major one which pissed Cy off more than me.

"I don't really know if I fancy it," I huffed.

"It wasn't really a question, darling." Michael frowned. "And it's not like you have anywhere else to be, is it?"

I couldn't disagree with that.

"And you and Cy are getting along better, aren't you? I thought there'd been a thaw in relations over the last few weeks. Anyway, it will be a great networking opportunity for me, so be mindful of what you wear and how you conduct yourself," he warned before turning to leave and as he reached the doorway turned back to face me once more. "El, I know things aren't right between us and who knows what awaits us around the next corner, but please remember that I have never had anything other than positive feelings towards you. That I only ever wanted you to be happy. Mainly just bear in mind that you are my wife."

I stared wildly, clueless as to what I should say. His tone was sincere and his words believable and yet there was something else there, something I couldn't name or pinpoint and then he was gone.

I did consider his words and wishes as I dressed, opting for black satin underwear consisting of a black satin mini brief and push up bra underneath an opulent fuchsia floral print midi dress. I had to admit, if only to myself, that the little cap sleeved, slightly plunging neckline that revealed my cleavage and the general skimming fit of the dress had also been chosen with Cy in mind. With a sheer skin tone pair of hold up stockings and dark blue heeled court shoes finishing off the look I smiled in the mirror. I wasn't and had never been a real fan of make-up, but in an attempt to look like Michael's younger, yet sophisticated wife I did put on a light and natural looking foundation, with just a hint of blusher and grey, slightly smoky eyes. As it was dinner rather than a party a single coating of brown mascara and a clear lip gloss seemed to fit and then I was ready to go.

Michael had dressed in a dark blue suit with a white shirt and equally dark blue tie.

"You look very smart," I told him as I arrived at the bottom of the stairs where my husband waited for me.

"Thank you." He smiled as I stopped on the bottom stair where I reached across to brush his once medium brown hair that was heavily peppered with grey at the temples and sides off his face like I would for a friend or even a child. "Come on," he added, passing me my clutch bag that was the exact same shade as my shoes. Not a Prada, which was a frequent companion of mine, but my clutch was right for today.

Chapter Fifteen

Pulling up at the Miller's house I felt butterflies fluttering in the pit of my stomach at the anticipation of seeing Cy, but cold fear coursed through my veins too at the idea that I might somehow give my true feelings away, reveal to someone present that Cy was so much more than my boss and the son of my husband's old friend.

Michael was already getting out of the car as I felt my breathing hitch at the number of cars already parked meaning this was not a small and intimate dinner. With a smile he opened my door and offered me a helping hand.

"You okay? Maybe you should have had a more substantial lunch," he mused as he took in my nervous, angsty disposition.

"No, I'm fine," I lied. "This isn't likely to a late night, is it?" I asked, hoping to feign fatigue if it all got too much.

"I have no clue, El," he sighed. "I thought I was supposed to be the old, boring one," he seemed to accuse before softening a little. "Sorry, this is important to me, so please, try."

I looked at him intently, wondering what any of that meant beyond the fact that I had just been told to suck it up whether I wanted to be there or not.

We were already at the front door as another car pulled up behind us.

"Hey, Michael, El," cried Tia, a little more excitedly at my name than my husband's.

Michael was kissing Tia on the cheek before she turned to pull me in for a long warm hug.

I liked Tia. We'd met a couple of times for lunch and I

considered her a friend, a new one, but a friend nevertheless. We were a similar age, just a couple months between us and shared similar interests; books, music, films and clothing. I took in her appearance and felt slightly envious of her relaxed outfit of black leggings, knee high boots and an asymmetrical tunic in a bright blue hue that seemed to emphasise her height and the enviable length of her legs.

"You look great," I told her as she opened the front door.

"Er, you look better, very sophisticated sexy," she whispered the last word which I knew meant, wait til Cy sees you.

I flushed a little, making her laugh, by which time we'd reached the lounge where there was quite a crowd of people in clusters of various sizes. I was hoping Michael might leave me with Tia, at least then I could have a drink and a laugh without having to try too hard, but no, he took my hand, gave Tia a farewell nod and led me to a group of people.

I stood at his side, smiling in all the right places, making the occasional comment, but for the most part my role was to stand and look pretty while Michael discussed various political, financial and business topics. After about twenty minutes I was struggling to maintain my focus never mind remain attentive which clearly showed when one of the men smiled at my stifled yawn sympathetically.

Once I was sure I was safe from revealing my yawn I returned his smile, just as Edward joined the group. I felt a strange awareness and apprehension of him. Initially I thought I didn't like him, but now, I didn't think it was actual dislike. There was an element of fear I decided as I shuddered when his glance landed on me, but it was more than that. I didn't trust him, nor his motives for reappearing in Michael's life. I knew I was hypocritical, judging anyone's intentions where my husband was concerned as my own were seriously compromised since my affair with Cy had begun and yet Edward just didn't seem *right*. Like he was hiding something or had an ulterior motive.

I sensed someone beside me before I turned to find Tia joining us. She seamlessly fitted in, contributing valid comments and thoughts before suggesting that she might just need to steal me. I nervously looked to Michael for his approval, which was given and with a lighter heart and a huge sense of relief I followed her to the refuge of the kitchen.

"Alone, at last," she laughed as she passed me a bottle of beer that I eyed with suspicion, reluctant to accept it. "Shit, El, what the hell are you doing here?" she asked seriously before returning the beer to the fridge where she grabbed a second soft drink, identical to her own for me.

Happy to accept the can and a glass to pour the contents into I looked at Tia quizzically.

"What?" she asked in response.

"Exactly, what did you mean, what am I doing here?" I asked feeling braver about the question than the answer.

"Precisely that! You are here with Michael. Your husband. A man who openly disapproves of the woman you are, or at least the one you're attempting to grow into and you're still here in my family home where you should be my mother's counterpart and yet you're not. We're the friends here and then add the fact that you're not only having an affair with your boss, my brother, but you are falling for him..." her voice trailed off as footsteps sounded behind me.

Turning, I was surprised to see Cy's vamp friend, Rhonda with a girl of around five, a near carbon copy of her, but with dark hair rather than Rhonda's perfectly coiffured blonde locks.

"Lulu," Rhonda said with a loving and warm smile for the little girl. Maybe I had misjudged the other woman, purely for being on Cy's arm and being an old friend. I had a horrible feeling that I knew just what sort of friendship they'd had. With a gentle stroke of the little girl's shiny brown, braided hair Rhonda continued to speak, "Ask Auntie Tia if she knows where you might find some candy."

"Really Mommy?" the little girl cried excitedly, already running towards Tia.

So not only was Rhonda an old friend of Cy's, an ex-girlfriend, I now knew she was a mother to the bubbly little girl beaming at Tia. I smiled at the exchange between Lulu and Tia and then smiled a little broader knowing Rhonda had clearly moved on if she was involved with someone else enough to share a child with them.

"Sure thing, Titch," Tia grinned, hugging the little girl.

"Hey. Rhonda," Rhonda smiled with a hand outstretched to greet me. "Cy's friend," she added with a wry smile that told me that she knew exactly who and what I was, but moreover she knew how I had felt about her, making me and our handshake a little awkward.

"El," I reciprocated. "Cy's P.A."

She arched her brows at my professional title, although she stopped short of correcting it.

"Then you have my sympathy and respect for lasting this long," she laughed. "He gets through P.A.'s like other men get through clean socks."

"I've heard a few rumours, but we're doing okay, I think." I smiled, suddenly wishing I had said something else because it sounded like we could be talking about our personal relationship rather than our professional one, although, maybe we were.

"Hey, this looks very suspicious," Cy called when he entered the kitchen behind us.

"Only to you," Rhonda retorted quickly making Cy laugh.

"You know me too damn well," he grinned with a cocky swagger as he sauntered to stand between us.

"You bet, and that is my cue to go," she laughed. "El, it was lovely to meet you, properly. I hope we'll see you again soon," she added, confusing me slightly as to why she hoped to see me, but also who *we* were, was it her and Lulu or her and Cy?

Shaking that thought from my head I noticed that Rhonda, Tia and Lulu had suddenly disappeared. Tia and the little girl might have disappeared before Rhonda and I had become reacquainted. Now Cy was stepping even closer and he looked and smelled divine. Dressed in dark blue jeans that were cut and stretched in all the right ways and a tight grey t-shirt that emphasised his firm body whilst hinting at the possibilities beneath the fabric. I knew I was staring at his abdomen, chest, arms and tattoo that seemed to be teasing me from its position, peeping out from one sleeve.

"Hey," he whispered, closing the distance even further until there was barely a hair's breadth between us. Me now pushed against the edge of the counter top of the island and Cy pressed against me, both of us oblivious to the potentially public venue we were in. My excuse could be blamed on my intoxication at his close proximity and the scent of the man; musk, cologne, clean, fresh and incredibly sexy all rolled into one. "Alone, at last," he said seriously, making me laugh. "That's really not nice baby," he chastened with a small frown.

"Sorry, it's just that was what Tia said when she rescued me from boring business talk."

"Ah, well as grateful as I am for her rescuing you, I think my motivation and appreciation in having you alone might be considerably greater."

"I can't think why," I teased deliberately.

"You pushing?" he asked with a twinkle in his eye.

"Like you wouldn't believe," I conceded, nibbling the corner of my lower lip.

"Oh baby, I have fucking missed you," he told me seriously.

"You know that it has been about twenty-four hours since you saw me," I reminded him, thinking that somehow it seemed much longer.

"Yeah, like I say I have fucking missed you. I'm thinking of changing your contract to a seven day week arrangement," he said as his lips lowered towards mine. He paused to tell me, "Oh, you look gorgeous by the way. I like this dress."

"Thank you and I can see the advantage of weekend working."

"Yeah?"

"Mmm, seven days a week," I whispered. "I missed you too," I admitted to myself and him.

His lips completed their journey, landing on my own mouth that was needy and greedy in equal parts. I couldn't believe that the house was buzzing with people, many of them unknown to me, but surely all of them known to Cy. Yet here we were, lips locked, my hands running through his hair and tugging gently while Cy's were roaming every inch of my back, shoulders, hips and behind through my dress. A single insistent press of his tongue was enough for my lips to part, inviting him in. Begging him to enter, which he did, stroking, probing until I was panting breathlessly.

"Where's Cy got to?" called his mother, already entering her own kitchen where we had just come up for air and fortunately had unhanded one another. Still, I was convinced that it must have been obvious where he'd got to judging by my immediate red flush, rapid breathing and guilty expression, which was the complete opposite of Cy. He was resting back against the counter top, his ankles crossed and his hands pushed into his pockets looking completely casual. "Oh, there you are. Your father said you'd arrived, but I somehow missed you and here you are with El."

She smiled, a slightly flat smile that unnerved me, especially when she chose to hold my gaze a little too long. She knew that there was more to me and Cy than work. God, she'd almost caught us snogging in the bloody kitchen, her kitchen while people, her friends and family were in neighbouring rooms, people including my husband. Cy had been right all of those weeks ago when he'd described us as a disaster-in-waiting and yet I couldn't stay away even if I wanted to and I didn't, because I loved him. Those words rang out loudly in my head and between them, my own arousal and excitement together with Elizabeth's knowing and disapproving eyes I wasn't sure my legs wouldn't give way beneath me.

"I needed a drink," Cy replied with a calmness I was in serious envy of. "El and I missed each other," he seemed to announce making me feel sick at his honesty before relief replaced nausea. "At the office. At the end of the day on Friday," he expanded, which was actually true. He had been called to a meeting late in the day and had insisted I should carry on home.

"I see, but sweetheart, you shouldn't really badger El with business talk at the weekend or at social events." Elizabeth frowned, but I was unsure if she disapproved of his lack of social etiquette or because she wasn't buying a single word of it, possibly both. "I'm sure Michael would disapprove," she added curtly, somehow reminding me that I was married and as such I should back the fuck away from her son.

"Come on, Mom," he cajoled, pulling her under his arm for a hug. "El is like me, that's why we work so well together. She's a seven days a week girl." He grinned with a wink at me for good measure as he reused our words from earlier. I stared across at him with a lax jaw and a wide stare.

"No more business talk today," she insisted, looking up at her son with nothing but love in her eyes.

"Whatever you say," Cy agreed, although we hadn't actually discussed business so his apparent compliance might not be too big a request.

"Mmm," the disbelief clear in her voice. "You're enjoying your work now, El?" she asked transferring her attention firmly to me.

"Yes," I nervously stammered, ignoring the inference that I hadn't been previously. Unless Michael or Denny had suggested as much.

"That's good."

"Mom, I thought we weren't talking business," interrupted Cy, "But for the record Ms Ross is the best P.A. I have ever had and we work well together."

I thought that would be the end of the conversation but as Elizabeth continued to speak she had other ideas. "I am pleased. Cy has difficulty keeping staff, although maybe you should get El to line up her replacement so at least she knows what candidate she's looking for."

"Replacement?" both Cy and I asked in unison, although I think my one-word exclamation may have been more of a shrill.

"Sorry," she began. "But people's circumstances change and I am sure once you start a family…" She smiled, looking at only me for a few seconds.

"No!" I protested, "I won't."

"You don't want children? I know Michael has children already, but you're young…" she suggested and yet I wasn't entirely sure that this wasn't some kind of test I was probably failing, completely.

"I do want children, really I do," I claimed with heartfelt insistence shocking her, me and Cy who was glaring at me, presumably angry because I had previously insisted that Michael and I would not be having a baby, which was still true. "But not with Michael," I blurted out. "We won't have children," I added, hoping to make this whole situation less uncomfortable for us all.

"Mother. I think you should probably stop right there, because if me talking to El about business is considered inappropriate then you grilling her on her family planning is definitely off the table."

I gazed across at Cy with tear filled eyes, grateful for his intervention but mortified at my own clumsy admissions.

"Of course. Forgive me, Eloise." She smiled warmly and put an arm around my shoulders with some genuine concern as she guided me out, away from her son.

****

Dinner threatened to be torturous as I followed a long line of fellow diners into the huge and professionally catered dining room; this was clearly the formal, entertaining dining room rather than the one I had eaten in on my last visit to this house. I had an arm linked through Michael's and felt totally at ease in this position, like I would with a girlfriend or one of my siblings. My husband seemed to detect my general unease and attempted to soothe it by gently stroking my hand that was resting on his forearm until he reached my wedding ring that only served to somehow make him as uneasy as me. I couldn't help but wonder, what the hell was the matter with my ring that it seemed to burn any man that touched it? Cy, and now Michael.

We were sat in what I thought was an obscure order as I found myself sandwiched between a middle-aged diplomat and Cy. Michael was opposite, flanked by Rhonda and the diplomat's wife alerting me to the fact the Rhonda must be viewed as Cy's date and just like that my irrational jealousy was back, assuming it was irrational.

I opted for the vegetarian choice and managed to avoid a glass of wine, instead requesting fizzy water. In my current strange and free speaking mood I knew alcohol could be a really bad idea and although the idea of confessing my affair, my feelings for Cy and lack of appropriate feelings for my husband was appealing, doing it here with such a large and varied audience was not.

I chatted to the diplomat initially, hoping to deflect Elizabeth's attention which had been quite rapt since my outburst in the kitchen. When my starter was placed before me, I turned to find Cy watching me, studying me.

"Are you ignoring or avoiding me?" he asked seriously.

Shaking my head, I waited for the waiting staff to move down the table. "No, but this is quite public," I replied in a hushed tone rather than a whisper in an attempt to avoid suspicion.

"I see," Cy replied, turning to the woman who was on his other side, making polite conversation with her for a couple of minutes before returning his focus back to his plate. "Do you think I'm pissed with you?"

I looked around before answering, just in case he'd been heard by someone else. Apparently not considering everyone else was deep in conversation with someone or eating their starter.

"I don't know, maybe," I nervously admitted, putting a fork full of risotto into my mouth. "Are you?"

"I kind of was, but once you'd clarified your baby plans, I was good."

"Good," I repeated and meant it as my reply and confirmation of his feelings.

****

For the remainder of dinner Cy and I chatted, to each other and to the other people around us. I found the diplomat on my other side to be funny, friendly and incredibly interesting, but every time I looked at him to speak I noticed Edward. He was on the other side of Mrs Diplomat, staring and yet again I was confused by his studious gaze that was beyond intense as it bore into me with something I still couldn't name. It was different now, but still unfathomable by me, almost as though he was seeing me for the first time after a long period of absence.

A sense of liberation came over me as we were able to leave the dinner table, ending Edward's scrutiny I thought as Tia came to my side and linked arms with me to lead me outdoors.

"Is it just me or is this like Groundhog Day? It's like this day is never going to end," she sighed, sitting on a low wall. She pulled me down to sit next to her.

I laughed at her observation but couldn't deny that this day seemed to be going on forever.

"Did Mom bust you and Cy? I tried to throw her off the trail but only stalled her."

I shook my head. "Probably a good thing you did stall her. By the time she came into the kitchen there wasn't much to see. We were talking, I suppose."

"Ah. Talking like we're talking or talking like you guys do with the breathlessness, the enforced distance and the looks that strip you down and fuck you?" she asked, startling me slightly with her description, but again I probably couldn't disagree. "I see, eye fucking talking," she grinned. "Did Mom say anything?"

I shrugged and gave her a summary of our time in the kitchen.

"Thank fuck she's going home this week or she wouldn't be able to stop herself from, interfering, I guess."

"You two look like naughty schoolgirls," Edward accused from behind a bush, startling us both.

"Hardly schoolgirls," Tia retorted while I sat nervously twisting my fingers.

"You'll always be a little girl to me." He smiled with genuine fondness, something I hadn't previously seen until now, until he embraced Tia.

"Whatever, Uncle Edward," she giggled.

"Aren't you girls about the same age?" He turned to me.

"Yes, almost. Just a couple of months between us," I waffled, making him frown and smile at me as someone called Tia indoors leaving me alone with Edward.

"I make you nervous?" he asked and stated with a slightly overconfident smile.

"No," I protested. "Unless there's something I don't know about you that should make me nervous."

He laughed at that which didn't reassure me at all, quite the opposite.

"I think there's a lot you don't know about me, and I you. So, let's fill a few gaps," he suggested.

I seized the opportunity. "How long have you known Michael?"

He looked amused and a little impressed at my taking the bull by the horns attitude.

"About thirty years I suppose. We met at a club of all places." He frowned, making me smile at his distaste. "Elizabeth and I share some distant relatives and about a month after I met Michael we met again at Elizabeth and Denny's and we've been friends ever since."

"How come I have never met you, or even heard of you until the fundraiser at the hospital?" I was really pushing for information.

Edward laughed with a shake of his head. "You're a tenacious little thing, aren't you? I have no clue why you've never heard of me, Eloise," he said enunciating each sound of my name. Like my dad had accused my mother of doing a few weeks before, during my last *lucid* visit. "That's something you'd need to ask Michael. We, you and I have never met because Michael and I had a little falling out. About six years ago and we were only ever friends, never business associates."

"What was your little falling out about?" I asked being blatantly nosey now.

"Again, ask your husband, you curious little kitty. My mother was called Eloise," he told me thoughtfully, changing the subject, ending my pursuit of knowledge. "Who named you?"

"My parents, I think. Although my dad recently revealed he doesn't actually like my name." I laughed, making Edward laugh with me and suddenly he seemed less cold, friendlier and genuinely interested in what I was saying. "So, maybe my mum."

"Then my compliments to your mother dear," he smiled, patting my hand.

"You were close to your mother, still am?"

"Yes, very. She died about six years ago." He looked down at the ground sadly.

"I'm sorry. Mine died about sixteen years ago." I sympathised with a reciprocal pat of his hand but couldn't help but wonder if Edward's falling out with Michael had anything to do with his mother's death, but that was a curious step too far, even for me.

"You're very kind, and my condolences. I can see why Michael tried marriage again with someone as sweet as you."

His words sounded as though he was suggesting that Michael marrying me was a mistake, maybe marrying full stop was. Yet there was a compliment in there for me, even if his expression was once more conflicted. He wore a smile that didn't quite make it as far as his eyes and a look that was almost pained.

"I think I could like you, Eloise," he declared with over enunciation of my name again. "Can I ask you something though?"

I nodded my acquiescence and he continued with a smile.

"Are you happy, with Michael?"

I wanted to insist that of course I was. Be offended that he'd ask me such an impertinent question and yet his eyes insisted on the truth. That he would know if I lied. Like a rabbit caught in headlights I had no clue what to say, but I needed to say something. Still no words came, all of them getting stuck in my throat. Daring me to lie. Daring me to tell the truth.

"I see," he said with a sad expression. "And with Cy?" His question caused me to panic that he knew about our affair. That possibly Michael suspected it and now Edward would go back and tell my husband.

"He's my boss," I managed to splutter.

"Of course," Edward agreed, leaving me feeling that I had been well and truly let off the hook. "I hope you find your happiness El, wherever you hope, but alas, I think it may be a rocky road."

"Edward, Edward."

We both turned to see Cy coming towards us with a concerned look on his face, presumably at the sight of us sitting together, in cahoots.

"Dad said to tell you that Bill is making noises about leaving."

"Ah, Eloise, lovely chatting with you, but business calls." He smiled getting to his feet and left me alone with Cy.

Cy immediately took the space Edward had vacated. "Are you okay? Was he hassling you?"

"No. He was nice. We chatted. I think he knows about us…"

"Yeah, he has hinted as much to me, maybe—" he said but was interrupted by Lulu barrelling across the grass towards us, laughing as she went.

She was being followed by Rhonda and Tia, both of whom were looking decidedly distracted. More confusing to me was their sudden look of worry, but why? Although, Cy and I were yet again putting ourselves in a very precarious position of potential discovery.

I heard Cy mutter under his breath as Lulu closed in on us, but I didn't quite catch what he said before the little girl's voice broke through.

"Daddy," she called with a huge smile on her face as she giggled and laughed.

I looked at the space behind us, where she was looking. There was nobody there. With a confused frown I looked up at Cy who was standing now and then at the pretty little girl who had just begun to slow as she almost reached us and then the world stopped spinning. The air thickened and my breathing became laboured. I was unable to stand or move.

"Baby, I can explain," I heard Cy say somewhere in the distance through the fog of my mind that was struggling to order and place everything in the right location. Add to that the sight of Lulu throwing herself at Cy and Rhonda and Tia appearing in front of me, looking concerned and sympathetically between us and then my distress and confusion were compounded.

"Daddy, Grandpa says I can go and stay with him and Grandma when they get home. He's going to take me to Disney World," she shrieked so loudly I thought my ear drums might burst.

"Wow! That is so cool. You're so lucky," Cy told her as I looked up and saw him holding her in his arms.

"Oh God!" I heard the cry on a wobbly exhale before I realised it was my voice. I had four pairs of eyes trained on me now and had no clue what to say or do next.

"Lulu, can you go and find Grandma and stay with her for a while?" I heard Cy ask the little girl.

"Why Daddy? I don't want to. Why can't I stay here?" she asked before turning her attention to me. "Why is the lady crying?"

"I'll take Lulu," Rhonda offered, already carrying the little girl away towards the house.

Tia shifted awkwardly on the spot for a few seconds, just enough time for me to rediscover the ability to think, to order a few thoughts and to speak.

"You have a child. A child you never mentioned. Not once!"

"Let me explain—" he began but I cut him off.

"Explain? Explain?" I shrieked without a second thought for anyone overhearing. I wasn't even sure if Tia was still there. Cy had my complete and undivided attention.

"What's to explain? You have a fucking child and potentially an ex-wife. Why wouldn't you tell me?" I asked but needed no reply as I continued blazing through the words in my head. "You could have told me, should have told me. I would have understood." I truly believed that I would have been fine with him having a child so long as he wasn't already married which I knew was hypocritical considering the fact that I was. "As you pointed out to me on a regular basis, I'm the married one, so you having a child would not have been an issue, would it?"

Tears were running down my face and I was at serious risk of choking on them when Cy took a step closer. Stretching out towards me, possibly preparing to pull me in, to hold me.

"No!" I yelled. "Don't you dare touch me," I warned him, feeling out of control, unsure what I might do or say next, especially if he came any closer. "I thought I was the one in the wrong. The married one. The cheater. The liar, and you allowed me to continue in that belief. You never once mentioned your child, never even hinted at her existence."

"We should talk about this," he insisted, but thankfully kept his distance.

"No, no talking. It's too late for talking," I snapped. "I should go. This is over." I got to my very shaky and wobbly legs and feet.

"This is not fucking over!" Cy snapped, grabbing my left

hand that he looked down at viewing my wedding ring with suspicion, as usual.

I pulled my hand free and went for my final fling in this ridiculous situation.

"You do not get to tell me anything anymore. When I think how shit you've made me feel about being married when all along you had your own dirty little secret."

"She is not a dirty little secret," he snapped back defensively.

"Whatever, Mr Miller. Is this your modus operandi then? You find a willing party and act all righteous and indignant?" I laughed ironically. "I think your, *I don't fuck staff or married women* spiel was a nice touch. I fell for that like you wouldn't believe and that whole distaste you had going every time you saw or felt my wedding ring touch you…maybe that's me though, plain old stupid, easily manipulated for other's needs. And to think I thought you saw me differently, that there was nothing in this for you, nothing ulterior." With a deep breath and a long sigh, I continued, "I need to go. I need you to back the fuck off and leave me alone. If you make a scene now everybody in this place will see exactly what we have been doing and for what? For nothing, because this is over. If you have any sense of decency or if I was ever anything more than a game you will let me walk out of here without making any more of a scene."

He nodded sadly.

"I really don't like you very much at the moment, but the worst thing is that whilst I hate you, I actually love you. How fucking ridiculous is that? I even gave you my name for your first-born daughter. That was surely the time for you to correct me, to tell me that ship had sailed, don't you think?" I really was done now. With a tear stained face, a dry, hoarse throat I turned away and walked purposefully, avoiding the house completely, instead walking around the grounds until I reached the front of the house.

I'd left Tia with Cy and heard her telling him that he should have told me and then her voice softened, becoming more comforting than accusatory.

Once at the front of the house I had no idea where to go or

what to do and then from the corner of my eye Edward appeared.

"You look like you might need a lift home," he said, already taking my arm and leading me to his car.

"Michael," I managed to say with clarity.

"I'll text him. Tell him you've had a turn and I've taken you home. That you didn't want to disturb him as he was discussing business. How's that sound?" He reached across to fasten my seat belt.

"Thank you," was a struggle to get out, the second word catching in my throat.

Chapter Sixteen

Neither of us made any further comment until we were entering the house.

"Michael has text back, he could be a while," Edward informed me with a disapproving frown.

I nodded with some relief as Balder turned the corner to see us. I laughed in spite of the situation at the big lolloping hound struggling to gain any traction on the smooth marble hallway that he was skidding on like some kind of cartoon character.

"Hey, Baldy. You are looking as handsome as I remember," laughed Edward as the dog first jumped up to kiss me then turned his very excited and happy mood to the man beside me who it appeared was an old friend of my dog as well as my husband.

We wandered through to the kitchen together where I opened the back door and let the dog out before turning back to Edward who was sitting on a stool at the breakfast bar looking somehow at home.

"You know Balder too."

"Mmm. Michael and I chose him together," he explained and suddenly looked as though he had a bad taste in his mouth.

I knew Michael had collected Balder a few months before we got together. About six years ago. The same time that Edward's mother died and the same time he had fallen out with my husband.

"Eloise…" he started but I was already speaking.

"Why do I think there is so much more to you than there appears to be on the surface?" I asked.

He shrugged making me smile that he wasn't going to deny it.

"Maybe you'll discover all of my secrets, over time," he suggested with some kind of inference, but I had no idea of what.

I stared for only a few seconds that seemed to last so much longer as his eyes never left mine and a sense of panic washed over me. Could it be that Edward thought I was an easy bet, a sure bet? He'd told me in the car, before we left the Miller's house that he had seen most of mine and Cy's exchange in the garden, before Rhonda told him about Lulu inadvertently outing my lover. My former lover as her father. So, did he now think he could pick up the pieces and what?

Clearly my face gave away my thoughts as Edward laughed. "You don't think very highly of me or my motives for bringing you home," he accused with a grin. "Eloise, you're safe with me. You're not really my type."

I let out a huge relieved sigh. "Too married?" I asked with assumption in my tone.

"Not really, but maybe too female for my current tastes sweetheart," he replied flatly making me stare a little wildly.

"I didn't know." My response, like me were awkward.

"No? My pink tutu and flashing tiara only come out on special occasions," he teased, making me laugh as the tension was relieved. "And it's not something I announce even though I am completely at ease with my sexuality. Plus, you are very young, so even with my appreciation of the female form, you're not my type."

Balder came rushing back through to where Edward sat back on his haunches to fuss the dog who obviously remembered his old friend.

Edward stayed with me for about an hour and we mainly chatted about safe subjects; the dog, Edward's work, his mother, my father, but we avoided subjects involving Cy, Michael and my marriage.

"Will you take my number?" Edward asked as he prepared to leave.

"I don't know." I hesitated. "After all, you're Michael's old friend and a member of the Miller extended family."

"Guilty as charged." He smiled. "But, I don't know. Look I am not known for my friendly demeanour and I don't go out of my way to make new friends, but you Eloise, there's something about you that makes me think that you need a friendly ear."

I shrugged. "And you want to be my friendly ear?"

"You seem so young, childlike almost, in a situation you don't really know how to resolve. Please take my number. You don't have to use it, but just in case you need a friend, a surrogate uncle shall we say, then call, in a day, a week, a month, whenever."

I nodded and allowed Edward to input his number into my phone before walking him to the door where he hugged me with a warmth I felt I could get used to.

"I am sorry that you got hurt," he told me.

I was unsure whether he was referring to my marriage or my relationship with Cy so nodded.

"I think I've made a bit of a mess all round," I admitted.

"I don't know that the mess is insurmountable," he smiled.

"Do you think Michael knows our marriage is over? That it's no more than a sham?" I asked causing Edward to turn on his heels to look at my face that might just have been as shocked as his.

"Maybe you should speak to Michael. Find out what he knows."

I didn't take Edward's advice, that night, nor the following morning having gone straight to bed with just Balder for company. I had no clue if Michael made it to bed or not, if he did, I didn't wake until the following morning when it was just me and Balder.

My husband had definitely been home at some point because there was a note on the fridge door that simply said:

Hope you're feeling better this morning.
Have some business meetings today.
Should be back later. X

I read and reread the words and could sense no more than

friendly concern in it. A paternal or avuncular affection that genuinely warmed me, and yet I felt cold as I realised that I couldn't really remember a time when Michael's feelings were anything stronger, if they ever had been.

****

Arriving at work on Monday morning, I turned my phone on and looking down I sighed at the number of missed calls and text messages from Cy, meaning work was going to be intense. Maya and I arrived at the lift within seconds of each other and travelled up to our floor together.

"You okay?" she asked, revealing that my face suggested I was anything but.

"Not really," I admitted, refusing to keep lying to myself and the people around me.

"You want to talk about it? Maybe we could do lunch," she suggested with a sympathetic smile.

"Maybe. Can I let you know?" I asked as the lift came to a stop.

We stepped off the lift together and headed for our own workstations. I busied myself with some tidying and organising before making Cy his tea. I had coffee, possibly just to be different to him, probably out of some kind of spite, or to prove a point. It was wasted I decided when I pulled a distasteful expression at my drink. I would have preferred tea.

Sitting at my desk I sensed Cy's arrival before actually seeing him, which only added to my irritation with myself and at him.

"Your tea is on your desk," I told him without bothering to look up.

"Bring yours in," he almost ordered, but somehow stopped short of making it an all-out demand.

"I don't think so," I snapped.

"It wasn't a request, Ms Ross," he replied as curtly as me now.

"It should have been, Mr Miller, and unless your need for me to come into your office is entirely and one hundred percent business you are in no position to make demands on me or my time."

"El…" he began, more gently.

I interrupted. "No. Don't you dare! If you're bored or at a loose end or whatever the fuck you were when you played with me then maybe you should find a new friend to fuck with because I am done." My voice was a virtual screech. "In fact you could give your daughter a call."

"Let me explain…"

"No. Like I say, I am done, we are done and the disaster-in-waiting, well it is no longer waiting for me because my life is one big, unadulterated disaster zone. Now, please, go and do whatever you need to, but leave me the fuck alone or I will tender my resignation forthwith, minus any notice and I can ill afford to be unemployed on top of everything else."

Cy looked at me, warily, nervously with a sad expression that looked poised to speak and then he turned away, closing the door behind him. That one action made my heart, head and soul ache, but I needed to remain strong in my resolve to resist any further advances from Cy, but also from any attempts on his part to talk me round.

****

My resolve remained strong for the remainder of Monday and well into Tuesday. Cy did as I had asked and kept our contact purely professional which didn't give me as much comfort as I'd hoped. Precisely, it gave me none. I declined lunch with Maya on Monday and Tuesday, but by mid-afternoon on the second day she appeared at my desk with cake. Cy was out and I agreed, well it was more a case of gave in to her suggestion of coffee and cake. We talked about a few different things including the weather before she addressed the elephant in the room.

"So, you look like shit, and I could guess what's wrong, but I'd rather you told me."

"It's complicated," I sighed, making her shake her head.

"Complicated? Meaning it's a matter of the heart, but is it Michael or the boss man?" She shocked me with her brazen inference, accusation, whatever it was about my boss.

"What?" I spluttered, but she was already waving my objections away.

"Please do not insult me by finishing that sentence," she warned. "It's as plain as the nose on your face El, yours and his," she grimaced pointing towards Cy's office. "You both look miserable, and you didn't, until yesterday, so I assume you and he have split."

I nodded as I fought the tears threatening to overflow. She offered me a sympathetic smile before pulling me into a huge hug that was the final straw for the tears that now flowed freely down my face.

We remained huddled together in the kitchen for long minutes and once I thought I was done with tears Maya let me go.

"What about Michael?" she asked with concern for us both I thought.

"I think it's over. It is, has to be, when I am in love with another man and have finally realised that as much as I love Michael it's not enough. Not even real compared to what I feel for Cy. It's a mess," I sighed before we both heard Cy coming through the door.

He came to a standstill and stared at us both, but said nothing.

Maya was the first to speak. "If you're okay I should get back to my desk," she said with a final squeeze of my arm.

"Thank you," Cy replied while I simply nodded. He waited until she'd left us and then he turned to me. "We can't carry on like this, I can't. I cannot, will not pretend that we did not happen. We did, and I realise and accept my fuck up. It happened and there will come a time when you will have to listen to me, and that time is coming soon, baby."

I picked up on the warning in his tone, but ignored it.

"Don't bet on it and don't call me baby."

We stared at each other, his eyes dark and cautionary. "You can tell yourself that, but trust me, it's coming. I know how much you like me calling you baby, so, I'm going to call you, baby."

I had no more to say so petulantly attempted to push past him, but his hand closed around my wrist and pulled me back. I gasped loudly at the sensation, the heat and prickling across my skin, scorching me, searing through me until I found myself gazing up at the beautiful eyes that had promised me so much, delivered so much and then cut me to the core. Seeing them now, seeing them sad hurt me a little more.

"This is not over, not by a long shot. No matter what you tell me, or yourself."

"Cy," I gasped. I wanted him to let me go, yet still wanted him to tighten his hold on me, pull me closer until I could almost taste him.

His description of us being a disaster-in-waiting was a serious understatement I thought as he lowered his face to mine. Oh God, he was going to kiss me and then I would be done for. Once his lips touched mine, I would be putty in his hands to do with as he wanted and he would destroy me next time, because next time I would be further invested, physically, mentally and emotionally and if I was questioning how I would recover from this now, well it didn't bode well for *next time*.

Stopping short of my lips he stared down and said one word. A warning, a reassurance and a notice all in a single word, "Baby."

I was packed up at the end of the day and as it was Tuesday I hurried away to be on time for my visit to my dad, something Cy allowed me to do with no further words or exchanges.

I entered the care home and felt the vibration of my phone as Angela's concerned eyes met mine. I smiled up at her warily before grabbing my phone from my coat pocket and found a message from Cy. So much for me thinking he was letting me have some space.

<Hope your dad is a little more like himself this week. Say hi from me...call me if you want to, need to>

I didn't reply because I had no clue how to respond. Also because all I could think of doing was calling Cy, morning, noon and night and then there was the fact that Angela was closing in on me.

"Hello El," she smiled warmly, but there was concern in her eyes too. "He's gone to bed."

"Already? Is he okay?" My dad never took to his bed so early, not even on a bad day.

"Today's been a toughie. He got up late, hasn't eaten much and went back to bed a couple of hours ago. He's been emotional, a bit disorientated, shouting at anyone he saw."

"Sorry." I smiled weakly feeling as though I was about to defend my errant son to his teacher.

"Don't be daft," she reassured with a rub of my arm. "I know he loves me really. Speaking of which…Jezza was asking about that man, the American…" She clearly felt awkward.

"Cy?" I asked, but felt sure it couldn't be anyone else.

"If that's his name; tall, dark and bloody gorgeous." She smiled and made me laugh.

"Yes, that's Cy, he's my boss."

"Hey, you don't need to explain yourself to me. Anyway, I thought I'd mention it, that he'd been asking after him, asking me to call him, but I don't have his number…"

"It's fine, probably for the best. I'll go round and sit with him for a while," I said, already leaving to make the short journey to my father's room where I found him fast asleep.

Silently I took the armchair next to his bed and watched him for a while before considering a response to Cy's message. I could ignore it, but that would be ungracious as he had only offered kind words and thoughts, so I composed my reply a total of eleven times until I felt I had found the right balance.

<Jezza's taken himself off to bed and is snoring away. Apparently today has been a rough day. Thank you for your text>

My phone alert sounded within what seemed like seconds and although my dad didn't stir, I switched it onto silent before I read the reply.

<Sorry it's not a better day. You don't have to thank me for showing you concern…I meant what I said about calling me, if you need to>

I sat for another hour and a half watching my dad sleep, checking emails on my phone and even reading his well-thumbed copy of *The Great Gatsby* aloud and smiled at the page it was on.

"He smiled understandingly, much more than understandingly," was the line I read and continued speaking words of a rare smiles that faced the whole world and then concentrated on you.

My dad stirred briefly at the words I was sure I didn't understand and yet they were calling to me, making me think of Cy and his understanding smile. I shook the thought from my mind and decided that it was time to leave as Jezza showed no signs of actually waking up. With a gentle kiss placed on his forehead I left and drove home.

****

Michael was already there when I got home, watching something on the TV that seemed to involve politics and share prices. He barely looked up as I entered the room, simply offering a small smile and a half wave as Balder rushed me. At least someone was genuinely pleased to see me.

I waited, although I was unsure what I waited for. A kind word, some show of concern for my dad or an offer of a cup of tea? There was nothing, zilch. If there had previously been any doubt in my mind that somehow I had changed, that my marriage had changed since I'd met Cy then tonight proved those doubts were unfounded. My marriage was over and all I had to do was say the words out loud and as we were both there, together.

"Michael," I squeaked out, but it was enough for me to gain his attention. "I was thinking, we should talk, about things, us things…"

"El, can this wait? I've been waiting for this next piece for the last hour." He frowned with irritation.

"Sorry," was my response. His annoyance had me simpering and recoiling. Why couldn't I find my bitch persona as readily with Michael as I did with Cy? "I'm not sure it can," I braved.

"El," he sighed as the phone rang and that was it, the moment was gone.

With a sense of irritation at myself I took Balder outside for a while and then we both went to bed where I text Cy.

<Thanks again for the earlier text. Angela said my dad had been asking about you, asking her to call you...he likes you>

<Please stop thanking me. I like Jezza too. Are you okay?>

Was I okay? Possibly not.

<Not really. I think my dad is slipping away>

I was crying as the words I was typing registered in my brain.

<Oh baby, I have no clue what to say or do to make this better>

<That's not your responsibility, but thank you>

I knew I was being unreasonable in my prickliness at Cy, although his secret child was the reason why he and I were estranged, but then again, he was my boss and I was married, so not exactly a love match by anyone's standards.

<Don't tell me what my responsibilities are and don't be such a bitch! Isn't Michael there to offer you some support?>

So now my prickly bitch was rubbing off via text!

<Takes an arsehole to know a bitch.>

<Asshole>

His correction made me smile in spite of the fuck up that was my life, and for a few seconds I forgot that we, Cy and I were no longer a couple. That I really had nobody.

<Michael is here, at home, but he won't even speak to me, so support might be too big an ask>

<I'm here>

I stared at the two words, but couldn't really trust myself to get caught up or carried away with the notion of him being anywhere for me.

<I'll see you tomorrow. Goodnight>

Chapter Seventeen

We plodded on for almost another week with next to no conversation, me and Michael, and me and Cy, and although I found the former reassuring the latter was difficult and painful. It was on my mind when I came downstairs where Michael was in the kitchen.

"Morning, El. Next week, any chance of you taking some time off?" he asked, throwing me into a tail spin.

"Nope. Too short notice I'm afraid, why?"

"The kids are coming to stay," he explained, causing me to gawp in his direction.

"Can't you put them off?" I didn't even think how it might sound.

"They're my children and grandchildren, so no." There was aggravation in his tone.

I had no response planned, none at all and yet I still allowed my mouth to open and words to leave it. Words that sounded hard and blunt, even to my own ears.

"I think we should separate."

The cup Michael was holding slammed down onto the counter top as his jaw dropped and his eyes widened. "What?"

He sounded pissed off rather than shocked or saddened.

"Separate. Please," I added a little pathetically.

"No. Eloise, this is a mess, I know, but, no, not yet…"

"Not yet?" I queried, needing more details.

"I realise things are difficult, but I need time. Please, you owe me that much."

"I owe you? How so?" Maybe I could do bitch with

Michael as well as Cy. Especially when the inference here was that our marriage was something I should be somehow grateful for.

"Everything you have is because of me; a home, clothes, money, job, friends…"

I laughed at the last two. "I have no friends Michael and my job I do well," I snapped.

"Do you indeed? Is that before, after or as Cy fucks you?"

I was stunned at the words he spat at me, partly because they were cruel and crude, but moreover because I thought he had no clue about the two of us.

"Exactly. Plus, you should think of Jeremy and his very, very expensive nursing home, unless you'd like Cy to pick up the bills."

"No," I whispered because I had no intention of allowing any man to buy me and leave me feeling obligated, not again.

"So, as I say, everything you have is because of me."

"And you got nothing in return?" I asked unsure if I wanted an answer.

"I thought I'd got a loving and faithful wife who wouldn't be solely driven by her need to find herself filled on such a regular basis."

I recoiled at his cruel words, their crudity cutting me deeper than I imagined.

"You did," I countered.

"I'd have to disagree," Michael said, making me angry because I wanted to argue that he had no right to disagree with the fact that I had been both loving and faithful, and yet maybe he did.

"You didn't exactly start out with a clean sheet though," I retorted. "Allowing my sister to procure you her virgin sister when she wanted you for herself. I paid in a very different way for whatever game you and Susan were playing. I might be the only one to have really paid the highest price."

"Oh sweetheart, I'd already had Susan and she was fun, eager to please," he seemed to taunt. "But still not quite enough for my tastes. When I first saw you and I made the connection it amused me, the possibility. We, well, I had ended things with her, she was too needy, too desperate to please and be the new wife I didn't want and then things changed...." he mused. "I picked things up with your sister, not to get to you as such. I told her that I needed more than she could give me, that I valued her loyalty too much to risk it with any more than a fling. She was okay with that. I knew she loved me, but she wasn't in love with me, that ship had long since sailed," he revealed leaving me confused as I had never known my sister to be in love with anyone who wasn't Michael. "We talked about my other wives and lovers, in bed. We actually discussed them in bed," he told me coldly and then laughed with more coldness. "Susan seemed intent on gifting me your hymen," he sneered showing me a snide side I never knew existed. His character flaw being as much of a shock to me as my slap across his face was to him, not that it even caused a flinch.

The greatest shock was the retaliating slap that he returned. He literally knocked me sideways. Balder was running around the garden and oblivious to the confrontation we were beginning.

Michael didn't even miss a beat as he continued to discuss our happening. "I wasn't entirely sure that you were a virgin, although Susan insisted you were. As a mature virgin I guessed other physical exertions actually claimed that little membrane, but your clumsiness and clear inexperience convinced me. Look, this is not how I wanted to start the day, and I did feel honored to be your first. I honestly thought I could make a marriage work with you."

Suddenly my husband, the man I fell in love with, believed I'd fallen in love with was before me once more. Oh, why did I think blurting out my desire to leave this morning was a good idea?

"But this is not working Michael and I can't believe you're any happier than I am," I aimed for reasonable as I remembered Edward's words to talk and ask.

"I don't know that I have ever been happy. Not as I was expected to be," he mused cryptically. "I can accept that things aren't working and as much as I could blame the fact that you are only too willing to drop your pants for another man, I won't.

For now."

I couldn't keep up with the many personalities that were now occupying my husband's body and mind. I didn't even bother to offer any defense against his words and accusations, I just wanted this to end, all of it.

"I will continue to keep you," he told me, making me detest the word *keep*. "You and Jeremy, and in return all I ask is that we remain as we are, for now."

I was struggling to know what to say or how to react.

"I'm not an ogre El, but I need some time. To explain to my family and to sort my new business affairs out and the latter would be easier with a wife. I'm sorry, that sounds crass. So long as you're discreet with Cy I see no reason to insist on your fidelity, although you've already proven that your fidelity can't be assured."

I found myself nodding in agreement, but was unsure if I knew exactly what I was agreeing to. "For now," I told him, hoping it might be the end of the conversation as Balder appeared.

"For now. We can talk again, after the children have visited."

With a nod I agreed.

"I'm away for a few days, at the end of the week," he told me as I rubbed the dog's head and grabbed my bag. "Oh, El," he said calling me back. "You and Cy, not here, don't fuck him in my house."

I nodded. After all, in this open world we were sharing it seemed silly to deny anything and I had no desire or intention to tell Michael that Cy and I were no longer anything beyond boss and employee, friends even and from Michael's perspective it was a fair request, I supposed.

****

Cy called me as I arrived at the office to let me know that he was out of town for a couple of days, business, family business, but that I should and could contact him if I needed to, wanted to. I resisted for the whole of Monday and Tuesday, with the exception of work emails, until I visited my dad who was still fading away before my eyes. He slept for the duration of my visit, again, and I knew Angela believed this was the beginning of the end, her face said as much. As I left the nursing home, in tears, again, I sat in my car and considered my future, whatever there actually was waiting for me. When I left, divorced Michael and my dad was no longer around, what that would leave me with? Where would I end up? My phone pinged with a wonderfully timed message from Cy.

<Hope I haven't interrupted your visit with Jezza. How is he? How are you?>

I smiled at his consideration but had no real clue how either of us were, not really.

<Just left him. He's the same as last week really, and me? I don't really know how I am. When are you coming back?>

I knew that the last part was a bit needy and pleading, but I didn't care, I'd missed him, wanted to see him and speak to him. No matter what else I felt with him, I always felt safe. Like nothing could touch me when he was there. I was seriously screwed with my brain insisting he was *everything* when we were essentially nothing to each other, not really. Even if I knew I loved and was in love with him.

<I really wish I was there. That I could do something to help, to make you feel better. I might not make it back until the weekend...I've hit a few snags here, family stuff>

My heart sank thinking that I might not see him for almost another week. I wasn't sure how I would get through it, and yet I would have to, this week, next week, every week from this one on.

Maya and I had just returned from lunch on Thursday when Tia appeared in the doorway to my office.

"Hi, how you doing?" she asked with a knowing expression.

"You tell me." I smiled, making her laugh.

"Okay, busted. Cy is worried about you and as I managed to get back before him, he asked me to check on you."

"He didn't have to do that, neither did you," I assured her.

"My brother would disagree with that. He really is worried about you being isolated, sad and alone and I do think of you as a friend, so I'm worried about you too."

"Thanks." I smiled weakly, thinking that we, Tia and I had become closer before the revelation of her niece.

She shrugged off my appreciation. "So tomorrow night, come to the club. I'll be working if I have to, but mostly I will be drinking and dancing with you, what do you say?"

I quashed my initial thought to dismiss the idea of a night out and decided that maybe I needed some fun, a break from work, home and thinking.

"Okay."

"Cool, bring your friend, Maya? If you want."

"Yeah, Maya. I'll see if she's free, but I'll have to go home first, get changed, feed and walk the dog, so about half eight, nine?"

"I'll be there. I've got to go, but I'll see you tomorrow." She smiled triumphantly before pulling me in for a hug and a kiss.

****

As three o'clock on Friday afternoon arrived I smiled to see an email land in my in box.

Good Afternoon Ms Ross,

I hope your week hasn't been too dull and that your bitch hasn't missed my asshole too much.

Normal service will be resumed next week.

Assuming there is nothing that can't wait until Monday morning you should go home for the day.

Have a good weekend.

Regards,

Denton Miller

CEO Miller Industries (Europe)

Mr Miller,

I think your week may well have been as dull as mine in the absence of my bitch to your ARSEhole.

I look forward to normal service.

Thank you for the early doors. I need to go and walk Balder before I go and meet Tia, but then, I think you knew that.

Regards,

Eloise Ross
P.A. to CEO Miller Industries (Europe)

I saw that my email had been sent successfully and grinned for possibly the first time in a week, two, almost three when the sound of my phone made me jump.

"Hello," I grinned broader than ever.

"Hey, just thought I should check if your last email was you pushing?"

The familiar words made me shake with trepidation and anticipation in equal parts and made my heart rate speed up as my breathing hitched. But then I remembered. I couldn't push because that would be inviting him to push right back and that was no longer part of our relationship. We didn't have one, not anymore.

"Thank you for the early finish," I said instead. Ignoring all references to anything *us*.

I was sure I heard him tense at the other end of the line. Somehow, what? Annoyed, hurt that I was ignoring the opportunity to discuss pushing and pushing back, but to what end? Cy had lied to me, about so much. About Rhonda, their past, their child and goodness knows what else I hadn't yet discovered. More things to hurt me more than I had previously thought possible. I reasoned that I was the married one, not him. But hadn't I always been honest about that? Kind of, considering we'd had sex before he knew of my marital status.

"El, I think you know there is more to this than an early finish. I told you we would be talking, that it was coming and believe me it is and you will listen to me, but not now and not over the phone. So, I will see you soon."

I stared down at the phone wondering how long I could avoid listening to his feeble excuses for having a child he hadn't told me about but my response didn't mention that.

"Well thanks anyway. I should go. Bye," I said, and with an equally curt bye from him the call disconnected.

****

I had gone straight home after speaking to Cy and with a quick change into running gear I had taken Balder out for a long and muddy run before giving him his dinner while I showered and dressed.

I opted for a dress I'd bought a couple of years before, one I'd never worn because Michael had thought it was a little tarty and cheap, but his opinion tonight was of no consequence so after putting on a slate grey, satin mini brief I put on the dress. I knew that Cy would love it, but this wasn't for him. He wouldn't even be there.

It was for me and I did feel pretty special in it. It was nothing special, just an off the rack item from the high street in the sale; it finished a few inches above my knees and was made from woven polyester that felt soft against all the naked skin beneath it, not that there was a huge amount of fabric with its deep plunging v-neckline and open back. It was secured to my body by the fitted waist zip closure and wide straps that lay across my shoulders, similar to a racer back. I had bought a pair of silver heels with an ankle, buckle fastening as well as a single strap across the front a few months before and tonight they fitted perfectly. My hair was down and straight whilst my make-up was natural and understated. With a clear coat of nail varnish to my fingers and toes I was done.

I took in my appearance in the full-length mirror in my bedroom. When did that happen? When did my marital bedroom become mine alone? The logical answer was a few weeks ago when my husband stopped sharing it with me regularly and more recently when he just stopped coming in here at all. If I was completely honest it had been weeks before then when Michael had begun sleeping in a guest room with some frequency. Around the same time I met Cy that first time at the bar. The same bar I was going back to tonight.

My wedding ring glistened in the overhead light, taunting me, maybe even challenging me. I rose to the challenge when I slipped it off my finger and placed it in a small jewellery box I kept in my drawer. I now looked a little bare so added a chunky silver bangle and dangly earrings, but chose to leave my neck naked. Grabbing my bag, I threw in my credit card, phone and keys and dashed down the stairs where I gave a sleeping Balder a pat before securing the house and then headed out to the taxi that had just arrived.

Beer and dancing were my only plans for the night.

Chapter Eighteen

As the taxi pulled up at the kerbside to the front of the club I saw Maya waiting for me. Maya and another woman, her younger sister, Cora, who I'd met a couple of times before, years ago.

"Hey, Cora was at a loose end. I hope you don't mind," she said almost apologetically.

I didn't care who was there. I was there for beer and dancing so as long as nobody got in the way of that I was good. Plus, from what I remembered of Cora she was fun loving and friendly, like Maya. I wondered what it must be like to have a sibling you shared that relationship with. A true sibling, a sister, because I didn't have that. Never had.

First stop was the bar where I ordered my first, guilt free beer, while my friends opted for more ladylike glasses of wine.

"Hey, you're here," Tia called as she arrived at my side and kissed me gently on the cheek. "Maya," she grinned, already reaching for my friend before turning her attention to Cora. "Hi, I'm Tia."

I allowed Maya to complete the introductions as I took another mouthful of my beer and grabbed a handful of nuts from the dish on the bar. It quickly became apparent that Cora had recently split up with her boyfriend or had some kind of falling out and tonight Maya was cheering her up. I didn't really mind that she, Cora might need cheering up. I just didn't want to listen to how terrible she felt or what she might do in order to get her boyfriend back because I knew that my misery was as great as hers, maybe greater and there was no way back for me, I couldn't make things right with Cy. We had nothing to *talk about* or *things to build on* which is what Maya was talking to her sister about as I drained my beer from its bottle and got to my feet.

"I might just dance for a while," I announced but was already heading for the dance floor and while Cora nodded, Maya muttered something and Tia looked aghast at the prospect of me being unattended.

I danced for an undeterminable period of time. I simply let time and music wash over me and pass by without worrying about anything. A couple of men danced with me, alongside me, whatever, but when they suggested more, a drink, getting to know each other better, I declined. They had nothing I wanted. None of them were Cy. I paused to get another beer only to find Tia watching me as I took the first slug.

"You okay?" she asked.

"Yeah. I'd forgotten how lost you could get in music," I replied, thinking back to the last time I'd been lost in music only to find myself discovered in Cy's arms.

"You look sad," she told me, pulling me down onto a stool next to her.

I shrugged because I had no words to dispute what she was saying and was disinclined to offer anything resembling an explanation. Also, I was one word away from tears. There was no point in discussing my mood that was down to my father's decline, my mess of a marriage that I had somehow agreed to end and yet stay in for a while longer. A while I had no clue how long would last and then there was my pathetically broken and betrayed heart that still belonged to Cy, my friend's brother.

"I'm okay. I will be okay," I corrected and hoped I sounded more convincing to her ears than my own. "Tonight I just want to dance, drink beer and not think about tomorrow or anything."

"I guess that makes sense, but be careful because you look seriously hot with your perky boobs and no bra," she accused, making me laugh. "That's better, now come on, let's dance."

I returned to the dancefloor with Tia and noticed Maya waving to me from her position in some tall, broad and fair-haired lap. Her sister appeared to be over her broken heart, temporarily at least as she attached herself to the friend of tall, broad and fair.

"Your friends seem to be having fun," Tia grinned.

"So I see," I grinned back.

"You could get yourself some of that action, there is a very handsome bodybuilder type checking you out, behind you, about twenty feet away with a couple of friends."

I turned to see the man she'd meant staring at me; he was huge, a real man mountain and yet quite attractive with sandy hair, spiked up a little and big eyes, pale eyes I thought, staring at me, through me, so much so that I felt almost violated. My head spun back so quickly that I cricked my neck making Tia laugh at my discomfort.

"It's not funny." I laughed too. "He's not my type." I continued, "Too big, too, just too…" I trailed off as I felt a body behind me and knew it was going to be *not my type*.

"Hi," he said in a deep boom of a voice that on a different occasion might appeal. "Joe," he introduced himself already coming to my front to face me, well so long as I looked up.

"Hello," I stammered nervously. "El, and this is my friend Tia," I told him hoping and praying to all things holy that he would go away.

"Can I get you ladies a drink?"

"No," I snapped.

Tia disagreed, "Sure."

With a glare for her, I still shook my head. "I'm fine, really."

"Okay." He grinned, clearly thinking I was aiming for hard to get. If only he would recognise that I was impossible to get, not hard. "So what's your deal? You don't like me, you find me unattractive or married? You're married?" he asked already raising my naked left hand where there was a mark where my ring had been for the last five years, until tonight. "Or divorced, newly divorced?" he seemed to ask and state while Tia stared wildly at my *unmarried* hand that Joe was putting down.

"I have no deal. I do not know you so neither like nor dislike you and you are attractive, I suppose. In a big way," I replied, making him laugh a slightly crooked smile. "I am married, sort of, not for much longer," I told him making him raise a slightly triumphant eyebrow now. "But I know someone, met someone. We're involved, not involved…it's complicated," I prattled on.

"Then he must be a fool if it's complicated and you're out alone." *Not my type* Joe laughed again at my horrified face but quickly turned to Tia. "So, are you attached, in a complicated relationship or can I still get you a drink?"

"No, no and hell yes." She smiled as she linked her arm through his and led him towards the bar.

I waved them off and continued to move to the music around me, fending off another couple of dance partners before visiting the ladies and the bar again where Maya and Cora rejoined me with their new friends from earlier.

"We're moving on," Maya giggled, making me giggle back.

"Together?" I checked.

"Yeah, we're going back to my place if you want to…"

"No, no," I waved her offer away. "Tia is around somewhere and I'm okay here," I assured her before they left.

****

It was probably only twenty minutes later when Tia appeared and pulled me off the dancefloor, through a door and up towards her office. Just the thought of that room had me blushing, clenching and dampening my pants.

"Why are we going back here?" I asked.

"A private drink in peace," she replied.

"Where's Joe?"

"He got called out. He works for a security company or something, but he left me his number and a little DNA," she smirked rubbing her thumb over her own kiss swollen lips.

I laughed as I protested. "Too much information, Tia!"

"No," she refuted. "TMI would be walking in on you and Cy when you're about two point three seconds from fucking each other's brains out!"

I laughed louder as I recalled how many times she had come close to discovering us.

The office door was opening before me as another woman's voice called, "Tia, five minutes please. Somebody's insisting they've been short changed."

"Sorry, El, five minutes, ten tops. Help yourself to beer," she said apologetically, already leaving me to dash back down the corridor.

I opened another beer from the fridge, my third, possibly fourth, probably fifth of the night and sat down on the sofa, the one I'd sat on once before. Maybe I should go away. On holiday after Michael's children had visited. To think, clear my mind, make some decisions, big ones, and maybe even get Cy out of my system. I found myself wandering around Tia's office as I waited for her to return, looking and somehow trying not to see anything that might remind me of Cy. Of my first time with him, here or the fact that there would be no more nights with him. Looking across at the window I could have kicked myself as my body responded to the memory, the way he made me feel, like nobody ever had before.

"Shit," I cursed myself, putting my half empty beer bottle on Tia's desk where there were several framed photos; one that must have been seven or eight years old judging by the youthful faces looking back at me; Tia, Cy and another man of a similar age to Cy, but nobody I recognised. The speed with which my heart began to hammer inside my chest suggested that getting Cy out of my system may take more than a bloody holiday!

My text alert sounded from my bag that was on the sofa still. I found it flashing with a message from Cy, his timing really was something else. I wandered around the office a little more before settling in front of the window where I gazed down at the throng of the crowd; dancing, laughing, drinking, having fun and being happy. Part of me knew I should envy the smiling faces below and yet I couldn't bring myself to channel any jealousy because if I did then that would mean I didn't want the pain and confusion I currently felt. If I wished away those feelings of turmoil then that would mean Cy and I had never happened and I could never regret what we'd had. With despair at myself I checked out the message that waited for me.

<Hey baby, how's your night going? Are you and Tia having fun?>

It was no surprise that Cy knew of my plans. He'd orchestrated Tia inviting me out, she admitted that when she'd expressed his concern and they were close, really close, so of course she'd tell him what we'd agreed. I'd said as much to him earlier on the phone and it would be no shock that she would have told him that I had turned up tonight. I admired his tenacity in some ways, although this whole getting over him might prove easier if he'd let me go. Just be my boss again, not that I was even fooling myself that's what I wanted, or that was what he'd ever been, but it had to be for the best, didn't it?

<I'm not your baby and my night is going fine. Fun might be overstating it, but have been drinking beer and dancing, so I guess it's fun-ish>

<I think my asshole contacted your bitch just in time. You are so prickly and more than that you are my baby. You are mine completely>

Yeah, this would be so much easier without him acting as though he was an irate boyfriend. I hadn't even had time to think of a suitable response when he sent another of his own.

<You look amazing tonight. I like your dress>

I spun round, half expecting him to be standing there, behind me, but there was no sign. I scanned the club below, but if he was down there I couldn't see him. However, he was here, of course he was. I should have predicted this I supposed. Another message.

<I'd like to unfasten your dress and watch it fall to the floor>

Shit! He couldn't keep doing this to me. I was breathless, turned on, desperate for his touch and his words inflamed me until I was on fire. Clinging to the glass window was futile, but that was what I did in an attempt to still my hands that briefly shook, actually trembled as I composed the most ridiculously naïve and unimaginative text ever.

<What?>

"I said, I'd like to unfasten your dress and watch it fall to the floor," he actually said and was behind me now, somehow having made his way into the room under some kind of stealth mode.

Slowly, I turned, almost scared that I might have still been alone. That I was imagining things. Losing the plot completely. Dreaming that Cy was here, for me. As I completed the partial revolution of my body he stood there, more attractive than I remembered, and I remembered him being damned attractive and he knew it. Standing there in a very well fitted pair of black jeans and a black t-shirt he looked divine. Even his casual black boots were sexy. Not as sexy as his devilishly handsome waxed hair though, how I wanted to touch it, play with it, and pull it.

"I really do like that dress and assuming you're wearing panties I might just be able to remain focused on the drive home."

The words he was saying confused me because he was doing that thing again, like we were a couple, together. That we were going home together like regular people did. I knew we weren't and yet no words left my mouth as he moved towards me. The only reaction from me was a hitch in my breathing, pebbling of my nipples and dampness between my thighs. In a couple of strides Cy was standing before me, over me. His fingers were brushing over my jaw and cheeks until he was sliding them through my hair, cradling my head and I knew what was coming next. Although my brain said I should stop, everything else was begging him to carry on.

"I missed you, baby," he told me as his face moved close enough that I could feel his warm breath on the skin of my neck and face.

"I missed you too," I almost cried and then his lips were on mine, moulding them to the shape and position he wanted them in.

With his lips manipulating mine and his hands guiding and tilting my head until it was in exactly the right position, Cy was in charge of everything. My body and mind couldn't deny that he knew what I needed, wanted and as the tremors began to heat my body to boiling point there was no way I could deny this, deny him. The sensation of a hand skimming my outer thigh all the way to my satin covered behind had me gasping into the kiss we were still sharing as my hands desperately reached up and found their way into Cy's hair that I was now pulling and teasing.

"I really, really like this dress and I can't fucking wait to get it off you," Cy told me when he eventually broke our kiss, leaving me panting and barely able to stand.

"I knew you'd like it." I smiled coyly.

"You knew I'd be here?"

Shaking my head, I explained, "No, not like that, but when I put it on I thought of you and I just knew that you'd like it."

"Ah. You were thinking of me when you were naked and preparing to dress," he grinned smugly, making me laugh.

"I'm a mess Cy," I admitted. "Everything about me is a mess. I've told Michael things are over."

Raised eyebrows followed by a smile were his response and then he seemed to quickly regroup his thinking. "Come on, let's go home."

"Home?" I queried.

"Yeah, home, my home," he expanded reaching for my hand to lead me away.

"I can't," I stammered. "You still have a daughter and then there's Balder," I told him stopping him dead in his tracks.

"What? My daughter and your dog? Look, I've told you we needed to talk and you've had enough time to think and to lick your wounds, so now we talk. So, what's the issue with Balder, besides the fact that he still seems fairly intent on removing my balls?"

"I agree we should talk, but no promises," I whispered.

He nodded, not that I was convinced he'd be this compliant if I tried to walk away.

"Balder is alone. I can't leave him all night, and Michael is away, business…"

"All night? Let's go back to yours," Cy suggested making me shake my head in frantic panic.

I had promised Michael that Cy and I wouldn't go there, to our home.

"What? No, that's not what I meant, baby. We'll go to yours and collect the damned dog and take him back to mine, and we'll talk, and then I am definitely going to unfasten that dress and let it fall to the floor. In fact, I might just stand and stare at you in just the panties I now know you're wearing, so, come on," he said, but was already grabbing for my hand and pulling me towards the door.

We drove back to my home and for most of the journey my hand was covered and wrapped in Cy's larger, protective one. Pulling up in front of the house seemed surreal, even by my standards. As Cy helped me from the passenger side of his car I decided it had not been made with the intention of housing a large, adult, male Great Dane like Balder. The dog rushed towards me giving Cy a suspicious sniff before falling into step with us as we entered the kitchen where the dog's day bed and water bowl was.

In the space of ten minutes Balder had managed to get a run around the garden, we'd gathered his things and I'd even managed to pack a small overnight bag, presuming I wasn't going to wear tonight's dress tomorrow too. Getting Balder into the back seat proved easier than I thought it might. Maybe the dog knew that things were changing and he was glad of it too, especially as he had witnessed rows between me and Michael, and a couple of moments of aggression. That thought took me back to the night in our bedroom when Michael had hit me, slapped me, for the first time ever, not the last though. Cy's hand covered mine again as he started the engine and with one touch, I was back with him.

Chapter Nineteen

I'd never been to Cy's home before, didn't even know where it was, although I did have his telephone number for the property. I wasn't sure what I was expecting from his home, but I was surprised because I hadn't expected this. I'd imagined a penthouse apartment or a large, new build house on an exclusive development, but not the wonderful Edwardian family home hidden behind leafy hedges in a very upmarket part of town. Okay, the last bit was not a surprise because everything about Denton Miller Junior was upmarket.

I thought it was probably about eight million pounds worth of prestigious house on a tree lined residential street. The gates at the roadside were opening as was the garage door beyond it.

Balder seemed to be on some kind of mission to smell everything in the garage before we entered the house through the integral door and security system that Cy was disengaging. With my hand in his and my bag in his other hand he was leading me through his home via the long hall into a huge open plan kitchen/diner. He opened the back door for Balder to explore before turning back to me.

"You might want to keep an eye on him. I have no clue whether any of the bushes and plants are safe for him to eat."

I nodded, wondering where Cy was going as he left me by the back door.

"Hey," he said reassuringly as he crossed the kitchen until he was back at my side. "El, I'm going to the car, to get the dog's things."

"Oh," I replied feeling more nervous than I thought I should at the idea of being here, alone.

"You can come with me if you want to," Cy offered, brushing a stray strand of hair off my face.

"No, sorry, I'm being silly. I'll watch Balder," I assured him, already turning away to look for the dog who was emerging from between two big green bushes.

"Two minutes and then we'll talk this through. We've got this baby," Cy told me with a sincerity and determination I hadn't expected, much like the single, gentle kiss he placed on my forehead.

****

Cy was literally two minutes and had set up a warm corner in the kitchen for Balder's bed and water bowl but encouraged him to follow us through to the lounge, a huge room with a bank of windows overlooking the extensive gardens beyond the dual level patio to the back of the house. We sat at opposite ends of a large sofa in a dove grey chenille fabric.

"This isn't what I would have expected of your home." I looked around at the feminine fabrics and colours surrounding us and then regretted the words and thoughts that were swimming around my head, all of them culminating in the woman who had added these touches to this house, this home.

Closing my eyes tightly I tried to banish the questions and the answers I was battling to conquer, but as I opened my eyes again I realised it was futile because right before me was a picture in the middle of the mantelpiece, Lulu. Beautiful big eyes, dark hair and a look of total happiness at simply being. Cy followed my gaze, his eyes briefly settling on the image of his daughter before returning his wary gaze to me. With a single stretch and a tug he was pulling me closer, so that we were sitting next to each other, but angled so we were face to face.

"Lulu, Tallulah. She is my daughter, but it's not quite as clear cut as you might think," he sighed. "I never intended to deceive you, not in any way. I never intended for you to become any more than, well, whatever the fuck we decided we'd be."

"I think we agreed to let it run its course, our disaster-in-waiting."

"And that would have been fine, had it run its course."

"Mmm, well it's certainly living up to its name, disaster-in-waiting, although I think the in-waiting might be defunct now." My reply was accompanied by a shake of my head.

"I still don't know exactly what it is but it's not a disaster baby, far from it," Cy said seriously before his expression softened slightly as he brushed a thumb over my cheekbone.

Even as I pushed into his touch, I wanted to hate myself for wanting, needing the contact, but I couldn't. I did despise my body slightly as it ignored my head and heart's reservations and responded in its Cy default mode which consisted of breathlessness, followed by a rush of heat driving through my whole body before coming to rest in my sex which softened, moistened, pulsed and prepared.

"I want to kiss you so badly," Cy told me which only spurred on my body to welcome the idea with even more gasping, heating, softening and everything else that followed. "But I won't," he told a very disappointed me. "Not yet, talk first. I want to explain, for you to understand and then, this will be the start."

"Okay." I almost panted as I wondered what this would actually be the start of.

He looked pained as he ran a hand through his hair with a sigh and then he began to speak, "I have never told anybody this, except Tia, she knows, and Rhonda of course, but nobody else. Not my parents, nobody."

I had no clue what we were talking about at that second but I felt sick as I saw Cy's tortured expression and considered the million different thoughts that were rushing around in my head about what could be so big that only three people knew about it and why that thing caused such conflict in the man before me. The same man who was always so confident. Cocky.

"I have a brother, Christopher. He's only ten months younger than me. We were close, really close until about six years ago."

"That was quick, ten months apart." I smiled thinking that maybe that was why the Miller's marriage had stood the test of time because they'd clearly had passion as well as love.

"Yeah, but I can kind of live without putting too much

thought into that. As I think I've said before, they're my parents."

I smiled at his discomfort at the idea of his parents not only having sex, but enjoying it, being overcome with passion only a month after his birth. I was really overthinking this. Cy turned conversation back to his brother.

"He went to college and while he was there he began to run with a dodgy crowd. He wanted to be a scientist, but unfortunately got a little too involved with the chemicals."

"Drugs?" I whispered.

"Lots of drugs. He graduated and got a good job in research. He kind of seemed to be okay. The drugs at college were mainly weed and the odd bit of coke."

I stared wildly, my eyes on stalks at the idea that Cy knew about this and seemed accepting of weed and the odd bit of coke. Although, I was the girl who had never so much as tried a real cigarette.

"He didn't seem to have a problem until about six, seven years ago when he lost his job. It was obvious he didn't have a handle on things at all. He overdosed on a concoction of fuck knows what. We had a call from the E.R. and things became apparent. My dad offered him a job once he was clean, paid for some seriously good and expensive rehab and it seemed to work, for a while. We even lived together, me and him and we began to see Rhonda."

I frowned in confusion at the introduction of Rhonda.

"Rhonda and I were friends. We'd been at high school together, gone to prom together and we'd dated for a few months, but it was never serious. Jeez, we never even slept together." He ran his hand through his hair again which I now recognised as a nervous, angry habit he had. "But he knew her through me and Rhonda and I still went out together as friends, and if one of us needed a date then the other would step in. So while I lived with Chris he and Rhonda became friends too. He'd been seeing a woman he'd met at work and one night they had a fight, a big one. Rhonda had called and asked if she could meet me at my place, she's a fashion designer and had a business plan she wanted me to look over. I got held up, but that was no biggy because when I called her she said Chris was home. Fuck!" he cried with another run of his hand through his hair.

I had no clue where this was going but it was clearly about to take a twist, a nasty one, I guessed judging by Cy's reaction. Suddenly, I felt guilty that I had somehow forced him to do this, to reveal all, not that I understood what this had to do with us and his deceit.

"She said he was in a weird mood, but I had no clue he'd been drinking and he'd relapsed and taken some kind of shit."

"What happened?"

"I got home about an hour later and found the apartment a mess. Like someone had broken in and ransacked the place, and then I heard crying, whimpering. Really pathetic whining, like a puppy in the middle of the night." Cy continued as Balder seemed to sense some kind of sadness and came to sit on the floor between us, resting his chin on Cy's knee. "Is this him about to make a challenge on my balls?" Cy asked, gently reaching down to stroke the dog's head, the same dog who repositioned himself so that he could lick the hand that had stroked him.

"No, he's being your friend," I assured him with a weak smile.

"Yeah, well thank fuck for that. Right, so I found the crying and it was Rhonda, bleeding, bruised and hysterical as I reached out to help her up. She was crying and screaming all kind of crazy shit about Chris. I somehow managed to calm her down enough that I could check out the rest of the place and I found Chris. Completely off his head on fuck knows what and surrounded by drugs paraphernalia that littered the place. I went back to Rhonda and I knew, even before she told me what had happened..."

"He assaulted her?" I asked nervously, desperate to be wrong.

"Yeah, well, raped her. What a fucking douche bag. I told her she should call the police, press charges and have his sorry ass thrown into jail, or else let me beat the shit out of him."

"She didn't?"

He simply shook his head sadly, looking like he might just

cry and then came another run of fingers through his hair.

"No. Her dad is a politician and there was a very good chance that he might be a future president at the time and well, shit sticks and my brother could easily have claimed consensual sex and the scandal… so, no, she didn't. I took care of her, took her home, stayed with her and called my dad. I only told him that I'd come home and found the place a mess and my brother off his face. Dad cleaned his shit up and I took care of Rhonda."

"What happened to him, your brother?"

Cy laughed at my question, but a dark sinister laugh. "Nothing, fuck all. He went to a new rehab facility and has been to countless ones since. My parents love him, he's their child, I get that and I don't know what they'd do if they knew what he'd done, but that's not my place, it was Rhonda's. She chose not to. I have minimal contact with him, none if I can help it, but when he's clean my parents have him around."

"What about Rhonda, did he admit it, apologise?" I asked and immediately wanted to slap my own ridiculous question. Apologise? For what, rape? "Sorry, that was fucking stupid, even for me…" I began.

"No, stop, don't put yourself down. It's a reasonable question, I guess. No, he never admitted it, he didn't even remember it! I am unsure if that makes it better or worse, if that makes him more or less of a danger. I tried to talk to him about that night and he didn't even remember Rhonda coming round. He even asked if she'd been the one to call me. That's why I had to tell Tia, because if he didn't even remember Rhonda being there then he was a definite danger to Tia who often, dropped in."

"Shit!"

"Yeah, and then some. Tia found it tough, we were all close, she's only a year younger than Chris, but she understands why I did what I did. Anyway, he went off to rehab, I moved apartment and a month later Rhonda appeared on my doorstep crying and pregnant."

"What? You mean?" I asked and then in a whisper continued, "Lulu is his?"

"Biologically yes, but in every other way he is nothing to

her. I couldn't let Rhonda go through it alone and we owed her, my brother, my family. So, after much persuasion from me we decided that if she didn't want a termination then her baby deserved two parents and if the baby looked like my family this would explain it. We told everyone we'd been together for a few months, which was believable and although we hadn't planned a baby, we were having one anyway. We began to believe our own lies and tried to make a relationship, but it wasn't right for either of us. There was no real connection beyond friendship and then when Lulu was born we gave it a few months and called time. In reality, we were never more than friends, with some benefits, although to the outside world we were engaged and lived together. As far as the world and most importantly, Lulu, is concerned, Rhonda is Mommy and I'm Daddy."

"I don't know what to say…you love her, Lulu?"

"Yeah, totally head over heels," he grinned. "Couldn't love her anymore if she was mine, but, well, she is mine. I never thought that I needed to tell you at the beginning and then I decided I was going to, but that fucking afternoon in the garden blew it out of the water. I am sorry for hurting you. I don't know if this makes sense, baby, but part of me didn't want to lie to you about who and what she was, and yet I didn't know you well enough to trust you with the whole truth which would have meant lying to you twice and that, in my mind would have been worse."

"But you trust me now?" I asked, ignoring everything else. This was what mattered.

"Well you know all the dirty laundry. So, yes, I trust you, baby."

"Was he something to do with you and your dad changing roles?" I suddenly asked thinking that the brother had to be involved.

"Yes, he was in rehab over here and then decided he was going to another facility in The States and my mom wanted to be closer to him.

"I'm glad," I blurted out and then realised how that must have sounded. "Shit, no," I panicked. "I just meant that you and your dad swapped."

"I figured that." Cy laughed, pulling me closer, into his lap, a move that Balder facilitated by moving back into a prone position in front of the fire. "And now, if you have no objections, I would really like to kiss you."

"And if I do?" I tormented as I teased my bottom lip with my teeth.

"You pushing?" he asked with an arched brow that made me smile a big toothy grin.

"So much that we might just end up in the next room if you don't start pushing right back."

"I really have missed you," he told me as his lips covered mine roughly.

We'd ended up almost eating each other on the sofa with hands and tongues everywhere; touching, probing, teasing until eventually I found myself burning with desperate desire.

"Cy, please, please touch me," I pleaded making him laugh as he pointed out that with his tongue in my mouth, one hand in my hair and the other skirting the edge of my pants but not quite breaching them he was in fact touching me.

"Inside, under my clothes," I clarified as I began to greedily fumble with his belt.

"I need to unfasten that dress and watch it fall to the floor," he'd reminded me as one of his fingers pulled on the edge of my underwear, almost advancing beneath, but not quite. Still teasing me, taunting me.

"You really are a fucking arsehole!" I yelled as I tried, and failed, to move quickly and precisely enough to trap his finger inside my pants.

He laughed again, definitely at me now as he pulled both hands away and held them up as if I was pointing a gun at him.

"It's asshole. And you are a testy little bitch when you're horny."

I made no attempt to refute his claim. Even if I had my bratty response would have disputed it, "Then fuck me!"

"Upstairs," he barked with a flat expression.

"At last," I sighed, already up on my feet and heading back towards the hall, not that I knew where to go beyond there.

Pausing at the bottom of the stairs I looked around at the

wood panels and high shine wooden floor and wondered whose
handiwork this was, it looked old and I had no clue how long Cy
had lived here, kept this house, whatever. My internal musing
was enough that I was distracted and didn't hear, see or feel Cy
until I was pressed against the panelled wall in front of me, my
chest and pelvis pressed firmly against the old, dark wood whilst
behind me was the hard, firm feel of something much younger
and warmer, Cy.

"Maybe I should bend you over and spank you before I fuck
you," he said as my skirt was hoiked up and I braced myself for
the contact of his hand, but it didn't come. "Maybe, later. I'm
pretty sure you're gonna keep pushing baby."

****

I don't know how I got upstairs. I think it was a
combination of being carried, running and tripping with a few
episodes of being pressed against walls as we went. Balder
seemed to be following us initially and then decided that he
didn't want or need any part of it so went back downstairs.

Standing in the middle of Cy's bedroom I fully realised,
acknowledged, that this was happening. I didn't even notice the
zip at my waist being undone. It was only as Cy pulled back
from me and was tugging the front of my dress to my waist that I
recognised my near naked state and Cy's intention to unfasten
my dress and watch it fall to the floor. He was already stepping
back to watch it slip past my hips and then his work was done. I
was standing in just my pants and shoes while my dress was on
the floor.

"Very fucking nice," he told me as he settled himself in the
middle of the bed, propped up on pillows, watching me, staring.

I was unsure what to do or say so I did and said nothing. I
simply stood there, almost as naked as the day I was born with
heaving breaths that only served to emphasise my chest that was
clearly aroused with pebbled flesh and erect nipples, aching to
be touched. I could feel that the moisture gathering between my
thighs once more, was responsible for how closely my pants
were clinging to me. A chill in the air caused gooseflesh to cover
my whole body, although I was honest enough to acknowledge
that arousal and anticipation were mainly responsible for my

heightened sensations and sense of being.

I looked up to see a smile pulling at Cy's lips.

"What?" I asked with a note of irritation.

"Mmm, definitely testy when horny," he taunted. "But I was thinking that I might have this become your everyday work wear. The thought of having you standing before me on a daily basis like this is making me feel very, very happy."

"I think H.R. might have something to say about that," I snapped but it only served to amuse Cy a little more.

"Then maybe I need to work from home more often, no H.R. here."

I made no reply to that. I simply stared. Still unsure of what to do. So I remained where I was, standing perfectly still. Time passed, not too long I didn't think, but enough that I became slightly uncomfortable. My legs began to tire and I found myself shuffling from one foot to the other.

"I think you should come here baby. Come to bed," Cy said, breaking the silence.

I mutely obeyed, crossing the short distance until I stood at the side of the bed, unsure if I should remove my shoes and single item of clothing. Before I had chance to decide if I should do anything, I found myself pulled down onto the bed and Cy was over me, blanketing my body as his mouth found mine and in that instant this all made complete sense.

My whole body was coming to life with an intensity I'd never experienced before. Maybe because up until a few hours ago this was over in my mind. There was no Cy and me, and now he was here, with me, over me, but maybe it was more than that. Could it be that this moment was truly significant and something I wouldn't ever be able to truly walk away from?

My hands were running over Cy's body, tracing the planes, lines and edges of bones, muscles and flesh. Greedily wanting to touch him everywhere. All of him, and yet he was doing that exact thing to me. His fingers traced a path down my body, from my lips, across my jaw, down my neck, teasing, caressing, my collarbone, chest, breasts, pausing a little longer to torment my nipples with squeezes, rolls and pinches before moving onto my ribs, the skin stretched tightly there as I arched off the bed into his touch. As he reached my navel I became aware of something else, softer, wetter.

"Oh God!" I heard myself moan as I realised that the warmth that was following the touch of his hands was his mouth, replicating every movement his hands and fingers had made. Somehow his mouth was a little softer and yet rougher at the same time. He was using his teeth. My pants and shoes were absent now, where and how they'd been removed I had no recollection of.

It was like Cy knew exactly what I wanted and needed even if I had no real clue and then he did it. The thing that made me freeze. Looking down I had no clue what to say or do as I found Cy between my spread thighs. His hands, which I had prior knowledge of and his mouth, ready to touch me, there, down there. I felt horrification mingle with my initial mortification forcing me to speak, to stop him.

"Hey," I called out nervously before running full steam into words I put no real thought or planning into. "You don't, I, erm, just come back up here," I pleaded with a huge sigh and a deep crimson flush to my skin as I attempted to close my legs that Cy remained within.

His hands were resting against my inner thighs now, so as I tried to press them closed his hands offered resistance.

"Cy!" I cried, making him look up at me whilst still remaining between my splayed thighs.

"Baby, what's wrong?" he asked me. "You don't want me here?" He released one thigh to run a finger the full length of me.

On a gasp that disputed that I didn't want him there, I shook my head. "I do."

My confirmation made him smile as the finger retraced its path until it was gently rimming and probing me before returning to circle my clit with my own moisture.

"Oh God!" I repeated as small shudders began to make everything below the waist gently quake.

"Now, where was I?" Cy asked himself as he lowered his face back towards me.

"You don't have to do that, really," I insisted with panic that stopped Cy dead.

"I don't have to? Baby, I am not doing anything because I have to. I want to, I want to lick you, right here," he told me with another sweep of his finger. "You don't like oral sex?" he asked with a confused frown.

If I thought my earlier embarrassment had caused me to redden then it was nothing compared to my current shade of pillar box red.

"No, maybe, I don't know," I stammered. "I know guys don't usually like to…" I trailed off when I saw Cy watching me with a dropped jaw.

"What do you mean, guys don't…has nobody ever done this…" he trailed off now and I was unsure whether he was shocked or simply disgusted by me.

I shook my head, not trusting myself to speak in case I made this moment any more awkward than it was already proving to be, or worse still burst out crying.

"And you think that guys don't what, do this, want to do this, like this?" he asked and again I responded with silence, but gave him a nod this time. "Let me make this clear for you El; I want to do this, I fucking love this. So this guy here, he does this. We might never have done this before but I can guarantee once I've had a real taste of you, I won't ever be able to get enough and knowing that I am the only guy to have ever done this is the best news I've ever had."

"Oh," I managed to whisper.

"Yeah, oh and then some. Look, there's a rule in our house, you lick it, it's yours, so," he said and then with no further words he pushed my thighs so that I was completely open to him and then he licked me, my whole length.

With that one movement I wondered how I had got to this age without feeling this sensation. How I might have gone my whole life without it had I never met Cy. I could feel his shoulders pressing into my fleshy inner thighs, keeping me wide while his mouth worked me into a frenzy; his tongue licked and lapped, then twirled, swirled and mouthed my clit that I was sure had trebled in size and then he did something I had no idea about, never even heard about, he stuck his tongue inside me, *there*. He was actually fucking me with his tongue, like it was his penis. God I really was naïve, wasn't I? Not to know this was an actual thing?

My hips were taking on a life of their own. They worked with his rhythm and movements until I could feel that I was on the edge of pleasure, teetering there. Cy pushed me to the precipice and then pulled me back, stopping me from taking the final headlong dive.

With my hands full of Cy's hair I began to plead with him, "Please, please, don't stop."

My body was primed, ready for the final push it so desperately needed, but I expected Cy to stop short, to draw everything out again. It felt as though he was as his tongue circled my clit and when he closed his mouth around it, sucking hard, I found myself burning as I was stretched by two, possibly three fingers invading me and with a final suck, possibly with the use of teeth I was incoherently calling to any deities in this world or the next with my whole body spasming, pulsing and twitching like I was having some kind of seizure. I was drowning in a sea of lights and beams, illuminating the room that had filled with stars or maybe I was just seeing stars as my body crashed from the higher plain I'd been lifted to before coming back down to this one.

Cy was crawling back up my body, cradling me, cuddling me until he was over me, covering every inch of my skin with his, then his lips were resting against my own.

"I licked it, it's mine now," he announced before gently kissing me, quietly. Gradually he opened me up for his delight and consumption while I considered his words and felt my heartbeat increase at the suggestion of being his in any way.

"Is that what I really taste like?" I asked, wondering how to describe the salty, oceanic flavour I'd never found on Cy's lips or breath like this before.

I was momentarily distracted by the feel of Cy nudging my opening.

"Sure is baby," he replied, kissing me again.

I had no idea if my question or his answer were normal, acceptable or whether this was another show of my naivety where sex was concerned.

"Condom," Cy muttered, beginning to pull away from my body.

"Wait," I whispered, holding onto him with my hands gripping his shoulders and my legs looping around his hips.

"I don't know that I can wait much longer." He grazed his lips over my collar bone.

"I thought maybe I could return the favour." I flushed.

"Favour? Which favour would that be?" He bristled with a frown. Clearly I had committed some kind of sexual etiquette faux paus.

"I know we haven't done it before that oral thing. I wanted to do it too," I snapped awkwardly, beginning to feel stupid.

My sense of stupidity seemed to turn Cy's brusqueness in a split second until he was smiling down at me. "I'd love that, baby, but not now. There's no rush and right now I need to be inside you. To feel you pulling me inside you."

He was gently teasing my entrance again, making me smile a little nervously as I nibbled my lip before deciding that I was on a roll for opening my mouth and just jumping right in, so I went for it, again.

"Do it then," I encouraged. "We don't need a condom. You know I'm on the pill, so I'm safe..." yet again my voice trailed off.

"You're sure?" he asked, but I was unsure whether he was asking me or himself.

I nodded. "Positive, if you want to. I never have without a condom," I revealed not thinking there was anything strange in that fact, although Cy's startled face suggested it might be, but it never had been anything other than normal for me. For me and Michael, because he had always insisted on condoms.

"Fucking hell, you are going to kill me." He grinned as he easily slid into me, slowly, allowing my body to accommodate and accept his presence within it.

Once we were coupled completely, he held still within my pulsing insides and then very slowly began to move. Having only ever had sex with Michael before Cy in no way prepared me for how things were between us and having never had sex without a latex barrier the sensations and feelings I was now experiencing were a huge shock.

"Oh God, I can feel you," I panted out as Cy's movements increased in number and speed.

"Fuck, yeah, baby, you feel so fucking good, so soft. Jeez, this is not going to last long," he seemed to warn me as I felt the first tremors of arousal reigniting.

Instinctively my legs moved so that my knees were at his waist, and if it was possible, I felt him even deeper within me, stroking and brushing nerve endings I didn't know existed.

"Yes, yes, yes," I began to chant.

"Come on El. I'm going to come baby," he told me with an unmistakable warning.

"In a minute," I replied, the ridiculousness of my words making us both laugh for a second before Cy adjusted his position and his angle enabling him to reach between us where he found my clit with his hand while his mouth latched onto one of my over-sensitised nipples, drawing it into his mouth, slowly, tantalisingly. It was enough, more than enough to send me into another orgasm, even more frantic than my earlier one. Maybe because Cy himself became more frenetic in his movements, bringing every nerve and muscle into sensory overdrive, inside and out and then I felt him swell inside me before he came with a deep groan of my name.

Chapter Twenty

It was four a.m. and I was lying in Cy's arms, in his bed, and it felt far better than I had ever dared dream. The feel of his warm body enveloping mine was divine, comforting, loving even, and really did feel like the most right thing I had ever experienced in my life. Although, as I thought about the circumstances that had brought us to this point I did feel a little guilty; the end of my marriage, any pain I had caused Michael, even my dad had contributed to this in his ailing days and then there was Lulu, a product of possibly the worst thing a man could do to a woman. I really had read that one all wrong.

I recalled that little girl rushing across the lawn to Cy in his parent's garden. Clueless that he was not her father. The world clueless to that fact, although he had pointed out to me a couple of times that she was his, in every way that mattered and I couldn't actually disagree with that. Somehow the vile abuse of her mother which led to her conception made her being easier for me because although Cy had lied to me, or at least kept her existence from me he had done it with her best interests at heart. I was now one of only four people who knew his family's dirtiest secret. I hated myself a little for such an awful thing to have made anything better for me, but as I lay there I couldn't regret anything that had happened from the first night I'd met Cy to this point. Nor could I regret his brother's most recent relapse as that had led to him and his father switching roles which ultimately led to him being here, being my boss and my lover.

"What are you thinking?" he asked, stroking his fingers up and down my naked arm.

"That I might not be a very nice person," I admitted honestly. Thinking that so many of my thoughts were selfish and coldhearted.

"I think you might be the nicest person I have ever met." Cy landed a delicate kiss to my shoulder.

"You wouldn't say that if you'd been in my head when I was thinking that I was glad that everything that had happened between us, to us and to everyone connected with us was some kind of kismet and I was glad of it."

"I see," Cy mused against my ear. "I think you might be doing your overthinking thing again, baby. I can understand why you would feel bad for feeling glad about some things that have led us to this point, but I get it, because I feel the same about us."

"Thank you," I whispered, glad that he understood and relieved he hadn't judged me.

Cy's hand was reaching for mine and for the first time he touched my ring finger, where no ring sat.

"Hey, you took it off," he stated with a slight start.

"Mmm, tonight. It didn't seem right to keep it on when all I could think about was how much I wanted to see you. How I'd missed you and how I couldn't see a way back for us."

"I approve, of the naked finger and all of those thoughts, except the last one because we never needed a way back. We never ended baby, you just wouldn't accept that."

"Maybe," I reluctantly conceded as Cy lifted my hand and kissed the space where my ring had previously sat.

"You know that this is real don't you, us?" he asked seriously.

"Yes," I acknowledged in a low whisper.

"Good. Do you remember what you said to me, at my parent's house about hating me?"

"Hating you, or loving you?" There was little to no point in trying to pretend that I hadn't declared my love for him at that awful, painful moment.

The sound of Balder moaning from somewhere beyond the closed bedroom door brought our conversation to a standstill momentarily.

"Maybe they're bedfellows, love and hate. Perhaps you need to love someone enough to ever be able to truly hate them." The sound of scratching at the door interrupted. "Let me go and check if your dog's okay, or if he's just letting me know that he's still pissed off that I'm in here with you and he's not. But he'll need to get used to it because there is no way he's coming in here and judging me."

I laughed at his horrified expression. "In case he finds you wanting?"

"Really? You're gonna push again so soon?" he asked pulling on his boxers.

"Maybe," I teased, making him shake his head with a lust filled smile as he picked my dress up off the floor.

Placing it on the back of a chair he smiled again, at me, a full-on megawatt, panty dropping smile.

"Unfastening that dress was far better than I thought it might be," he told me before turning to open the door where Balder sat waiting for him. "Come on," he called to the dog who dutifully followed him. "We really need to reach an understanding buddy."

I laughed to myself at his conversation with the dog before rolling over in the bed that seemed far too big now that I was in it alone. Glancing around, my eyes stopped on the image of my dress on the chair and I couldn't temper the smile or the flush of colour to my face as I recalled its journey from being on my body as I sat in Cy's lap downstairs to its current resting place.

"We've never done this before," I muttered with a smile as Cy returned to bed and I rolled over in his embrace to look up at him.

"I know it's been a couple of weeks before tonight, but…"

I giggled as I slapped his arm playfully. "Not that. I meant in a bed."

"Ah, I see, and is it all you'd hoped for?"

"I didn't say I'd hoped for it at all," I protested weakly.

"Baby, you keep pushing and you won't be able to walk, sit down or pee in comfort for the next week," he warned me with a smile.

"All I'd hoped for and more," I conceded, already softening

as Cy pulled me closer.

He leaned down to kiss my lips gently before turning off the lamp that was the only source of light in the room. "Go to sleep and in the morning you can push some more and I'll push right back. And talk. We'll talk tomorrow, today," he corrected as he pulled the covers higher but refused to let me go.

"That sounds like a plan," I agreed.

"Goodnight, baby. I love you too," he told me and although the room was in darkness my beaming smile might just have lit up the night sky outside as Cy bestowed his love upon me, never mind illuminating the bedroom.

****

Saturday was spent naked for the most part, with a few clothed moments to eat, watch TV and play with the dog in the garden. Everything was relaxed, calm and natural, something I hadn't expected really. Not that I'd given much thought to this. A day, a night, in Cy's house. Just us, plus Balder. I had been shocked to find the ridiculously decorated hall and landing on the first floor where the carpet matched the wallpaper. I still couldn't believe I hadn't noticed that on the way up to the bedroom, although I had been so blind to everything that didn't involve bodily contact between us that the floors and walls so close to the bedroom hadn't been high on my attention to detail list.

"Do you need to let Michael know where you and Balder are?" Cy asked as we walked over the heath on Sunday morning, hand in hand with Balder enjoying the open space and freedom to run.

I shook my head as I began to speak, unsure how Cy was likely to react to what I was about to say.

"He's not back until later. I don't think he'll even consider where either of us have been all weekend, me, nor Balder," I clarified.

"I see. Look, if you need somewhere to stay, you're welcome to stay with me…"

I interrupted, needing him not to complete that sentence when there was so much he hadn't heard from me yet. So much we hadn't discussed but had kept insisting we would, but time was running out today.

"No, no. I can't move in with you, Cy. We work together, we're sleeping together but it's too soon…" I trailed off.

"Okay, okay," he laughed. "I'm sure Tia would give you her spare room until you decide what you want. I understand that divorces take time and can't be sorted overnight."

"I haven't really thought beyond the next week."

"The next week? What's happening in the next week?"

"Ah," I sighed.

"What? Just tell me," Cy pleaded, causing a wave of something akin to guilt to wash over me. I wondered why I felt guilty about the impact of my marriage on my affair, on Cy, but not how my affair was impacting on my husband and marriage.

"We haven't discussed a divorce yet. I told him we should separate and he agreed."

"But? Come on, there's a but, we both know it. What the fuck have you agreed to, uh?" he asked angrily, angrily enough that Balder came running back and positioned himself directly between us, protecting me.

"He has a new business thing and it would be better for him to be married." It sounded lame to my own ears now, but when Michael had said it, it all sounded so plausible. I thought that maybe I'd been manipulated again and Cy's expression confirmed it.

"That's a crock of shit baby. Fuck, he is playing you at every turn and you are still falling for it," he sighed.

"Sorry, maybe. It's not just that, the kids, Michael's kids and grandchildren are coming to stay tomorrow. For the week, and they don't know how things are."

"So for the next week you're going to play happy families, with him? Fucking hell, Eloise!" he cried, my full name demonstrating how frustrated and angry he was.

His emotions had his face contorting and his hands flailing, the latter making Balder even more protective of me and suspicious of him. Sufficiently suspicious that he growled at Cy, baring his teeth to prove his intent. I felt self-conscious, being in a public location with other people aware of our *domestic,* but I also felt guilty that I hadn't explained the situation to Cy before we'd slept together. Especially after he had shared so much about his situation. The guilt extended to my dog who was now clearly mistrustful of anyone who moved too erratically around me. Obviously a little wary too of the arguments, raised voices and occasional physical altercations that Michael and I had been engaging in recently.

"And what is his problem?" he gestured to Balder. "What does he...shit," he suddenly softened. "Come here," he called opening his arms but resisting the temptation to pull me to him.

Calling to the dog I petted him gently and then leaned down to kiss his head, giving him a sign that things were alright. That Cy posed no risk to me. Willingly, I went into the warm and welcoming arms that waited for me and melted a little.

"Balder thought I was going to hit you," he decided while I nodded my agreement. "I wasn't, never would, not like that." He seemed to correct thinking about the occasions when he'd spanked me, which didn't count as a bad thing in my book. "Which begs the question, how many times has he seen you being hit?"

"I know you never would," I replied, unswerving in that belief, although I avoided his question. "Look, I have agreed to stay at home for the next week, but after that it's done. We're done, Michael and I. He knows about us, he told me, and he knows that our marriage is over. I can understand why he wants to tell his children properly rather than them turning up and me being gone and the business thing, I'm unsure if I believe that us being apart would make a difference to that. Maybe that's an excuse. Perhaps he's syphoning his money away to keep me from taking it in the divorce, but I don't care about that. He's agreed to pay the bills for my dad's care, at least for now so long as I am discreet and remain at home."

"He thinks he's got you over a barrel."

I shrugged, not entirely sure Michael had, or indeed if he believed he did.

"It doesn't matter, none of it, except for my dad."

"I could help you," Cy began.

"No, no, please don't. I don't want to feel that money has paid any part in anything between us, so no. And if Michael stops paying my dad's bills as soon as I leave, I will sort something out."

"We'll talk some more, later. We've got this baby, even if I don't like it, okay?"

I nodded, grateful for his understanding and support, yet still felt as though I should say something. The sound of a voice calling our names stopped my thoughts of what I should or shouldn't say. Turning, I saw Tia running towards us with someone following her, Edward.

"Hey you two," Tia called as Balder moved closer, still feeling a little protective.

"Baldy!" called Edward with a huge, warm smile for the dog who was already rushing towards him, almost knocking him over when he got there.

"What the hell?" Cy asked against my ear as Tia hugged us both tightly.

"Old friends," I replied in explanation as to why my dog and Edward were currently enjoying another loving reunion.

"How? When? Where?" Cy asked, thoroughly confused, but before I could answer Tia was grinning at us.

"So, good night on Friday, weekend, whatever?"

"None of your business," her brother chided with a grin.

"There's a café, over the road, fairly dog friendly if we sit outdoors," Edward called, still disappearing beneath my overzealous dog.

"Why not?" Cy sighed as he slid his hand over mine, following the others towards the café.

We sat at a table outside, the largest table they had, near the door. As Edward had said they were dog friendly, providing bowls of water and dog biscuits that arrived with the human's order that for us was a selection of biscuits and various coffees. Edward and I each had a plain, butter shortbread while Cy and Tia seemed intent on devouring anything with chocolate until they were faced with the last one that my, my what? What was he now, boss, yes, lover, definitely, boyfriend? Oh God, I had a boyfriend. I also had a husband I reminded myself. For now I had a husband. My relatively pointless wondering was broken by Cy who not only grabbed the final biscuit but licked across its chocolate coating.

"Eww! You are such a pig," Tia shouted making people look across at us, mostly in amusement.

Cy laughed, as did Edward and I. I loved seeing the relaxed, silly and juvenile persona beneath Cy's more serious, businesslike outer.

"You snooze you lose," Cy told his pouting sister. "And you know the rules Tia Mamoda," he smiled, making me think back to those flowers I had to send her and now I suddenly wondered why she was called Mamoda by Cy, but over the door of the bar she was named as Tia Miller. What was it with Miller offspring that nobody used their actual name?

"Yes, I know the damn rules," Tia snapped. "You lick it, it's yours!" Her response made it clear that those words did actually make up some kind of rule in the Miller household. When Cy had said them to me I hadn't imagined that he meant his words literally. He did and now I was blushing deeper and deeper shades of pink and red until I resembled a beetroot I shouldn't wonder.

"Told you," Cy whispered against my ear causing further redness to afflict my complexion. "In fact I might need to remind you just who you belong to when we get home."

I almost choked on the essence of coffee I was inhaling as my lips rested against the cup I was holding in a death defying grip as I recalled the feeling of Cy's tongue and mouth on the soft, sensitive, intimate tissue that was currently dampening and quivering in anticipation despite being sore and swollen after spending almost a day and a half in bed.

My thoughts scrambled as I faced the problem of having such a large dog as Balder. He didn't really fit into small or compact spaces, like in coffee shops, under tables or at someone's feet. He had been happily sat at Edward's feet but as he saw another dog at the table opposite with a young family he decided to introduce himself, almost dragging Edward with him, much to our amusement. Edward returned after offering a profuse apology to the family, whose dog, a rather timid little schnauzer was now sitting on the lady's lap, a move Balder seemed to like and replicated it as soon as Edward sat back down.

"You might need to tell him that he is not a lap dog." Edward smiled, patting the dog's head that he was peering around while his behind was wedged into Edward's lap.

"I don't think he'd believe me. Maybe you should tell him. You and he are friends." I laughed and then asked with probable randomness, "Who are you?"

Cy and Tia looked at me with confusion, which was understandable considering the fact that I knew who Edward was, but he knew what I was asking. Who was he to Michael, and where did he fit in?

He looked as though he might be about to answer when my phone began to ring in my bag. Pulling it out, I sighed at the name Susan flashing on my screen.

"Hello." I answered abruptly causing everyone present to look startled.

After three or four minutes it became apparent there was no cause for her call beyond wanting to check up on me. To see if I was playing the good wife, none of which was any of her business. After allowing her to lecture and bemoan me for another couple of minutes, I cut her off.

"Look, I appreciate your call, but I need to go. I'm with friends." She made several comments to dispute my claim before I snapped again, "Friends. Nobody you know. Just friends. My friends. My own friends."

With her about to let rip and go into full flow, I hung up, turned my phone onto silent and threw it into my bag before returning to the people around me.

"Sorry," I offered, unsure why and then with sudden unease at the wary and curious glances aimed at me I got to my feet. "Sorry," I repeated. "Would you mind if we called it a day. I have a few things to do. Things I need to do."

Chapter Twenty-One

With my abrupt departure from the café, I returned to Cy's and began to pack up my belongings in preparation to leave. To go home to the last place on Earth that felt like home. My phone remained on silent, not that I didn't hear it vibrating in my bag. Despite my protests Cy took me and Balder back home to the empty house that Michael hadn't yet returned to.

I was relieved to find the house empty, that I didn't have to suffer a confrontation or worse, a polite encounter between my husband and my lover. Fortunately, Cy wasn't insistent about remaining with me. He dropped me off, escorted me in and kissed me. A gentle delicate kiss to my forehead and then he left.

Balder and I went for a run, then I had a shower before preparing dinner for me and the dog which took us up to late evening. I went upstairs and arranged my things for the following day and upon returning to the lounge I braved my phone which was littered with texts, voicemails and missed calls from Susan, all of which I deleted, a brief text from Michael confirming his return that evening and finally a simple text from Cy.

<Hey, forgot to say, I love you baby x>

I grinned inanely at the I love you and the kiss before replying.

<I'll forgive the lapse in memory because I love you too xx>

<Are we competing with kisses? xxx>

<I don't know, are we? xxxx>

<I think someone is pushing xxxxx>

I giggled as I decided that yes, I was pushing and knew that if I were still at Cy's house we'd be back in bed forthwith, or he would at least be in me, but we weren't there. He was, but I wasn't.

<You might be right xxxxxx>

<We will pick this up tomorrow Ms Ross, and we'll decide on our kiss cap! x>

Michael chose that precise moment to return looking less than thrilled with life.

"Have you eaten?" I asked feeling uncomfortable in the company of a man I had known for almost six years and shared a home with for over five.

"Earlier," he snapped. "I'll have something later."

I shrugged my acceptance and got to my feet, but had no clue where I was going. The kitchen, the garden with the dog or even to bed, alone, well except for Balder.

"Are the children's rooms all ready?" he asked reaching for my arm as I came alongside him.

"Well the beds are made up, as they always are," I replied earning myself a loud tut.

"Haven't you checked everything, aired the rooms? What have you been doing all weekend?" he asked with irritation.

"Michael, the rooms are as they always are. I will open some windows in the morning, plug in some air fresheners. It'll be fine," I told him, hoping to placate and reassure.

His response clearly indicated that neither of my objectives had been achieved.

"Fine? It'll be fine? What have you been doing all

weekend?"

"I've been out," I said, unwilling to share anything more.

"Out where?" he persisted with a raised voice that caused the dog to look up.

"Just out."

"You've been with him, haven't you? Too busy screwing your boss to make sure the house is ready for our family," he accused. "Where? Where have you been?" he asked turning a very strange colour, something between damson and puce.

"I don't think I need to discuss that with you..." I began but was cut off.

"You don't think you need to discuss it with me. You are my wife, mine, not Cy's, mine and for this week you need to act it or I will ensure that you leave here with nothing. Do I make myself clear?" he demanded to know rather than asked.

I made no reply, this conversation was escalating out of control quickly and the last thing I wanted was to be arguing all night, or worse, fighting.

"You should start by putting your wedding ring on Eloise, now. We can hardly expect the children not to suspect something is amiss if you parade round with no ring on. Oh, and do not plan any late nights this week."

"Except Tuesday," I said firmly. This was my non-negotiable here and honestly, if he pushed me on this then I would walk from here now in only the clothes I stood in.

"I said any night," he sneered with a curl of his lip that made me want to leave immediately.

"And I said except Tuesday. Unless you want your children to turn up tomorrow to find I've already left you."

I had no clue where my words or determination were coming from. I was just grateful that they were.

"I'm unsure if Jeremy will understand having to move to another home. A different place, a cheaper place, with strangers. I doubt he'll get the same care..."

My glare fixed Michael to the spot briefly as I realised he was attempting to blackmail me into not seeing my dad on Tuesday night, although I suspected it was more a case of him trying to prevent me seeing Cy, having sex with Cy. This was a step too far for me, my dad, not Cy. I brushed past him, picked up my phone, purse and car keys and called the dog to me.

"Goodbye Michael," I said coldly and left without looking back until I reached my car.

"El, love," he called to me, "Balder stays here. He's my dog, unless you come back inside and do as we agreed, and then, when we sort the details you can take him with you."

I turned and faced the man who was physically so familiar and yet I barely recognised him. He was blackmailing me with the dog and as I slammed my car door shut, I conceded that I was allowing him to do so. I couldn't, wouldn't leave Balder behind like this.

Walking back through the front door I allowed my husband a final scowl before he asked me, "So, opening windows and air fresheners, is that your best offer?"

I had a near overpowering urge to fly for him, to hit him, punch him, to hurt him badly. To end his smug, triumphant expression and tone, but I didn't.

"Not my best offer Michael, my only offer," I told him. Just about managing to hold onto my perilous grip on my self-control. "Balder," I called behind me and at nine o'clock I went to bed.

****

I woke early, very early, spent some time outdoors with the dog and managed to avoid Michael before heading into work where I knew I would be the first to arrive.

It was barely half-past seven when I found myself in the kitchen making myself a cup of tea when I felt someone behind me, approaching before an arm reached around my middle. I smelt and felt a body I knew was Cy. I just knew it was him or at least my body did.

I was pleased to be here. Beyond pleased not to be at home. Thrilled to be here with someone who genuinely seemed to want to spend time with me for just being me, unlike my husband and really all I wanted to do was to forget and get lost in something that didn't involve being married, manipulated or controlled in some way.

"Are you sure we're not having a competition for who can

get into the office first," Cy whispered against my ear he was nuzzling. "Because if we are you need to cut me in on the rules."

I knew he was smiling, I could feel it and still I reacted with total irrationality snapping at Cy, taking all of my angst out on the one person I not only wanted to be with, but the one person I was as far removed from angry at than anyone else in the world.

"No! No competition!" was my surly response to my lover's jovial comment.

"The bitch is sure as hell back this morning," he told me with a less than gentle nip to my ear that had me flinching a split second before pulling away enough to turn and face him, preparing to storm past him, but not without another barbed comment.

"Fuck you, arsehole."

My intention to storm back to my own desk was seriously ill thought out as I found my wrists roughly bundled together as I was pressed back into the nearest wall with Cy's body pushing into me.

"It's asshole, and that is some serious pushing you have going on this morning. Or else you're deliberately trying to antagonise me. Pushing my buttons to bring on a fight. So which is it?" he asked, rubbing his front against mine, bringing it to life, my nipples pebbling against his chest and my belly beginning to warm at the sensation of his erection rubbing against it.

"All of them," I admitted tearfully. "Cy, please."

"I see. What do you want baby? What do you need, huh?"

"You, just you," I admitted as I attempted to capture his lips that were teasing me by merely being out of reach of my own, and with my hands and arms still securely contained in one of his much larger hands I had no way of forcing his lips towards my own.

"Okay. Assuming we don't want interrupting when Maya arrives," he said, already pulling me with him to his office that we were quickly locked inside of.

My breathing was rapid and shallow at the same time, so much so that I was seriously worried that I might hyperventilate if I didn't gain some control over it. Standing against the back of the door seemed a strange place to still be when Cy was already sitting on the sofa, his jacket cast aside with his tie and the top two buttons of his shirt undone.

"Baby," he called to me with a strange, confused expression on his face.

"What?" I seemed to snarl.

"Exactly what I would like to know. What the fuck is your problem? This whole bitchfest you have going on is not going to do it for me, not unless you were hoping to be put across my knee for the spanking of your life."

I stared for a matter of seconds, but it seemed much longer as I considered the option of receiving the spanking of my life. Maybe that's what I needed. Something to centre me. To make me cry and release all of the mixed up feelings inside my head. However, I knew that he deserved a response rather than waiting while I considered his hand on my arse.

I shook my head. "Sorry. I didn't sleep very well. I missed you," I added tearfully, because I had and the truth of it was that the few short hours I had spent sleeping in Cy's bed, Cy's arms a couple of nights before had been the best, most restful sleep I had enjoyed for a very long time and last night, well that was the complete opposite in spite of the greater number of hours.

By the time I had acknowledged those facts Cy was in front of me, tilting my head up so that we were gazing into each other's eyes.

"The only thing that got me through the night was you. Memories of the weekend and thoughts of today, and tomorrow and the future."

His words were sentimental and loving, his tone sincere and kind and yet those were the words that proved to be my undoing. The idea of a future with him, worse still, a future without him. Tears were silently running down my face, having already breached the dams of my eyes. There was an increasingly serious risk of me choking or hyperventilating now with my strained breathing, crying and inability to speak.

"Hey, come on. Don't cry, baby."

I quickly found myself disappearing beneath Cy's arms and body that was cradling me, carrying me to the sofa where we lay, holding each other.

Time passed by while we lay together, Cy behind me with my back pressed against his front while his arms held me and his lips rested against my neck, gently kissing and stroking the sensitive skin there. My eyes closed of their own accord, possibly mimicking sleep as a cover for my intention not to cry again. My faked sleep at some point became a reality I found when I awoke at the sensation of Cy's absence. Rubbing the sleep from my eyes I began to sit up just as Cy appeared in the doorway.

"Hey," he smiled warmly.

"Sorry," I replied before he cut me off.

"Stop, there's no need. You feel better?"

I nodded as he reached me, bending down to brush his lips over mine, preparing, I think, for a gentle kiss. I still needed more. I still needed a distraction from the thoughts in my head so reached up for him. Grabbing his shirt that still had the two buttons undone I roughly fisted the material.

"Cy," I gasped into his mouth, urging him on, not content until he was sitting on the sofa with me straddling him.

It felt as though we were doing battle. I fought with his belt, zip and remaining buttons while he attempted to slow my rapidly flailing movements. He attempted to regain some control and I had to admit that one of us should probably have some degree of command over the situation and I certainly had none.

Cy was almost incidental to this now. I had my mouth on his, licking and tasting, sucking the length of his tongue while my hands flitted between tugging on his hair, stroking and roughly groping his skin and removing the barrier of our clothes. In the distance I could hear him calling my name, but it was too far away from the thoughts hammering away in my head that were deafening me, drowning out any other sound. I needed this. I needed to feel something and think nothing. I needed right here, right now. Where there was no Michael. No unhappy home to go back to. No Susan. No nothing. Not even me and Cy and certainly no disaster-in-waiting.

Somehow, I don't know how, I managed to release Cy from his trousers and boxers, freeing a large and desperate looking erection that contradicted the objections I had somehow heard him making, albeit half-hearted ones. I had managed to sheath him, stretching around him and as I was barely ready for this physically the stretch of my skin was more intense, painful, but in a good way. I hissed as I lowered over him, taking no time to allow my body to adjust, moving immediately. Rocking, circling and then full on riding, up and down, faster and faster.

"Oh God," I heard myself cry and moan. I was close, so close and so soon.

Relief flooded through me as I realised that in spite of my mind my body was functioning properly, moving into Cy default mode. It knew what it wanted, needed and it was taking it. I was also dreading this moment ending because once it did, I would be forced to face up to real life which today was going to be a full day here and then a whole night of playing happy families. A family I didn't belong to and an emotion I didn't feel with them.

The sound of my name being called broke my thoughts as I saw Cy looking at me, angrily. In the second he gained my attention I was being flipped over and pressed into the sofa on my back with Cy still inside me. He lowered himself towards me, one arm braced on the sofa and the other reaching for my face, cupping my chin and gripping my jaw so that I had no choice but to look at him. To see him for possibly the first time since he'd kissed me. He was thrusting into me still, pounding against me so that all that could be heard was skin slapping against skin, our laboured breathing and my whirring mind and then he spoke.

"I am not a fucking distraction here! You want to fuck, we fuck, but the *we* would be you and me. Not you on your own and not with anybody else. So whilst it might be my dick in your slick little pussy it certainly isn't me in your head, is it?"

"Sorry," I muttered, knowing his accusations were accurate. "I just needed to forget everything," I admitted, unwilling to add any more deceit to this moment. "Oh God," I cried again, louder, slightly more strung out now as I realised just how close I was to release.

"No," Cy snapped, still driving into me. "You want to forget me, then do it, but don't fucking do it while I am balls deep in you. Oh, and if you're going to use me to forget him at least have the decency to remain here with me," he snarled, angrily removing his braced arm from the sofa before he pulled out of me. Immediately he took himself in hand and stroked his length. Once, twice and then he was coming over me. My thighs, pelvis and my sex, my pussy as he called it.

I couldn't take my eyes off him. The almost pained expression, the streams of creamy liquid streaking my body and the loud breathing sounding around us and all I could think of now was him. My mind and my body buzzing with thoughts of Cy. My body burned for him, for a touch, but it didn't come, neither did I. Clearly, he was seriously pissed off with me and with good reason. I knew that. Accepted it, and in turn I accepted his annoyance and my punishment. He was standing now, redressing and then he was heading for the door.

"I'll give you some time to clean up," he said and left.

****

As far as Mondays went this one had to rank up there in the top ten of hideous, fucked up ones by anybody's standard. I had, as Cy had suggested, cleaned up and when he returned to his office twenty minutes later there was coffee waiting for him on his desk while I sat at my own. We didn't speak until lunch time when he announced that he was out for lunch. I nodded. Not entirely trusting myself to speak for fear of making the day worse, if that was possible. With my luck it was probable rather than possible if I opened my mouth.

My lunch hour was spent in a coffee shop around the corner from the office, with Maya.

"El, El," she called in a sharp shout. Clearly that hadn't been her first attempt to gain my attention.

"Sorry, I was miles away," I explained unnecessarily, my absence clear to us both.

"Mmm, but where and who with?" she asked with only concern in her voice.

"It's complicated. Very, very complicated, and Cy and I had an argument this morning. He's still pissed off with me, and I deserve it."

"I see, well I don't. I can see you're fond of him and him

263

you, but surely you knew banging the boss was only ever going to be a bad idea."

Maybe I should have been offended by the inference that I was *banging the boss*, which I was, but her words only served to amuse me.

With a smirk and a shrug I revealed a little more, "My marriage to Michael is over and I like Cy, really like him. But it's all a mess and like I say, complicated. Anyway, enough about me, how did your Friday night end?"

"It ended in a very crumpled and sweaty bed this morning," she said already adopting a smug expression.

"No way! All weekend?" I asked, watching her nod seriously. "Wow, I can't deny I'm very jealous that your weekend lasted all the way to Monday morning."

"But not of my bed companion?" she asked with mischief in her voice and was in no way surprised when I shook my head. "Chad, that's his name by the way, he's an Adonis," she grinned making me laugh.

"And Cora's friend?"

"She shagged him on Friday and on Saturday went to make up with Maddox, her boyfriend." Maya winced.

"You don't like him, Maddox?" I asked curiously, thinking Maya was usually really laid back about other people's choices and lives.

"He's okay, but I worry that they're too different, Cora and Maddox, and that eventually she'll end up alone, but will it be before or after a broken heart, and with or without a couple of kids in tow." She sighed. "You know sometimes when you can just see that things are nigh on impossible to succeed, a bit like you and Mr Stanton," she added boldly, taking me aback.

"Really?"

"Yes!" she sighed with exasperation. "I like Michael, he's a nice man, a good man to work for. Before you, there were three wives, four kids and God knows what else, so clearly, he was flawed and you, well you were young, sweet and obviously innocent. You and him, you just never seemed right for each other. Now, with the boss, well you couldn't look more right together and the fact that you two are hot for each other permanently."

"What?" my startled voice mustered up, making Maya laugh.

"Oh God, El! Don't tell me you thought that you and he weren't like open books." She laughed. "Look, I expect to find you shagging on your desk most mornings. The way he looks at you should be illegal and don't get me started on the thickness of the sexual tension I wade through every time I come into the office. Then there's the wedding ring you're not wearing, haven't been wearing since Friday…just be careful. I would hate you to get hurt any more than I think you already have been."

"Thanks," I replied, suddenly centred and a little more balanced.

****

Returning to the office after lunch I did feel a little apprehensive at the thought of facing Cy, but with Maya's words, *you couldn't look more right together* still bouncing around my head, words I agreed with, I realised that we probably just needed to clear the air. Like couples did after they'd had a row. That thought was a revelation in some ways because until recently Michael and I hadn't really rowed and before Michael nobody was ever serious enough to bother clearing the air with. Cy was claiming another one of my firsts.

I heard voices as I approached my desk and a glance at the open doorway confirmed that Cy was deep in conversation with another executive who had only relocated to this floor that day.

I busied myself, providing regular offers of refreshments in between working my way through my workload; emails, phone calls, photocopying, collating and compiling reports.

Before I knew it, the new exec', Darius, was leaving and it was almost home time, again.

"Thanks for the coffee," he smiled at me. "Remember me to Michael."

I nodded my agreement before wondering how well he knew Michael as I had never met this man before, professionally or socially, but then I hadn't worked here for some time before my current post.

"You need to get off?" Cy asked resting his behind on the

edge of my desk.

"Yeah," I confirmed after a glance at the clock showed it was just turning five o'clock.

"I was hoping we could talk," Cy sighed.

"I know." I nodded. "Me too."

For no particular reason I reached up and rested a hand on his knee and immediately a larger hand covered mine, stroking the space where my wedding ring had sat until recently. The same ring that was in my bag, ready to go back on when I got into my car.

"I am already fucking hating this week."

"Me too," I agreed, horrified to feel tears burning my eyes and throat.

"Sorry if I was an ass this morning," he whispered against the top of my head that he was gently kissing.

"You weren't. I was a bitch though. I am sorry. Using you that way was unforgivable."

"I wouldn't go that far, baby, but we'll talk about it. Maybe think of how we're going to deal with the shit that's undoubtedly going to happen and fuck with your head."

Again I mutely nodded with gratitude.

"I was thinking," he mused. "Tomorrow, how about we work from home?"

Panic and bile were rising at a similar pace at the mere suggestion.

"No, no, please. I can't. No. Shit! The idea of just being confined with them all and having to play the loving wife I no longer am is bad enough, but the reality," I cried. "And then he might try to stop me visiting my dad and I have no idea how many visits I will have," I sobbed, almost stamping my feet that were now holding me upright.

"Fucking hell, baby. I didn't mean you at his home. I meant you and me at my home, together. We can work and talk, and whatever else we need, want to do," he told me, pulling my shaking body into his arms, between his open legs, holding me tightly against his warm and firm body.

"Oh," I whispered.

"Is that oh as in yes?"

"Yes, yes please," I replied with a smile spreading across my face. A happy, excited, enamored smile.

"Then I will see you in the morning. As early as you like, Ms Ross." He grinned down at me.

****

My journey home was easy and far too quick. When I was about ten minutes away from home, Michael's home, I pulled into a layby to text Cy. Just in case I didn't get a chance later.

<I might not be able to call/text later so, sorry about this morning, really I am x>

<No need to keep apologising. We can make up with real 'in person' talking tomorrow x>

<There is. I was in the wrong and I am sorry, really sorry. I keep thinking about something you said earlier x>

I felt sick when I sent that message. I knew what I was thinking of, had been since he'd said it and I was fairly certain he'd know what I meant.

<What? X>

Yes, he probably knew what I meant and was possibly going to force me to acknowledge it and say it to him.

<You said, when I was having my bitchfest…X>

<Tell me…what did I say? What are thinking about baby? X>

Yes, he knew and he was going to make me say it.

<Tell me, now! X>

"Fucking fine!" I muttered to nobody but myself.

267

<You asked if I was hoping to be put across your knee for the spanking of my life…it's all I've thought about since you said it, and maybe that is what I needed, wanted, deserved, 'the spanking of my life' X>

<We'll talk tomorrow X>

<Talk…or spank? X>

Who was I? And what had happened to the real Eloise Ross? I asked and also answered. This was her. I was her and I clearly wanted spanking!

<I will see you tomorrow. I love you baby and if you need me, call, day or night X>

"Bastard!" I muttered, but wore a huge grin.

<I love you too. I might make a very early start tomorrow X>

<I think you're pushing! Tomorrow…early X>
****

Several deep breaths were needed before I ventured out of my car which was parked farther away from the door than usual courtesy of the numerous vehicles belonging to the visiting guests, Michael's guests. The distance seemed apt, as though my car moving away from the house signified my own withdrawal. The feel of my wedding ring on my finger was constricting and tight, almost as though it shouldn't be there, that it no longer belonged to me, which it kind of didn't.

I entered the house in near silence, although with the amount of noise that was coming from indoors I doubted anyone would have heard me if I had been accompanied by a brass band and a troop of majorettes. The cacophony of sounds resonating around the house consisted of adults; Michael, his daughters Sophie and Nieve, their husbands, Drew and Rod, Callum and Moses, Michael's sons, all shouting to be heard over the sound of the children, a baby crying, six-month-old Rosie and the other children squealing, Jake who was just two and four-year-old Delilah. The only one I couldn't hear was the dog, which was unnerving, considering the fact that he was normally the one shouting when I returned home.

With a very deep breath and a quick pep talk I took the bull by the horns and called out, "Hi, anyone home?"

I turned into the lounge and found people and things everywhere; bags, cases, toys, plates, cups, mess. And then I heard the dog, from the other side of the kitchen door, scratching and whining. Communal calls of hi and El were the responses I caught as I met Michael's eyes.

"Where's Balder?" I asked, already knowing where he was meaning my real question was why?

"He's in the kitchen," Michael replied sheepishly and then saw fit to expand, "He's erm…"

Sophie interjected, "Dad shut him in the kitchen. Jake is into everything," she informed me. "And whilst that can't be helped, I don't really want that everything to include dog hair, drool or, well anything dog."

I could feel tears burning the back of my eyes at the thought of the dog being surplus to requirements or that he might feel sad, scared or unwanted, although he didn't really have much to do with children so was not really into them, I reasoned in my own mind. Reason was quickly overtaken by a sense of unjust on his behalf when I remembered that Balder was not in the kitchen out of anyone's concern for him, quite the opposite.

With a huff that seemed to startle everyone present I turned on my heels and entered the kitchen, deliberately leaving the door open, allowing the dog the choice of where he went in his own home.

"Hey boy," I called cheerily as I bent down to pet him.

"El," Michael said behind me as the door closed again, only serving to irritate me further.

"What?" I snapped.

"You said you'd do this, this week," he snapped right back.

"I am, but you didn't include shutting the dog away for the week in your blackmail."

He glared and glowered at my unpleasant word, but I didn't really care. "Grow up," he growled in a low tone. "He has been shut in the large, warm kitchen that he's rather fond of with water, toys and a bed. Strangely, I thought that he might be happier in here than out there with all the noise and fuss, especially as Sophie was on the verge of disinfecting him. He, Balder and I get each other, love each other and I would never deliberately do anything to cause him harm."

"Oh," I whispered, his words resonating with me on several levels. Clearly Michael had taken Balder's wellbeing into consideration and I had misjudged him. "Sorry, long day," I said as an excuse. "Dinner? What's the plan?"

Michael, fortunately, allowed me to change the topic easily and shrugged. "I had suggested dinner out, but apparently Jake is likely to eat the waiting staff. Everything goes straight in his mouth," he said dryly as he did a very good impression of his oldest and slightly uptight daughter.

I laughed. A real, genuine laugh of amusement at Michael and for a second was reminded of the man I married.

"I've missed that sound El," he said with heartfelt sincerity as a hand came up to stroke some stray hair back off my face.

"Please don't," I replied, pulling back from his touch as we both heard Balder let out a low, warning growl.

"I've made a real mess of this, haven't I? I never ever wanted to hurt you, El, but I suppose I always knew…"

That moment seemed to be unfolding into something real, substantial and potentially honest, but his words were stemmed when Callum appeared with Moses, who at fourteen looked less thrilled than me to be in the midst of children and noise.

"Sorry." Callum smiled. "We have now moved onto the effect of too much fresh fruit on Jake's bowel habits." He grimaced, making me laugh.

"Heads up, it's loose, green and odorous," Moses added making me and Michael laugh.

"I'm guessing Thai green curry's off the menu then!" I frowned.

"Yeah, for the rest of my life," Callum agreed.

"Michael, dinner?" I asked again.

"Whatever, I'm easy," he replied using words I'd never heard him say before.

"Pizza," suggested Moses.

"Okay, pizza," Michael agreed while I looked on wondering if I'd ever get my head around the ever-changing personas of my husband.

I managed to spend half an hour or so being sociable and chatting in the lounge before I got changed and took Balder out for a good run before returning in time for the pizza delivery. With his dinner, a run and a play Balder was happy to retreat to the kitchen while we ate in the lounge that looked slightly tidier after I came downstairs freshly showered. Rosie was already fast asleep and safely tucked up in her travel cot. A freshly bathed Jake seemed to be on the verge of losing consciousness but was determined to see off another slice of Margarita before giving in to it. That just left Delilah who I rather liked. She was Nieve's eldest daughter and pretty, bright, friendly and very sweet.

"What's that?" she asked as she glanced over at Sophie's monstrosity of a pizza.

"Pizza," Sophie snarked.

"What's that stuff on it?" the little girl persisted.

"Smoked mackerel, squid and kale," her aunt replied.

I knew my face had given away my total and utter disgust at the three items she'd named but I was glad that it was Delilah and not me who actually expressed their undisguised horror.

"Eww!" she cried. "That is nasty."

I laughed and when Sophie looked at me, I explained. "I love pizza, hate fish." I stopped short of expressing how much I loved beer and as if by magic Drew spoke.

"We're just missing beer."

Both Rod and Callum agreed but Michael dismissed them both. "No beer in this house. We don't drink it, do we?" he asked giving me a look that dared me to disagree.

I reminded myself that there were children present and reined in the near overpowering urge to dispute his words but said nothing.

"Maybe we can pick some up tomorrow," Rod suggested as the pizza passing down my throat seemed to form a ball and get stuck.

The remainder of the evening was significantly easier with all the children bathed and put to bed and adults unpacking and settling down in comfy clothes in front of the TV where warm, familiar and friendly banter ensued.

"So, how's work back at Stanton Industries?" Nieve asked with a warm smile at her use of the company's old name, her father's name.

"Fine, although it's no longer Stanton Industries," I replied, avoiding introducing Cy's name, albeit his surname in the company name, unlike Michael.

"No, it's all rebranded now under the banner of Miller Industries."

"Of course it is," Nieve smirked, already knowing who Michael had sold the business to.

"How is Denton?" Sophie asked, her ears having suddenly picked up.

"Fine," replied Michael as I threw the half-eaten slice of meat feast back onto my plate.

That had been my husband's concession to pizza. It had to be eaten off a plate. But the prospect of discussing anyone called Denton or Miller with Michael's family had me fighting a huge wave of nausea from the pit of my stomach to the back of my throat that was burning.

"Although, Denny has gone back to The States."

I somehow felt as though I was being set up by Michael. Like a trap was about to be set to ensnare me.

"So who's at the helm then?" Nieve asked.

"His son..." were the only words Michael got out before both of his daughters spoke in stereo.

"Cy? Cy is over here and working in your old company?"

"Yes," Michael confirmed to the two giggling women who were irritating the hell out of me now with their adolescent sniggering and blushing act aimed at my lover.

This was seriously messed up, even by my current standards. We were pushing into Greek tragedy, surely.

"Is he still drop dead gorgeous?" Nieve asked with a wide-eyed stare. "Oh God, do you remember him in just swimming trunks?" she giggled as she waved her hands in a fanning motion.

"That is burned on my brain," Sophie stated salaciously and while their father, husbands and brothers laughed, I didn't. Far from it. I imagined my face must look like a bulldog chewing a wasp as my dad used to say when Susan was in a huff over something.

"You okay, love?" Michael asked me. His false sincerity made me want to punch him, tell him to shut the fuck up and then go out and buy beer. Yeah, my inner bitch was being channeled to the max.

"Fine. Tired. I have an early start and a late finish so I think I'll turn in," I replied with a forced smile and yet I found that I was unable to leave. Maybe to keep my bitch company I had an inner masochist. How did these two know Cy? When had they seen him in trunks and just how well did they know him? How bad was that, if either of them, both of them knew Cy like I knew him?

"Oh, okay," smiled Sophie. "Maybe I could pop in and see you, meet for lunch?"

I wasn't convinced that my pizza wasn't going to put in a reappearance very soon judging by the churning and pulsing in my stomach as I imagined Sophie or anybody turning up at the office tomorrow only to find me missing in action, me and Cy.

"Meet El or reacquaint yourself with Cy and his teeny tiny speedos?" Nieve laughed. Again, unlike me.

"Be still my beating heart," whispered Sophie.

"Erm, hi, remember me? Your husband, father of your child," joked Drew, making everyone look across at him.

Sophie looked suitably guilty, as if the mere memory of Cy in speedos had made her completely forget her married status and her husband, much like me after meeting Cy.

"I love you," Sophie told him getting to her feet and hugging her husband.

"But he had a bum to die for," Nieve interjected, which really was my cue to go, but in my emerging masochistic state I stayed and foolishly allowed my mouth to open.

"You know him that well?" I asked. I was hoping for

friendly disinterest yet only managed to pull off a jealous and resentful snarl.

Michael threw me a knowing glance with a clear warning to mind my step. Nobody else seemed to notice. Anyway, this wasn't my fault if it all turned unpleasant as I hadn't brought Cy into this. I refused to remind myself that I was the one who had started shagging him behind my husband's back.

A cackle resonated as the two sisters laughed, either at my question or what they knew the answer was.

"We all sailed the Med, it must be fifteen, sixteen years ago. Callum was only little," Nieve explained glancing across at her brothers, possibly explaining Moses' absence. "Do you remember it, Callum? Your mum was there with us and the whole Miller family, Tia, Cy, and the other brother. Easy on the eye but a bit sulky...Christopher, that was him, wasn't it?"

"Yes," somebody confirmed as I shuddered at my knowledge of sulky Christopher.

"But then Dad and Trish split up and things seemed to go a bit weird with the Millers until after he married your mum," Sophie told Moses. "Then we met Denny and Elizabeth a couple more times. I think Elizabeth likes you married," she smiled at her dad. "Because when you and Nadia split they kind of disappeared again until you were selling up and obviously married to El."

I was on masochistic overload with all that information swimming round in my head and the urge to stay a while longer. I realised that I really needed to listen to myself more carefully, especially when it came to leaving conversations as Rod changed the subject.

"It was nice to see Edward again. He looked well. I don't think we've seen him since we got married."

My mind was racing again at that nugget of information. Rod and Nieve married just before Michael and I started seeing each other...six years ago. Why did everything keep coming back to six years ago? It was most likely a coincidence yet somehow it felt much more deliberate, like there was an invisible common thread connecting all things from that time; Edward and Michael's falling out, Edward's mother dying,

Balder becoming Michael's dog and Edward's friend, Michael seeming to pick me out of obscurity with a little help from Susan and the recurring distance between the Millers and Michael.

"You saw Edward?" I asked in a confused croak.

"Mmm, we almost missed him," Rod told me. "We made good time, and got here an hour ahead of schedule. Edward was just leaving.

"Here? Edward was here?"

"I thought you were going to bed El, with your busy day," Michael interrupted, sounding almost as awkward and deceitful as he looked.

He was definitely up to something and all roads kept coming back to Edward and/or six years ago. Maybe he'd always been a sneaky bastard in business and I'd never seen that side of him, but now I was getting a ringside view privately.

"Yes," I replied meekly. "Goodnight and I'll see you all tomorrow night, but don't hold dinner up for me. I visit my dad on Tuesdays. It can get late."

Chapter Twenty-Two

It was dark still. I felt hot, too hot, and restricted. Balder was mumbling and groaning nearby, and watching me. I could feel his protective gaze on me and then I felt it, a body next to me in bed. In my bed. It was a dream. It had to be because I slept alone, had done for a while now, since Cy really, but it couldn't be a dream because as I leapt up in a panic, I was one hundred percent wide awake and lying next to me was Michael.

"What the bloody hell are you doing?" I asked haughtily, pulling the duvet up and gripping it at my chest, hiding my modesty like something from a Jane Austen adaptation.

"Sleeping in my bed, with my wife." He sounded as outraged as me.

"No. You sleep next door. Not here and not with me."

"Eloise, I am not sleeping in another room when my children are here. They might find that odd."

"But they won't find it odd when you tell them we're ending our marriage. In fact, that might give them something of a hint," I suggested more gently.

"Goodnight El," was his response as he rolled over.

I lay there, rigid in the darkness for another forty minutes before deciding that I wouldn't, couldn't do this. Quietly and quickly I got out of bed and grabbed the clothes I'd laid out the night before. I dashed into the bathroom for a quick wash before throwing on my clothes. Balder followed me downstairs, watching me closely. Probably wondering why I was washed, dressed and ready for work at quarter-to-five in the morning. With a final fuss and a kiss for the dog I headed out to my car.

****

It was only half-past five when I pulled up in front of Cy's house that, like a normal person's home, was in complete darkness. I pulled my phone from my bag.

<How early is too early? X>

About a minute passed before my message was read and then a reply came.

<How early are you planning? X>

<As I've just pulled up outside your house…now early? X>

Suddenly lights began to come on all over the house and then the gates opened, clearly inviting me in. By the time I was parking in front of the garage doors the front door was opening, revealing an almost naked Cy. He was standing there with his just woke up face and hair, a little bit of a five o'clock shadow that I was desperate to kiss, lick and nibble. I allowed my eyes to dance down his shoulders, chest and abdomen until they rested on his black designer boxers that clung in all the right places, including the bulge at the front. The smile on my face broadened until I remembered Sophie and Nieve's reminiscent memories of Cy in speedos.

"Baby, get your ass in here. I'm fucking freezing my balls off and I don't think either of us wants that." He grinned and just like that I was back in my happy place, which it seemed meant any place Cy was.

"No, I need your balls exactly where they are," I agreed as I reached the space before him and rather bravely, brazenly cupped his balls and stroked along his length.

"I think you should make an early start like this every day," he told me before his lips came down to crush mine as the front door slammed.

Our kiss was deep but brief. Lips against lips, tongue against tongue, his body pressed firmly against mine.

"Yeah, this is officially my preferred start to the day," he grinned, his lips and forehead resting gently against mine.

****

By eight o'clock on a Tuesday I was normally ready for the business day to commence with tea for Cy already on his desk, but this morning I was naked and wrapped inside the cocoon of Cy's arms in his bed.

"I don't think working from home together is likely to be very productive. Not work wise anyway," Cy whispered against my neck that his face was buried in.

"I've always liked work, but this has some real advantages," I giggled back.

"Mmm," he agreed, his nose rubbing through my hair. "You smell fucking divine," he told me on a deep inhale.

"Cy," I moaned as the arm around me loosened enough to allow a hand to snake up my body cupping one breast and then the other before honing in on a nipple. "Oh God," I cried as my nipple came up in a stiff and aching peak, still sore from the earlier administrations of Cy's tongue, fingers and teeth.

"Too much?" He was already firming up his grip, his pinch.

"No, no, no," I stammered. "More," I begged.

"More what baby?" Cy allowed his other hand to find my neglected nipple until both were being expertly manipulated, until all I could think about was some kind of relief from the burn in my nipples that was making me hot all over and thirsty, not to mention wet between my thighs.

With my hips bucking and everything else flailing I was sure I might come from this alone.

"Baby," he repeated. "Tell me what you want, what you need."

"You. Touch me more," I told him, burning with embarrassment as well as the heat engulfing my body.

"But where, where should I touch you?" he taunted.

I had read in my romance novels that when aroused, a woman's skin becomes flushed and red and although I had no idea if it really did, having never seen a real woman aroused from that perspective. I now hoped to God that this was true and not a myth because at least that way my mortified embarrassment might be disguised. A sharp nip against my ear made me squeal but also reminded me that Cy was waiting for an answer.

"You are such a fucking arsehole," I told him as I rubbed my behind against his hard and naked erection.

"Only for you baby, and it's asshole," he whispered with a strange sincerity to his tone. "Now be a good bitch and tell me what you need."

I smiled as I realised that this was part of us, the antsy bitch with the churlish arsehole. Together we completed the other.

"Your fingers," I whispered as my face burnt like a beacon but my leg was already cocking over Cy's, opening myself to him, for him. "Inside me, finger me," I whined with a red hue covering my whole body I imagined at my strangely crude and immature phrase.

"My absolute fucking pleasure," he replied and immediately complied with my request. One, two and possibly a third finger stretching and filling me. "Touch yourself El. Play with your tits, pretend it's me, baby. Not too hard. I feel like teasing you," he told me with a lick along the shell of my ear making me think of his magical tongue licking me lower, much lower.

I had no idea how much time had passed by the time I was begging, actually begging for the final touch I needed to find my release, but again I was denied.

"Not yet, baby. It will be worth the wait. Now get those hands back on your tits and tease those nipples some more for me."

With his fingers still filling me but pumping away in earnest, I wasn't sure how long I could actually wait before my body would overrule my lover's desire for some delayed gratification for me. My movements were becoming even more erratic as my senses went into overdrive, chasing the inevitable conclusion of climax. My legs were splayed wide, one of them still secured over Cy's, encouraging and demanding his attention.

"Oh God," I began to chant as my forefingers and thumbs continued to squeeze and roll my own nipples.

"Ssh, soon…slow down baby, not so hard, gently, tease

yourself, like I would," Cy's whispers encouraged as if he was a mentor of some sort.

"I can't," I cried as the burn in my belly began to spread.

"Sure you can," he disagreed. "Take your hands off."

"No, no, please," I pleaded, unsure if I was actually going to cry if he stopped me from coming again.

"It's okay. We're going to take this home together, but I want you to let go."

With his reassuring, comforting words I complied.

"Good girl, and for that, next time I am going to fuck you really hard and make you scream until you're hoarse and the time after that I'm going to lick you all over until you're coming in my mouth, but first…put your fingers in your mouth and suck them, lick them and make them really wet."

Cy's movements slowed. He clearly knew how close I was, but I did exactly as he asked, told me, and once my mouth was full of my own fingers and wet, I waited for my next instruction.

"Circle your nipples with your fingers. Make sure your fingers are really wet and then circle them."

Again I complied with the instruction given and whined at the sensation of my warm saliva bringing my flesh to life further and then the feeling of my flesh puckering, rising and chilling as my spit dried, the additional sensations being almost enough to push me over the edge of pleasure, but not quite.

"That's it," he cooed as his fingers began to pick up speed while his thumb began to circle my clit that felt too sensitive and too swollen.

"Cy, oh yes, no, don't stop," I called incoherently before losing myself in an electric storm that carried my body up, coiling and twisting in a hurricane of sensation and pleasure that verged on being painful and yet I couldn't get enough, couldn't absorb it quickly enough, deeply enough. I was sure my nails were going to snap as my hands fisted the sheet beneath me and then my hands were reaching out for Cy, to touch him, hold him, but our position prevented that. It felt as though this was never going to end and that my pelvic area might never recover from the tense burn that just seemed to keep intensifying until I realised that I was still coming, orgasm after orgasm, one rolling into another and then, eventually when I was incapable of speaking, barely able to breathe and totally and utterly spent the unrelenting storm I had been caught up in spat me out.

"I told you it would be worth it," Cy told me, wrapping me in his arms, rolling me towards him where he held me, cradled me, laying gentle kisses on my closed eyes.

"Hmm," was as much as I could manage in response as we lay together for countless minutes lost to lust induced sleep.

Our moment was broken by the sound of a phone ringing, not mine, Cy's. Adjusting his position and loosening his grip on me, he reached for it.

"Hi, Rhonda, you okay?"

The sound of the other woman's name woke me fully from my sex induced coma and although my initial response to her calling was jealousy, I quickly remembered that she was an ex, not even that, not really. An ex in name only for all intents and purposes. Fidgeting, I rearranged my position so I was nestled more tightly into Cy's side, an arm draped over him and my mouth littering gentle kisses to his side, chest and then nipple.

He let out a low hiss before continuing his conversation. "No, that's right I'm working from home. Yes, with El."

Hearing his flat tone was like music to my ears. He wasn't trying to hide me from Rhonda, nor was he playing down who I was. In fact, he was offering nothing in the way of explanation which I took to mean she knew we were back on and that possibly I was more than the stereotypical secretary he was shagging. His reward for making me feel that way was my tongue lapping at his erect brown nipple. Cy's free hand snaked through my hair until he was gripping my head, holding it to his chest, encouraging me to continue.

"Oh, okay. No, it's fine. I'm at home and she is my daughter too. Do you want to bring her here?"

Shit! His daughter was coming here. What did that mean for me? Should I get up or get ready for the office? I was unsure if he read my mind or maybe my body language was giving me away, but with a slight pull he was forcing my head back so I had to look up at him.

"Stop overthinking," he mouthed, his words barely audible.

With a smile I focused my attention back on his body that I was now straddling. I shimmied down his body. Kissing, licking and occasionally nipping I made my way down as far as his erection that I suddenly remembered hadn't been given any relief when I almost passed out.

His conversation continued as I consumed him greedily, desperate for his pleasure to be mine.

Muffled words were coming from his mouth. "Lulu...an hour or so...no problem...of course El won't mind...things are good...better than good."

My mouth was forming a tight suction around his arousal as I sucked long and hard before reverting to a licking motion from the base to the tip and then I began to sweep my tongue around the head. He was already leaking his pleasure and I was greedily consuming it, gently lapping at the weeping eye as I fisted him, oblivious to anything else. Shrieking, I found myself being pulled up until we were eye to eye. Cy's deep brown pools almost black, smoking with arousal.

"Really?" he asked with a broad smile.

"Uh-huh," I replied nibbling my bottom lip.

"Oh dear," he chastened with a mock sternness that didn't reach his eyes and that was the last thing I saw as I was unceremoniously flipped over, face down onto the bed.

Cy's body quickly blanketed mine and with a slight lift of my hips he was sliding into me. Yes, this was definitely the way to work from home.

****

Sitting with Cy eating a breakfast of eggs and toast seemed like the most natural thing in the world to be doing even as my stomach somersaulted at the thought of Tallulah's imminent arrival.

"Please don't look so worried. She's a good kid. A little bit wacky, but good. You two should get on just fine."

"But is it too soon? And what if she asks about Michael or sees me with him?" I asked, rambling in my panic.

"Baby, she is unlikely to assume you're married. She's five years old and too soon for what? To introduce you two? That's all I'm suggesting."

"Okay," I agreed, slightly more reassured.

"And why would she see you with Michael when you and he are playing happy families for one week only?"

It was a fair question and a valid point made at the same time, but I was unsure why I wasn't convinced that this week would be the end of it. With that in my mind I remembered my horror at waking up to find Michael in bed with me. Obviously, my face, its colour or expression must have revealed some of my worry, concern or discomfort at finding my husband in my bed for the first time in a long time because suddenly Cy's beautiful face was transformed into a manifestation of anxiety.

"What? What are you not telling me? Have you renegotiated your deal with him?"

He'd misunderstood. He'd assumed I was moving the goalposts on my remaining time with Michael rather than the actual reason for my disconcerted demeanour.

"No," I insisted. "Not like you mean. We haven't discussed anything, but last night, this morning, he, erm, didn't want to raise suspicion and got into bed with me."

"What do you mean, he got into bed with you? I thought the two of you didn't share a bed anymore?" Cy asked flatly, but I could already see the annoyed fury flickering in his eyes, but were those emotions directed at me or my husband?

"We don't, haven't for a while, but because the kids are at home he didn't want to raise suspicion."

I relayed the details of my fairly one-sided conversation with Michael and explained that my discomfort and desire to put some distance between us had resulted in me arriving at Cy's house ridiculously early that morning.

"Oh baby," Cy whispered, already pulling me to my feet and enclosing me in a warm and gentle embrace. "A week and this is all going to be over, and in the mean time you feel free to turn up here at any time of the day or night."

"Thank you," I replied on a long exhale.

"He didn't touch you, did he?" he asked nervously.

"No, no he didn't. If you recall touching me wasn't really his thing, so I think I'm pretty safe."

"Okay. Well not okay, but you get what I mean."

A gentle kiss landed on the top of my head as the doorbell rang.

Awkwardness was probably the most apt description for how I felt when Tallulah arrived with her mother.

Rhonda explained that her daughter had some inset day at school and her meeting had been sprung on her. She seemed apologetic at the interruption her daughter's presence was to our day which only made me feel slightly more uncomfortable, especially as she had witnessed my meltdown when I had inadvertently discovered her daughter's connection to Cy, her father. I wondered whether Rhonda was aware that I knew the truth behind the little girl's parentage. The horror of it.

As the other woman began to kiss her child and give her all those instructions only parents would think of; behave, don't forget your manners, make sure you do as you're told, I felt even more uncomfortable at the prospect of Rhonda leaving because I was in no doubt that she was the one supporting and scaffolding this meeting and once she left I was unsure how this might pan out.

An hour later, I sat watching Beauty and the Beast, singing along to the songs and agreeing with Lulu that Gaston, was indeed a very nasty man. We ate popcorn and drank what Cy and his daughter insisted was soda. I decided that my earlier reservations had proven completely unfounded. I was having fun, right up until the point where the little girl began to ask questions.

"El, are you Daddy's girlfriend?"

I looked to Cy for some interjection or support in dealing with this particular question, but as he sat down next to me, pausing to kiss my temple, reaching around me to pinch a handful of popcorn from Lulu I assumed I was on my own.

"I think you must be because Daddy just kissed you," the little girl giggled. "And you're wearing one of his t-shirts," she added, reminding me that I was wearing a plain white t-shirt of Cy's that I had found in his bathroom after I'd showered with him. I was wearing it with my own black suit trousers I'd left home in, under the guise of being dressed for work...my whole life was becoming a farce again. "Why were you crying at

Grandpa's house? Did you and Daddy have a fight? Did he make you sad, or mad?" she asked and fortunately Cy did rescue me now.

"Lulu, please stop. You're making El feel bad now," he told the frowning little girl. "El is my girlfriend and at Grandpa's, yes, we had a fight, but that is none of your business. Now, are we watching Beauty and the Beast or shall I see if I can find some baseball?" Cy reached for the remote control that Lulu was desperately grasping for, but I intercepted, securing our viewing.

"Beauty and the Beast," I called triumphantly.

"We will be discussing your loyalties later, baby," Cy whispered against my ear, causing chills and goosebumps to wash over me.

Rhonda's meeting was clearly running over I decided when I found myself sitting at the table in the kitchen for lunch with Cy and Lulu just after one o'clock.

"Daddy, can I have peanut butter and jelly?" She eyed the pasta salad with suspicion.

"What would Mommy say?" he asked with a grin that said he knew exactly what Mommy would say.

"She would say," the little girl appeared to pause for thought. "She'd say that it's full of sugar and additives and that it's not exactly healthy, but maybe so long as I eat it and brush my teeth afterwards."

This kid was good. Totally honest and yet at five-years-old had just set up a situation to get what she wanted.

"Then I guess you'll be having peanut butter and jelly," he replied.

"Yes!" she cried triumphantly with an air punch too. "You're the best Daddy," she cried sincerely making me smile between her and her father.

"You bet I am baby." He bestowed a kiss on Lulu's head before landing a slightly longer one on my lips as he leaned down towards my inclined head.

"El," Lulu said, preparing a question for me. "Have you seen Daddy's tattoo?"

I resisted the urge to explain that I had seen it, kissed it, and licked it all over as recently as that morning. "Yes, yes I have."

"I'm going to have one too," she began as her sandwich appeared before her.

"Like hell you are," Cy muttered as he turned to collect our salad.

"Daddy's tattoo is about me. Well some of it is."

"Really?" I wondered how I'd missed that part of it.

"Maybe if you stay his girlfriend he'll have one for you. He doesn't have one for Mommy though..."

"Eat your lunch before Mommy gets here and decides you should be eating salad," Cy warned making me laugh.

"Okay." The little girl sighed. "Do you have a tattoo?" she suddenly asked me.

"No, I don't." I hoped that she wouldn't want me to get one about her too. I could feel Cy's eyes on me so decided to play him a little. "Although, I think I might get one."

"Like hell you are," Cy repeated a little louder making me laugh. "Oh baby," he grinned picking up on my tease.

"Show El my tattoo Daddy," Lulu said, pulling at Cy's arm from her position on the opposite side of him to me.

I expected him to tell her to eat her lunch or make an excuse not to. I was wrong. Immediately he was turning towards me pulling his t-shirt clean off, revealing his hard, toned, torso. Oblivious to anything or anyone else I reached forward and stroked the top of that 'v' muscle that was predominantly hidden beneath his jeans before moving up his abdomen, across his ribs, rubbing a thumb over his nipple and finally coming to rest on his shoulder and upper arm where his tattoo sat. Cy's eyes bore into me as my fingers remained on him, touching, stroking his skin, feeling it warm beneath my touch.

"Daddy, my tattoo," Lulu reminded him impatiently.

"Okay, okay," he agreed moving my forefinger over a series of lines on his skin, stopping on what I could now see was an eye. "This is Lulu," he told me proudly and suddenly it actually looked like her. "When Tallulah was born and placed in my arms for the first time she was fast asleep, or so I thought, but as soon as I spoke to her she opened one eye."

"Aww." This sweet and sentimental paternal side to Cy was calling to me on what could only be a hormonal level. I was actually picturing him cradling a tiny, new-born baby. My baby. Our baby, I realised with a start.

"You okay?" He frowned as I nodded. He continued tracing my finger further across his skin "This is her date of birth in Roman numerals. It sits within intertwining lines around a heart, my heart," he told me and for the first time I could really see that this little girl was his, totally his. Regardless of who her sperm donor *father* might have been.

"That is so sweet," I told him with emotional sincerity.

Putting my hand next to my fork Cy replaced his t-shirt and winked at me. "Hey, don't worry, baby. Normal service will be resumed once half pint is out of here."

Half pint didn't actually leave until almost three in the afternoon when a very apologetic Rhonda came to collect her.

"Sorry baby, this is really not what I had in mind when I suggested working from home."

"It was fun, especially when Lulu and I designed our tattoos," I teased from my position standing on the opposite side of the sofa to Cy. I knew that although Cy had light heartedly told us both *like hell* when we'd suggested tattoos, he was deadly serious.

"I think somebody is doing some pushing right now."

"No," I protested, although we both knew I was. "I really think the pink unicorn might be my favourite, maybe on my arse cheek." I grinned, picking up the badly drawn sketch I had done and stared down at it.

I was so busy grinning that I didn't see Cy moving until he had rounded the sofa and was about to grab me. With a start I squealed and attempted to run away, only managing to get as far the bottom of the stairs before Cy caught me around the waist, causing me to stumble to the ground, landing on the stairs where he soon joined me, between my splayed legs. We both laughed before the air thickened leaving a tense, palpable energy between us. My breathing grew louder as my chest heaved while Cy's eyes darkened until they were almost black, gazing down, scorching me with the heat there.

"No fucking tattoos!" he told me seriously. "Nothing marks this skin, except me." He grazed a finger across the slither of exposed skin on my belly courtesy of his t-shirt I was wearing hitching up in the fall. "This is perfection. You are perfection and nothing could improve it, so…"

"So?" I panted.

"No tattoos."

"Okay," I appeared to concede. "For now," I added with a nervous nibble of my lip.

"Oh baby, I fucking love it when you push."

The shake of Cy's head was followed by his lips hungrily finding mine to greedily feast on before my legs wrapped around his hips, then higher around his waist until I was tightening, pulling him in closer, tighter before I got lost in the moment, in him, in us.

****

"I really should go," I admitted reluctantly.

"You might want to get dry and put some clothes on before you do," Cy replied making me laugh as I gently slapped one of his thighs that was bracketing me in his huge bath as my back rested against his front.

"I figured that much out, but I really don't want to. It's like some little bubble we've got here."

"Mmm," Cy agreed, pulling on my ponytail to hold me closer. "Five more minutes. I like being here with you."

I closed my eyes, enjoying the moment, the peace and quiet and the contentment that washed over me in the fragrant water, fig and orange I thought. Cy's lips, kissing, caressing my neck and shoulder made me sigh. I became more content with every breath I took.

The sensation of lips and teeth against my over-sensitised skin brought back memories of our encounter on the stairs; I remembered the way he had gone to work kissing and touching me before I found myself pinned to the stairs with clothing flung everywhere to allow the intimacy we both craved. Quickly it all became primal, the end goal being all either of us could see. Cy pushed me higher and higher and then higher still until there was nowhere else for me to go but head first into an intense release. Somehow he held back on his own pleasure and moved us both until he was the one underneath me with me straddling him, except reversed. The memory of seeing our reflection in the large mirror in the hall was more erotic than the incident itself. I watched my own body and expression as I moved up and down, along Cy's length, arousing myself again with shocking speed, even by my standards. His position allowed him to watch us too, or at least watch me watching us as he looked over my shoulder at the reflection before us. As I came the contractions within my own body seemed to be Cy's final undoing and then we'd managed to get up here to share the bath, even though all I wanted to do at that point was to crawl into bed.

The sensation of an ache, a slight throb in my neck, no, more my back or shoulder, was it called the trapezius? I smiled at my own internal musing as the discomfort refocused my thoughts, like a bruise that hadn't come out yet.

"I'm sure I'll regret asking this, again. What are you thinking about?" Cy wore a smile, I was certain.

"About earlier, on the stairs," I admitted with burning cheeks.

"Hmm, unexpected, but fucking marvellous."

I laughed but couldn't deny the truth of his words.

"I've never had sex on the stairs before, nor facing the wrong way," I clumsily admitted while Cy pulled me closer to massage my shoulders.

"I love that baby."

"Yeah, well I've never had sex in the shower before you, oh and never shared a bath."

"Seriously, seriously loving that baby, but if you continue speaking you may never leave here," he teased, maybe. "I'm gonna guess that would also mean no sex on the beach, in public or in the sea…"

With a spin that undoubtedly sent water splashing over the side of the tub I faced a startled looking Cy. "Speaking of beaches and the sea," I interrupted, "I've also never sailed the Med!"

"What?" asked a confused and perplexed looking Cy.

"Let me clarify. Do you make a habit of sailing the Med with other women?" I was referencing my uncomfortable conversation with Michael's daughters the previous evening.

"What? What the hell are you talking about?"

"I am talking about a conversation I was privy to last night when Michael's daughters took a little trip down Memory Lane with a yacht, the Med, one summer and you and some Speedos I believe."

"Me? When?" He moved into a less relaxed position, splashing water around us both until I think I saw the penny drop and like that he lay back down in the bath, pulling me closer, kissing me. "Ah, I remember," he smiled, releasing his hold on my head. "That was years ago, fifteen years, maybe more. Sophie and, erm, the younger one…"

"Nieve," I added.

"Yeah, Nieve, and the boy and his mom, but he was only a kid." Cy shook his head, a move that suggested it was a distant memory he really had forgotten about.

"Clearly you in Speedos was more memorable for them than —" I stopped, knowing that I was about to go down a road paved with bitchy comments for Michael's daughters and some kind of fishing mission for me. Both things I knew I'd hate myself for.

"Baby, they were girls. I was a boy, I noticed, but honestly the older one was too much of a princess for me, even then, and the younger one was precisely that, young. Too young. We have no history beyond being stuck on a holiday together, and a few chance encounters courtesy of our parents."

"You know I'm younger than the younger one," I pointed out triumphantly causing an arch to Cy's brow as if sensing a challenge of some sort.

"And you know that if you continue to push at this relentless pace you really won't be able to walk. Oh, and she was too young then. Just like you would have been. But now, well, you're fair game baby."

Cy was wearing a big, sexy grin as he ran a hand through his damp hair, but suddenly I felt cold. His words made me cold. *But now, well, you're fair game baby.* The giddiness I usually felt when he called me baby was absent. I could only focus on the *fair game* part.

"Hey, what did I say?"

"Nothing, sorry. I really need to go or I'll be late," was my best reply as I scrambled to vacate the bath tub.

I heard a *what the fuck* behind me before footsteps began to follow me.

"Will you stop? Talk to me," Cy almost pleaded as I finished drying myself off and put on my underwear.

"Nothing to talk about. I just need to go." I reached for my blouse that Cy got to before me.

"Bullshit! Something happened and I deserve to know what the fuck it was," he insisted, holding my blouse aloft, well out of my reach.

"Would you please give me my blouse?" I asked as I fastened my trousers, ignoring his demand for answers.

"Yes, when you tell me what is going on here."

"Nothing. For fuck's sake," I snapped at a defiant looking Cy. "You know what, forget it. You won't give me my clothing, I'll leave without it." I snarled, grabbing my shoes.

"Like fuck you will," Cy told me, already covering the distance between us and grabbing me so that somehow I ended up flat on my back on the bed with him over me. "I love you, even your bitch, but she only usually comes out to play when I am being an ass or you are trying to get a rise from me. Right now I don't think either of those is true, so I either need to be worried or suspicious and I haven't needed to be suspicious of you before, have I?"

I shook my head because he hadn't.

"We, you and I, we don't lie to each other. I don't and I believe you don't, unless you're scared, like with your dad. So, I said or did something that freaked you out."

"Cy," I cried.

"Talk to me, please."

"You said I was fair game." I felt a little foolish when I heard the words out loud but continued. "When I first started dating Michael he joked that he had deprived the boys my own age of my company..."

"Go on," Cy encouraged with a stroke of my cheek.

"I brushed it off, tried to. I struggle with compliments, but he insisted that he had, but he didn't care because I was fair game."

We stared at each other for what seemed like an age.

"Sorry, I don't know why I reacted that way or why it made me think of that. I felt shitty when he said it and now, knowing some of the things from back then makes it even worse."

"I can't know everything that's ever been said or done to you, certainly not with Michael so you have to tell me. Don't do that stalking off and saying it's nothing or lying that you need to fucking go when you're hurting."

"Okay."

"Good. Look, another week and you will be out of there and things will be better, but in the mean time you just remember that he doesn't deserve you, he never did and he'll never love you like I can."

His eyes were full of emotion, love. For me. I was taken aback at the intensity of his gaze as his words registered and then I laughed.

"What?" he frowned making me laugh harder. "El," he said crossly.

"Sorry, that sounds like a song lyric, *just remember that he doesn't deserve you, he never did and he'll never love you like I can.*"

"Maybe I should diversify into song writing," Cy replied dryly. "I could do a follow up to that one with, You Lick It, It's Yours."

"That one might not get much air play," I suggested with another laugh.

"Couldn't give a shit, but I see your point so maybe I'll save that one for you, baby. After all, I licked it so it's mine," he told me leaning in to brush my lips with his.

"Cy," I whispered.

"I know." He gently pushed my hair back. "Come on, let's go. Put your blouse on because there is no way you're leaving here naked, and Jezza will be waiting.

Chapter Twenty-Three

It was shortly before lunch and I was stuck on a call with another P.A. who was telling me how busy her boss was and that Cy would have to rearrange his schedule to fit in. I smiled as I imagined using one of my boss' favourite phrases to explain how wrong she was, *like fuck he will.*

She was clearly going to keep going on this subject so I let her, and took the opportunity to let my own mind wander to several other times and places. First, I went back to the previous night, after we'd left Cy's house. He'd insisted on coming with me to visit my dad and seemed rather familiar with Angela and a couple of the other residents. My dad had been tired and grouchy which also meant he became disorientated sooner and last night that had evolved into a situation whereby he decided that Cy and I were there to rob him, having broken into his house.

We left early, with Angela calming my dad down and Cy comforting me, again. We stopped at a pub near Cy's house where I'd left my car, at my request as I didn't think I'd ever bring myself to leave his house if I'd returned there last night. I was distressed before I had to return home and as I bent to get into my car, Cy had pulled me back and pointed out a love bite he'd noticed on the back of my neck. It explained why it had felt so sore and sensitive when he'd been mouthing the skin there in the bath.

I'd gone home late enough that after a run around the garden and some ball throwing with Balder I could legitimately go straight to bed. I wore pyjamas in case Michael descended on our bed again, the top of which had a collar to hide my love bite. Could my life get more complicated? Unlikely.

Michael had joined me in bed, and when I'd woken to find him there at half-past five, I'd gotten up and made another early start where I'd caught up with a few things from the previous day I'd spent at Cy's house.

The voice in my ear was still telling me how busy her boss was and that if my boss was intent on meeting in person before contracts were signed then he would need to go to Dublin for a Saturday breakfast meeting.

"I would suggest that if that is your only availability then Mr Parker will need to contact Mr Miller direct as you're attempting to schedule out of office hours," I told her, although Cy had pre-warned me that Mr Parker liked people to jump through hoops and make really inconvenient appointment times.

"Are you his P.A.?" she asked haughtily.

"Yes, but as you're talking Saturday breakfast…."

"Leave it with me and I'll see what I can sort," she retreated and hung up.

"Told you. Jump through hoops," Cy said from his position in the doorway.

"Mmm, well we'll see, won't we?" I yawned.

"Tired baby?"

"A little."

"We could schedule a little lie down." He grinned with a wink, making me laugh but seriously consider his offer.

"Lying down with you usually leaves me more tired."

With a cocky shrug he offered no further words on the topic, switching back to business. "Where and when did Parker suggest?"

"Breakfast, Saturday, Dublin."

"He must be mellowing," Cy smiled. "The last time I met with him he wanted Bueno Aires at Thanksgiving."

"Did you go?" I asked curiously but more than that I was enjoying his chatter, his sharing.

"No, I didn't. My office base at the time was New York and I was planning to go home for Thanksgiving. We met the following week, in New York, so I won't be going to Dublin."

He looked ready to say something else when we both became aware of voices and sounds before Maya appeared with Nieve, Delilah and Rosie.

"Oh, hello," I stammered as Delilah came rushing towards me.

"Nana," she laughed as she hugged me in my now standing position.

"What?" I shrieked at her form of address, a new one.

"Grandad says I can call you Nana," she explained still giggling.

Cy and I exchanged a glance that was basically asking why he would say that when we were splitting up in a matter of days. Unless he was cooking something else up.

"Yeah, well Grandad was wrong, and El will do me just fine," I told Delilah as I kissed the top of her head gently.

"Okay," she agreed as we both watched her mother thrust Rosie upon me whilst she thrust herself upon Cy.

"Long time no see," Nieve cooed as she hugged him.

I smiled as he reluctantly returned her embrace.

"Yeah. What is it, fifteen years?" he asked looking over at me mouthing *which one is she?*

"Nieve," I called, but she barely looked at me.

"Delilah, this is my boss, Mr Miller," I told the little girl hoping to prise her mother off my lover.

"Hello," Delilah said awkwardly.

Cy was oblivious to Nieve as he stared at me with Rosie wedged on my hip, jigging the little girl up and down as I spoke to her in a high, singy voice. Maybe this was too much for him, my husband's family. People he used to know turning up out of the blue.

"Hi." He smiled at Delilah. "So, what brings you here?" he asked nervously as he managed to unhand himself from Nieve, briefly.

"I thought we could catch up and say hi and maybe take El to lunch," she replied and although my horrified expression was behind her, Cy's was still above her as she now seemed permanently attached to my boss and lover. "Or maybe if she's busy and you're not..."

"No!" I seemed to screech, startling everyone except for Rosie who looked up at me and laughed. "I'm free, was just about to go to lunch," I added in a slightly calmer tone I hoped would hide the fact that I would have done just about anything at that point to get Nieve away from my lover. As far away as possible, even if I knew and believed that she wouldn't do anything with her kids here and a husband she was totally smitten with. But now, more than ever I needed Cy to be mine and nothing to do with Michael and his family.

"Then I will see you later, Ms Ross." He smiled with relief. "Nieve," he added with a step away from her, a step towards me where Rosie thrust her arms up in his direction. Yeah, my man was a woman magnet.

Cy didn't even pause as he scooped the baby girl from my arms and held her, gently at first and then more *roughly* as he threw her around. I was sure I was gaping and drooling at this vision. Cy and a baby. My womb and lady hormones were going into overdrive as Rosie's face disappeared and a beautiful little boy with dark hair and dark eyes was superimposed on her baby body, if only in my mind. My baby boy being held by his daddy. I was sure I could hear my own laboured breathing and there was definitely wetness and swelling between my legs. Is that what I wanted? A baby. Cy's baby. Is that what he wanted?

Delilah tugged on my arm firmly with a call that suggested it wasn't the first time she'd called me. "El, are you ready?" the little girl asked. "I'm starving."

"Yes, of course, sorry." I smiled in my partial haze of the future. A future. My future.

"Nice to see you again," Cy said to Nieve who was kissing his cheek and then grabbing Delilah's hand to walk away with me following.

"Baby," Cy called throwing me into a panic that he had called me that within earshot of Nieve.

"What?" I replied in a hissed whisper as I spun on my heels.

"Baby, the baby." He grinned looking down at Rosie who was babbling happily as she looked up at Cy.

"Shit!" I muttered wondering how me, Nieve and Delilah had forgotten Rosie.

"If that's her first word it will be your fault," Cy chided as he handed the little girl to me, transferring her from his arms to mine. A simple, necessary and perfunctory move and yet it felt like one of the most intimate moments we'd shared. "You okay?" he asked with a small frown as I adjusted Rosie's position on my hip.

"Hmm, this is all a little unexpected and, erm, weird," I admitted.

"We can talk, later." He smiled and seemed as though he was about to lean in and land a kiss on me, but he pulled back, held back.

"El," Nieve called to me. "Rosie!" she cried in panic.

I laughed at her realisation. "I've got her," I called back and left for what I feared would be a very long lunch.

****

Twenty minutes into lunch Delilah had eaten and was throwing herself into the ball pit of the pub we were sitting in. Rosie was fast asleep in my arms leaving me to eat one handed, which was okay with a chicken salad. Nieve was devouring a huge burger topped with a dozen different items.

"Hungry?" I asked with a laugh.

"Starving, permanently, pregnant hungry…if it's not nailed down, I eat it," she grinned.

"Wow, congratulations. Does your dad know?"

"Thanks. No, nobody. I thought I'd tell you all at once. It wasn't exactly planned, but we're happy," she revealed.

"Then I'm pleased for you all," I told her and meant every word of it. I liked Nieve, and Sophie, although Nieve was the easier of the two to like.

"You're not wearing your wedding ring."

I glanced from my bare finger to Nieve's expressionless face as her blunt and flat sounding words hit me.

"El," she sighed. "My dad is a wonderful father but we, Sophie and I have lived through four of his marriages and three of his divorces. He's a shit husband and a very hard man for a wife to love."

"It's complicated." I sounded lame to my own ears.

"Always is with Dad. Let me tell you a few things about

297

him…"

"Nieve." I attempted to stop her. These things she was going to reveal might not be for the best.

She waved away my attempt and continued.

"He married my mother because she was a good choice, the right choice. She loved him and thought it would be enough. That in time he would love her as she loved him. He didn't, although he loved her in his own way. He had countless affairs and we all knew when they were happening."

"How?" I asked, enthralled now.

"He changed when they were occurring. Initially he would be attentive, to us all. The perfect husband and father and then the husband role would slip a little. He was never abusive or anything like that, but..." she whispered, drawing me across the table we shared. "Once his affair went beyond whatever mark means it's more than sex he would become faithful, to his lover, not his wife."

"Wow," I replied, unsure whether Michael had cheated on me and if that was why sex between us had stopped. I realised that almost from the moment I'd met Cy I had moved beyond the mark Nieve spoke about. I had only wanted to be with Cy from that first night in the club.

"My mum always suspected that there were a couple of recurring ones. One especially. I think whenever his marriage ended he would throw himself into the affair and then find it came up short. Probably because it would be viewed negatively, his affair or maybe they weren't suitable as any more. You know what a snob he is."

"Yes," I agreed and thought she was right. Michael's greatest issue was other people's opinions, along with image and appearances. All of his wives had been of a type I realised; educated, attractive, sociably competent and fitted the acceptable mould for a man in his position. I was the nearest to an exception with my considerably younger age, but clearly my virginity and naivety had cancelled that out.

"You were probably the best and worst choice of wife for him, no offence." She half-smiled.

I ignored her comment and certainly didn't take offence. I

agreed with her and didn't need to hash out our potentially differing thoughts on why.

"Has he said anything to you? About us, me and him?" I hoped he'd at least hinted at our impending separation.

"No, but the night before last was tense and as my daughter sleeps soundly in the day but not at night I've been aware of you being up very, very early in the morning. Usually within an hour of Dad going to bed."

"Shit!" I whispered and laughed as Rosie smiled in her sleep. "I'll apologise now if it's her first word."

"El, I like you and I love my dad. When you and he married I was concerned, me and Sophie. You were younger, pretty, in need of rescue and he was very well off, able to rescue you and presumably flattered by your attention."

"It really wasn't like that," I said defensively. "Although I understand what it might have looked like."

"I know it wasn't like that, I really do. I remember seeing you on your wedding day. You looked so beautiful." She smiled and I smiled back. "And yet there was something not right."

"What do you mean?" I wondered if there was something wrong that far back, at the beginning.

"I love Rod, with every fibre of my being. He is my husband, my lover, my confidante. I trust him implicitly with even the worst of me. I know that no matter what I do I can lean on him. Depend on him. When I met him it was instant, the lust," she told me making me laugh again. "And then it became more. Emotions became involved and the lust along with that made it better than ever. By the time we married, although it was a whirlwind, but by the time I walked down the aisle to marry him it was all I wanted, forever. I ate, slept and breathed Rod. Me and Rod and our future together. I had never chosen to love anyone as much before. I remember that at one point I was dragging Dad down the aisle, I couldn't wait to get there. You didn't behave like a bride who was unsure she'd be able to take her next breath without her groom being her husband, El. You looked beautiful, pained and resigned. And Dad, he looked like he'd just pulled off the deal of his life, and he might have."

"Shit!" I said again as one of Rosie's eyes flickered open

making me smile and then remember Cy and his tattoo. Lulu's eye tattoo. "I did what I thought was right, Nieve. I loved your father and I thought it was the right love between a husband and a wife. I now know it wasn't. He did take care of me, rescue me, and somehow those things and love and duty and responsibility got rolled up in a ball with Susan and your father and before I knew it I was married. He has been a good husband, I can't say he hasn't. But I changed, grew without him and before I knew it we were poles apart with very different needs."

"So, what are you doing, staying with him?" Nieve asked flatly, startling me with the lack of emotion in her question.

"I've told him I'm leaving but he wanted me to wait until you'd all been and he insists there's some business thing."

"He wants you to stay for business reasons, and you agreed?" she asked, slightly outraged now.

"Kind of. I agreed to this week. For him to tell you all and then he has agreed to continue paying my dad's medical bills until I am sorted and Balder, I can take Balder with me."

Nieve stared without a single blink for several seconds.

"Let me get this right. He got you to stay by using your father's bills and access to the dog?"

"I wouldn't put it like that…"

"No? I would. Shit! I spoke to Mum a few months ago about a friend who was getting divorced and the husband was a bit of a masochist, or so I thought. He turned everything so that it was about him, what he'd done for her and the sacrifices he'd made. How their marriage failing would affect him. Everything came back to him and his suffering."

"Hence the masochism?"

"Exactly, but Mum blew that out of the water and insisted he was a sadist."

"How?" I frowned.

"You'll see. Mum explained that Dad had been like that when their marriage was failing. He wanted their marriage to work, but only on his terms and he did that thing of pointing out all the things he'd done for Mum and provided for her, his sacrifices."

"A masochist?" I warily asked.

"You'd think, like my friend's husband, but no. Mum insisted that they were both sadists. You see this is the thing, when they were insistent that they had made sacrifices, only wanted the best and bent over backwards to give it my mum reckons they both did that with one reason in mind. To inflict guilt and in turn pain and then they'd sit back and watch. Enjoy the hurt they caused as they continued to wield the power. Look, I have no reason to dispute what my mum said, and you know better than I do if that's how things are between you and Dad, but I saw him with Callum and Moses' mums and I can remember moments like that. That sail around the Med. He was vile to Trish and he only mellowed when Edward appeared in Spain."

"I see," was all I could manage as I thought that Nieve, or at least her mother made real sense and again the mention of Edward made me suspicious.

"Like I said El, I like you and I love my dad, but if he is using your dad and the bloody dog to make you bend to his will…you deserve to be happy and so does he, although I have no clue what would make him truly happy, not sure he does…"

"Hey, look who we've found here," came Edward's voice as he sat down between me and Nieve. "Suits you," he smiled as he looked down at Rosie in my arms.

"I might just check on Delilah." Nieve was getting up and kissing Edward on her way out.

"What the fuck are you doing here? Are you following me?" I asked, knowing I must sound crazy at best.

"Mind your mouth in front of the baby," he chastened firmly.

"Sorry." I felt genuine remorse rather than pissed off as I thought I would have been on the receiving end of correction from Edward.

"I am not following you. I spoke to Cy. He said Nieve was out for lunch and Tia is on her way."

"What? Why?" I sighed.

"To chat and catch up?"

I eyed him with suspicion again. "Who are you, really?"

"I don't know. I haven't decided yet." He smiled as Tia

appeared.

"Hey, do we get to play too?" she asked, pointing to the ball pit as Nieve returned and with a squeal was hugging and reintroducing herself to Tia.

I watched on for a few more minutes until Rosie woke and then prepared to leave, handing the baby to her mother. Slipping my jacket on I flicked my hair free of the collar and leaned in to kiss Nieve.

"By the way you have a love bite on your neck. Maybe wear a scarf," she whispered without judgement. "And remember, everyone deserves to be as happy as me, and find a Rod to love and be loved by."

I had no clue if she suspected the love bite was her father's handiwork or not, but I had no intention of asking. Although, I loved her idea of me finding a Rod, or a Cy, as it would be for me. Edward kissed and hugged me warmly while Tia walked me to the door.

"You okay?" she asked. "Cy called and as Edward and I were having lunch at mine..."

"You came to rescue me?"

"Maybe. Oh, you might want to tell Count Cy that he's left a hickey on your neck, back, kind of."

"I know," I snapped and immediately regretted it. "Sorry. I know. He knows. You know and so does Nieve. I have no idea if she thinks it's off her father. I have to go."

****

I arrived back at the office and found Cy's office door open, allowing me to hear his voice. Just his, meaning he was on a call. Walking into his office I was already casting my coat aside and banging the door shut behind me causing him to look up with a frown.

"No, my P.A. was right. You want to meet me out of office hours, and she can't make that call Parker, so..."

I had already pulled my jumper off and was unfastening my skirt that was falling to the ground as I reached Cy's lap that I straddled. He was smiling and staring, but mostly he was confused. Holding a finger up to indicate that he needed just a minute I took the receiver from Cy's hand and with confidence and bravado I didn't know existed within me I spoke to Mr Parker.

"Mr Parker, this is Eloise Ross, Mr Miller's P.A. I gather you believe I should have been able to schedule my boss' appointments?" I paused to allow him to reply, he didn't so I continued. "I am inclined to agree with you. So how about this, Mr Miller will meet with you on Monday morning at nine a.m. here, in his office. No trips to Dublin or anywhere else and definitely no late night, early morning, weekend or public holiday meetings."

Cy was sitting back in his chair, hands at his side, looking at me as though he didn't even recognise me. Mr Parker was still silent, so I spoke again.

"I should probably tell you, Mr Parker, I am about to leave my husband, doubtlessly resulting in an acrimonious divorce involving emotional blackmail and a custody battle for a Great Dane. Oh, and my period is due and there is no sign of chocolate in this building."

"Put Miller back on," the man at the other end of the phone demanded.

"He'd like to speak to you," I told Cy, nerves kicking in suddenly, me astride my boss who was fully dressed whilst I sat in my underwear having just acted in the most unprofessional way of my career with a rich, influential business associate.

The nerves that had begun in my stomach were crawling up my gullet into my throat, threatening to propel my chicken salad across Cy's chest as he said nothing. Not a word, and then he hung up.

"Cy, I, sorry, I, erm…" was as much as my stammering would contribute.

"I have no idea what the fuck has happened during lunch, but Parker will be here at nine a.m. Monday, and as a man who's been married for twenty-three years he seriously recommends that I get my ass to the nearest store to stock up on chocolate for the next week," Cy laughed. "He also made an open job offer to you. Clearly, he likes your bitch baby, but he doesn't realise that you're my bitch. Only mine."

"You're not angry?" I nervously enquired, not caring about

job offers. I only wanted Cy's approval and understanding because he was right, I was his bitch. Only his. Forget the bitch part. All I was belonged solely to him.

"I dunno, maybe, but more than anything I am as horny as fuck and you appear to be almost naked baby."

"Oh yeah," I grinned with a nervous nibble of my bottom lip. "Maybe you ought to shed a few items, unless you want me to feel self-conscious."

"No fucking problem," Cy replied, already getting to his feet, taking me with him. Depositing me on the edge of his desk, he began removing clothes.

****

I finished my work and although we hadn't spoken about my return from lunch and my mood, we both knew something significant had occurred.

"You wanna get some dinner? Out or we could go home and cook." Cy smiled as he waited for a response. I really wanted his smile to remain. I didn't want to make him sad. I loved his smile, especially the one he wore now. The one he only ever wore for me when things were good and settled between us.

"You know I would love that, but I gave him this week."

"And next week?" Cy asked taking a seat on the corner of my desk.

"Are you asking about Michael or dinner?"

"Are you being deliberately awkward and argumentative or has your inner bitch not had her fill with Parker?" he asked with only a frown. No smile now.

"I was asking a serious question. Hoping for some clarification of exactly what you were asking." I sighed. "Oh, and my inner bitch is back now only because of your arsehole."

I knew I was wearing a scowl and a pout and didn't really care.

"Sorry," Cy offered with sincerity that saw his hand covering mine, gently stroking and caressing the skin to life. "I thought you were trying to piss me off."

"I wasn't. So, dinner next week? Yes. Any night you want, and I would love to cook dinner with you, and Michael? I agreed to this week, so next week, no agreement. I actually have no idea what the hell I am going to do, where I am going to live, but it has to be done. Nieve made me realise I was being manipulated still."

"Shame she didn't visit sooner." Cy smiled. He pulled me up to hold me against him. One hand reached for the back of my neck while the other one found the small of my back and settled there.

I inhaled the glorious scent that was Cy and allowed my nose and mouth to nestle in his neck where I sniffed and then gently kissed him. "I love you," I whispered.

"Me too, but I am guessing you're about to tell me that you have to go."

"Sorry."

"No need, we just need to get through this week and then it's just you and me, baby."

"Mmm, I can't wait."

Chapter Twenty-Four

Throughout the remainder of the week I broached the subject of our marriage, our separation and Michael actually telling his children what was happening. He shut me down at every turn. By Sunday lunchtime I was beginning to think he wasn't planning on telling any of them, even though Nieve knew and I assumed Rod was aware of the imminent end of my marriage via his wife.

I made an excuse to go upstairs and took the time to begin looking through my belongings, deciding what I could and should take with me. I had two piles accumulating on the bed when Michael came in, closing the door behind him.

"What's this?" He waved his hand at the bed.

"Sorting, with a view to packing."

"El, don't be ridiculous," he sighed with exasperation as he pushed one of my piles so that it merged with the other. "You're not leaving," he said with confidence. "Once the kids have gone, we'll talk, but business is taking a while longer."

"Michael, I don't care about business, or talking. We're done. I am done, and it's over."

"You don't mean that because if my business doesn't take off, I might not be able to meet all of my commitments, like, ooh, Jeremy's bills…and let's not forget Balder, he needs stability and routine and here is where he'll get that."

I turned on my heels and shook my head. "You think I wasn't expecting this? I wasn't when we first made this agreement for the week, but then I realised, well a lot of things, so the week is up tomorrow and I will be going, Michael."

He gripped my arm tightly, too tightly making me wince.

"Dad," called Sophie from somewhere downstairs.

"This isn't resolved, Eloise," he snapped and left.

Michael may have had some unresolved issues still, but not me. I had decided that my father's care would have to be met, one way or another. Surely between me and my siblings we'd be able to pay the bills without Michael's money and then there was Balder. I loved the big dopey boy, but Michael had been right when he said that he needed stability and routine, which I might struggle to give him immediately meaning he would undoubtedly be better off remaining with Michael in the only home he'd ever known. Even if I'd cry like a baby when I had to leave him. Maybe I could get some kind of visitation. I guessed that depended on Michael. I needed some legal advice about canine access, quickly.

'The children' were all leaving on Monday, after I left for work so I bid them all farewell, thinking I might never see any of them again and although that saddened me, I accepted it if it meant I could move on with my own life and it was understandable that they would take their father's side if battle lines were drawn.

****

At half-past eight on Monday morning Maya appeared in the doorway with a very attractive man of around forty-five years. He wasn't Cy, 'oh my God that degree of gorgeous should be illegal' attractive, but more of an 'I am successful, powerful and know my way around the female anatomy well enough to make you scream' attractive. I felt a grin spread across my face and wondered why I hadn't noticed attractive men before I met Cy as frequently as I did now.

"Morning El, this is Mr Parker. He has an appointment with Mr Miller at nine," Maya informed me as I flushed at the memory of my previous conversation with the man standing before me.

"Ah, Mr Parker. Eloise Ross, Mr Miller's P.A." I said, extending a hand in greeting.

"Ah, Miss Ross, soon to be divorced and fighting for custody of the dog. How lovely to meet you," he replied with a

307

serious expression, although his eyes twinkled with good humour making me laugh in spite of my embarrassment. "And the period? I assume it arrived safely and the mood has lightened along with the homicidal thoughts at the idea of no chocolate in the building." His words made me laugh loudly while Maya gawped at us both from the side-lines until an awareness washed over me. The awareness that was Cy.

"Hey, Parker, my staff are not for hire. And if they were, this kind of conversation would be highly irregular and more than a little inappropriate. Shall we?" he asked, already shaking the other man's hand and guiding him into his office. "Some tea and coffee please, Ms Ross."

"Yes, Mr Miller," I replied as the office door closed leaving me with Maya who was still gawping, most likely at the revelations she'd just witnessed including details of my menstrual cycle.

"You and Michael, Mr Stanton are divorcing?"

"Yes, eventually. Although my leaving him is imminent, like tonight or tomorrow imminent," I replied, feeling a little guilty that one of my few friends in the world had just heard about my marriage ending from a third party neither of us had ever met.

"That's, erm, quick," she replied, following me to the kitchen where I needed to make tea and coffee for Cy and Mr Parker.

"I suppose, but there's no going back for me, not now that I've realised I don't love Michael as a wife should, never have, and he knows I've been having an affair with Cy."

"An affair?" Maya queried. "Is that what this is, between you and the boss man, an affair? Because if it is you can come back from that. If you want to, if Mr Stanton wants to."

I sighed as the coffee machine began to chug the hot liquid into the jug.

"I love Michael like an uncle, a friend of the family. I didn't realise that wasn't how I was supposed to until," I trailed off, scared to say the words out loud. Afraid to see the expression on my friend's face when the words were out in case she looked at me with pity, disbelief or worse still, as though I was stupid and delusional. I slowly looked up and faced Maya to finish my sentence. "Until I met Cy. Until I fell in love with him and discovered how you're supposed to love a man, a boyfriend, lover..."

"Shit! Then you're doing the right thing," she confirmed with a smile of support and encouragement. "You moving in with him?"

"God no! In fact, I have no clue where I'm going. Michael knows this is happening and he has managed to delay it a few times with one thing and another, including a little emotional blackmail, but I can't just rock up at Cy's front door with my possessions. It's too much too soon."

Maya nodded and then with a hint of accusation asked, "Is that what he says, the boss, too much too soon?"

"No, the opposite. He'd be happy for me to move in, but I don't think that's wise and he's suggested that his sister would let me stay with her but again that may not be for the best, after all, she is his sister."

"You get on though? You always seem friendly."

"Yeah, but if Cy and I argue or things end, where does that leave me? Sorry, I probably sound a bitch; I want to leave my husband, have nowhere to go and am being picky about my options." I smiled wryly. "Michael currently takes care of my dad's bills, but I think he's going to go back on his offer to continue quite quickly once I leave and he won't let me keep the dog," I added thinking I probably sounded quite pathetic and a little immature with the last comment.

"Stay with me. I have a spare room and two can live almost as cheaply as one," she offered.

"I don't expect a freebie."

"Okay, pay what you can, share the housework and if you need to pay your dad's bills for a while there's no pressure from me. Oh, and if you get to see the dog I have a garden." She smiled. "Seriously El, I hate being on my own for the most part so maybe we could do each other a favour until you get things sorted and find your own place or whatever."

"Are you sure?" I asked with excitement. This was probably my best option, my only real option.

"Course. Think about it and let me know." She pulled me in

for a brief hug before turning towards the door to leave.

"Maya, yes. Yes please, thank you."

"Cool, let me know when. The spare room is all made up so whenever you're ready is good for me, and honestly, I have wondered what the boss man looks like without his top on and maybe now I'll get to see if my imagination has done him justice." She grinned before leaving me with tea and coffee to take through to Cy and mental images of the boss man topless.

I sat at my desk for the two hours Cy was with Mr Parker, Lance, as I knew his name to be after he introduced himself to me during my second coffee run that had also involved pastries. I flitted between real work and list making for my departure from my marital home. I even dropped a text to Michael asking if he would be home that evening for us to talk. He had replied with what I thought was a curt and irritated, *yes, of course, this is my home.*

My list mainly consisted of things to pack and take with me and if I was honest it was a relatively short list with clothes, toiletries, photos and very little else. I was staring down at my list and wondered if this really was all I had accumulated in five years of marriage. I had my car, which was mine, all registered in my own name and had no connection to Michael at all. It was unnecessary to add my car to my list, but I did add cheque book and savings account book. Thank goodness I'd kept separate bank accounts from Michael that my salary was paid into and from that my savings had accrued. He, Michael, had paid all of the bills and in doing so had allowed me to gather some savings which I would need to keep and hopefully increase for when, rather than if, I needed to pick up my dad's bills.

Cy's door was opening and the sound of laughter was filling the space around me.

"You drive a hard bargain Miller," Mr Parker accused with laughter.

"Mmm, well it would have been a much harder bargain had you insisted on Saturday in Dublin," Cy retorted making the other man laugh.

"You know I like to make an occasion of these things and Martha will schedule my appointments when I desire," he grinned, looking at me now.

"Martha?" I queried.

"My P.A. You and she spoke, briefly," he smirked with a cock of his head.

"Yes, we did. She was very, erm," I paused, struggling for the right word. "Persistent. She was very persistent."

Mr Parker laughed, throwing his head back revealing his neck that I could imagine his wife or maybe Martha wanting to lick and bite, like I did with Cy. I flushed, I could feel it at the thought of Cy's neck and my mouth and my lover could clearly see that I was thinking of less than professional things judging by his raised eyebrow and questioning glance.

"Well, persistent is one word, but Martha is worth her weight in gold, as I think you are..." he began but was cut off by Cy.

"I have warned you, Parker. Back off from my staff," he told the other man quite seriously.

"Your staff? Okay." Mr Parker grinned mischievously before he winked at me. "But with a divorce, a clean start might be the way to go."

I laughed at his cheek and Cy's annoyed expression, but then Lance Parker slid a business card across my desk, leaving it to rest between my hands. Glancing down I was ready to set Mr Parker straight on where my loyalties and professional future lay and then stopped.

"Georgina Parker?" I asked.

"Yes, Georgie, my wife, an excellent divorce specialist, legally speaking. I just thought if things turned sour and there was an innocent dog stuck in the middle."

"Thank you," I whispered, hoping not to cry at the reality of this situation, my situation.

"I don't know you, Ms Ross, not beyond our brief interactions, but I know your husband, Michael, in business terms. He can be a tough nut to crack. A very, very tough nut, so you'll want the best, Georgie." He smiled proudly then turned back to Cy, "As usual it's been traumatic! I'll call you later in the week to seal things." He reached for Cy's hand to shake before heading out towards the lifts, escorted by Cy leaving me alone with the number of an apparently eminent divorce lawyer.

****

Cy had been stuck on an overseas call when it was time for me to leave. As I loitered near his open door it was clear that he wasn't going to be done anytime soon and I really, really needed to go home, to my marital home, briefly at least. I grabbed my things and by the time I reached the lift Maya was already waiting. Looking up she smiled and gently rubbed my shoulder.

"You okay? I'm guessing not, but my offer stands, if you still want it."

"Yes, yes please. I would love to take you up on the offer of your spare room, thank you." I smiled as we stepped into the lift together. "There is so much in my life that I am unsure of. And in the middle of that is your offer that I am certain of. I need to go home and talk to Michael so I'm unsure when I'll need to move in, tonight or tomorrow."

"Either is good for me El. Call me tonight and let me know what the plan is. If you need me to come and grab some of your stuff or just give you a bit of moral support let me know, please."

"Thanks. I might take you up on that, especially as I can't really call on Cy to come over," I said with a half-smile I didn't really feel.

We reached the car park and were about to go our separate ways. "I'll get you some spare keys cut at the supermarket on my way home, so whenever you're ready," Maya said with another sympathetic rub of my shoulder.

****

Before I entered the house that by now should have been empty of visitors, I dropped Cy a quick text. Apart from anything else I didn't think he'd be too thrilled that I'd left without telling him and also because I just needed to get this over with and a conversation with Cy would only have delayed that.

<Sorry I left without speaking to you, but you seemed stuck on the phone. I have gone home, unsure whether I will remain there tonight, but the week I gave is over. I have somewhere to stay…will call you later, when I know what's

what. Please don't be mad at me, I love you X>

<Not so stuck that I couldn't have spared some time for you, but you know that, you wanted to go without me! I'm not happy that you're back there alone baby. Where are you going to stay? You already had somewhere, several 'somewheres' but we can talk about that later. I am giving you two hours and if I haven't heard from you by then I am coming over. I can't say that I'm not mad. I love you too X>

I slipped my phone into my bag without replying further and walked to the front door, slowly. More slowly than I ever had before and found Michael in the kitchen talking to the dog.

"Hello," I whispered nervously as I tried to imagine just how this might pan out.

"El, are you okay?" His question threw me a real curve ball that left me confused and more nervous than I'd already been. "Shall we have dinner? I could prepare us something," he offered.

"I'm not hungry. I'd rather just sort things between us, Michael." I really wished I hadn't come back alone.

"Tea. Let's at least have a cup of tea and see if we can't sort things between us, how about that?"

"Okay," I conceded, thinking that a cup of tea couldn't be any more than, well, a cup of tea.

We sat opposite each other at the table in the kitchen and while Michael stared across at me, I stared at the dog, the floor, my hands, anything other than my husband.

"El, love, talk to me, please. Tell me what you want, what you need from me?"

That certainly got my attention. The idea that he was willing to listen and consider what I needed from him.

"I never wanted things to turn out this way," I began. "I loved you. Thought I loved you as a husband should be loved and I was happy, but I can't say that anymore."

"I see." He responded with a slight bristle.

"Maybe we were always too different. You were so worldly wise, and I wasn't. I just allowed myself to get caught up in other people's plans rather than figuring out my own plans and making them a reality."

"That doesn't sound like love and happiness."

"Sorry, I really am. I don't blame you entirely," I admitted with honesty because I did blame him for his part in where we were now as well as my manipulation. "I accept my own portion of blame and Susan's."

"Susan loves you. She wants what's best. I was best. Still am, if only you could see past this ridiculous fling you're involved in," he said quietly, but there was no disguising the snarkiness. Clearly, I had hit a raw nerve I realised with his next bitter comment. "Maybe you should try thinking with your head."

"I'm not doing this Michael, taking the blame for everything and allowing you to absolve yourself and Susan for where we are now and as for my fling..."

Cutting me off Michael said, "Are you about to tell me that this is different, that it's not a fling? You are!" he laughed incredulously. "It would seem that I am not the only one who saw naivety in you if he has you believing that. Has he told you that you're special, different or that he loves you?"

I stared across at Michael, refusing to speak, unwilling to defend myself against these, these what, accusations? Even with the acknowledgement to myself that I loved Cy and believed he loved me I would not do this. I would not attempt, and undoubtedly fail to ratify that what Cy and I had was real because there was no way Michael would accept that. If I was being fair to him, that was understandable. I had been having an affair behind my husband's back, betrayed him and as such he needed, maybe for reasons of pride or dignity to condemn and dismiss the importance of what Cy and I shared. I was prepared to allow him to do that, but I refused to be drawn into it further.

"We agreed that I would stay here last week, until your children left and they've left, so now I am going to do the same," I said flatly, already on my feet and turning towards the door.

Part of me was expecting Michael to follow me, to say something to stop me. A threat, something, but there was nothing until I returned from upstairs with two large suitcases packed.

"You're actually doing this?" he asked with sheer disbelief in his voice.

"I told you I was."

"Eloise, this is ridiculous. You must know that. Where exactly are you going, or is the answer to that an obvious one? Trading my bed for his?"

I shook my head. I wanted Michael to understand that I was leaving him for me, not for Cy. That our marriage had failed because of us, us and possibly Susan with a large dose of circumstance. I might have begun an affair, but it had become something that brought me clarity and indirectly led me to this place, at the foot of the stairs with two suitcases packed.

"I'm going to stay with a friend, not Cy."

"How honourable." Michael sighed. "There is no need, we can make this right El."

"We can't."

"We can if you want to. Tell me what you need; a holiday, a new house, a baby, whatever you want," he pleaded, making me feel guilty again because I was fairly certain that Michael and his needs had changed very little in the last five or six years, unlike mine.

I shook my head.

"Is it sex, is it that basic, the problem we have between us?"

Sex had been an issue. I had enjoyed sex, making love with my husband, but over time his interest had dwindled to nothing and although he cited health problems, which were genuine I was no longer convinced that those things were at the root of our problems. Then there was the fact that I had never known that sex could be like it was with Cy. That I could be so affected on an emotional and sensory level by such a physical act. If I was aiming for melodrama, I would now be acknowledging that Cy had indeed ruined me for any other man.

"I will see a doctor. There are things that can be done, tablets," he offered and for a split second I loved him all over again for offering that. It can't have been easy for such a proud man who cared so much about things being right and proper, but he continued to speak. "If we can address the physical aspect of the problem, I think I can ignore my lack of interest."

Had he actually just said that to me? That essentially Viagra would equip him to fuck me physically in spite of his lack of interest in me, my body and any combined sexual pleasure? Yes, yes he had, and even with my horrified stare in his direction he was making no attempt to clarify or dress it up a little more attractively. He simply stared back as I imagined what Cy would say if I asked him how he felt about having sex with me.

I remembered some of the things he'd already said about it; that first night we met, on the dance floor when he was pressed against me and had asked me, 'Do you have any idea how close you are to getting fucked right here, right now?' Then there was one time when we'd had a bitch/arsehole moment and he'd told me, 'I can't get you out my head, I want to touch you, kiss you, fuck you, it's all I can do not to rip your panties off, bend you over and fuck you senseless whenever you walk into the room.' He wanted me, he had a natural interest in me, maybe on the most animalistic, base level, but his interest was real and undisguisable. I recalled his realisation that sex between me and Michael had become non-existent when his reaction had been instantaneous and honest as he'd said, 'That is a fucking crime baby...I can't imagine living with someone like you and not permanently planning on fucking you, actually fucking you or recovering from it.' I was sure that as far as classically romantic lines went that wasn't acceptable, but I'd loved it when he'd said it and I loved the memory too. We'd discussed Michael's suggestion that we could have a baby, an idea I'd dismissed and assured Cy that I was still on the pill. I could feel a smile pulling at my lips as I replayed his words, 'And rest assured if I wanted to start a family with you we'd be fucking twenty four seven with no protection.'

My mind was suddenly awash with Cy and the mess that was here, before me; Michael, my failed marriage and what I suspected would be a messy divorce with a fallout of horrendous proportions was becoming less significant.

"El," he broke into my thoughts. "I'm trying here, love. I know I haven't been perfect in this and I want to put it right.

Let's try again, me and you. We could, should have a baby. You'd feel differently if you were a mother, and you'd be a wonderful mother."

He was serious and genuine in his attempts to keep our marriage intact, I could see that, although his reasons were still suspect as I believed this was about appearances and little to do with love, real love.

"It's too late, Michael," I replied firmly, not wanting to offer anything resembling hope. "You want to be married, but I think I'm incidental to that. You have three ex-wives and children with each of them and they failed. I don't think a baby to paper over the cracks is the way forward for us or it."

"Okay, you don't want children. I can respect that." He nodded thoughtfully.

Clearly my face revealed the answer to that question because in an instant Michael's posture straightened stiffly.

"Oh, you do want a baby."

I nodded.

"Just not with me."

I nodded again.

"El, I'm scared for you, this thing with Cy won't last, can't last. He will tire of you, become bored and leave you. Do you honestly think you're the first office fling he's engaged in?"

I didn't reply because I believed Cy when he'd told me that married women and employees were not something he became involved in. My words were unnecessary anyway it seemed as Michael continued to speak, at me more than to me.

"Stay, give it six months. I'll get this business thing off the ground, inject some serious time and cash into it and you can see how this thing with Cy really is. Nobody need ever know…"

And there it was, the most important things in this whole situation for Michael, business, money and appearances. I just needed to leave. This was pointless, all of it. The clock chimed next to the door and I realised I had been here for almost two hours and if I didn't leave soon, leave and make contact with Cy, he would be rocking up here and that would be bad, for us all. Not least my poor confused dog who was watching me and Michael closely from his position about six feet away.

"Somebody once gave me the perfect definition of wanting to get married," I told Michael, already replaying Cy's words in my head from when I'd asked him why anyone got married.

"Because you can't bear to be without the other person. Because you can think of nothing else, day or night but them and the idea of them ever being with anyone else drives you to the verge of insanity. That you need to make them totally and utterly yours. Without them at your side for the rest of your life would mean your life would be less fulfilling and more painful than anything you can imagine, and as a man I personally love the idea of that someone taking everything I am, especially my name. Or am I wrong?"

"What's yours?" I asked and waited for a few seconds.

"See, this is where your naivety morphs into simple immaturity," he replied angrily, clearly getting pissed off with my constant refusals to bend to his will, something relatively new in our relationship, well as new as me and Cy. "Now, enough!" he snapped. "I have been nothing other than reasonable, but enough is enough. You are going nowhere aside from back upstairs to put your things away. We both know that you're far too sensible and loyal to risk Jeremy's future care."

"Goodbye Michael," I said flatly. He was right, enough really was enough.

"Eloise, don't you dare do this. Don't you dare walk out on me after all I have done for you, you selfish little bitch!" he snarled, pulling on my case so that I was forced to face him.

"I will be in touch, to discuss Balder and handing over the cost of my dad's care..." I began.

He laughed, throwing his head back, like a comedic villain. "You'll be back, sooner rather than later. When Cy finds himself someone new, younger, less naïve and needy, you'll come back and I will laugh at you, you and your desperation. You will promise me anything and everything to take you back, and I might, but I assure you if I do you will pay for this. For tonight, your biggest mistake ever, for every day from this day on."

I could feel my eyes widening until I was gawping and gaping at the man I had once pledged my life to and again I barely recognised this new facet to his personality. I could also feel my phone vibrating somewhere in my bag that was resting across my body. Fortunately it was on silent otherwise it may have made this hideously ridiculous situation a whole lot worse.

"Nothing to say? Maybe that will be a stipulation, that you remain silent unless I grant you permission to speak." He sounded as I imagined a Victorian father would. "Or maybe I won't take you back because by then I will have ruined you, you and your reputation. You won't have even reached the car tonight before I am calling Denny and Elizabeth, sharing my plight. My heartbreak. How do you think that will go down? Elizabeth already suspects the worst of you and I am going to confirm that for her before you make it to her son's bed tonight and that will leave exactly zero chance of her ever allowing you anywhere near her son or family. She will ensure that you are out in the cold and you will have to watch as Cy moves on. Sit back as he finds a nice girl of his mother's choosing. A girl he'll ship back home with him to marry and have his babies and she will be as far removed from you as anyone could ever be."

Unshed tears were stinging my eyes as Michael's words were cruelly expressing my own fears. From the beginning Elizabeth had done nothing to hide her distaste for young, pretty girls on the make, taking advantage of old, stupid, rich guys. Those had been Cy's words before he'd realised that I was one of those young, pretty girls on the make, if only in his mother's mind. How could I ever have been so stupid to think that we, Cy and I could have a future, a real future that extended beyond the duration of an affair? What was it Cy had said very early on, let this thing run its course, get it out of our system? Despite the fact that he had since said things that led me to believe he saw us with permanence I couldn't shift that statement, Michael's words or the heavy, sick feeling in the pit of my stomach.

With a click of his fingers in my face, breaking the trance I was lost in, Michael spoke again, "Don't let me keep you El. Balder and I are off for a long walk in a while, so let yourself out...oh, I'll take your keys," he sneered, already reaching into my bag for my bunch of keys that he was pulling the house keys off. "Balder, say goodbye to El, she's tired of us."

I wanted to protest that I wasn't leaving Balder, not through choice, ridiculous as I knew I'd sound, but I couldn't be trusted to speak, not without crying and I refused to give Michael the cruel satisfaction of seeing my tears. The tears he'd caused, not when I knew his sole mission had been to hurt me, possibly as some kind of revenge or retribution for the hurt I didn't doubt my actions and infidelity had caused him. Was still causing him.

"I'll be sure to remember you to Susan," he stated as I reached the front door, having given Balder a single pat to the top of his head.

I refused to be drawn on Susan because we both knew that when she found out about me leaving Michael, she would flip out good and proper and we also both knew that I wouldn't be the one to tell her what was happening. Even if I did she'd never believe my version of events, not when Michael's account would differ so much from mine.

Chapter Twenty-Five

Determination coursed through my veins as I began the drive to Maya's home. Determination not to cry and determination to push Michael's words from my head. The tears were at bay, for now. The words, not so much so. My phone that was still on silent in my bag, vibrated like crazy. The thought of Cy turning up at my former home felt like a bad idea on every level, so I pulled into an all-night supermarket car park and retrieved my phone. There were several text messages and missed calls from him. I skipped straight to the most recent text.

<Can't deny that I'm panicking baby. You have precisely 15 mins before I head over to check on you. X>

Checking the time of the message showed me it had been sent exactly fourteen minutes ago.

"Shit!" I hissed as I composed a message.

Even typing the message proved emotional judging by the dampness coating my cheeks. My attempts to keep the tears under control had failed and Michael's words were still swimming around in my head, so much so that I was drowning in the sea of my mind.

<I have left, sorry it took so long and I wasn't able to answer your calls sooner. X>

<I'm glad. Where are you? Where are you staying? Shall I come to you or are you coming to me? X>

This was going to go downhill fast, but I couldn't cope with Cy tonight. I needed space to think or at least order my thoughts and cry, and I would do that alone. A call arrived as I tried to compose the right text to Cy. Could this night get any worse? Considering Susan was calling me, no, no it couldn't. I rejected her call.

<I need to be alone. I'm tired and just need some space. Susan is now calling me so Michael must have called her. We can talk tomorrow. X>

<You do not need to be alone. You need to be with me. I need to be with you. For fuck's sake, I don't even know where you're staying or who with. Forget Susan, for now. I don't know that I can give you space, you know that. You're overthinking Ms Ross, stop. X>

"Fuck!" I knew this was not going to be as easy as me simply saying no to Cy.

<Please, support me in this. I am going to turn my phone off until the morning and attempt to get some sleep. I am overthinking, Mr Miller. I need the space. Please respect my choice. X>

I didn't wait for another response. I turned my phone off and drove the remainder of my journey to Maya's small house. My new home. Maya welcomed me, literally with open arms and hugged me until my tears ran dry and then I went to bed, still with my phone off and amazingly I slept, a deep but restless sleep until six the following morning.

****

With a long and exaggerated stretch I took in my surroundings fully. It was a light and airy room, with pale yellow walls. The curtains I didn't remember closing were a similar pale yellow to the walls with a tiny blue flower pattern that was a perfect match to the duvet I was lying beneath. It was a fairly typical guest room; double bed, single wardrobe, chest of drawers and a bedside table, but lacking in personal touches. Not that I was complaining. There was a small vase on top of the chest of drawers containing fresh daffodils. Bless Maya, not that I was sure I deserved her hospitality or friendship at the moment. Not when I had just landed her in the middle of the gigantic mess that was me and my life.

With a final stretch, I managed to make my way out of the comforting warmth of the bed to pad downstairs, still refusing to turn on my phone and face up to the aftermath of turning it off.

I put the kettle on and threw a teabag into a mug I hoped it was okay to use and waited, wondering what all the little creaks and noises in this house were. Was this what it was like, house sharing? Because I'd never done it, I had no real clue what was involved. All I'd ever seen of it was on TV shows where the contents of the fridge were labelled and the biggest arguments stemmed from eating someone else's banana when claiming not to even like bananas. With I smile, I added some boiling water to the mug and jumped as I was joined by Maya who was reaching into the fridge for some orange juice.

We sat together with our drinks. "Do you want the bathroom first?"

"I don't mind. It's your house."

"You're usually in the office before me so I don't mind taking the second shift," she smiled.

"I might take a few days off," I announced, surprising myself with that idea. An idea I didn't know I'd been considering, although the truth was that I was hoping to hide away and avoid the world for a while.

"Oh, okay. Will he want me to cover for you, the boss man, or will he arrange a temp?"

I shook my head and shrugged, clueless as to what Cy might do if I didn't bother going to work. With a second shrug, I gulped down another mouthful of hot tea.

"What do you mean?" Maya frowned. "Ah, you haven't told him. Look El, I want to support and help you in any way I can, but that does not extend to lying to my boss. You lie to him, what's he gonna do, refuse to shag you? I lie to him and potentially my days are numbered. I like my job. Need my job. So, if you choose to take time off and he asks if I know where you are?"

"You'll tell him."

"Sorry."

"No. I'm sorry. I shouldn't put you in that position. I'll shower first and head into the office. Maybe I can get some time to myself before he arrives."

****

My plan for some alone time didn't quite work out. Cy was already in his office when I arrived, nervously brushing my navy peplum dress down unnecessarily as I paused in his open office doorway where he was on the phone, talking animatedly until he looked up and saw me.

"I have to go," he told the person at the other of the phone, preparing to hang up. Seemingly, they had other ideas. "No, no. I'll call you later, bye." He hung up, even though I could still hear a distant voice speaking. "Hey, am I pleased to see you." He smiled.

"You look tired," I told him, and he did.

"And you look amazing, considering."

"I'm sorry I couldn't speak to you last night..."

"No. I'm sorry," he whispered, already closing the distance between us.

Cy's arms wrapped around me and I could feel my chest tightening for a dozen different reasons; fear, love, apprehension and more I couldn't quite name. I felt stiff against him and hated myself for allowing the fear of what our future might never be to settle between us, preventing me from enjoying this moment. A kiss settled on the top of my head as a hand ran through my hair before settling on my chin, where a thumb stroked my cheek gently. Then my head was being tilted up, forcing me to look up and face him. In that split second where our eyes met, he could see it. I knew he could see it all, the doubts and the fear of Michael's comments.

"What's going on in your head, besides overthinking, baby?"

"Nothing," I lied and seeing his expression harden at my

324

attempt to deceive him I conceded a little. "This is all a lot to take in and last night became unpleasant…"

"Did he hurt you? Because if he lay a finger on you, I will…"

"No. He didn't touch me." I couldn't deny that Michael had hurt me, just not like Cy meant. "This is all just much more… intense, complicated, and maybe harder than I thought it would be."

"You're having regrets?" Concern was etched across his beautiful face.

"Not like that, no. I regret decisions that led me to this point, but not putting an end to it." I reached up to stroke away his worried frown. "I thought that it would be a relief, and nothing else, but now? Everything is just spinning around me, like the earth is spinning on one axis and the one I'm on is spinning in a very different direction."

"I get that, I think." He smirked at my ridiculous rambling. "But us, you don't regret us? We're not one of those things, are we?" he asked without any hint of amusement.

"No, never," I protested as the first of today's tears began to escape down my face. "I just hope you don't," I stammered through a face wet with salty tears and snot which I was embarrassed to realise I really didn't care about.

"Hey, come here." Cy pulled me back against him. A move I softened into this time, refusing to believe that anything that felt this good and natural could be anything other than the future. My future with Cy. "I don't regret a second of the time I've spent with you. Not even when you were being a complete bitch."

With a smile I held onto his waist a little tighter. Too scared to let him go, fearful of a new reality I may not like.

"Baby, if you need to take some time."

"No. That might just give me too much time to think. Although I did consider not coming in this morning until Maya said she wouldn't cover for me and if you asked her she'd tell you where I was."

"So, you're staying with Maya? I had no idea where you were or where you might go. I assumed you'd got a friend or family member to fall back on. Are you staying there long?"

Shrugging, I wasn't entirely sure what to say as the truth was that I had nobody to fall back on beyond Cy, not until Maya had offered me her spare room the day before.

"I don't know. We haven't discussed time frames. She's offered me the spare room as long as I need it."

"You really don't need it. I told you that you could, should, come and stay with me, or Tia."

I pulled back, scared to be discussing this, in case I said the wrong thing and made Cy realise sooner rather than later that this, that I was a mistake. I really should have stayed away today with Michael's ideas still filling my head.

"Don't overthink it Ms Ross, and please don't deny it because I can hear the cogs turning. Overanalysing and turning all of this in on yourself. I get why you don't want to move in with me, or Tia, but when you're ready, baby, we'll move you in together."

In that one sentence, or at least a few words in that sentence my heart filled, overfilled with love and something else I hadn't had for a long time, possibly never had, hope. Hope that Cy really did see me in a permanent way. That he imagined, envisaged a time when we would live together and now I was crying again, but happy tears now.

"I love you, but we should probably get some work done and then, then we'll make plans for later. Dinner after our Tuesday night Jezza time," he said, and I felt a smile on his lips as he pressed them to the top of my head again.

"Thank you. I love you too."

"No need for thanks. Always the need for your love though...fuck, that was lame. Go, work, tea."

And like that, for the time being at least I was grounded and centred.

"And baby, turn your phone back on. See what you're up against."

Eventually, and after several prompts to do so, I turned my phone back on and found my screen flooded with alerts and notifications; voicemails, text messages, missed calls, the lot and some of each from Tia, Cy, Maya and a couple of missed calls from Michael. Then worst of all, too many to count attempts to make contact from Susan.

"Fuck!" I hissed as Cy appeared in the office, returning from a meeting with a couple of new execs who had moved onto this floor over the weekend.

"Problem?"

"No, maybe, probably. Susan. Michael told me he was going to call her and we both knew what that would mean, but honestly, I really don't feel prepared to deal with her just yet."

"Then don't deal with her, but decide when you will," Cy suggested.

"What if that's never?" I grimaced, making him smile as he sat on the edge of my desk, facing me.

"Unacceptable. You will have to deal with her, but not today. Maybe you could make a to-do list and schedule her a place on that. Make her a priority, but tomorrow."

"Okay," I sighed, thinking that if Michael had followed through with his threat to call Susan, he may have called Denny and Elizabeth.

"What?" Cy asked, taking my smaller hand in his larger one, holding it in his lap.

"Nothing."

"Let's try that again baby. Your face does this thing like you have a bad taste in your mouth when something comes into your head that you don't want there, so what?"

Gazing up I smiled. Not exactly thrilled that Cy read me so well, but a little warmer inside for that knowledge. I liked that he cared enough to bother to get to know me, to pick up on the signs I clearly gave off, albeit subconsciously.

"He, Michael, said he'd call Susan, but also your parents…"

"He needs to accept that he fucked up by marrying you in the first place. That you were never his, not really. Not like you're mine. So, he can threaten to call who the fuck he wants, because he is done as far as you are concerned."

"Thank you," I began as Maya appeared and I immediately knew why she was there.

She had been fending off my sister's attempts to contact me via the office number and judging by her face Susan had somehow upped the ante.

"Sorry El, there's a call. Another call, your sister. She sounds really angry now…"

Yeah, she'd upped the ante with anger, rather than just pissed off.

"Maya, tell El's sister that she is now out of the office, may be out for a few days but you will pass her message on requesting that she calls her tomorrow."

I looked between Cy and Maya and could see that my friend was waiting for me to confirm what she had been told, but seemingly my boyfriend, if that's what he was now, was.

"Maya, El is leaving, now. We both are so she really won't be in a position to take any calls."

"Leaving?"

"Yes baby, we'll get some extra Jezza hours in."

"Okay. Thanks Maya. I'll see you later, back at yours," I smiled, unlike Cy who presumably wasn't expecting me to stay anywhere other than with him.

"Sure thing, and El, it's not mine, it's ours," she said with a smile to match my own.

"El, get your things," Cy muttered grumpily, on his way to grab his own things.

****

The journey to visit my dad was quiet, a little too quiet, meaning Cy was still unhappy with me. Unhappy at the idea of me being at Maya's tonight and I needed him to be okay with it because that was where I was going to be living for the time being and on top of everything else, I couldn't be worrying about his mood over that of all things.

"I was thinking," I said as I turned in my seat so that I could see Cy in all the glory of his profile.

"Hmmm," he replied, oblivious to my staring. My staring that was becoming a distraction from my thoughts. "El, what were you thinking?"

"What?" My distraction threw me off track. "Oh, yeah, sorry. Most recently I was thinking just how beautiful you are," I admitted clumsily, causing Cy to take a sideways glance in my direction. A glance that showed his eyes dancing with amusement and a curl to his lips while I simply blushed.

"Beautiful?" He smirked.

"Yes, bloody beautiful…too beautiful…should be illegal beautiful!"

My flush was getting deeper shades of red as my own words caused me further embarrassment while Cy laughed.

"Anyway, before your face distracted me, I was thinking about something you said last week about going home and cooking dinner and spending the night together."

"I remember, baby, and I remember you saying no last week, but this week…"

"Exactly," I confirmed. We were on the same page. "So, tomorrow, I was wondering if you were free. Maybe I could come to yours."

"Consider it a date, baby." He smiled, beaming at me before suddenly frowning. "Is that your way of giving me the brush off tonight?"

"No. I thought, if you wanted to, you could come back to Maya's, to mine," I said aloud, trying the words out for size. "For dinner. You could stay if you wanted, unless it's weird because Maya will be there."

I exhaled thinking I needed to breathe but happy that I had given him a get out for tonight if it was going to be awkward for him.

"Assuming Maya and you don't share a room I think we have another date planned."

I giggled, but confirmed that my friend and I didn't share a bedroom.

With my hand safely tucked in Cy's we walked into my dad's home where Angela greeted us.

"Hello, you two. You couldn't have picked a better day to come. Jezza is firing on all cylinders."

"A good day?" My optimism perked me up and made me grin broadly.

"Yeah, the best I've seen in months." Angela seemed almost as pleased about it as me. "Have any of my siblings been in?" I asked, already knowing the likely answer, the usual answer because none of them really came here.

"No, sorry. Mary called on Sunday, like she usually does."

"I just wondered." I attempted to put a brave face on things as Cy squeezed my hand in reassurance. "Is Mary okay?" I asked, thinking I shouldn't be asking one of my dad's carers about my sister's wellbeing.

"She seemed fine. Normal," Angela replied with a warm smile. "Go through, he's in his usual chair. I'll be through shortly."

Walking away I pulled back and turned, calling to Angela, "Is the business manager or someone who deals with fees around?"

I felt Cy's gaze fixed on me as Angela's own eyes widened, but I needed to do this, to know that if Michael was going to pull the financial rug from under my dad that I'd be able to sort it, manage, alone if need be.

"I'll send her through to find you before you leave."

"Thanks." I smiled, before turning my attention to Cy, "I'll fill you in later."

Entering the day room, I saw my dad immediately, sitting in his usual space with a couple of other residents nearby, near enough that they were all chatting. He seemed to pause before he looked up and found me.

"Here she is, my baby girl. Come on Muffin, over you come. I've saved you a space," he called, patting the seat next to him.

"Hi Dad," I whispered, leaning down to place a gentle kiss on his cheek before taking the seat next to him.

"Come on, you too," my dad continued, summoning Cy to the empty space on my other side.

"Mr Ross," Cy said with a hand outstretched.

"Mr Ross, bloody hell. I feel like I'm meeting with the bank manager when you call me that, especially in your polished shoes and fancy suit," he chided, making his friends laugh before Cy and I joined in. "That's better. Jeremy, please," he said taking Cy's hand that he shook with an odd familiarity.

"Jeremy." Cy smiled, caressing my hand with his thumb before returning it to his lap.

My dad chatted amiably, spreading his conversation between me, Cy and his nearby friends. One of them, May, insisted on making us all tea, something she did very well.

"If you need a job May, you be sure to call," called Cy as he took the first sip from his cup. "Your tea is up to its usual high standard."

I was momentarily confused that he knew what her usual standard was when my dad began to address Cy again. "So, my Muffin's tea isn't up to scratch? I feel I should apologise," he said before patting my knee reassuringly with a wink for good measure.

"No, no," protested Cy. "You clearly taught El well because that first cup of tea each morning sets me up for the day."

I smiled at the easy, friendly conversation between the two most important men in my life.

My dad was, as Angela had assured us he was, very lucid. He chatted about life at home when my mum was alive. When things were good. He laughed and smiled as he reminisced. He shared stories about my childhood, embarrassing stories that made me cringe while Cy howled at the image of me asking the vicar at Sunday school why, if God made us all in his image why we didn't all look the same, in a white gown with a white beard. I had a very vague recollection of that incident.

"Reverend James was pretty good about it until I asked if women were really men because God had made man in his image, or did it mean that women were aliens? I then went on to discuss the likelihood of God making aliens."

"Oh baby, you really are priceless." Cy laughed, brushing amused tears from his face as he raised my hand to his mouth that he gently brushed with his lips. "Priceless," he repeated.

"Ms Ross." A lady I recognised as being the person who dealt with charges was coming to a standstill in front of me.

"Yes, and you're?" I queried, unable to recall the woman's name.

"Saskia Montague. You wanted to speak to me?"

"Yes," I confirmed, already on my feet and following the other woman to a nearby office with a word for my dad. "I'll be back in five."

"She always says that," he chuckled. "And then five minutes turns into twenty or thirty when she gets talking," my dad told Cy with a loving shake of his head that made me smile broadly as I watched them both over my shoulder before making my heart lurch at the image of how my life could have been.

****

Ten minutes was all it took to find out that Michael had already cancelled future payments for my dad's care. He'd cancelled first thing. Clearly, he was wasting no time. Saskia explained that fees were paid quarterly and as such no further fees were due for eight weeks, which was something I supposed. She was very empathetic but made no attempt to dress up the fact that the home expected fees to be paid promptly. I was confident that I had enough money to cover the next six months, but beyond that, it would be a struggle to make the payments on my own.

"Shit," I muttered as Saskia offered me a tissue for the tears I hadn't realised I was crying. "I've just left my husband and I don't earn as much as my dad's care costs."

"You could speak to our social worker here. Your dad's benefits can be used in part payment."

Relief washed over me that the costs could be offset. However, it still meant I would most likely still need some support from my siblings to do it comfortably.

"Is the social worker here?" I asked optimistically.

"No, she's off sick, but I will update her on things when she's next in and she will call you."

"Thank you. I should get back to him," I'd already got to my feet. Turning I added, "I was named here as next of kin, but my husband was a secondary contact. I'd like to change that."

"Who would you like adding as secondary point of contact?"

"I don't know. Can you leave it as just me, for now?" I asked, sad that I couldn't automatically add Cy because more than anything, I knew he liked my dad and I trusted him to only ever act in his best interests.

****

Returning to the day room I noticed how tired my dad

suddenly seemed. His good day was taking its toll.

"Hey, baby." Cy pulled me down into the seat next to him. With a kiss to my temple he asked, "Sorted?"

"For now." I smiled weakly before turning to my dad. "Are you okay? Do you need anything?"

"Fine. I've got everything I need when I have my Muffin," he told me so sincerely the tears I thought had finished in the office were back. "Hey, come here, don't cry," he said, pulling me close across the arms of the chairs until my head was pressed against his chest. "You've done enough crying my girl. No more. Not for me. Not for any of them. They don't deserve your time, never mind your tears."

I had no idea if he was still lucid or not.

Then he continued to speak, but to Cy, "You take care of my girl and stop them all from using and hurting her."

"Jeremy, that is at the top of my list right now," Cy replied as I felt my dad's whole body tense followed by the sound of my sister's voice breaking this moment, this beautiful if heart breaking moment.

"Michael said I'd find you here," she snapped, stomping towards us.

"This is not the time or the place," I told her, concerned that her pending outburst might just send my dad back into his confused and disorganised place.

"If you'd been bothered to take my calls, we wouldn't all be here. So that would be down to you, and only you," she snapped back.

I stared up at her and wondered why she was doing this here, with Dad watching. More than that I wondered why she hadn't even spoken to him yet.

"Are you okay still?" I asked my dad who looked angry rather than startled or disorientated.

"I will be once *she's* gone," he replied, sneering the *she.*

"Does he even know who I am?" Susan asked coldly and yet the flicker in her eyes that only I might have seen suggested she was as scared as the rest of us by our dad's erratic mind.

Even seeing that hint of fear, I refused to allow her to speak about him that way, as if he wasn't even present or not important enough to be considered. "Don't fucking speak about him that way. He is still our dad, even if I am the only one to remember that on a day to day basis."

"Muffin, don't swear," my dad chastened. "Have a word," he said, confusing me until I saw he was addressing Cy again. "I thought you had a handle on her."

"You think? Only when she allows me to," Cy replied making my dad smile.

"That's my girl, keep him on his toes!"

"And then some," I heard Cy mutter as Susan glared between my dad and me.

"You've brought him here? How could you do that? I am totally at a loss for words on that one," Susan said with a disapproving shake of her head and then her glare turned to Cy who was getting to his feet to face her.

"El has already told you that this is neither the time nor the place and Jeremy doesn't need to be embroiled in whatever ridiculous statements are likely to leave your lips once you rediscover the power of speech you claim to have lost so, I would suggest that you take this elsewhere. That you enjoy your visit with your father and then, later, if you want to speak to El, you do so. But understand, when I say speak, I mean talk, not scream, shout, berate or try and force her to do your bidding in anything, or I promise you your next meeting with her will be your last."

I couldn't remember anyone ever speaking to Susan that way; she had always been quite standoffish but in an authoritative way personally, and professionally she had carried positions of responsibility that demanded respect so nobody had ever dared. Nobody except possibly Michael. The look on Susan's face suggested she couldn't quite believe anybody was speaking to her this way now. She seemed to take stock as she got over the initial shock of Cy's words and his greater authority than hers, if only over me. She turned to me for a split second with the expression I suddenly realised was her default with me, something between disapproval and sadness.

"You really have downgraded here Eloise." She returned her eyes to Cy's that merely held her gaze with a cocky smirk and the lift of a brow.

I noticed Cy's expression change at Susan's introduction of Eloise and although I was unsure what he was thinking, I heard it, the exaggerated pronunciation my dad hated so much. He had confused them, my mum and Susan, that day when he'd rambled about my name and his distaste for it weeks before.

"Don't call her that," my dad suddenly snapped, having somehow managed to get to his feet and although he was older and frailer, he managed to still look like my dad. The one from my childhood, my hero. "You call her El, not Eloise," he sneered. "It was a name that screamed pretentious and ostentatious when she was lumbered with it and that hasn't changed, and neither have you. I know what you're here for. Well, you can't have it. You do not get to take my baby's life away, not again. Not when she's finally begun to live it properly, as she should; being loved, feeling loved and valued for who and what she is. You took it all away from her and you didn't give a shit what happened to her so long as that fucking hideous excuse for a human being smiled at you favourably, patted you on the head approvingly and presumably shagged you."

I was agog, truly catching flies, as was everyone else in the room, including Angela who was making her way round with the drugs trolley.

"Jezza," she called with touching concern for my dad who was shaking like a leaf.

"It's her. She was a good girl," he said seeming to defend Susan. "Dumpling, my Chunky Dumpling!" he squealed with tears brimming his eyes. "That's who she was and then she went to work, worked hard and made her way up the ranks…I was so proud, me and her mother until we realised just how she was getting her breaks and promotions. From the start she decided she was cut out for better. Decided she was too good for the likes of us. It was all about her fancy friends and posh restaurants and clubs until all her chickens came home to roost and then who got to pick up the pieces? Us, and we did. She was ours and we loved her. I hated what she'd done but forgave her." He laughed as he shook his head. He turned to me to smile and then he was looking back at Susan. "We forgave you. It was the best thing any of us did and then…well you picked yourself up, got a new job and worked your way up. Like I said, not in the best way, until she was working for him, Michael," he scoffed as he uttered Michael's name. "And when that man had taken exactly what he wanted from you, when he thought you had nothing left to give, you gave him Muffin, your own…"

"Dad, please," I interrupted thinking that as his distress increased and Susan's horrified expression intensified, enough had been said, maybe too much, too much that couldn't be taken back. "Daddy, please," I pleaded as my first attempt had been ignored. "Let me take you to your room?"

He nodded. "Not her though. In fact, don't let her come anywhere near me, not today. Not ever!"

"Dad," Susan called, her own face wet with tears.

"No. fuck off, all of you, except Muffin and her Yankee mate. I like him. He understands me, we have an understanding." He wagged his finger in gesture between me and Cy but clearly confusion was setting in again.

"I'll be through in a minute," Angela told me as my dad linked his arm through mine and we left.

I'd blocked all the other voices out as we left the day room and only became aware of anyone other than us when Cy appeared next to me in the chair near my dad's bed about twenty minutes later. My dad had suddenly become exhausted once we returned to his room, exhausted and confused. I helped him to change and put him to bed where he now lay, sleeping peacefully.

"Hey, baby," Cy whispered kissing the top of my head gently. "Angela got held up, but she'll be here soon. How's he doing?"

"He's okay, tired. I think all that shouting exhausted him. I guess we know where my inner bitch comes from," I offered with a weak smile. "Is Susan still here?"

"She left, but assured me she'll be in touch with you."

"Great, can't wait. At least she came alone," I huffed.

"You thought she might come with Michael?" Cy frowned.

"No, more likely a brother or two, although that would require them visiting."

"Sorry, I got delayed," whispered Angela as she joined us. "Bless him, he's all tuckered out. Arguing and laying the law down must be exhausting," she said with a small smile for me. "I think I might just love tough guy Jezza even more after today's show."

I laughed a short, single laugh and then watched the rise and fall of my father's chest, wondering how many good days like today he had left. Good as in lucid, in fact how many days full stop.

"He seems out for the count. Maybe you should get off, you look beat," said Angela with a rub of my back.

"What if he wakes up?"

"I'll stay with him for a while. I'm due my break, but I don't think he'll wake for some time."

"Thank you," I cried, knowing tears really weren't very far away at the simple show of kindness Angela was showing my dad, had always shown him.

Chapter Twenty-Six

My head was still awash with the madness of my evening as Cy drove back towards home. Fortunately, I had no calls or texts from anyone, meaning I was at least being given some respite.

"I need my car," I suddenly panicked.

"Leave it at the office. We can travel in together in the morning, if you still want me to stay at yours," Cy said almost nervously.

"Of course I do. That's the one thing I am certain of right now," I admitted honestly.

"I might be beautiful baby, but you say the most beautiful of things."

"Are you going to let me forget calling you beautiful?"

"Never." He grinned, reaching for my hand that he kept in his for the remainder of the journey back to Maya's. "We'll take some takeout back with us."

With a brief detour via Cy's house to grab clothes and toiletries and then the take away collected, we landed safely at Maya's where we found her preparing to go out.

"Is this why you didn't want take away, better offer?" I smiled looking down at her outfit that consisted of high boots, short skirt and tight top.

"Maybe, Chad called and offered dinner."

"Oh, okay," I replied wondering if me or Cy being there was a factor in her sudden change of plan.

"Maya, is this too weird, me being here?" Cy enquired. "It's not a problem for me to leave later."

I smiled at what I knew was a genuine offer he was making.

"No, really. Chad has been working away the last week, so that's the only reason for my change of plans," she assured us both. "El, please, make yourself at home and I will see you both in the morning." She leaned in to kiss my cheek and took the chance to whisper, "Don't forget I want naked chest with breakfast."

I laughed, loudly, at her cheeky grin and wink as she rushed through the front door.

"Right then, baby, you go and sit down or get changed. Whatever you want and I will put dinner on plates and crack these open." Turning, he showed me two bottles of beer.

"You think of everything." I grinned inanely.

"You bet I do. And I have some really dirty and depraved thoughts for after dinner, now go."

Just the thought of what he might have in mind had me frozen to the spot, staring at my beautiful man while my body reacted in its usual way; my nipples were beading and pressing against the lace fabric of my bra, my tummy was flipping and turning in the most delightful way and between my thighs was the familiar throb as I squeezed my legs together which offered no comfort. It simply emphasised the dampness that was already coating my swollen folds.

"El, we need to eat. I need you to eat and this is getting cold, so do what you need to, and I promise I'll make it worthwhile."

Dinner proved easy and natural, as if we had done it a million times before. Even as we sat at the kitchen table in what was essentially a stranger's house, my new home, it felt right. With the washing up taken care of we retired to the lounge. We sat huddled together on the smaller of Maya's two sofas, me engulfed in Cy's arms and wrapped around him at the same time. I could feel my eyes fluttering closed as he gently stroked his fingers through my hair. Neither of us spoke, there was no need. We each knew exactly what was being said in the silence between us. This was the beginning of something, something good and if we were really lucky something permanent and honest. Something built on love and trust.

"How you doing?" Cy asked, and I knew he was referring to

my feelings after our visit to my dad, more specifically Susan's appearance.

"Okay," I said on a relaxed exhale. "I mean it was pretty horrendous to watch but I refuse to let them take my visit with Jezza away from me. Tonight was like he had never been away," I smiled. "And I was really, really glad that you were there to share it with me."

"Me too baby, me too." He moved us both so that I was being hoisted up onto my feet. "Come on, bed time."

"I'm really not tired," I protested with a frown making Cy smile.

"All the better because I have dirty and depraved plans for you and it really has been too long since I was inside you."

"Take me to bed."

"That is never going to get tired," he grinned, leading me towards the stairs.

****

Waking the following morning whilst still wrapped within Cy's arms felt like the most natural place to be in the world. He had complied with my request to take me to bed where he had made love to me more than our usual carnal sex, although it had still managed to be a little dirty and depraved.

I could feel a huge, smug smile spreading across my face, although the throb between my thighs dared me to get too smug. Even a few days without Cy seemed to be enough for my body to almost forget how to accommodate him, causing this ache I was feeling now, not to mention the sheer endurance this man displayed where sex was concerned. Even though Cy was older than me I realised that he was a younger man compared to Michael with a younger man's stamina to match. My smile was expanding into a grin as I realised that my body very quickly remembered just what it needed to do to adjust in order to house him within it.

When we'd gone to sleep, a few hours ago I had been unsure if my body would be able to maintain consecutive nights with Cy, but right now I was throbbing against new, slick arousal and wondering if I should reach over and wake my glorious lover. After all, it might be that my body really just needed more practice, to be honed and programmed so as to minimise the sweet ache I had begun my morning analysing. Although, maybe I liked the ache, the reminder of what we'd done. What Cy had managed to incite and driven my body to do. Things that were unique to him. Things I hadn't even known were possible in me or anyone else.

The sensation of Cy's breath on my neck was quickly followed by one of his hand's stroking up my body until it was cupping my breast, teasing it, teasing me with the brushing of a thumb bringing my nipple up into a stiff peak that had me moaning.

"What are you doing?" I asked with a smile.

"You woke me up with your funny little whines and sighs," he accused and although I hadn't realised I had made any noise when I pondered what my thoughts had entailed so far, I didn't doubt sounds had escaped me. "I fucking love your horny noises," he added as I heard the sound that had just left my lips without warning. "I also love the idea of waking up with you each morning, finding you warm and naked next to me."

"Oh God!" I whispered as I felt Cy's teeth nipping a path to my ear, goose bumps rising all over my body.

"I fucking love making you crazy for me, baby," he told me as his tongue began to lick the shell of my ear.

"Cy, please," I pleaded as his other arm had stretched beneath my neck and both of my breasts were now being manipulated into longing and desire for more.

"What baby, what do you want?" he asked. Teasing was clearly his primary aim.

"You know," I whispered, suddenly bashful and blushing.

"Maybe, tell me though."

Why couldn't he just do it, do what he knew I wanted and needed from him, all the things I liked? I was suddenly irritated by the fact that he was teasing me, when all I needed was for him to touch me, to continue talking in my ear and working me up into more of a frenzied ball of arousal.

"You are such an arsehole!" I snapped, already trying to break free and put some distance between us.

"It's asshole!" Cy snapped back and somehow manoeuvred

us both so that now I was flat on my back with him wedged between my thighs as he held my wrists over my head in one of his hands. "And you are being a bitch because you're not getting exactly what you want when you want it."

I could hear my shallow breathing echoing around the room as my chest heaved and my mind began to predict what his next move would be, my body and brain reacting to Cy's physical presence as well as his words. The sensation of his naked erection pressed against my mound would be my undoing, knowing exactly what that one part of his anatomy could do to me. Cy began to lazily push his length back and forth, brushing my clit with the base of his dick while the tip of it was pushing into my belly.

"Now," he said, lowering his face to mine. "I know how much you like it when I tell you what I'm thinking, what I plan to do, or just what I'd like to do. When I tell you exactly how you're going to feel and react, well, you just cream yourself, don't you baby? Your pussy gets wet for me, doesn't it?"

"Yes," I whispered, not taking my eyes off his, and becoming even more turned on. With Cy's body wedged between my thighs I was certain my creamy wetness was undoubtedly apparent to him and most likely leaking onto him, coating him in my desperate arousal.

"You see baby, I love how embarrassed and flustered you get when I take you out of your comfort zone, but it's not just that. When I say things to you, whisper in your ear," he said, actually whispering against my ear, throwing in a groan for good measure. "Well I like it too. I like to hear you, to hear what you're thinking, how it feels, what you want, it excites me as much as my words excite you and you are pretty excited right now, aren't you?" he asked, rubbing himself in the pool of arousal overflowing my sex and running down my thighs."

"Yes, I'm sorry," I stammered unable to control the evenness of my voice.

"Mmm, should I fuck you baby, touch you and stroke you until you're coming undone for me?"

"God yes," I cried, far louder than I had planned.

"But do you deserve it?"

I was pretty sure he was teasing, his own arousal was hard, surely painfully hard and currently leaking across my belly meaning he'd need to finish this off.

"Please, Cy, please. I love you," I told him, attempting to pull his lips to mine.

He laughed at that, which did piss me off, but I had no intention of risking the orgasm I desperately needed.

"Ah," he grinned far too cockily. "You're reining the bitch in for me, for you, for…" he paused as a hand was pulling at my knee, raising my leg to open me.

As he continued to rub himself up and down against me, a finger was dancing through the wetness that must have been causing a wet patch beneath me.

"Oh baby," he cooed as his finger stretched inside me and bent forward to find something that shot sensation through me causing him to chuckle.

"Fuck!" I shouted and immediately regretted it when I heard the squeak of floorboards on the landing the other side of my bedroom door. With my hands still bound in one of Cy's I couldn't even smother my own voice so instead bit down into my lip in an attempt to at least stifle my noises.

Cy hovered over me, lowering and raising his lips from mine, refusing to allow me to capture them. The ball was back in my court and I needed to make this a shot of a lifetime.

"Please, please fuck me, make me come, fuck me hard, I need you. I woke up thinking about last night and how you make me feel." It appeared that once I'd found my voice there was no stopping me. "Nothing has ever felt like this, like us. Nobody has ever made me feel like you do. Even when I thought I might be too sore, too sensitive this morning I immediately wanted you, wanted to wake you up by touching you so that you could touch me. I want you to kiss me until I'm dizzy, to caress every inch of my skin until it's over-sensitised and almost too much to bear. But I want you to be dirty and depraved," I grinned as I used his own words from the night before, giving myself a metaphorical high five for that when I saw his face; eyes like saucers, his pupils so dilated you could be excused for thinking Cy had black eyes, his lips and mouth suddenly dry, his tongue darting out to lick across his lips. How I envied those lips being on the receiving end of that talented tongue. "I want your tongue on me, sucking against my skin, drawing my nipples between your lips for you to lick them and bite them."

I knew this was far more than Cy had wanted or expected when he'd pushed for it but the jerking and pulsing from his oozing erection was certainly appreciative of my efforts.

"I love your tongue, the way it tastes when it does battle with mine, but most of all, I like the way it feels when your face is between my legs, licking my..." my what? I didn't use those words, only in my head or as an insult, but not out loud like this and I refused to call it my vagina as I wasn't in GCSE science. Again, I decided to take a leaf out of his book. "My pussy, when you lick my pussy, flick my clit. I think I could fall in love with just your tongue for that alone, well that, and the way you fuck me with it. Please," I exhaled thinking I had no more to give.

"I would have settled for the bit about fucking you hard, but now, I am going to be rock hard all fucking day, so you probably shouldn't bother with panties, they'll only serve to delay me, but now..."

"But now?" I asked optimistically.

With a grin and a couple of quick movements, I was being impaled on Cy's entire length in one thrust.

"Fuck, fuck, fuck," I squealed biting my lip again when I heard the bathroom door open and close.

"You better believe it baby," he said as he virtually pulled all the way out and then rammed his way back in, buried to the hilt making me groan, cry and shout something inaudible at the same time followed by a harder bite of my lip, hard enough that I was sure I'd broken the skin resulting in a muffled exclamation of pain. "What are you doing?" Cy asked with confusion as he thrust again making me turn my head and attempt to bite my own shoulder as my hands were still bundled together in his. Suddenly, Cy froze. "El?"

"They'll hear, Maya and Chad if he stayed," my concern revealed in a whisper, the reason for my biting and attempts at silence.

"So?" He frowned. "I want to hear you baby. What it does

to you when I fuck you, when I make you come."

"I know, I do too, but I'm a little uncomfortable. Do you want Maya to know what we sound like, how you sound doing *it*?" I asked with more immaturity than even I knew I could muster.

Cy shook his head. "Don't give a shit, I lived in a frat house," he told me as a hand skimmed down to my breast to squeeze my nipple causing internal tremors and external moans.

My only knowledge of frat houses came from American youth or comedy movies where there were lots of Greek letters being used, Delta, Beta, New, or Nu, whatever and lots of buff jocks with large breasted cheerleaders. The image of a college Cy was appealing, unlike the thought of him with cheerleaders queueing round the block for their turn. In the movies the men in these houses, brothers, would share their experiences in graphic detail, so I suppose I could imagine Cy discussing the noises his friends may have heard emanating from his room, but that was then, and this was now. He was possessive and alpha male generally, so I didn't think he'd want anyone else privy to my sex noises.

Cy was thrusting again and driving me on to what I hoped would be a serene orgasm, although all indicators pointed towards something toe curling and intense.

"Cy, please," I pleaded on another loud groan. "I don't want Chad to hear me. Just you. Nobody has ever made me make these noises. You're the only man I ever want to hear them," I told him with sincerity and honesty, not intending to manipulate him unduly.

"I fucking love you, baby," was his unexpected response as he released my hands and with a shift in position he needed just three move stroking thrusts to trigger the mind blowing orgasm that had me shaking all over as I raked my nails over Cy's shoulders and back, clawing him as I pulled him closer and closer. Yet there was no noise from me, confusing my addled mind and debilitated boneless body until I realised he was kissing me. At the split second my climax broke, he covered my mouth with his and absorbed each and every sound I had made, claiming them as his own. God, could this man kiss, right up until the second his own climax hit him with a final swell I was sure I felt deep inside me as he emptied himself inside me and then it was my turn to take his hisses and groans as he froze above me, my hands still wrapped around his back while his were laced through my hair.

"Now that is my idea of good morning," he told me as he rolled onto his back giving us both some recovery time.

"Yeah, well, you be sure to remember those good mornings are exclusively ours."

"Too fucking right," he agreed leaning across to kiss me before silencing his alarm that had just begun to sound.

****

By the time we got downstairs Maya and Chad were already sitting at the small kitchen table.

"Morning," Maya grinned as she took in the appearance of a topless Cy who seemed oblivious to his effect on anyone when all he wore was a pair of loose-fitting track pants.

"Morning," Cy replied before looking down at Chad to introduce himself as Maya got up.

"Breakfast?" I asked from my position next to Maya who was in front of the fridge now.

"I'll have whatever you're having, baby," Cy replied as Maya continued to grin at me.

"What?" I mouthed as the fridge door opened providing a privacy screen from the men who were currently chatting about something I couldn't quite figure.

"Oh my God!" she silently shrieked. "He is glorious," she whispered making me giggle. "And tattoos, thank you, thank you, thank you," she told me in continuing whispers, making me laugh out loud until Cy appeared as the fridge door moved.

"Baby, are we eating before we shower?" he asked, viewing me and Maya with suspicion.

"Mmm, yes," I confirmed as I reached into the fridge for some juice and milk.

Cy returned to the table leaving me alone with my friend again who was back to her mouthing whispers. "Fuck! He wants you to shower with him. You're never getting to work early again."

I laughed loudly, well more of a cackle really, causing both men to look up and stare at us with simple confusion.

"Oh, El, you might never be able to leave me alone," she smiled, unlike Cy who had a frown fixed to his face. Clearly, he didn't like the idea that this might be anything more than a temporary home for me.

****

It came as a surprise when it was mid-afternoon and Susan had made no attempt to reach me via telephone or in person. I found that, despite how busy the day was, I still kept checking my phone to see if I'd missed a call or a text, even though Susan wasn't really a fan of text messages. It seemed inconceivable that she would leave things as they'd been left the previous day or given up in what would undoubtedly become a one woman mission to mend my marriage or at the very least ensure I was back in it, one way or another. No contact was very un-Susan-like.

Maya was in the kitchen, she'd passed by me a couple of minutes before and now she was heading back towards me with a cup of coffee she was placing on my desk.

"Since when did you make my afternoon drink?"

"Since you paraded semi-naked boss man around the kitchen," she replied with a smirk as she sauntered back to her own work space.

"Yeah, well next time make boss man one too," I muttered as I got up and went to make Cy a drink too.

Upon returning to my desk via Cy's, where he was reclined in his chair with his feet up on his desk talking on the phone, I found Susan's name lighting up my screen and now my confusion at her lack of contact was replaced with nausea at dealing with her.

"Hello," I answered nervously.

"Eloise, we should talk. Just the two of us."

"There really isn't anything to say," I told her.

"I disagree. I could meet you after work," she demanded more than suggested, and as much as I knew I needed to deal with her, to see her and talk, I couldn't face it, nor allow a meeting with her to ruin my first night with Cy at his house as a single woman. Not single as such because I was more attached now than I might ever have been, in my head and heart.

"I can't tonight." I heard a loud sigh at the other end of the line as Cy appeared at my desk and stood, patiently waiting. "Hold on Susan, sorry. Are you okay?" I covered the mouth piece on my phone as I watched Cy toying with his car keys in his hand.

"Sorry baby, something's come up. I need to pop out. Meet me back at mine after work."

"You're out for the rest of the afternoon?" I frowned, thinking there was nothing in his diary.

"Yeah, I think so. I'll see you later."

"Are you okay? Is everything alright?" I could hear the concern etching my voice.

"Yeah, yeah, don't worry. Later." He smiled weakly before dipping down to kiss my cheek gently.

I watched him leave and was reminded of my sister's presence by her speaking.

"I think he may be tiring of you already."

I was hurt and annoyed by her words and bitchiness. What had I ever done to her to make her this much of a bitch?

"Susan, sorry." I could have kicked myself for my own apology. "Look, I can't, won't do tonight, but tomorrow. Lunch, dinner, whatever."

"You should come here."

"Here? Precisely where is here?" I shrilled, already knowing what she was going to say.

"With Michael, at his house, your home."

"No. No fucking way!" I snapped and was sure I could feel her wince at my expletive.

"Eloise, really."

"Susan I am hanging up now and won't be accepting further calls from you. Neither will I be meeting you at Michael's house or with him present. So, you consider that and let me know when you want to meet. Just us, lunch or dinner, drop me a text," I told her with a self-satisfied smile in the knowledge that having to send a text would irritate her no end. I hung up, somehow able to return to my work almost blocking out her suggestion that Cy might be tiring of me already, but not quite.

Chapter Twenty-Seven

Cy didn't make it back to the office and as I turned into his road, I hoped he'd at least made it home. With no way of getting in I would have to wait in my car at the roadside on the wrong side of his security gates. Relief washed over me at the sight of Cy's car parked on his drive and as soon as I buzzed the gate's intercom he answered. I parked my car next to his and by the time I reached the front door it was open.

"I like this," he smiled as he tugged me through the door before slamming it shut and pushed me against it with his body. "You coming home here, to me," he told me, his voice hoarse and then he was kissing me. This was like no homecoming I'd ever known or dared dream of.

The idea of this being my home scared and thrilled me in equal parts, although I couldn't really allow my mind to go there, to a real future here with Cy and my yet to be conceived family when I had left my husband a matter of days before.

"Cy," I moaned as he came up for breath briefly. "I can smell something," I told him between kisses and nips that littered my lips, jaw and neck.

"It's the smell of desperation, baby," he replied before resuming his consumption of me.

I was ready to disagree. To interrupt the movement of his lips kissing their way down my body; caressing and teasing through my clothes until he was on his knees and pushing my dress up my thighs where he wasted no time in pushing the tiny scrap of lace that was my underwear out of the way of his tongue that immediately began to lick along my length that was already ripening and opening for him.

"Fuck!" I cried out as his tongue lapped forward and found my clit. "Oh my fucking God," I squealed as Cy went from gentle circling and flicking to drawing my tight bundle of nerves into his mouth and then began to suck.

My hands were fisting in his hair, pulling him closer and trying to push him away as the intensity built while my climax rolled towards me like a runaway train. A finger and then a second slipped easily into me and with a simple curling motion I was coming in a series of expletives that were only broken by the sound of an alarm, specifically the smoke alarm.

"Shit!" Cy shouted as he leapt to his feet and ran towards the kitchen, leaving me to readjust my clothing until I was decent again.

"Whoops," I smiled when I joined Cy in the kitchen looking down at the charred remains of nothing recognisable. "Told you I could smell something," I told him smugly.

"I still think you only smelt desperation, yours and mine, but I think stir fry is off."

"Sorry," I said and genuinely felt remorseful that somehow I had caused the ruination of dinner, simply by arriving when I had, actually just being there.

"Hey," Cy soothed, closing the distance until he had me wrapped in his warm embrace and his lips kissed the top of my head with reassurance and reverence. "You have nothing to be sorry for. It's stir fry. No more. Maybe it's a blessing in disguise that we can't eat now."

"You don't like stir fry?" I could think of no other reason for our ruined dinner being a blessing of any sort.

"No," he grinned down as he pulled back to ensure I could see his face. "I love stir fry, but I love fucking you more and now I get to take you to bed and fuck you until we can barely stand and then we'll order take out and then we'll fuck some more."

"Oh," I whispered, unsure what I should or could say to that, making Cy cock his head with more than a hint of his cocky swagger I loved and yet always wanted to knock down a little, spurring me on to find something more to say. Something to take his swagger down a peg or two. "Except maybe I wanted dinner and take away food is very high in fat and salt…it's been a long day and I am hungry, in need of my appetite satisfying," I teased with a coy smile as the smoke alarm stopped of its own volition.

With the pan of burnt remnants of dinner already thrown in the bin and the pan in the sink Cy had both hands free and made quick work of hoisting me up onto the counter top, his hands gripping my hips as he stepped between my slightly spread thighs.

"Pushing?" he asked, his fingers tightening on the soft flesh around my hips.

"No." My protestations half-hearted at best causing his cocky swagger to move straight up to sheer arrogance with a simple arch of an eyebrow.

"No?" he asked with a smirk.

"Maybe a little," I conceded and was rewarded with his hands pushing my knees apart, allowing him to move closer. Clearly not close enough for me I realised when my legs instinctively wrapped around his hips until my ankles were crossing on his behind.

"A little?" he asked, teasing a strand of my hair around his finger.

"Maybe a little more than a little…or a lot." I nervously nibbled my lip before reaching forward to grab a handful of Cy's shirt, allowing me to pull his chest to mine where my nipples immediately responded to the contact, stiffening and beading in anticipation beneath my clothing.

"So are we on the same page baby, fucking, eating, more fucking, possibly some sleep and then definitely more fucking?"

"Yes, please…here?"

"Here? I think the smell of burnt vegetables might just ruin the mood, so now we go to bed. We'll christen the counter tops another time though."

With that I found myself being lifted up by hands on my arse and carried through the house until we reached the bedroom.

****

I had no idea how much time had passed and I'd lost count of the number of orgasms I'd achieved at Cy's hands, mouth and dick. Lying breathless and sated whilst wrapped around each other, my belly began to grumble making us both laugh.

"So, fucking done, then a little more fucking so we have deviated from the plan meaning we really need to eat before a little sleep and then some more fucking."

"I thought you said we'd barely be able to walk during round two. I am going to need adaptive equipment at this rate," I told a smiling Cy whose chest I was burying my face in, kissing his soft, fragrant skin.

"Baby, I will fucking carry you everywhere if I need to, but if that's not your chosen mode of transport for the next couple of days I suggest those lips have a word with themselves otherwise there will be no food or sleep. Just fucking. Hard, ferocious and unforgiving fucking."

Although the idea of hard fucking was in no way a threat, there was no disguising the warning tone being aimed at me and even though I in no way objected to some more sex, some more orgasms, I was sore and tender, and very hungry. Another roll of my stomach chipped in, confirming my state of hunger.

"A pleasure debating with you, as usual, Ms Ross," Cy replied to my unspoken response.

"You are such an arse," I accused with a broad grin.

"It's ass! We really need to get you fluent in American English baby."

"Or you could just speak English correctly," I countered as Cy's phone burst into life, startling us both.

Reaching across to the bedside cabinet where he'd put it after pulling it from his trousers when he'd stripped earlier, he frowned. "My mom. I've missed a couple of her calls," he explained as if asking for permission to answer his call.

"Then you should answer. It could be important. I'll go and shower…"

"You stay," he commanded before connecting the call. "Hey Mom."

I smiled at the warmth and love in his voice in those two simple words.

"Yeah, I'm good. Thanksgiving? I can't say I've given it much thought…it's not recognised over here beyond Black Friday and it's not for weeks yet, but I guess we'll come home."

I lay there, no choice but to listen to the conversation but did so absentmindedly. I wondered what dinner was likely to be, questioning what time it might be and then I thought about Susan and my impending meeting with her. I shook my sister from my mind as I heard Cy making his Thanksgiving plans; how long would he be gone, him and Tia. I assumed the holiday would likely be a long weekend but once travel time was added it would surely be a week or so. A week without him in the office. A week without seeing him, touching him, sleeping with him, being able to inhale his scent, which I realised I was doing as I tuned back into his conversation.

"I'll get back to you on the details, once I've spoken to Tia, Rhonda and El."

I bolted upright as if I'd been burnt by his words that suggested he expected me to go home with him for Thanksgiving with his family. His family and the ex and presumably his daughter. It seemed that if I had been shocked at that suggestion then Elizabeth was stunned with a liberal helping of outrage and offense for good measure judging by the raised pitch and volume of the voice I could hear coming down the line, escaping from Cy's phone. He allowed her to let off some steam and then she said something, something I didn't hear, but I didn't need to. The words were a step too far for Cy and his intervention clearly revealed the gist of his mother's sentiment.

"Mom, you're being judgemental and unfair. You know nothing about El beyond what Michael has told you…yeah, well, I guess that leaves a few extra spaces at the Thanksgiving dinner table then because if El isn't welcome then I won't be there and I very much doubt Lulu and Rhonda will make it there without me."

His words were resolute and his tone firm. He actually meant what he was saying.

"Shit," I whispered, possibly only in my head as I pulled free of Cy, unwilling to lie there and listen to any more of her words or insinuations.

I already knew what she thought of *girls like me.* Cy had reassured me previously that her opinion was incorrect or unimportant. He was clearly wrong on both fronts because as he allowed me to leave his bed, I turned to find some clothing, Cy's t-shirt and that is when I saw his face, his sad and conflicted expression. I was already coming between Cy and his family, but I refused to stand there and cry while Elizabeth remained on the phone, obviously pointing out each and every one of my flaws in minute detail while my lover attempted to rebuke his mother's opinions. Unsuccessfully.

I made my way back downstairs, alone and chastened myself for being stupid and naïve enough to believe that this was possible, me and Cy. Immediately, Susan's words from earlier, along with Michael's came back to taunt and haunt me. Would it be this simple, that his mother's words, thoughts and ideas would be the final straw causing Cy to tire of me or at least to realise that there was no point in continuing with this futile attempt at a relationship with me?

Michael had warned me, although I still didn't doubt that he had his own agenda for his warning shot, but could he have been right that I would never be the right permanent partner for Cy? Would he go home and find himself a girl that his mother would approve of, a woman who had no ex-husband and questionable reasons for ever having had a husband? Would he marry her, make a home and a future that would see beautiful babies and a happy ever after I didn't think I'd ever be worthy of, not with Cy anyway?

"You're overthinking. I can hear it from here," Cy said, his interruption making me physically jump as I stood in the kitchen, gazing into the darkness of the back garden where Balder had run around and frolicked just a few weeks before. "Baby, talk to me, tell me what you're thinking because I can guarantee the reality of things is nowhere near as bad as whatever you have in your head."

I turned, slowly, and hated myself when I saw the genuinely pained expression that greeted me.

"Shit!" Cy sighed as he took in my tear streaked face. He began to close the distance between us, his concerned expression replaced with one of annoyance when I held my hand up, an attempt to halt his movement and his intent to what? Pacify me, convince me that his mother didn't hate and mistrust me and probably always would or was he simply going to try and make me believe that this was possible, us?

"Don't, I'm fine."

His face dispelled my ridiculous words as did the horrendous sounding sob that caught in my throat as I wiped away the tears running down my face.

"You are far from fine." Cy ignored my halting hand and words to fold me in his embrace.

I said nothing for a few moments. I simply enjoyed the warmth and closeness of Cy's naked skin that was searing through his t-shirt that I still wore. As we stood together, his hands wrapped around me while I secured mine tightly around his middle I wondered how to move forward, what to say or do and after coming up short on responses I eventually managed to speak.

"I allowed my mind to wander, to a few weeks ago. To Balder running around here," my voice broke and I hated myself a little more, not for being upset about the lack of the dog in my life now, but because I was being dishonest now, lying. There were many reasons causing me pain and sadness and Balder was just one of them and it was unfair of me to suggest that he was solely responsible for my upset.

"I am calling bullshit here. These tears are not for Balder, maybe a few are, but we both know that there's so much more going on here, baby. So, let's order takeout for dinner and we can eat and talk."

I pulled away a little, needing some space and distance, enough that I could imagine how this would be long term, not having Cy here, with me, being held by him and protected by him.

"I should go," I sniffed.

"No fucking way. You are going nowhere, and I am not allowing you to do this to me, to us. Now, decide what the fuck you want to eat and prepare yourself for talking before we go to bed, here, together."

There was no room for discussion or argument even, this was non-negotiable and as much as I wanted to remain here, I couldn't help thinking this was a bad idea. That it was prolonging the agony of our inevitable separation.

****

After moving my dinner around my plate for twenty minutes I felt sick. Sick in the pit of my stomach even though the three small mouthfuls of kung pao chicken that had passed by my lips were stuck somewhere between my throat and my chest.

"You need to eat some more," Cy told me firmly as I pushed my plate away.

Looking up I saw his plate was clear, meaning that either this situation didn't worry him as much as me or maybe he just didn't care as much.

"I'm not hungry," I told him as I intercepted my plate that he was pushing back towards me.

"Just eat a little more then, before we talk," he insisted with a small smile tugging his lips. "Unless you want me to feed you."

I stared across at his words, thick with suggestion and inference, his eyes beginning to flicker with desire and heat as our gazes met.

"Cy…"

"Another time then. Now eat, please," he added, softening the hardness of his insistence.

I managed another four mouthfuls before I pushed my plate away again and sensing further objections I intervened. "Cy, I can't eat any more, not unless you want me to cover the space between us in vomit."

"Okay, but you're going to need to have a very big breakfast in the morning, baby."

I nodded and waited for the thick ice that was between us and encasing my heart to be broken, but Cy said nothing, he just waited.

"I love you," I managed to stammer as I decided it was obviously down to me to break the aforementioned ice.

Still Cy said nothing. He just continued to stare, meaning I needed to continue.

"Your mother doesn't like me. From the first time she saw me, maybe even before then, when she heard about my marriage to Michael. She wasn't the first to think I was a gold digging whore and she certainly won't be the last and it didn't matter to me, not really."

"And now it does?" Cy asked flatly, his face and expression offering no insight into his thoughts or feelings on my words.

"Yes," my whispered reply confirmed. "When I married Michael I believed I was doing the right thing. I wasn't. It was doomed from the outset, but I didn't know that. I hate that the mistake I made then is going to haunt and threaten my future."

"Why? How is it going to affect your future?"

"It already is," I sighed. "You once said that her opinion didn't matter unless you were planning on getting down on one knee and I know we're not there, nowhere near, but then, when you said it we were simply letting this run its course, getting it out of our systems and now things have changed. Love was never part of that old plan."

Cy nodded and gestured for me to continue, his expression one of understanding and acceptance of my words.

"Look, your mother hates what she believes I represent and I don't see that changing any time soon. It's already coming between you and her. She wants you to go home for Thanksgiving and she doesn't want me sitting at her table…"

"I want you sitting at her table," Cy interrupted.

"And how do you suppose that would pan out, for me? How uncomfortable I would feel, knowing I was there under duress and her stomaching my presence only because of you. Her love for you."

"She'll be fine. She just needs some time and once she gets to know you."

"No," I shouted, springing to my feet. "You don't know that. I deserve better than having to put up with somebody's snide comments and judgmental glances, just putting up and shutting up. I thought I was done with that."

"You are, that's not what I meant," Cy told me from his position still sitting. "Please carry on."

I was surprised he hadn't got more to say, more objections,

but none were forthcoming, not yet.

"She might hate me for the rest of her life and in turn that will shape your relationship, it already is. The fact that we're even having this conversation is proof of that. We should stop things now. Everyone else can see it, and we're the only ones in denial on this whole fucking mess! I married a man I thought I loved correctly, and I remained with him through illness and the demise of our marriage. If I had wanted a quick payday I could have left him months, years ago, but I didn't because I believed my marriage was happy. You changed that. Only you, and yet falling in love with you only makes others more suspicious of me. Like I've traded one payday for another." Realisation dawned on me. "Is that what she thinks? That I see pound signs when I look at you? But why would I have stayed with him if I wanted money? Unless—fuck me, she thinks I was that calculating that I was waiting for him to fucking die for a bigger pay out?"

Looking across at Cy was enough to tell me that Elizabeth had thought exactly that.

"So why did I ditch that plan for you?" Curiosity had got the better of me.

Cy made no attempt to reply. He simply sat there looking uncomfortable, refusing to fill in the gaps, although I was more than capable of doing that for myself.

I laughed a brittle, sardonic laugh. "Ah, I see. He didn't drop dead soon enough. I couldn't quite manage to fuck him into an early grave so I found myself someone richer, younger. Meaning what? That I string you along to pay my bills, sort my divorce and then what? Marry you then divorce you too, and presumably my half share of your wealth would be more than enough to set me up?"

"Not quite. You're overthinking, baby," he told me, pulling me down into his lap where I cried, unsure if I could do this, doubtful that I was cut out for any of this. "My mother is suspicious of you, of your motives for marrying Michael and for your apparent sudden change of heart, trading him for me. Yes, she thinks his money was a factor in your choice to marry him, and it was. You made that choice because you loved him how you thought you should, but you also made that choice for other reasons, for your father, your sister, your brother..."

"So what? You fucking agree with her?" I screeched, back on my feet again.

"No. I fucking don't agree with her! She doesn't even agree with herself. She doesn't dislike you. She dislikes your possible motives and she is worried about me. She's my mother, that's her fucking job. Until you, we, prove her wrong she will continue to harbour those feelings and thoughts and your constant intent to throw this all away will only ever prove all of those people who doubt you, who question your motives right," Cy told me in a hard and loud tone, but still not quite a shout as he stood in front of me. "Now, if you don't want to be with me then you say now and it's over, but if you love me, as you claim, and I sure as hell love you, we need to toughen you up and prepare to weather this shit storm. So, are you in or out?"

I stared up at him knowing he was giving me a final get out. One I didn't really want and yet I couldn't shift the idea that this was somehow doomed, that I would never be the right girl for him and for that alone we would fail, but if we did I knew I wouldn't recover. The pain would be too great.

"I keep thinking about what Michael has said, and Susan and your mother..." I began but was cut off abruptly.

"They're not the ones I was asking to vote in or out, and they, all of them, anyone that isn't us, they're the shit storm, baby. I love you, so much it seems too overpowering, too intense and I know it will burn me if we fuck this up, but it's the one thing I don't think I will ever find again. Us. What we have, so are we doing this? No more threats and attempts to bail, in or out?"

"People might try and mess things up," I said, even though every thought in my head and fibre of my body was screaming to simply say in. I wanted nothing more than this, than him, him and me forever.

"Let them try. No secrets between us, no lies, and then they won't be able to. Although if they try and make you cry again, I may have to kill them. So, for the final time, in or out?"

"In, totally and utterly in, please, thank you."

A huge grin broke out across Cy's face as he stepped closer and cupped my face with his hands, gently cradling it.

"I'm going to kiss you now and then, well we can make it up as we go along." He moved closer and then paused. "Oh, and for the record I don't ever want to hear the words, you, Michael and fuck in the same sentence again, okay?"

I frowned briefly and then recalled that I had suggested that Elizabeth had thought I might have planned to fuck Michael into an early grave.

"Okay," I agreed easily.

"But the early grave is optional," he said a little too seriously.

I smacked his chest with some force. No matter what had happened between me and Michael he was essentially a good man, I truly believed that and I didn't wish him dead, never had.

"Maybe that was uncalled for, but I am definitely going to kiss you now. Enough talking."

Immediately his lips closed over mine, reassuring me, giving me a sense of belonging that I hadn't felt since I was a little girl, maybe not even then, not like this. There was no doubt in my mind that all other decisions before this one had been trivial and simple, whereas this one was either the best choice of my life or the worst. Time would tell which.

Chapter Twenty-Eight

The next few weeks passed by in something of a blur, but a good, comfortable blur.

I had met with Susan the day after Cy had given me my final out. My sister had been subdued, worryingly so, like the calm before the storm. I'd waited throughout the lunch hour that had turned into an hour and a half but felt much longer as we both avoided addressing the elephant in the room. I couldn't quite believe it when I returned to the office unscathed and none the wiser as to what my sister's plans or intentions were.

That week had got ever more surreal when Edward called me the following morning as I ate breakfast with Cy at Maya's. He wanted to meet up, for no obvious reason, and although I had considered putting him off he had mentioned that he was going to be walking Balder later that day so I agreed to meet with him, mainly to see the dog, but also because although I was still wary of Edward, I somehow felt drawn to him in spite of my fears of who and what he was. Seeing Balder had been wonderful, I'd missed him and judging by how he'd bounded towards me and knocked me flat on my behind to cover me in sloppy kisses, it was reciprocated. Edward still seemed to have no real reason for meeting up, and yet I still managed to agree to meet with him again, which I was going to do later, for dinner. Just the two of us, no Balder, sadly. Although, as I had cried for three hours solid after leaving him on our last meeting that might not be a bad thing.

"Hey, there you are. What time are you going out?" Cy asked, interrupting my thoughts while lying in his huge bath.

"Edward said he'd booked a table for eight," I replied as I watched Cy shedding his own clothes with a small smile I couldn't hide as his tattoo was revealed.

"You fancy some company before you leave?"

"Always," I conceded freely and honestly. I really couldn't get enough of my handsome boyfriend.

A bigger grin covered my face as Cy cast his remaining clothes aside until he was completely naked.

"You need to explain to your face that if it doesn't rein in its 'come fuck me til a month Sunday,' Edward will be eating dinner alone."

"This is not my come fuck me face," I protested with a pout as I scooted forward to allow Cy to climb into the bath behind me.

"If you say so." Cy laughed as he lowered into the water before pulling me back against him.

"You know that my girlfriend going on dinner dates with other men is a very limited group, don't you?"

"I imagined it might be." I smiled at the sensation of soft lips kissing my neck and shoulder.

"Should I ask who is in that limited group for your girlfriend?" I giggled, still unaccustomed to that title.

"You think I'm joking?"

"Not about the dinner thing, but I was amused at you calling me your girlfriend."

"Ah, I see. It's weird, huh?"

"Yes, it is and it has been a very long time since I've been a girlfriend. Now tell me who you have in this little group of men I can have dinner with."

"Me, obviously, Edward and Jezza."

"And?" I asked with curiosity as to who would pass muster.

"That's it," Cy told me far too seriously. "Now, I think we need to get a little dirty before you get clean." He encouraged me to flip over so that I was straddling him, my groin loitering over his. "You're going for the big prize right off then?"

"I've missed you," my husky voice told him as a finger traced the lines of his tattoo before coming to rest on Lulu's eye. "I can't wait to get my first tattoo."

That was it. I was being raised and then dropped down onto his erection, my skin stretching to accommodate Cy just a little too quickly causing a burn that had me hissing through gritted teeth.

"Keep pushing baby!" he warned as his hands settled on my breasts, teasing and easily coaxing my nipples to stiff peaks.

"If this is where it gets me, I won't ever stop."

A sharp and intense sensation shot through my nipples following Cy's unspoken response to my words that had him squeezing my nipples in a twist movement. As I cried out it transformed into a warming pleasure that shot straight through to my clit which in turn caused my hips to rock while my internal muscles squeezed the dick that was invading my body.

"God, I'm sure that anything that feels this good must be wrong."

"Does this feel wrong?" Cy asked as one hand dropped between our bodies where he found my clit standing proud, not requiring further coaxing.

"No. Never. Please, Cy," I pleaded as his free hand held my hips still.

"What baby? Tell me what you want? What you need?"

"You, all of you, inside me. Fuck me, make me come and then fuck me some more until you're coming inside of me…oh God," I cried in a higher pitch than I'd ever heard from my own voice before as my own words sent my horny arousal into overdrive.

"You had me at hello." Cy grinned, causing my already flushed complexion, courtesy of some embarrassment and lots of anticipation of pleasure to come, to deepen. "Ride me baby," he told me as my hips were freed.

I rose and fell in quick succession and felt complete satisfaction at the sight of Cy's hooded eyes full of arousal and increasingly ragged expression. I followed his eyes as they lowered, coming to a halt at the point where our bodies joined. I slowed my movements, allowing us both to appreciate the sight of my body taking him into it, drawing him in, encasing him, preparing to milk him as I squeezed and pulsed around him, pushing us both towards the most primal desire. His expression was one of desire and darkness that only served to raise my own desire for him and need for the end game to this. As I lowered, I rotated my hips, ensuring that my clit brushed against the firmness of his body triggering ripples of pleasure. I repeated that move another three or four times while Cy lazily rested his hands on my hips.

"You like that baby?" he asked, already knowing by my body's reaction that I loved that.

"Mmm," I replied dreamily.

"Come on baby. I want to see and hear you coming as you fuck me. Nothing could ever feel better than this. This is home baby, here, buried inside you...."

I didn't hear anything else. His words undid me until I was falling apart on every rise and fall that carried me through the intensity of my climax. My own release had only driven Cy even closer to his and with his hands on my hips, lifting me up and down in quick succession I knew he was close. With one hand I reached behind me where I found Cy's balls hanging loose and large in the warm bath water. Cupping and caressing them I felt them tighten and with a loud groan and a hiss, his fingers were digging into the soft flesh of my hips as his own body was thrusting up and then he froze, buried inside me, spurting his seed against my internal walls with a simple cry of, "El."

Falling forward against his chest we both struggled to catch our breath, cocooned in the cooling water without a care or a thought for anyone or anything beyond us.

****

"Sorry, am I late?" I asked a slightly annoyed looking Edward who was standing to greet me as the waiter escorted me to the table at the back of the rather swish looking restaurant I'd never been to.

"A little, but I suppose I can forgive you. You look lovely," he smiled, placing his phone in his inside pocket as the waiter seated me opposite Edward who too had taken his seat once more. "Did you drive?" he asked flatly, confusing me as I nodded and then realised the reason for his question when he ordered water for us both which I assumed meant he too was driving. "I half expected Cy to arrive with you." Edward smirked with an arched brow. "He's incredibly protective of you."

I shrugged an acknowledgment that his statement was true before the waiter returned to take our order. Neither of us spoke beyond ordering and laughed as we ordered the exact same meals; a risotto, rib of beef main course with an option on poached pears with a soft cheese and honey cream for dessert.

"So, how do you come to be alone, dressed to stop traffic?"

I looked down and although I had liked the image looking back at me in the mirror, I wouldn't have said I was likely to stop traffic dressed in the simple sleeveless dress I'd chosen to wear. Even with the high heeled peep toe nude shoes and matching clutch that perfectly complimented the pale pink and beige floral print. However with wrap front skirt and ruching to the bodice it was flattering. My makeup was simple, natural with just tinted moisturiser, a hint of blusher, lip gloss and mascara confirming that I was wearing any at all. I felt my face flush as I remembered that this dress had been the reason I was late. It was also the reason I had found myself spread across Cy's desk at his house with his face between my legs. That might also be more of a factor in my rosy glow than the blusher.

"Earth to Eloise!" Edward called making me blush even more that he had somehow caught me in thoughts of Cy.

"Sorry," I smiled with a deeper blush, relieved when Edward politely began to chat about the weather.

With main courses finished we chatted whilst awaiting dessert.

"So, who knew our tastes would be so similar?" Edward asked and stated, yet there appeared to be more to his comment than I could see.

"Mmm," I agreed. "I was a little concerned by all the fish on the menu."

"You don't like fish?"

"Nope, although my sister and Michael always insisted that I did, and wine, they reckon I like wine too," I revealed almost clumsily.

"And do you?"

"No, not really. I can tolerate it and occasionally I find one that's pleasant, but it's not really me."

"And Cy, what does he say you like?" Edward asked with an amused smirk.

I resisted the temptation to say Cy says I like being fucked a month til Sunday and I like being held, kissed and touched by him at all times. He might also say I like being a bitch, enticing his arsehole to do battle, but I said nothing of that, I stuck to the mundane things my husband and sister were so desperate to control along with everything else.

"He doesn't. He accepts what I do and don't like, including my dislike of fish and wine and my love of pizza and beer."

"You could have been a much cheaper date if I'd known that," he laughed.

I didn't laugh with him, his words causing me some concern, that he expected to pay tonight and his idea that this was a date. It wasn't, not for me, and surely not for him as he was mainly gay.

"I don't expect you to buy my dinner and I don't think Cy would like this being a date, nor me," I waffled with a crimson hue that made Edward laugh louder.

"Oh, my dear Eloise, your expectation is of no consequence. I'd like to buy you dinner and I meant dinner date, no more. I thought we'd established that you weren't my type."

"Sorry, God I am such a prat!" I chastened, myself rather than him.

"There's really no need to insult yourself," he said quite firmly. "You misunderstood my words, no more, dear. Right, change of topic. Have you spoken to Elizabeth since you and Cy went public?"

He probably knew I hadn't. Clearly, he knew that I was a bone of contention as far as Cy's mother was concerned and whether he was fishing or genuinely interested I had nothing to hide.

"I haven't spoken to her. Cy has, a few times. She's not really a fan, of me, not Cy."

"She is a wonderful woman. She loves her children with all she is and I suppose if you're impartial you can see why she might question your motives for being with Cy. He is a very eligible bachelor."

"I am impartial in that view and I get it, but sometimes I tire of listening to her berate me to Cy. It's more than that though. I try to act like it's okay, that I believe Cy and that she'll get over it, when she gets to know me..."

"You don't believe that?" Edward asked, cocking his head to view me more intently.

"I dunno. Maybe she could grow to like me, once she sees I love her son, but what if by then I don't care and her comments no longer make me cry," I revealed a little too candidly but had committed this far so continued. "What if by then Cy has already grown tired of the comments and accusations, that the gap between them is too wide to close? That he opts for the easier life?"

"You're even more like me than we realised. You're an overthinker, planning for the next disaster before it's evolved."

With a smile I nodded, but couldn't miss the irony of his disaster reference, after all Cy and I were *the* disaster-in-waiting and as the waiting was over.

"Cy always tells me not to overthink, but I can't help it, it's who I am I suppose. I wouldn't have you pegged as an overthinker though. I thought you were super confident and simply strode through life making decisions without looking back, like Cy."

Edward shrugged. "No, not really. When I was a little boy I was the apple of my mother's eye, but not so much my father's. He really was a strider through life, making decisions without a second thought. My mother was the thinker. I get it from her. Anyway I saw firsthand what it looked like to stride confidently and as my father saw the overthinking as weakness I quickly learned to emulate him until I was alone and then I thought things through, too much. My father was old school. Children should be seen and not heard, know your place and don't move from it and although I might come across as that man I'm not, never was so we clashed, a lot. I am the worst card player in the world because I keep changing my mind, overthinking my hand, should I fold, take a hit or go all in?"

"I'm the same, although I have no clue where I get it from

because my parents nor my siblings are that way. So much of my life was planned without me, right up until I met Cy really so I didn't get the chance to think."

"So, how are you and Lulu getting along?" he asked almost randomly as dessert arrived.

The waiter presented our food to us and once he'd gone again, I replied.

"We get along okay." I laughed and felt obliged to continue. "She has this thing about tattoos."

Edward joined in with my laughter, clearly aware of her fascination with getting inked.

"She loves Cy's tattoos and is insistent that she's going to get one when she's older. We like to design them."

"We? I hope you're not seriously considering getting one," he seemed to challenge.

With a shrug that received a frown I continued, "I haven't really considered it, not seriously, but it drives Cy mad."

"Ah, you're a tormenter."

I gave another non-comital shrug making Edward smile and shake his head. "He really is going to have his work cut out with you, isn't he?" He laughed again. "He loves it though, he loves you. Anyone can see that. Elizabeth will see that. I'm just glad I'm here to see it."

Although I still didn't fully understand the relationship between Edward and the Miller family, I loved that he cared about Cy. It meant there was someone beyond Tia this side of the Atlantic in his corner, even if he had acted as an advocate for Michael on one occasion. I couldn't deny that his apparent like of me might also be an advantage in my hopes to overcome Elizabeth's objections to my relationship with her son.

"So, what about you?" I asked causing a frown to crease Edward's face that was growing ever more familiar, as if I knew him, in the past and he was like a memory coming back to me.

"What about me?"

"I dunno. You seem to know so much about me and I know nothing, well, very little about you. Do you have a partner? Are you in love, ever been in love? Close friends or family, someone who has your back?"

"Yes. You're definitely a curious little thing, although your questions are becoming more direct."

I recoiled a little at the accusation I perceived as being critical and as I prepared to backtrack and apologise, Edward continued with a warm smile and a squeeze of my hand.

"That wasn't a criticism. I like direct. So you want to even things up by knowing my deepest darkest secrets...let's see," he mused and with a more comfortable ambiance settling over me I relaxed while he continued. "I have four sisters. I was the only boy. My parents are both deceased, I have lots of nieces and nephews I'm close to. Now, love, let's see. I have no significant relationship at the moment, not really," he added the last two words as something like an afterthought. "Have I ever been in love? Yes countless times, although only twice truly, once with a woman and once with a man. I was a young man of probably twenty-three or twenty-four when I met the most beautiful girl in the world, on a train of all places," he sighed, making me laugh. "I assumed, and she encouraged the assumption that she was older, twenty-ish. She wasn't. She was sixteen."

I could see he was unhappy about that. Her age, even now. "Six or seven years is not so bad," I suggested.

"Maybe not. Maybe not today at least, but then, almost thirty years ago it was, and sociably it was frowned upon. Plus she lied about it on more than one occasion. We dated, discreetly, for almost a year and when I was confronted by her father it all came out, her age."

"Did you see her after that?" I hoped he had and yet knew even if he had the outcome hadn't been a happy one.

"Yes, one last time. I confronted her lies about her age and circumstances and we, I ended things there and then."

"I'm sorry." I smiled sadly, but sincerely. "Is that when you discovered your gay side?"

His face was as amused as mine was horrified by the ridiculous question I had just asked.

With a laugh he shook his head. "No, my gay side had always been there!"

"So you are bi-sexual then?" My whispered words made him laugh again.

"I don't know that there is such a thing. Surely bi-sexuality is code for greedy and indecisive."

It was my turn to laugh now. "I guess, but if you have known men and women…"

"One woman, she was my one and only woman. Men, there have been more, but only one I truly loved. Still do, but after all these years he is still not ready to admit what he is, not even to himself."

"That seems awfully sad, to not be comfortable enough in your own skin to admit who and what you are," I mused and quickly realised that I too had refused to stand up and be counted until I met Cy.

"Quite." Edward smiled as if he could read my mind or at least agree with my own thoughts.

With dessert cleared away and the coffee drunk, Edward and I stared across the table at each other for a matter of seconds, but it seemed longer. As Edward had been the one to do all the running up until this point I knew I needed to extend the hand of friendship, let him know that all of his efforts to reach out had not been in vain.

"Thank you, for tonight and for inviting me to see Balder, it was lovely, thank you," I repeated.

"I figured you both needed it and as I may have mentioned, I like you. Cy was less sure of the merits of your Balder visitation as it distressed you…"

"He told you?"

"Mmm, somewhere in between telling me he wouldn't have me causing such upset on a periodic basis, so unless I could make it a regular thing and give you both some consistency I should think carefully."

"Sorry," I grimaced.

"He loves you and wants you to be happy. You can't criticise him for that, well I can't and he's right, any contact with Balder needs to be regular, for you both, but Michael doesn't see that."

"He doesn't know," I stated rather than asked.

Shaking his head, Edward frowned at me.

"Ah, then thank you even more." I smiled with a little too

much enthusiasm judging by the tight sensation in my jaw and the eyes filled with sorrow looking back at me. I needed to take legal advice. I needed to add Georgie Parker to my to-do list, to the top of my list. "We should do this again," I started, moving back towards my earlier goal of extending the hand of friendship.

"I'd like that. Maybe we could invite Tia and Cy along, Lulu too?"

"Sounds like a date." I smiled, genuinely pleased at the idea of making plans with Edward.

"But not a date, I'm not good with angry, alpha male boyfriends," he teased, making me laugh. "Then we're agreed. Let me pay the bill and I'll walk you to your car, assuming Cy isn't going to magically appear."

"No, he's safely ensconced at home with Lulu and all things pink, furry and glittery."

"Lulu's weekend with Daddy?"

"Mmm, it's debatable who gets most excited by her visits." I smiled. "Him, her, or me. She's very sweet."

"Yes she is, and the fact that you're allowed within fifty feet of her will tell Elizabeth just how special you are."

"I hope so." I smiled. "But if not, I still get some Lulu time."

Chapter Twenty-Nine

Pulling onto Cy's drive, having used the fob for the security gate I felt happy, ridiculously so. I parked my car and once I was standing at the front door, I eyed the keys in my hand with apprehension and excitement. I had never used a key to Cy's home before, never needed to. We'd previously arrived here together or I had arrived when he was already home. I still wondered why he'd given me a key tonight as he was inside with Lulu, unless he was concerned I might wake her because it was past her bedtime.

I entered the house and after a quick look around downstairs and no sign of Cy, I headed upstairs where I could hear voices, two of them.

"Baby, if I read you another story you have to go straight to sleep at the end," Cy said sounding tired.

"I want to see El," the little girl replied insistently, melting my heart a little more. "But it's so boring to wait so we can have another story and if she still isn't back we could draw some more tattoos."

I stifled a fit of the giggles at her assiduousness and imagined her father's face at that precise second.

"Honey, El might be really, really late. It's already really late." I heard him sigh. "You have to go to sleep and you can see El in the morning and then we'll have the weekend together, all of us, but one more story is all I'm offering."

A broad grin spread across my face listening to Cy parenting as if he was negotiating a business deal in the boardroom. Listening to the little girl's response it seemed to be working.

"Okay," she agreed with what I imagined would be a pout on her lips. "But I'm going to need the whole of The Jolly Postman, and all of the letters and voices," she renegotiated.

"Fine, but if we could get started…"

"If El comes back soon though…you know what Daddy, I think you might need to give El a curfew."

"You know what Lulu I think you may be right."

With boggle eyes and a nervous sweat that they were both serious I decided that was my cue to make my presence known, to say hi to Lulu and once her story was done she'd have no further excuses to remain awake. Surely she was exhausted as it was at least two hours after her usual bedtime.

"El does not need a curfew!" I saw them both jump from my position in the doorway.

The scene before me made my heart skip a beat; Lulu was in bed, a beautifully crafted white wooden bed frame dressed in pretty unicorn emblazoned linen in multi-coloured glittery tones. The rest of the room screamed worshipped little princess, with pictures and prints of characters, mainly princesses and more toys than a small toy shop including a rocking horse and a doll's house. Cy was sitting next to Lulu, with his legs up on top of the covers, but stretched out, overhanging the bottom of the bed slightly. He really did look like an advert for sex with his loose fitting jeans and tightly fitted white t-shirt while his feet were bare. He had one hand between him and Lulu, holding the book he was preparing to read and the other was fingering his sexily mussed hair. God, how I loved making that hair messy. They both wore big grins at my intrusion. Cy straightened slightly while Lulu leapt from beneath the covers and was now bouncing excitedly on the bed.

"We'll see," Cy said as I reached the bed where Lulu flung herself into my arms.

"Yes we will," I agreed as Lulu began to tell me about her evening that had begun after I left for dinner.

"And then we made some more tattoos. Daddy helped me," she excitedly told me making me laugh at Cy's sour expression.

"Daddy drew some pictures, not tattoos," he insisted.

"You say tomato." I smirked briefly. Briefly because Cy's

expression turned dark before my eyes, not scary dark, but horny dark and I had no clue why.

"Daddy, can El read my last story to me?" the little girl asked, reaching over to her father who was now standing next to her and with one arm around his neck and the other around mine she pulled him in for a kiss.

"If El wants to. I'm kind of all read out after five stories in the last hour."

"Just you and me then kid," I told her and settled us both down on the bed for her final story before Cy leaned in for a kiss from each of us and then left us alone.

****

It was half an hour later, with The Jolly Postman done and dusted and one very tired little girl completely out for the count when I found Cy downstairs with a beer in each hand.

"For you." He smiled with a bottle extended in my direction.

I closed the distance to take the bottle, although I needed more than a bottle of beer right now. Close enough to smell and touch I pushed up on my feet and with my free hand I cupped Cy's chin and brought his lips down to my own and kissed him. Gently I drew his lower lip between my teeth, encouraging his mouth to open for me, which it did, freely, willingly. Carefully I allowed my tongue to invade his mouth as my hand that had drawn him to me slid up until it was pushing through his hair.

Apparently my dominance in this moment ended right there. I found myself lifted up by hands cupping my arse and the kiss I'd instigated as the aggressor was being replaced by a hot and ferocious kiss that savaged my mouth almost daring me to challenge it. I didn't, I simply whimpered as my legs did their own thing and wrapped themselves around Cy's hips, pulling him closer, feeling his thickening length pushing through the denim of his jeans and pressing into me through the fabric of my dress and tiny pants. I was unsure how I managed to keep hold of my bottle of beer, but Cy's had gone judging by his hands that were cupping my arse still, one full globe in each hand being squeezed and caressed as he continued to pull me into his arousal that surely couldn't thicken or stiffen anymore.

Breaking the kiss saw me breathless, but not Cy who was grinning broadly. "For you," he repeated, pulling me into his body a little further. So his dick was capable of thickening and stiffening some more, I could feel it.

"The beer?" I grinned.

"That too."

I really loved this Cy. The smiling, playful one, at home, chilled and happy, the father, the boyfriend, my boyfriend.

"You wanna discuss your curfew now?" he asked with a tilt of his head.

"No chance." I frowned with a smile still.

"We'll see," was his confident response.

"Long night?" I asked still wrapped around him but minus the beer that I had now placed on the worktop nearest to me.

"Like you wouldn't believe. By the time I was on my third happily ever after I was ready to kill Prince Charming off and leave the Princess to die alone and unloved in the tower," he replied flatly, making me laugh. "Not even joking there, baby."

"Have you decided on tattoos for me and Lulu yet?"

"Pushing?" he asked with a cock of his eyebrow.

"Mmm," I admitted and physically pushed myself against him, prompting his erection to jerk against me. "And maybe I can deliver a happy ending if not a happily ever after to make amends for your inadequate story telling."

I'd given no thought to my use of the happily ever after phrase until Cy responded. "Baby, I love happy endings with you and we will have a happily ever after, I promise, but not now, now we go to bed," he said with a wink before carrying me upstairs.

Everything about me was loose and limp, not to mention achy, in the best way possible as I lay in bed, on my side, watching the beautiful man beside me.

"Why do they call you Cy?" I asked, wondering why it had taken this long to ask even though it had sprung to mind a dozen or more times before this moment.

"It started when I was a baby and was named Denton. My grandfather wasn't overly keen on the name I don't think. It came from my grandmother's side of the family but he knew of a

Denton Young, known as Cy Young, a baseball player and he loved baseball. His father had seen Cy Young play and told my grandfather about him when he was inducted into the hall of fame, Cy, not my great grandfather. It helped that my great grandfather and Cy Young were both from Ohio. It just stuck and everyone called me Cy, like I told you at the beginning, my friends and family. Nobody calls me Denton, not in familiar terms."

"And Tia?" I asked wondering why she was known as Tia Mamodo when she was actually a Miller.

"Tia? That's her name." He frowned with confusion.

"When you had me send her flowers that time you told me to send them to Tia Mamoda."

He laughed now. "Ah, I see. It's just a joke, a sibling thing. Chris and I were into anime, had comics, books and watched it at weekends. I don't think Tia was as into it as me and Chris, but she wanted to be. There was a character Tia Mamodo who was sweet and loyal but was betrayed by someone she thought was a friend and then found a true friend in Megumi," he laughed loudly. "Chris and I used to call any friend Tia brought home Megumi, which usually pissed them off, or at least confused them. God we were asses, but the Mamodo stuck and Tia likes it."

"And her friends, do you still call them Megumi?"

"I don't really know her friends anymore. She's kind of picky, although there's you now. Do you want to be Megumi?"

Laughing I shook my head. "No, I'll stick with bitch or baby I think. I like that whole baby thing," I admitted.

"I know you do," he replied with a cocky grin. He reached for me and pulled me closer, "Baby."

****

I found that the weekend was relaxing and stressful in equal parts. It was wonderful to spend time within a family unit, a strong and happy unit, and yet it also proved painful. My memory searched to remember being in Lulu's position; happy, content, totally and utterly resolute in the knowledge that she was loved, nurtured, encouraged and completely adored. I did remember happy times and I never doubted I was loved and the weekend was almost therapeutic in making me remember that I wasn't always part of a single parent family, where my remaining parent had their own considerable mental health issues. A time and place where I was still a child, able to be a child.

However, it also threw up the dreams and ambitions I had held. I had once been like Lulu, a happy ever after kind of girl. I remembered dreaming of growing up and getting a job, one I loved and although I enjoyed my work, I had never wanted to be an office worker. I changed career each week as a child and went from doctor to zoo keeper, teacher to air hostess, actress to journalist, dancer to social worker, the final one being an actual ambition until I had finally taken the job Susan got for me. The realisation that even that dream had been manipulated from under me was a bitter pill to swallow as was the one where I recalled believing in Prince Charming and castles in the sunset I'd ride off to where I would live happily ever after with my prince and beautiful bouncing babies.

I was sitting on a park bench with these thoughts when disillusionment washed over me. I was twenty-eight years old, about to embark on a divorce from a marriage that had never truly offered my happy ever after or Prince Charming. I had no children. I didn't even have the dog. My living arrangements were essentially flitting between the spare room in a recently reacquainted friend's house and sleeping in my lover's bed, the lover that was the biggest factor in the end of my marriage. The same man who was everything I had ever allowed myself to dream about and more. The same man who was coming under familial pressure to make a wiser choice than me.

"El, come on the teeter-totter with me, Daddy's too heavy," Lulu called making me frown up from my private thoughts and worries.

"The what?" I called back, but was already making my way over to where the little girl stood with her father.

"Honey, go and play on the swings for a while and then I am sure El will be happy to ride the teeter-totter with you."

"Okay," the little girl agreed, running off towards a vacant swing.

"What the hell's a teeter-totter," I asked with a smile on my face that was only slightly forced.

"Over there. The see-saw you'd probably call it."

"Ah, I see, although I'm not sure I would ever have got it without the help."

"Hey, happy to help out and as I've said before you really need to become more fluent in American English. You're gonna need to be. Now, why don't you tell me what had you looking so sad just now on the bench?"

"Nothing." I attempted to push past Cy and brush him off at the same time, but he intercepted my intentions and with a grip around my wrist holding me steady, he shook his head.

"Baby, I thought we'd moved past this, trying to feed me a fine line in BS."

"Sorry. Honestly, it was nothing other than thoughts and some self-pity, but I am having a wonderful time. I really am."

Cy studied me for a few seconds, mulling over my words, maybe questioning the truth of them before smiling down at me as he brushed the hair off my face. "I'm glad you're having fun El. This is as near to perfect as I've ever known, you, me and Lulu," he told me as he leaned down to kiss me. His lips landed and mine responded when we were interrupted.

"Daddy, can you push me please?" called Lulu loudly, drawing our attention to her and everyone else's to us.

"Coming, honey," he called to the beaming little girl then turned to me, "and you need to get ready for the teeter-totter."

"See-saw," I called after him as Cy ran towards his daughter who was sitting almost stationary on the swing.

"American English baby." He grinned over his shoulder making me laugh and every woman within ogling distance of him gape and stare. God, he really was beautiful and seemed almost oblivious to it.

When Rhonda arrived a little after tea time, I was already beginning to think about going home, to Maya's. I hadn't seen her since Friday at work and hadn't slept in my own bed since Thursday making me feel a little guilty that I was in some way abusing her hospitality. I kept looking for an ideal opportunity to excuse myself without appearing rude or abrupt and it was Lulu that gave me my chance.

"Did Mommy tell you that Grandma called and invited us to stay for Thanksgiving?" the little girl innocently asked her father who shook his head but seemed less than surprised by that piece of information.

"No, and Mommy told you that she would speak to Daddy to check what his plans were, him and El," Rhonda replied with a smile in my direction.

"We have no plans, nothing concrete anyway," Cy explained and that was my cue because I could see the surprise on Rhonda's face.

"I have a few things to do," I awkwardly began. "I've had a lovely weekend Lulu, thank you for letting me spend it with you."

"No problem," the little girl grinned before meeting me as I prepared to exit and flung her arms around me for a squeeze. "You're good to ride the teeter-totter with. Daddy's just too heavy."

"Any time," I replied and offered her mother a smile as I headed for the stairs.

****

The quietness of the bedroom was a welcome relief, not that I hadn't enjoyed the weekend with Cy and Lulu. I had, and yet I needed some quiet to reorder my thoughts; the ones about my father, my sister, my husband, Cy, my divorce, Thanksgiving, my whole life really. The problem was that when I was with Cy everything else ceased to exist. I was protected in his world, he protected me. If Michael decided to give me shit then Cy would advise, guide and ultimately deal with it, same with Susan and my dad, as much as he could with my dad.

We hadn't discussed my divorce beyond my intention to divorce and contact a solicitor, Georgie Parker, who I believed was the best, but had researched her enough to know she may be a little too expensive for me. I knew if I discussed that with Cy he would sort it. These were the things that I needed to sort out in my head and then follow through, for myself and with Cy so close by I wouldn't be able to do that, so we needed a little distance...just a little.

The whole Thanksgiving thing refused to go away; Elizabeth just kept pushing for the answer she wanted to her invitation and that answer was Cy minus me. He was digging his heels in, stating that he wouldn't go without me and as much as I loved him for that, I wished he'd just agree with her demand, it would be easier, for us all.

I definitely needed to go home and spend a few hours in my own bed and head and make a few decisions. I could even call Susan, prepare her for my divorce and broach the subject of our father's care and the fees that accompanied it.

Cy appeared a short time later and seemed to be leaving me to it. He watched me putting my things back into my bag from his position sitting on the bed. I was nervous and he wasn't behaving how I'd expected. He wasn't saying anything, he just kept watching and I couldn't help thinking that this was the calm before the storm.

Eventually he spoke, flatly. "I've had the best weekend, thank you."

"Me too," was my response. Two words were as many as I could risk without tears which was ridiculous considering that I planned on seeing him again the following morning, it wasn't like either of us were going off to war.

"You want to go back to Maya's?" he asked gesturing to the bag I was struggling to fasten.

"Hmm."

"You need some help?" he asked, already reaching for my bag and proceeded to fasten it with ease.

"Thank you."

"No problem, baby. I need about an hour and then I'm good to go, or I could come over later," he began with certainty.

"No, sorry," I stammered. "I think I should go alone."

"No."

"Cy, please. I have a head full of shit to sort out. I need a few hours to straighten things out," I pleaded.

"What shit? Am I one of those things that needs straightening out, uh? I think I have a right to know, don't you?" he asked, angry now rather than his previous reasonable. "This is what was going on at the playground before, wasn't it? The

BS about thoughts and self-pity?"

I felt guilty as I watched Cy's expression morph into one of concern and worse still, disappointment. I hadn't lied to him earlier and despite his accusation that I had been feeding him bullshit, I hadn't been, not really, but here I was, kind of going back on my earlier claim that I was okay.

"It's not like that. I have had a fantastic weekend. This is something I haven't done, not as an adult, been so tightly involved in a family unit like this and I have loved it. I love you, and Lulu, but it's kind of scary because all I can see when I think about it is all of the missed chances and all the mistakes, my own and other people's. That's why I need tonight Cy, to really think about my future and what that involves."

I watched him physically bristle as he misunderstood my words and then attempted to turn away.

"No!" I cried, already moving so that I was in front of him again. "You are seriously misunderstanding me." My insistence seemed to register as his face softened slightly.

"Then explain it to me because I am fucking flailing here. This is as new to me as it is to you and we can't afford to fuck it up."

I nodded, he was right. As much as I looked to him to ground me, to centre me, enable me to move forward, make decisions and choices, I didn't do the same for him and he was as out of his comfort zone as I was out of mine. He was always certain in business and I thought that maybe I needed to remember that the man before me was not the same man who could spend several million pounds in one deal and not blink. He was actually a man, not just a man because I could never describe Cy as *just* anything, but he was a man, my man. He was a father, a son, a brother, a boyfriend and he was currently juggling a lot of plates that were at risk of falling and breaking all around him so I needed to help him to keep them in the air like he did for me.

I was sitting on the edge of the bed where I pulled him to sit beside me.

"Right, let me try again. This afternoon I was lost in thoughts about lots of things, and then I did go on a little bit of a path paved with self-pity, that was true. I need to stop burying my head in the sand with Michael, Susan, and my dad, all of them. Edward and I chatted and he seems kind of sad because his two great loves never worked out for him. He's missing something, someone and I don't want to end up that way."

"You won't, baby. I am going nowhere," Cy reassured with his forehead resting against mine. "You're mine. I love you."

"I know and I love you too, but lots of people love and lose. Anyway, I need to speak to Susan and to contact a solicitor and begin divorce proceedings, assuming I can and Michael doesn't contest everything. I have a feeling he may want to divorce me as a point of principal, probably on the grounds of my adultery, with you."

I left that one hanging there and imagined Elizabeth's horrified expression when that particular gem became common knowledge.

"Let him. I couldn't give a shit and if it means you're free of him…"

"We'll see. And Susan needs to understand that whatever she's plotting isn't going to work and more than that I have to tell her that dad's care is expensive and will need paying by us. I don't hold out much hope of money from the boys, but Susan earns good money and Mary will chip in."

"Who's Mary, I heard them mention her at the care home."

"Our other sister. She moved to Australia after a huge row and rift between her and the others, something nobody ever speaks of," I explained with a wry smile at the cloak and dagger nature of the rift.

"Families are great, aren't they?" Cy stated, making me laugh.

"Oh yeah. Anyway, the days of them all using me and in turn Michael are over. I just need to sit down and draw up a list or a plan of some sort and I can't do that here, with you?"

Shit, he was pissed again, his face said as much, but reaching up I stroked his jaw and cheek until he looked at me, his eyes on mine.

"I thought I was the overthinker. The reason I can't do that here, with you is because when it's us none of those things exist.

You, we, distract me, and all I can see and think about is us, right here, right now and a future for us, our happily ever after. The ending I always wanted, but first I have to sort my shit and remember who I was, before all of the shit, or at least who I should have been."

"Okay, I can deal with that and I know it's going to take more than one night to sieve through the crap, but tomorrow night you'll be with me."

I nodded, I didn't want or need days and weeks apart.

"You know I'll cover Jezza's fees, but I know you don't want that, so for now you deal with your family over that one, but attorney? You need to call Georgie Parker. Even though her husband likes to jerk people's chains he was right about her, she is the best and if you can't afford her I can."

"Cy," I interrupted to protest.

"No, nothing to say, or else I call Jezza's people tomorrow and pay the next year's fees up front, meaning the money you were going to use for them will pay for Georgie. Your choice, baby."

I stared at him and could see clear and cold determination on his face, this was his immoveable object persona in all its glory and he'd been doing so well with his reasonable one before.

"I'll call Georgie tomorrow."

"Thank you." He smiled and my concession was worth it, just for the glorious smile illuminating his features.

"Thank you," I replied getting to my feet. "I should go," I said not even convincing myself of that intention.

Before I could compute anything else, I was being pulled into the space between Cy's open thighs and brought down into a straddle across his lap.

"I need some alone time with you first. I love Lulu more than life itself but she impacts on our one on one time, in the best way, but if you're doing all that thinking and planning stuff later, I need my fill of you now."

"Your fill of me or you need to fill me?" I asked with a cheeky grin and a cock of the head.

"Good point, Ms Ross. I will never get my fill of you so I

think I'd better stick to filling you baby." Cy grinned back until I took advantage of my higher position and covered his mouth with mine, leaving us both happy, grounded and centred again, for now at least.

Chapter Thirty

Georgie Parker was my first call of the day and with her office only a couple of miles from my own I arranged to see her the following day. My sister on the other hand was being elusive, deliberately so I suspected. So, with my plan of action written down in my diary and engrained on my brain I changed tack. With my beautifully expensive handbag reinstated as my bag of choice for work I pulled my phone from it and selected a name and number I hadn't called in a while. The ringing tone seemed to sound forever before my call was picked up.

"Hello," my husband's voice answered flatly with only the tiniest hint of curiosity at me calling him.

"Hello, it's me, El," I explained, slightly unnecessarily as I was certain my name would have come up on his caller ID, unless he'd wiped my number from his phone.

I did stop short of introducing myself fully, Eloise Ross would have sounded as if I was making some kind of business call and being deliberately antagonistic. As much as I had a genuine reason for using Michael in this way, I wasn't that hard or that much of a bitch that I would do that, infer that somehow I had forgotten who Michael was and what we had once been, all the things I'd hoped we'd be.

"El, what can I do for you?" he asked.

Maybe this was going to be a formal conversation, from his end at least.

"It's a courtesy call really," I began and decided that yes, we were both treating the other like it was a professional associate and I didn't want that so adapted my tone and demeanour, but remained succinct in my words. "I have spoken to a solicitor this morning, about us, our marriage. I'm going to meet her tomorrow and discuss divorce. I didn't want you to hear about it from her or in writing."

I meant what I'd said, I wanted Michael to hear my plans directly from me, but his sharp intake of breath and pause on the other end of the line told me he was not expecting this move which made me feel guilty. However, I also knew that Susan would be aware of my plan before much longer and she would be disinclined to ignore me armed with that information.

"A divorce?" Michael asked when he eventually spoke. "Should I assume that you plan on divorcing me?" He laughed now. "We'll see then. Thank you for your call Eloise, goodbye."

I stared down at the phone that was in my hand, minus my husband at the other end of it and still slightly shocked I put my head, face down on my desk as Cy appeared in the doorway.

"Problem?" he asked, making me jump. Raising my head I saw he was wearing a deep frown.

"I'm not entirely sure," I admitted honestly. "Susan is ignoring all of my attempts to make contact so I took a detour to her via Michael."

The last word only served to make Cy's expression one of irritation.

"Go on."

"I've called Georgie Parker. I'm seeing her tomorrow and as Susan is avoiding me I thought I'd call Michael, partly to tell him about engaging a solicitor but also knowing he will tell Susan and that information will ensure she speaks to me."

Cy shook his head, but at least his frown and maybe his irritation were softening. "Don't play games, baby. With either of them," he seemed to warn. "You're not a player, not like they are so do not take them on in this."

"That wasn't my intention," was my reply, I hoped in defence of myself. "I thought Michael should hear of my plans from me and if it rattles Susan's cage a little."

"I get that, all of it, and now he knows and she…"

The sound of my phone ringing interrupted Cy. We both looked down and exchanged a glance when we saw Susan's name flashing across my screen.

"Mission accomplished," Cy said. "But no more games. Their games will hurt you if you get caught up in them. They will hurt you, again. So no games, okay?"

"Yes, I didn't think."

"Answer your call before she goes AWOL again." Cy smiled, although I knew she'd be relentless in her pursuit of answers and information once she knew of my divorce plans and suddenly, I wished I hadn't pushed for this so soon, but I had.

"Hello," I answered a little nervously. "Susan, I thought we should talk." I watched Cy walk back into his office, affording me some privacy and the choice on how to proceed, albeit with our normal service of *office door open* fully resumed.

Susan was clearly on some serious medication or had at the very least had a personality bypass judging by how calm and reasonable she was on the telephone when we arranged to meet that evening, to *chat*. Seriously, I didn't believe my sister had ever had a *chat* with anyone, ever!

****

"I still don't know why you didn't just invite her here." Cy pouted from his position lying on the bed, propped up on pillows looking delightfully tempting in just a pair of track bottoms while I stood in a short, satin robe that covered very little beyond my nakedness.

I looked over my clothes, trying to decide what I should wear as I replied. "Yes, you do know. We've had this conversation at least four times since we got here." I frowned, thinking that meeting Susan here, at Cy's house, would have been easier in so many ways, but unwise. Turning, I could see Cy was still unconvinced. "Right then, let me run through this one last time." I returned to the bed. Crawled up it until I straddled Cy's hips.

My fingers were tracing the lines of his tattoo while my naked and warm sex rested against his clothed groin, my own body immediately softening, heating and moistening, but I needed to focus on our conversation.

"Reasons meeting Susan here is a bad idea. Firstly, I don't want her to think that I live here, and before you go all alpha man and bang your chest, I mean that I don't want her to make assumptions about us and my reasons for leaving Michael. Secondly, she has no place here, with us. She will make this dirty and sordid, with looks and comments and here, with you, this place, your home is a happy place."

"So you're not ashamed of me, or my home?" He smirked a little cockily.

"No. Although, that hideous carpet and wallpaper combo you have going on out there." I cringed with a flick of a finger in the direction of the door and the decorating beyond.

With a squeal of shock and surprise, I found myself thrown so that I was flat on my back with the weight of Cy on me. Holding me down. Pinning me there. His body was hard, almost crushing me in a really, really good way. A hot way that certainly had me flushing, heating and panting.

"I was thinking of decorating, or at least getting someone in."

"Really?" I enquired, wondering whether I'd had anything to do with that decision.

"Yeah, really. But I think you should have at least one positive memory of it so I am going to fuck you up against the hideous walls until you develop a fondness for out there."

"Fond of the walls or the fucking?" I asked with a groan as I felt Cy pressing between my thighs, his erection obvious to us both as it rubbed across my mons before jabbing into my belly, my nakedness offering no barrier to the stimulation.

"The fucking is already taken as read so I guess that just leaves the walls."

"And the carpet?" I asked, almost gasping with the need for more than the gentle rubbing I could feel against my immobile body that was a prisoner to my gorgeous lover in every conceivable way.

"You have no idea just how tempted I am to send you to meet your sister with fresh carpet burns on your ass, or even your knees."

"Or both?" I grinned, thinking of nothing other than this. Us, me and Cy together with nobody else waiting to throw a hand grenade into the middle of my life. "And it's still arse."

"Pushing?"

"Most definitely, and I am hoping you're about to push back," I said with a sense of optimism that was well placed judging by the darkening of Cy's eyes and the twitching of his dick. Yeah, we were definitely about to have ourselves some serious pushing going on.

"I fucking love you, baby." He grinned down at me. A real panty melting grin with his perfect teeth and a twinkle in his eyes that had the desired effect if the rush of moisture from my body was anything to go by.

"I love you too. Oh, and there was another reason for me not meeting Susan here," I told him, suddenly and unexpectedly finding my sister back in my head.

"Go on."

"Thirdly," I began, still counting the reasons. "This whole reasonable meeting could indicate an ambush—"

"Ambush? What the fuck does that mean? Forget what it means, you are going nowhere to be ambushed," his interrupting protest made me laugh a little as Cy leaned back until he was staring me down rather than simply holding me down. "I am not joking so you have no need to laugh."

I laughed again before explaining my words. "I didn't mean a band of outlaws coming to hit me over the head to leave me in a cellar, gagged and bound."

"You are giving me some seriously perverse ideas thinking of you gagged and bound." Cy smirked, earning himself a slap to the chest, but a huge smile too.

"No gagging," I said firmly, honestly, thinking of my gag reflex that barely tolerated my toothbrush in my mouth some days. I grinned as I wondered why something as small as a toothbrush could trigger gagging and yet the feel of something considerably bigger, something like Cy didn't pose the same problem.

"I am totally on board with whatever you are thinking right now, but before your ass gets out of here you'll need to explain this ambush to me."

"Now?" With just the lift of an eyebrow he confirmed that yes, I needed to explain, now. "It could be Susan and Michael, but I doubt that. He will leave Susan to do his bidding and deny all knowledge of that in the future. I was thinking she is likely to turn up with one or more of my brothers, but they won't literally ambush me. They'll most likely be all for me working my marriage out. Michael is a wonderful benefactor for them in times of need," I said with a real bitterness I hadn't expected. "I meant no more than that."

"I get the stuff with Jezza and you've intimated on more than one occasion that your brothers have gained from your marriage, but never been specific."

"You are killing the buzz here," I accused with a huff and a frown making Cy smile.

"I'll get your buzz back, baby, I promise. I'll fuck you any way you want and make you come as often and as hard as you need, now spill."

"Any way I want?" I clarified and received a confirming nod. "And come hard?" I grinned, already becoming reacquainted with my missing buzz.

"You bet, and as often, so?"

"Edited details because I am needing to be on all fours, with the feel you inside me, making me come, really, really hard."

"You really need to speak, quickly," Cy told me, his tone cautioning me.

"Wayne, Gary and Neil are my brothers. Gary is ten years older than me, Wayne twelve years and Neil is the oldest of us all so has twenty years on me. Wayne and Gary got into various scrapes, usually without too much in the way of repercussions until Gary got himself in with some big boys, armed robbery kind of big boys. He was the driver, not that I'm suggesting that his role in anyway lessons the severity of his wrong doing. Michael and I were seeing each other when he got arrested and charged, the whole gang did. They all called the duty solicitor and applied for legal aid, and then Michael intervened. He called a top brief and Gary was the only one not to be held on remand. He asked me to marry him shortly after that, and I agreed for reasons of my perceived love and gratitude. Dad was then put into a home and when Gary's case came to trial, he had a very expensive barrister who got him off. The only one not to get a significant sentence. So in Gary's mind he owes Michael, and I am guessing his debt payment looks a lot like me. Michael even gave Gary a job. The boys all owe Michael one way or another, he's helped them all. Gary has his freedom, Wayne developed a gambling habit, a big one, and Michael helped him, paid his debts, kept his house for him and got him professional support."

"They owe him, not you. What's Neil's story?"

"Not much to tell with Neil. He has four ex-wives and children with them all, some grown up now, but he struggles to make ends meet most of the time so Michael has helped him with cash at times, a divorce solicitor who was able to negotiate favourable settlements and access arrangements. He absolved them all of responsibility for my dad, financially at first and then as time went on and I was his primary visitor and next of kin they didn't even have to think of our dad's needs. If Michael and I divorce and he cuts them and my dad off…"

"They're screwed."

"Yes, to a point." I nodded. "And they are genuinely grateful. Susan will be fine, she's not dependent on Michael for anything beyond Dad and she can probably contribute more financially than the others. Plus, she and Michael have a genuine relationship, friendship, whatever it is they have between them, which is what motivates her to make me right for him again."

"You sure you want to meet her off home turf?" He landed a gentle kiss to my forehead without delving further into my messed up family.

"Yes, positive."

"And you don't want me to come with you, even to wait nearby?"

I shook my head. "No, no thank you."

"Okay, but call if you change your mind," Cy told me firmly with a smile. My response was a short and conciliatory smile. "So, what now, baby?" A more confident and self-assured Cy was already lowering his lips to mine, preparing to graze them

"I want you, need you, I told you," I pleaded and with my legs no longer pinned down I began to raise them, spreading them in order to wrap them around Cy's hips. "Inside me. I want you inside me," I expanded and felt my whole body shudder when Cy reached down, pushed his trousers down his legs and freed himself.

****

I was still coming down from my third, or maybe fourth orgasm, and was at serious risk of losing track of time completely which would only serve to infuriate Susan further if I rocked up to meet her late. Especially if I ended up looking disheveled from sex with Cy. Timekeeping was pushed from my mind completely as I found myself flipped over onto my hands and knees, face down and arse in the air, with very little pause before Cy was pushing back into me. It was at a different angle than before, the position and sensation suddenly deeper and more intense. Cy quickly set the rhythm and pace, fast and regular which brought me to the brink in no time at all. His hands began to tighten their grip on my hips, possibly leaving his prints on me.

"Oh yeah, baby. This feels so fucking good, you feel so good. I love watching myself sink into you," he groaned, making me moan in response as I imagined the view he was enjoying right now. The primal and base image of us coupled, joined in the most primitive way.

I still found it odd to think that at almost twenty-nine years old and married for over five years that I was unaware of feelings like this, physical and emotional feelings.

Early in my marriage, sex with Michael had been pleasant, satisfying at the time for the woman I had been, but it had also been predictable and formulated. We had a routine. We rarely had sex anywhere other than in bed. We kissed, briefly, and then Michael would touch me, stroke down my body, with a few gentle caresses for my breasts. Occasionally he'd add a suck or a lick to my nipples and then quickly he would settle a hand between my legs where he would stroke me, for what I now realised was quite a long time until I came. Then he would put on a condom and make love to me, gently, often in missionary or on our sides, him behind me. Either way it would usually end quickly. Sometimes with a second orgasm for me before Michael shuddered and then he was gone, disposing of the condom and showering. Washing all evidence of me and us

393

together away.

With Cy, everything was different. My body reacted differently to and for him, and when we were together everything was unpredictable. There was no formula to anything we did, especially not sex. I knew that we were limited on time and yet this, what we were sharing, could actually turn out to be anything but a quickie, unlike my married sex which with hindsight was always a quickie and whilst I loved a quick and rewarding shag, I also appreciated a longer, drawn out session and right now I had no clue which way this was likely to go.

I had been so clueless, as Michael had said, clumsy and he had exposed me to experiences over the years we'd shared and yet Cy had shown and taught me more, including unleashing enough confidence for me to tell him what I wanted. Things I had no previous knowledge of. Perhaps I was discovering myself as Cy did. Maybe he was discovering me quicker than I was finding myself because he certainly seemed to know what I needed better than I did. As if to prove that thought, he lifted my behind as he pushed my middle down, lower to the bed and immediately my whole body came to life. Every nerve end reacting and intensifying with such a simple movement. My head turned, peeking over my shoulder where I found Cy's eyes on mine, one hand released my hip and lowered until it had found my clit that was already swollen and primed.

"Keep your eyes on me, baby. That is so fucking horny, you watching me and feeling me," he told me as his finger began to make firmer, tighter circles that had my internal muscles flexing and my breath catching.

"Oh God, Cy, like that, it feels so good," I moaned, earning myself a smile.

"What do you want baby. Right now, what do you want?" he asked. I gave no thought to my response. I simply answered, desire causing complete honesty from me.

"Make me come. Make me come until I scream and then come inside me."

No more words were exchanged, just looks, glances and then bodily fluids.

Collapsing into the middle of the bed, we were a heap of

limbs and sweat. I ached in all the best ways and could think of nothing more appealing than staying right there, entangled with Cy. Maybe even taking a little nap before waking up and rediscovering each other, a little less frantically, maybe a slow build up...

"Hey, you okay?" Cy's words and a gentle kiss on my shoulder interrupted my thoughts of staying in bed.

"Mmm, really okay," I replied with a grin.

"Good. I love lying here with you, El, but you probably need to get dressed if you want to meet Susan on time. Remember, you need me, call."

Chapter Thirty-One

Susan was already waiting for me in the bar of the hotel where we'd agreed to meet. As suspected it was an ambush with both Gary and Wayne sitting with her, but no Neil. I smiled at them, a rather flat and subdued smile as I reached them. None of them stood to greet me, nor did anyone return my smile. It was going to be a long evening. I purposely sat on the outside of the table, somehow feeling reassured that if I needed to I could make a quick escape.

"Have you eaten?" Susan asked before even considering hello as an opener, although I supposed checking on my diet meant she was still showing concern for me.

"Yes thanks. You? Have you all had dinner?" I asked in response, moving into my default mode of facilitating fulfillment of other people's needs, my family's needs.

"We're fine, we're all fed," Susan replied, not giving either of the boys an opportunity to speak. Perhaps they'd already agreed how this was going down. "You seem different," my sister accused. Apparently different was wrong.

"Possibly," was all I could think of to say as a waiter arrived with drinks that had been ordered before my arrival. The night was already taking a turn for the worse I decided as I accepted my glass of wine, rosé. "Look, I think we know why we're all here. I have left Michael and I won't be going back, regardless of what any of you say which means we need to be responsible for our own lives and that includes Dad's care home fees."

They all stared at me, probably wondering who the hell I was because their baby sister did not speak to them this way.

This bluntly or concisely. She dressed things up and then gave in, doing exactly as they wanted.

"Don't be hasty, El." I shook my head that Gary thought any of this was hasty compared to my speedy marriage.

"Gary's right, you're throwing your marriage away for what? A fling, an affair that's likely to fizzle out once the novelty wears off?" my other brother chipped in.

I shook my head at Gary again, whilst throwing Wayne a withering glance for thinking, suggesting that I would fizzle out of Cy's life. That I was a novelty.

"I think what they're inarticulately trying to say is that, well, this is ridiculous. Ending a marriage shouldn't be taken lightly, certainly not a marriage to Michael." I could have sworn Susan cooed and swooned a little as she said my husband's name. "Now, I have managed to convince Michael that you have been manipulated and that this is not your fault, that he should forgive you, which he has agreed to do. You might need to rediscover your dress sense though Eloise," Susan told me with a half sneer as she took in my appearance which, while it wasn't anything special, I hardly looked out of place in black leggings, knee high leather boots and a casual, soft grey tunic.

My cringe surely couldn't have gone unnoticed at the over pronunciation of my name on my sister's lips. I stared at them all, moving my gaze from one to the other and back again.

"You all need to stop," I snapped with a sharpness I wasn't sure I was capable of until that split second. "I am not going to change my mind. My marriage to Michael is over and Cy has never manipulated me, unlike the rest of you. Now, this cash cow is out of milk so you all need to grow up and take responsibility for your own lives and Dad's. I have spoken to the care home and they've said his pension and benefits should be able to be used in part payment for fees, fees that Michael is no longer paying, but that will still leave us considerably short. I'm sure between us we can make up the shortfall—"

"Whoa, hang on a minute, I've got kids and bills to pay," Wayne protested first.

"We've all got commitments," I countered. "But he is our dad, ours, all of ours. I've spoken to Mary and she is happy to contribute—" Again I was cut off, by Susan this time.

"Mary? How dare you consult her on this, you have no right."

"I have every right. She's my sister too and she is his daughter as much as you or I, so I have the right to ask and she has the right to know."

Susan seemed to be preparing something else to say, but stopped short.

"El, I don't have the money to help out and neither does Wayne, nor Neil, you know that," Gary began. "You're right, he's our dad, but we can't do it. If you and Mary can cover it with Susan, fine. If not, he'll have to move somewhere cheaper, somewhere his benefits cover."

Gary looked genuinely saddened by his own words but also expectant, as if I was about to wave my magic wand. I ignored him and looked across at Susan.

"I know how much that place costs and I don't have it, El. I relocated and between my mortgage and living expenses, well, I can't pay a third of those costs so if you insist on doing this then it will be down to you and Mary alone."

"You know Mary won't be able to cover half," I told them with a sense of sadness and disappointment.

They were all looking between themselves and then back to me, as if somehow this was panning out quite nicely. That they were ensuring my dad's costs would be covered by one person only, Michael, and there was only one way that could or would happen.

"Unless your new bloke," Wayne suggested but shut up when he found himself pinned down by the matching glares of me and Susan. I wouldn't have Cy step in and pick up where Michael had left off and it seemed that at least on that, my sister and I were in agreement.

Getting to my feet I knew this was over, the discussion at least, and our family at most. Looking down at them I shook my head and was unsure what I should say right up to the point where my sister's sense of righteousness and necessary decorum rose up.

"Eloise, sit back down and do not even consider making a

public scene. You have embarrassed yourself and poor Michael enough already, wouldn't you say?"

I laughed. Not because I was in any way amused but because this situation was ridiculous.

"El, please. If you and Michael have problems maybe you need to find a way to work them out," Wayne suggested with what sounded like genuine affection and concern.

"Come on sis," Gary joined in. "Sit back down. We don't want you to be sad, but with Michael, well, you'll never want for anything. He'll take care of you, of us all, but mainly you. Will this new guy? Really? Forever?"

"I don't want to argue with you, any of you, but my marriage is over. I am sorry if that causes problems for you, but they're your problems, not mine. As for Cy, I have no clue what the future holds, but even if I end up without him I can't give up the time we do have together and the chance of a future I really, really want. Michael is a good man and he deserves to be loved, truly, madly and one hundred percent. Just not by me. I can't give him that. I thought I could. Thought I did. I couldn't and I didn't, but I can and I do with Cy."

My brothers both nodded, understanding, believing and accepting.

"You're being foolish and selfish," Susan told me with a shake of her head.

"No. I'm not. Possibly for the first time in my adult life I am not."

"What about Dad? Are you going to put your own needs ahead of his?" Susan asked, unable to resist a bitchy side dig.

"You need to stop right there," I warned with a slight raise of my voice, hinting that if she didn't want a scene, she needed to consider her next move very carefully.

"I'll take that as a yes." She still couldn't resist another tart and snide comment.

The gauntlet had been thrown down.

"Do you know what? Fuck you! All of you if you think my only purpose in life is to be used as currency in order to relieve the rest of you of your own responsibilities. I am getting divorced and one way or another Dad is staying where he is for the time he has left. What's the worst that can happen? That I have to prostitute myself to achieve that? Oh wait, that ship sailed when you all decided that setting up your twenty-three-year old virgin sister with a man thirty years older was the way fucking forward!"

Having just revealed my virginal status to my horrified looking brothers, not to mention the occupants of the bar I was sure I should feel in some way embarrassed. I didn't. With my head held high and my shoulders back, I prepared to leave.

"This is done and I do not expect to discuss my marriage or my divorce with any of you. Oh, and for the record, I don't like wine, I like beer and I hate fish, but love pizza. I am Eloise Ross and I am perfect, just as I am. I know this because Dad told me that on one of my frequent visits to spend time with him. He also told me that nobody has the right to tell me what I like and what I don't like. Oh, and he also said that if anyone did, I should tell them to fuck off, so in case there was any doubt, this is my fuck off. You…" I stared at my sister, "Let Michael know he should expect to hear from my solicitor, Georgie Parker, very soon."

I turned towards the exit and with precise and purposeful strides I made my way out with the sensation of dozens of sets of eyes on me, following me and although my use of expletives had been slightly over the top, it was an inflammatory two fingers up to the world, specifically my sister and brothers.

Reaching my car, I climbed inside and locked the doors. I needed the security and safety of a confined space for a few minutes and then I drove away, to Cy's where I knew he would support me in whatever choices I made.

****

Sitting in the plush waiting area of Georgie Parker's office proved more nerve wracking than I had thought it might. I hadn't expected it to induce nervousness at all and yet I found my hands wringing, feet tapping and knees virtually knocking. It wasn't like I'd changed my mind or had any doubts about ending my marriage. I knew this was the right thing to do, and yet it had a sense of finality that frightened me, and my pride was hurting at this failure, but also that I had been so stupid, naïve and manipulated by so many.

"Eloise," a voice called, drawing me from my thoughts.

Looking up I was faced with a very elegant looking forty-something woman who was smiling at me kindly. She wore an obviously expensive trouser suit with a startling white blouse and shoes that must have cost more than I earned in a week.

"Come through," she summoned with an extended hand to greet me from her position on the threshold to her office. "I'm Georgie Parker, good to meet you. My husband has told me that I need to take extra special care of you." She still wore a smile that reassured me that she didn't perceive me as a home wrecking whore with a penchant for married men who was going to try and seduce her husband and that his words about taking care of me were innocent. Although, she was sexy, classy and seductive as hell, so maybe she knew she had absolutely no worries where her husband was concerned.

Following her into the office, I sat opposite Georgie who still smiled, but had a more business face on now.

"So, Eloise, may I call you Eloise?"

"Yes, well El is better, if that's okay?"

"Fine and call me Georgie. I don't think we need to stand on ceremony, do we?"

I nodded and let out a huge sigh of relief and underlying anxiety.

"Look, El, I know that this is a big step, for anyone to end a marriage and it shouldn't be taken lightly. If you're having any second thoughts, you should voice them now."

"No, no. No second thoughts. It's right and my marriage was possibly never right." I had a sense of panic that Georgie might turn me away and refuse to act for me if she thought I wasn't going to go through with this.

"Okay. That's a relief." She frowned. "I've been contacted this morning by Hector Rosefield."

"Michael's preferred divorce lawyer," I said.

"Mmm. Your husband has served a divorce petition."

"He wants to divorce me?"

"He does." She grimaced but this was no surprise to me. I'd said as much to Cy and knew that no matter what happened our divorce would be played out as our marriage had been, with all focus on appearances, image, other people's opinions and most probably money. "This is where divorces can get unpleasant and expensive, El, with the details, scoring points and saving face. He intends to divorce you on the grounds of your adultery with Denton Miller Junior."

My face fell. I felt it. Not because I was ashamed of my relationship with Cy, even if socially or morally I should be, nor was it about saving face or scoring points. It was Elizabeth, what would she think? I stemmed the words and thoughts in my head about exactly what she would think about her son's name, her family name being dragged through the mud by me, because of me.

"Look, let's start by you telling me what brings you here," Georgie suggested and like that I told her my life story from childhood to present.

"Sorry," I offered, thinking my life story was not what she wanted or needed to hear and yet had been forced to endure it.

"No, that's fine, really. So, we have two choices, we accept your husband's divorce petition and in turn you would be accepting his accusation of adultery or we counter petition him on the grounds of irreconcilable differences. If he contests that this could drag on for years and become very expensive. Sorry if that sounds a little grim and blunt," Georgie added with a small smile.

I shook my head. "I appreciate the direct approach. I really do not want Cy dragging into this, his mother," I sighed on an exhale. "But I don't want this to drag on and the cost is an issue for me," I revealed, although I knew we were both aware that it was Cy that would be signing her cheque.

"Then think about it. There's no rush and I like my clients to be entirely happy with what we're doing. Take a few days, as long as you need. I can respond to Mr Rosefield confirming receipt of their intentions."

"Thank you. I just need to think. It's not like I expect to take anything from my marriage, not even the dog."

"I know the dog is important to you and I can try to negotiate something, but from what you've said the dog was Michael's property before you came to the relationship."

"You mean I have no claim to him?"

Georgie nodded.

"And I'm going to guess that if I attempt to make him a battle ground, demand access or fight for custody that will prove timely, expensive and probably see me committed to a mental institution?"

"I wouldn't have added the last bit, but yes," Georgie confirmed. "Unless you believe he is at risk of neglect or abuse and then you could contact the authorities."

"No. Michael would never knowingly neglect Balder and he would never abuse him," I said, defending my husband with a true belief that what I was saying was true. It had only been of late when things were fraught between me and Michael that Balder had experienced anything other than a totally happy and settled home where his every need was taken care of.

"El, go home, think about everything and let me know how you want to proceed. Talk it over with your friends and family."

I nodded, not that I had family I could discuss this with or would want to hear my thoughts. They were the same family that would push me back into the marriage I was hoping to dissolve. Then there were the friends I didn't have; of course there was Maya and Tia, not to mention Cy, but I wasn't sure any of them would be impartial. Maybe Edward, except he was Elizabeth's friend and I wasn't sure he could really be a friend to us both in this situation. The same with him and Michael, although it always felt as though he was kind of on my side.

By the time I left Georgie's office it was approaching the end of the business day and Cy had already told me not to bother returning to the office. The plan was that I would meet him later for dinner. He had some people he needed to meet first and I was due to visit my dad, but I really didn't feel much like dinner and in some ways, I didn't relish the idea of seeing Cy to discuss my divorce, whichever way it panned out. I sat in my car and carefully composed a text knowing that hearing Cy's voice would be enough for me to cave in and agree to a full and frank discussion over dinner.

<Hi, Georgie seems nice and is happy to handle my divorce. I just need some time to decide how to proceed. Let me know when your meeting's done. I don't really feel like dinner out tonight. X>

Clearly his meeting hadn't started, or he didn't care because he replied straight away.

<I would have thought the procedure was set, you serve him, divorce him and then you are no longer linked. Will let you know as soon as I'm done and we can eat dinner in. I can come straight to you. And don't worry...I can hear your overthinking from here Ms Ross x>

I laughed at his text, not the assumption that dinner in was the only alternative to having dinner out, maybe I needed to secure some time alone, possibly just once or twice a week. That was going to be much easier said than done, I knew that. As I digested that thought I turned the key in my ignition when another text arrived.

<Give Jezza my best. I love you. X>

Nope, alone time was going to be a real challenge when he was so thoughtful.

****

My dad was awake when I arrived in the day room but he had no clue who I was. He chatted to me and another resident who he assumed I was there to visit. He even referred to his friend, Carol, as my mother at one point. I didn't correct him. What purpose would that serve? My mind was buzzing with divorce thoughts and a sadness that being here was a wasted visit because my dad didn't even realise he had a visitor. He got up before I was ready to end my visit and told me and Carol that he had to run, he was late for work and Stella would be cross if he got into trouble with his boss. I smiled as I remembered my mum giving him a roasting when he cocked something up.

"You needn't laugh, young lady. You wouldn't be so amused

if you knew my wife," he chided before going to find his car keys, leaving me and Carol together, Carol who was as out of it as he was.

"Right, I'd better be off. I've got to pick the kids up from school," she told me as she literally staggered to her feet.

I watched her disappear and selfishly prayed to all things holy that my father's dementia wasn't hereditary because I didn't want to forget anything in my life, the good, the bad and the downright ridiculous. Life really was cruel and I was done with the shit it kept throwing at me. Maybe I'd needed this visit to sort my head out.

Chapter Thirty-Two

By the time Cy called to say he was out of his meeting I was already at home and showered. Maya had decided to go to Chad's where a romantic dinner for two awaited her meaning Cy was able to come over for a home cooked dinner and a night together.

During the time since I'd left my dad, I had made several decisions; firstly, I didn't need to be away from Cy to make decisions, although I might need a little thinking space from time to time. Secondly, I was going to get a divorce, one way or another and if it took years to do it then so be it. It had, after all taken me almost six years to realise that the marriage was all wrong. Thirdly, and most difficult of all was the decision to stop worrying about Elizabeth, well, as much as was possible because she was and always would be Cy's mother. But I was going to stop beating myself up about what she thought of me and accept that all I could do was to love her son and hope that one day she would see that I really did care for him and I wasn't simply on the make.

I realised, as I made my life plans that I knew very little about Cy's past, his romantic past and assuming it had been fairly straightforward and uncomplicated before me, then this with me was going to be something very different for him to contend with. By his own repeated admission, employees and married women were not his thing and yet here we were, here I was, employed by him and married. I really needed to be more considerate of him and his needs in all things us, I reminded myself, not for the first time, but this time I would remember it and show him that we were in this together, working it out together.

With dinner in the oven and Cy due any second I quickly checked my appearance in the hall mirror, not that there was much to check as all I had on was a black silk robe that covered a set of black lace underwear consisting of a very brief thong and a half-cup bra that pushed everything in and up. I was freshly showered so had nothing in the way of make-up on, but looked fresh faced rather than washed out and my hair hung loose and a little damp, just how I knew Cy liked it. He'd once told me that my damp hair left loose always made him think about how it had got that way; naked in the shower, swimming in a pool or the sea wearing very little, possibly nothing. Even getting caught in a rain shower without a coat or umbrella when the rain would simply soak through my clothes, something white on top that would become transparent with the addition of water leaving me almost naked. There was a definite a pattern emerging.

I recalled that after him telling me that we had ended up tangled together for quite some time. My nipples began to bead at the memory alone and as my thighs began to squeeze and tense too, the sound of the doorbell interrupted. With a final shake and ruffle of my hair and a quick lick of my lips I opened the door and found Cy standing there, looking impossibly tempting. Thank goodness dinner was going to be a while.

"Hey," he seemed to drawl, making him even sexier.

"Hey yourself." I grinned, desperation encouraging me to simply grab him and drag him in. Encouragement I ignored, just.

"It's a good job we're not eating out. You seem a little underdressed." He smirked as he crossed the threshold, a simple move that made me inhale deeply. The inhalation doing nothing for my arousal as it only served to fill my nostrils with a clean and sexy Cy.

"Less to take off," I told him, nervousness settled in my stomach as I realised my temptress skills were sorely lacking. I briefly allowed Michael's words about my clumsiness and inexperience to penetrate my mind, then pushed them away. I refused to allow the girl I was to mould the woman I wanted to be. Furthermore, I refused to allow others, the ones who had moulded me to their liking to continue to do so.

Cy stepped closer, stalking me almost with a very dark look, full of intent and promise.

Before he reached me, just, and with the negative thoughts pushed from my mind I undid the belt of my robe and dropped my arms. I allowed the garment's soft satin to slip down my arms until it lay in a pile on the floor.

"I thought we were having dinner?" Cy asked with a cock of his head and a half-smile.

"We are, it's gonna be a while, so…"

No further words were required. I turned away and began my ascent of the stairs revealing my thong and globes of my arse that were quickly being cupped by Cy who had dutifully followed me, but only far enough that he caught up with me. I quickly found myself spun round, lifted and pushed against the wall on the stairs where I was crushed by Cy's body.

"I think all home cooked dinners should be like this," he told me before his lips slanted over mine and he captured my mouth completely.

****

The journey upstairs to my bedroom took much longer than usual with multiple stops to kiss, touch and lose clothes, Cy's not mine, so that by the time we reached the bed we were both in our underwear. Somehow Cy had even managed to lose his shoes and socks. His hands were sliding through my hair, a little roughly, tugging against the strands as his mouth devoured mine, possessing me completely. I heard a groan echo in my own mouth as Cy's fingers reached the damp ends of my hair. My own hands were focused on Cy's body, his chest that I was stroking, grazing across his shoulders and arms, tracing his tattoo before sliding each hand under his arms so that I could hold onto him, pull him down, closer to me. The feel of his mouth leaving mine left me relieved that I could breathe and yet strangely bereaved at its loss. My grief was short lived as I felt hot breath travelling down my body; along my neck and collar bone, across my chest before settling on the lace that still covered my hot and aching breasts.

"Yes," I moaned, tightening my fingers that were now in Cy's hair, encouraging and pulling his mouth closer.

His response to my one-word statement, suggestion and plea was to pull down the fabric of my bra. He sucked on a nipple, pulled it until I wanted to cry and scream with despair, longing and desire. Cy's mouth pulled away despite my protestations in the form of more hair tugging, but not before he dragged his teeth over my sensitive peak that was harder and more painful than I had ever known it, worse than the other neglected one that was about to find itself subjected to the same merciless, divine torture that my lover was so accomplished at delivering. While his mouth was closing over my other nipple the first was being treated to a gentle stroke from his thumb, then a slightly firmer rub before settling for some pinching squeezes that had my legs almost buckling. At the same time, I squeezed my thighs together in some vain attempt to find some kind of relief, not to mention trying to stem the flow of arousal that was escaping from me and quite probably drenching my underwear.

"Cy, please," I cried, totally unaware of what it was I was asking for.

His mouth released me as he dropped to his knees and landed several tiny, gentle kisses to my belly. Butterflies danced across my skin and somersaulted inside me and then he probed my naval with his tongue. Firm and persistent jabs that sent my excitement soaring once more. Surely that wasn't normal, the invisible string that was currently attaching my belly button to my clit that was throbbing with every touch. My moans and groans clearly gained Cy's attention when I gazed down to find his eyes fixed on me and his mouth clear of me.

"You greet me at the door almost naked, flaunt your sexy as fuck ass at me and you will now have to accept the consequences, baby," he warned me as his hands gripped my ankles and softly stroked their way up my legs until they were rubbing against my inner thighs, pausing at my intimate folds that were evidently hot and wet, the small barrier of my lacy thong hiding nothing.

I resisted the temptation to correct his ass to arse, just. It really did need saying.

"Oh baby," Cy sighed. He pushed his face between my thighs, inhaled and then kissed me. At that second, I forget about any correction to his use of the English language. "I find you dressed like this and clearly horny…it's only going to end one way and that is with you being fucked real hard until you can't think, see or move," he explained, although I figured, consequences like that I could live with. "I'm going to taste you baby," he told me as one hand pressed between my thighs quite firmly, causing me to press down against him, desperate for some pressure and relief. His eyes flitted between my face and my groin. Cy seemed to enjoy the image of me pressing myself against him. The way I rubbed myself, slid against his hand, the added friction of my lace underwear only added to the rising pleasure that just needed to crest and break. I managed to drive myself to the brink before the hand I was using like some kind of animal, driven only by my most basic need was withdrawn.

"Cy, please," I cried as I reached down for his hand to finish the job it had started.

"Uh-ho." Cy shook his head at the same time that he grabbed my hips and tilted me into a sitting position on the edge of the bed.

I watched as his hands reached for the sides of my thong and with a thumb hooked in each leg, he began to draw them down and with a lift of my behind he uncovered exactly how aroused I was. With a flush of embarrassment, I glanced towards my underwear that carried more than an adequate coating of the slickness from my body. My embarrassment was short lived when I saw the darkening of Cy's eyes that told me how pleased he was by my state of excitement. I was slightly uncomfortable at the sight of my underwear being lifted to his face. He inhaled deeply before he tossed them aside.

"You're so fucking wet," he told me, moving from his haunches onto his knees, affording me a glimpse of his own arousal, hard and erect. It pressed against the soft jersey fabric of his own underwear, dampness evident at its tip. I wasn't the only desperate one here.

"I want you," I stammered.

"You have me, hook, line and fucking sinker," Cy replied as

his hands pushed my knees apart, opening me up for him.

I hadn't really been awfully clear in my meaning of wanting him. I wanted him in my mouth, wanted to taste him on my tongue. Preparing to speak, I didn't feel his hands moving higher until he was running two fingers along my length, back and forth a couple of times before they sunk into me, pumping in and out and then the same two fingers were on the move again. They honed in on my clit that they circled and teased until I was panting. I was clueless as to how I had remained sitting up, rather than flat out on my back, but I had and now I was looking down watching Cy's hand.

"I mean, I want you," I repeated as I felt everything below my waist tightening in preparation for the waves of my pleasure to wash over me. I really needed more words. "I want you inside me," I gasped as I reached forward for Cy, for his hair that I was yanking on again as I felt the first tell-tale sign that I was going to come, very soon. "In me, in my mouth." I huffed and hoped to fend off my orgasm a while longer.

"I want that too baby, but not now. Now I need to feel you come around my fingers, and then I am going to drink everything you have for me as I make you come on my tongue and then I am going to fuck you until you scream my name, so maybe you get me in your mouth after dinner," he told me with no option for debate as his other hand joined the party again.

With a finger, then a second and a third entering me I felt full, stretched, but the other hand, the stroking one was still.

"Spread your legs, baby," he told me and I complied, or thought I had. "Wider, as wide as you can, and do not close them." I spread a little more and with a frown shot in my direction I spread them again, until my hips kind of hurt. "Don't close them, you'll get bruised," Cy warned me and although I was sure I should be alarmed at the idea of what he was about to do that could bruise me, I wasn't. I had no clue what he was doing or how it might cause bruising but I trusted him.

I nodded and received a smile before he positioned himself between my obscenely spread thighs. He shuffled closer until my legs were being held open by his broad, muscular shoulders. Now I got the bruising thing. My thighs would be no contest for

411

Cy's arms, shoulders and chest that were holding me open.

"Watch me baby, watch how you come for me," he whispered, his soft, cool breath brushed against my exposed skin making me tingle.

The three fingers inside me began to move, slowly, in and out, gently arousing me again as the burn of my stretching skin made me hiss a little.

"Don't stop," I warned Cy, thinking that my hiss of pain, not pain, discomfort, slight discomfort that also felt amazing had made him pause briefly.

His other hand, the two fingers that had been circling my clit resumed their work, slowly, gently. I needed more. The strokes needed to be firmer, faster, I was nearly there. No words were needed, Cy knew what I needed as well as I did, maybe better. The circling picked up pace as did the pressure, firmer more decisive touches pushed me closer to the edge. Even though I had a ringside seat to the action unfolding, I was beginning to struggle in my attempts to compute which sensation belonged to which action. Everything blurred, including my sight as my clit was squeezed and pinched at the exact same time the fingers inside me pressed and curled, demanding a reaction, and what a reaction they got.

Instinctively as my release broke, I attempted to shut my legs and was met by the immoveable object that was Cy's body. Yeah, I was going to be bruised tomorrow, possibly inside and out. My climax was intense and seemed to be never ending; my toes curled against the rug beneath my feet, desperate for some kind of traction, my head was thrashing from side to side. Internally, everything was pulsing and throbbing, wringing every last ounce of pleasure from me and my hands, well they acted on their own accord because at no point had I consciously cupped my own breasts and begun to touch myself, which is what I did as my climax slowed and calmed. I had no clue how long my hands had been stroking and caressing my own flesh, nor how long I had been rolling and squeezing my nipples, which I was still doing.

"You really are something else," Cy groaned as his face dived closer to my body, clearly there would be no come down and gradual re-climb, we were going straight into number two.

My body threw itself back on the bed so that I was literally sprawled, laid out like a feast. Cy's arms were wrapped around the tops of my legs so that he had a sufficient grip to move and reposition me. He pulled me down so that my behind hung off the edge of the bed slightly, then he spread me open. With a single kiss to my inner thigh he moved in fully and began with several gentle licks that were just the right side of uncomfortable for my still sensitized folds. After the first half a dozen were out of the way he began his task in earnest, licking and lapping with a straight and stiff tongue. My body responded immediately, moistening further and softening as the long strokes became shorter, delving into my leaking core on each passing, not stopping until it became better acquainted with my clit that was in receipt of a succession of licks, laps, flicks and nips.

All the time that Cy devoted to the space between my thighs I continued to play with my breasts. I teased them to stiffer and stiffer peaks until I thought I might lose my mind if they didn't gain his touch on them again soon. My touch was nice, effective, but nothing compared to his. I felt I was on the precipice once more. A final touch in the form of his lips closing around my clit and squeezing gave me the last push that really did have me seeing stars.

The feel of Cy's body crawling up my own, covering it, dispersed the haze that had descended. I could feel the nakedness of his erection already nudging me, my own moisture ensured an easy entrance. We were face to face now, eye to eye and suddenly nothing and nobody else existed. This moment was all that mattered. Gentle kisses traced a line from my jaw, down my neck and shoulders as slow, relaxed thrusts began to rouse my body once more.

"Jeez, baby, this feels so good," Cy crooned as his mouth settled against my ear.

I made no verbal response, but my body tightened around him, pulled him in.

"This really isn't going to last if you keep squeezing me," he told me with a note of regret.

"I don't care," I told him honestly. I didn't care, this wasn't a demonstration of stamina. This was an experience of spiritual proportions we were sharing. He'd already brought me so much pleasure since he'd arrived here that I wanted to reciprocate. For him to feel a small percentage of what he'd given me.

"I do. I want you to come again, baby, with me."

"Together," I whispered my single word reply meaning so much more than the sex we were having and the orgasms we were each likely to experience. My together was not just tonight. It was tomorrow, next week, next month, next year, a lifetime filled with shared experiences, holidays, homes, and children. I wanted it all and I wanted it with Cy.

"Together," he repeated and I thought that maybe he understood the feelings, wishes and emotions of my own word and shared them too.

Chapter Thirty-Three

"We might need to eat at home more often if this is what I can expect," Cy said, taking his seat at the table in the kitchen.

"You mean dinner?" I asked with a flush as I recalled all that had happened between him arriving and us descending the stairs about fifteen minutes before after sharing a shower following our final shared orgasm on the bed.

"Dinner is a bonus, baby." He grinned as he accepted the plate of slowly cooked lamb and vegetables in a sauce I remember Susan cooking when I still lived at home with her.

"How was your meeting?" I asked, already panicking inside at the prospect of the divorce discussion.

"Okay." He didn't sound convinced. "I'm going to need to go away." The reason for his hesitant *okay* revealed.

The sound of cutlery clattered off crockery. My crockery, my cutlery. I wasn't expecting his revelation.

"For how long?" I asked flatly with a small painted on smile. I hoped against all hopes it was just going to be an overnighter. I knew it wouldn't be. When the last-minute meeting he'd had was revealed there had been no mention of who he was seeing or why it was necessary, meaning it was private. Which was fine, except private meant family, which in turn meant America.

"Not sure yet. I'm flying back home the day after tomorrow and we'll take it from there. It's Chris, rather than actual business." He frowned apologetically. "Sorry, baby. I really want to be here. With you. For you."

"I know." I nodded, feeling overwhelmed and tearful. "It

can't be helped. I can at least hold the fort."

"I've got someone coming in, to kind of be at the helm…" he trailed off with a guilty expression.

I knew that if someone else was filling in then this business was big, important, complicated and as far removed from an overnighter as anything could be.

"Are you leaving me?" I pushed my plate away, my appetite suddenly non-existent.

"No. Fuck no!" He circled the table to sit next to me. "Never. Chris has gone AWOL. *Escaped* his rehab and nobody has a clue where the hell he is. Dad's worried sick and Mom is permanently on the verge of hysteria. The police can't, won't do anything because he is a grown man and not considered to be a danger or in danger. I have no clue what they think I can do beyond physically looking for him, but if that's what they need…" He kissed my temple and returned my plate to me. "This is good, eat. I plan on using all of your energy later." He smiled and returned to his own seat.

"I'll miss you."

"I know. Me too, but this isn't forever. I am not leaving you, ever."

I nodded, desperate to believe that.

"How did things go with Georgie Parker?" Cy asked as a forkful of food entered my mouth.

"Alright," I replied before taking a mouthful of water to wash down the food. "She's going to act for me and sees things going one of two ways."

"Go on," Cy encouraged. He got up to retrieve two bottles of beer from the fridge, flipped the lid off one and passed it to me then did the same to his own.

"When I got there Michael's solicitor had already contacted Georgie to serve me with a divorce petition," I began and then faced with his confused look I realised that Cy was oblivious to me having told Susan who my solicitor was. "I told Susan I was seeing Georgie."

"You see, fucking games," he snapped. "I warned you, didn't I?" he demanded with anger and concern in his voice.

"Anyway, I can still serve him on grounds of irreconcilable

differences, but he might contest that, I'm almost certain he would. More than that I think he wouldn't agree to me divorcing him willingly which would effectively mean I would need to wait two years and then divorce him regardless of his feelings."

"Two years?" Cy shook his head. "You need to wait almost half as long as you've been married. Hold on, you said he had already petitioned you meaning he is agreeable to a divorce, so…"

My face must have given away the fact that I was holding back.

"Come on El, spill. What ace does he think he has up his sleeve now?"

"I think I'd rather wait the two years." All earlier thoughts of riding the storm that was Elizabeth gone. Having one junkie son skipping rehab and calling the other one back to find him was quite enough for one woman to contend with, without me having the non-missing son's name dragged through the divorce courts and possibly the gossip columns as my fornicating lover.

"Really? You want to be left dangling on a fucking string, or more likely elastic for two more years? I don't believe you. So how about you cut the bullshit and tell me what the fuck Georgie said and what Michael's petition said."

His tone was hard and the volume raised, but demanded that I complied, and honestly I wanted to. I didn't want to add to Elizabeth's woes but my earlier thoughts were right, I needed to stop beating myself up and lay all my cards on the table or at least throw them in the air and see exactly where they fell.

"Michael wants to divorce me, on the grounds of my adultery with you."

There, the words were out and I felt a little lighter. Cy stared across at me studiously, studying me.

"And what? You think I'm going to be pissed about that?"

"I don't know, but it's not nice. Georgie said if I agree this will be a quickie divorce with a division of assets, assets I don't want. If I refuse, I know he'll make me wait the two years, if only to save face."

"It's not nice and people will make judgements about you and speculate about just how many affairs you've had in the past, but two years baby. Is that what you want, to wait?"

I shook my head as the first tear breached my eyes. "No, of course not. I want to be divorced, to be Eloise Ross again and to have no obligations anymore. I don't want his money or anything else. Georgie said I have no chance of getting Balder and there's nothing else I want, so I will leave with nothing except my name and myself."

"So why not respond through Georgie to that effect?" he asked and then realisation dawned. "Me?"

"You," I admitted. "He will name you as the person I have committed adultery with and when I accept that, everyone will know that you have been shagging your married P.A. breaking both of your rules."

"Fuck my rules! They needed breaking if it meant we could be here like this. Look, El, I didn't go out looking for a married woman any more than you set out to have an affair and fall in love. We had one night that became more because you happened to be my P.A. We tried to let this thing just pan out, run its course, but the disaster became anything but and for that I am thankful."

"But your parents…"

"Will get over it. They already know you're married and that we are together."

"Your mother…"

"Will get over it," he repeated. "Tell me that you don't want a quickie divorce and that changes everything, but if you want to be divorced within a year then this is the way to do it. I think Michael acted all kinds of wrong in taking you as his wife, but honestly, I get his need for the last word, to save face a little. I'd probably act in exactly the same way in his position."

"You don't mind?"

"Of course I mind, but only because it hurts you. It's another manipulation of you, but it will be the final manipulation. I am sorry you don't have a claim on Balder, but I'm glad that you can make a clean break. Nothing left to keep drawing you back in. I know it's not the same, but when this shit is over, I will buy a litter of puppies if that's what you want."

I shook my head, feeling a little disloyal at the idea of

replacing Balder but knew that Cy was right about everything really.

"We should clear the shit and then re-plan and re-group."

"Whatever you want baby." Cy pushed his empty plate away with a grin.

****

"So, who is going to be filling in for you? Anyone I know? Please tell me it's someone nice, reasonable, not an arsehole that is going to insist I collect his dry cleaning and remember his wife's birthday and her favourite flowers," I said taking the seat opposite Cy in his office.

With a cocky *I know something you don't know* smirk he watched me as I attempted to cross my legs, a move that made me wince. The same legs that were covered in trousers today because the sensation of inner thigh skin against inner thigh skin was far too uncomfortable to bear. Cy laughed at my discomfort.

"It's not funny," I protested, only serving to amuse Cy further and incite more laughter. "You have fucking broken me. My inner thighs are black and blue and walking is a far greater challenge than it ought to be. I have carpet burns on my knees and arse meaning I look like I have piles or rickets or something equally as fucking attractive."

"Baby, I will take the blame for many things, but your black and blue thighs are because you didn't keep them spread when that was your one job. However, I will accept some responsibility for the knees and ass."

"Arse!" I corrected petulantly causing a raised eyebrow.

"Ass, like it was yesterday in the bedroom before you tried to get off on my hand," he pointed out, causing me to flush crimson.

"I knew I should have corrected you then," I snapped before he continued.

"So, your knees and ass. I offered no protest when you couldn't wait to blow me on our brief visit back to mine this morning, only getting as far as my hideous wallpaper and carpet combo, so for your knees I apologise. Your ass, too, although I am unsure whether it was being fucked against the wall or later on the carpet with your ankles over my shoulders that did the

419

most damage, but whichever it was, I am sorry."

"Don't talk about sex to me," I told him, and if I was honest I wasn't even convincing myself with my half-hearted protest.

"Why? Scared you'll want to go again?" Cy taunted, but actually read the situation perfectly. Even in such a delicate and bruised state all I could think about was the previous night, the playtime we'd shared in the shower and our early morning detour to Cy's home that morning. I was aching already and was sure I could feel my sex becoming moist with anticipation. Previous thoughts of damage and my inability to walk or have anything against my skin forgotten.

"Rest assured, Ms Ross, if I want to talk about sex to you, I will. And if there was any doubt, you will be fucked soundly before the end of the business day and tonight, I have no plans beyond fucking you, over and over, because if I am going on this fool's errand of finding my wayward brother I am going to need something to get me through, and that something is you. Memories of how you look, smell, sound and taste as you come on my fingers, tongue and dick will get me through, so tomorrow, by the time I am boarding a plane to LA you will be lucky not to need some kind of emergency medical intervention or walking aids."

A single low moan of longing, anticipation and apprehension left my lips as a cough behind me alerted me to someone else's presence.

"I'd ask if I'm interrupting, but…"

"Shit," I muttered, mortified to have been overheard, more mortified that I had no clue just how much was overheard. "You," I began accusatorily as I glared at Cy but said no more, I just turned my attention to our disturbance, Edward.

"Edward, come through, we've been expecting you." Cy smiled, already on his feet and preparing to greet the other man.

"Have we?" I whispered, thinking my life was reverting back to farce. The vicar was going to lose his trousers again at any second. I smiled thinking that it had been a while since I'd done that whole, if my life was a movie what genre would it be thing.

I too was standing, turning to face Edward with a crimson

hue of inferno proportions to my face.

"El, Cy," he smiled warmly, shaking Cy's hand and then kissing my cheek gently. "I take it El is oblivious?"

"I was just about to tell her," Cy replied.

"Tell me what?" I felt anxious irritation simmering.

"Edward has agreed to hold the fort here, with you," Cy replied, his concise explanation taking a few seconds to sink in.

"Really?" My startled response not shocking any of us. Cy had always stressed that Edward was little more than a family friend really and had also seemed a little mistrusting of his motives in things. So why would he allow this to happen? Unless it wasn't his choice. Maybe Senior was calling the shots on this one. "Can I get anyone tea, coffee?" I offered, unsure what else I should say or do as my emotions threatened to take over and overrule everything else.

"El," Cy began, sensing my unease and potential to have a meltdown. I knew he was going away, he'd told me and yet this was proof that he really was and not for a few days if he was shipping someone new in and I really didn't want him to.

"It's fine," I lied. "I'll get drinks and then if Edward needs to, he can let me know what he'll expect of me."

Edward and Cy remained in the office for another couple of hours and as it approached lunch time they appeared before me.

"Can I shout you lunch?" Edward asked me. "Both of you, if you fancy it?"

"Maybe another day," I replied. "Snowed under," I lied.

"You do know that I know what your workload currently is, don't you?" Edward asked with a chastising shake of the head that made me feel foolish.

"Sorry. I'm not very good company today," I told him, a little more honestly.

"I understand, El. How about this, tomorrow after work we'll have dinner and see how this is going to work between us? It really is a short term fix, me being here." He smiled with a kindness and understanding that told me he knew exactly what I was thinking and how I was feeling.

I looked up at Cy, unable to remember what time his flight was.

"I'll be gone by eleven in the morning, baby," he reminded me, someone else able to read my mind.

"Yes then, dinner. Thank you."

****

Three days after Cy's departure I faced a weekend alone and had no clue how to deal with that. My last night with Cy had been intense, moving from gentle and loving to primitive and basic and then back to gentle and loving. I smiled as I recalled it and was still struggling to decide which I preferred.

The morning of Cy's departure hadn't been any of those things. It had been sad and melancholy, for us both, although Cy was better able than me to fake a light-hearted persona. I settled on miserable with the threat of tears ever present and was still in that same funk, truth be told.

Edward had been very kind and taken me to dinner as we'd agreed and kept me busy during the days since. He'd also offered dinner each night, but I didn't want to become overly dependent on him while Cy was away, plus I'd stayed at home with Maya the second night and enjoyed a girly night in, possibly my first. I'd been out with Tia the night before to some wine bar that had recently opened up near her place. We went under the guise of checking out the competition. Cy called me each morning and evening, although he'd warned me that morning he might not be able to maintain that as he had a few remote leads on where Christopher might be hiding out.

With no idea how to fill a weekend alone, I washed, dressed and shopped for a couple of hours. I bought nothing beyond toothpaste and sanitary products. Cy had left me a key to his house with an invitation to stay whenever I wanted. I didn't want to, not yet, maybe when I knew he was coming home, coming back to me.

Somehow, after shopping I found myself sitting opposite my dad who was beyond confused. He shouted and ranted at invisible people, startling the actual people there. For the first time he didn't resemble my dad at all. Previously, no matter how disorientated he was there was still something that was him, something in his eyes that let me know he was still in there, hidden, buried by this horrible and cruel disease, but not today.

Another rant followed, this time at a sophisticated and graceful looking man. He was visiting someone else and probably only five years older than me. His insults involved words like bastard, selfish, stuck-up, posh and Nancy boy and then he turned his attention to me. His last words had made me laugh, unlike the recipient of the insults, but I had never heard anyone call someone a Nancy boy before. Maybe it was my laughter that had drawn my dad's attention. My laughter was short lived as he unleashed his anger on me.

"And you, you disgust me. You whore!" His shouts caused everyone to look at us.

"Dad," I whispered and hoped against all hopes that I could reach him, wherever he was.

"Don't you call me that. I'm ashamed to admit you're my daughter. Whore!" he shrieked. "You and him, what possessed you? You let him do that to you, well it's over," he said with serious finality that suggested that whilst his words meant nothing to me they made perfect sense to him.

"Dad," I repeated, calmly, more calm than I thought I'd be capable of in this situation.

"Stop calling me that," he snapped. "Anyway, as I say it's over. I've been to see him. Marked his card and blacked his eye, but don't worry I kept your dirty secret from him so he'll have no need to come and bother you again. I told him he wasn't the only one you allowed such liberties. He didn't believe me at first, but I convinced him you'd never be good enough to take home to his mother, and you're not, because you're a whore." He screamed again, somehow rising to his feet with a steadiness I hadn't seen for some time and was turning away from me, about to leave.

"Please, Dad." My words infuriated him further, just as Angela and another nurse appeared, presumably having been alerted to his agitated state by another visitor or possibly his shouts.

I had no clue what had happened as my head spun and the world darkened before I hit the floor. Clearly I should have listened when he told me not to call him Dad. It was one Dad too far I realised as I shook my head hoping to reorder my thoughts and clear the fuzz that was descending over my brain. I became aware of the other nurse, the one I didn't really know crouching beside me while Angela reached for my dad's arm.

"Jezza," she almost whispered, as if soothing a frightened animal which he kind of was.

If my dad heard her, he ignored her, choosing to look down at me. "Tell your mother I've gone to the pub and I'll be back later."

Those were his final words before he turned away and took Angela's hand. He began laughing with her, then struck up a conversation as if the last ten minutes hadn't even happened. Maybe they hadn't in his mind, but unfortunately for me I didn't think I would ever forget them or the image of the gentlest man I had ever known lashing out at me, and with that I began to sob.

Chapter Thirty-Four

It was another couple of hours before I began to get over the events of the afternoon. Angela had settled my dad before returning to me and the other nurse, Tanya, who had got me an ice pack and was chiding me for not keeping it on my swollen face. They were both wonderful and even provided me with sweet tea, something I despised, yet it actually made me feel better, a little. The next thing I knew we were being joined in the office by Tia and Edward.

It was only now, two hours later that I was questioning why they had turned up and how they knew that I needed someone. Tia kept looking at the clock on the wall in Edward's kitchen, as if she really needed to be somewhere else.

"So, just how did the two of you come to be at my father's care home?" I finally asked as another cup of tea was placed in front of me on the table I sat at.

I watched them exchange a glance before Edward explained. "Cy was concerned that you might need someone."

In my head I heard that the home had called Cy, making him aware of what had happened.

"Shit! No, please tell me they didn't call him," I sobbed. "But they don't have his details, his number—" Confused once more, I held my head in my hands.

Edward pulled my hands from my head and tilted my chin so that I looked up at him. Tia pulled her chair closer so she could easily put a reassuring arm around me.

"Some weeks ago I believe your father voiced some need or desire to contact Cy. You told him as much," Edward began.

I nodded as I recalled that moment, but hadn't given it any more thought.

"Cy contacted one of the staff there and left his contact details, in case your father asked to see him again or in case of an emergency."

"So they called him?" I asked wearily.

"No, no. Cy contacted them again, with my permission to leave my details while he's away, just in case."

"So Cy doesn't know about this afternoon?" I wondered why I wasn't more interested in why Cy had left his details behind my back. Although I knew the answer to that. He loved me and wanted to take care of me. I wasn't even too interested in the fact that Edward was now on Angela's people to call list. I just needed to know that Cy wasn't worried about me. I needed him not to ditch his search for Christopher in order to come home and check on me. I needed him kept in the dark until he came back. Then I would tell him and not piss off Elizabeth unnecessarily.

"No," Edward and Tia replied in stereo.

"That's the way it needs to stay. Both of you need to promise me that you won't tell him. This has been a shock, but it's nothing compared to what he is going through right now. Promise me," I implored, my gaze switched between the two of them until they both, reluctantly agreed to my request. "Thank you."

"I really need to go. Edward and I were only meeting up for an hour or so," Tia began. "Do you want me to call Maya or something?"

"No, she's away. Chad has taken her to the country for the weekend."

"Then you should stay with me," Edward told me.

I shook my head. I had been a little hysterical earlier, but I was okay now, except for the bruised cheek and black eye I was undoubtedly going to have come the morning.

"I insist. You've had a nasty shock and a significant blow to the head. I would never forgive myself if anything happened to you," Edward said with a warm smile and a pat on my hand, but I still thought his request was unnecessary.

"I will be fine, really." I was insistent but ill prepared for his next words.

"Eloise, it wasn't a request as such and if you insist on going home to an empty house, I will have no choice but to seek further advice, from Cy."

Tia looked away, clearly uncomfortable, unlike Edward. His expression never wavered.

"You promised," I reminded him.

"Yes, I did, and I meant it, but you seem to be forcing my hand. I have strict instructions to take care of you, keep you safe and to call Cy immediately if there is a problem. I promised him, so you stay here and we have no problem. You insist on going home…"

"Problem?"

"Exactly. Are you staying?"

"Yes, of course I'm bloody staying," I snapped and got to my feet to strop off into the lounge.

****

Tia left shortly after and Edward drove me home to collect an overnight bag before returning to his house. Sensing my ongoing irritation, he began to speak as he handed me a cup of tea and a slice of lemon drizzle cake.

"Eloise, please don't be angry with me." His pout broke the ice and made me laugh. "Thank goodness," he grinned back. "See this as a getting to know you weekend that allows me to keep you safe."

"I suppose," I grudgingly conceded.

"Good. Let me sort dinner for us and if you'd like maybe we could take Balder out for a couple of hours tomorrow."

Tears stung the back of my eyes at the mention of Balder. I missed him badly.

"Do you think Michael would agree?"

"To me taking the dog for a couple of hours? Yes, I do it fairly regularly. I love the big lad."

"But with me?"

"I don't think we need to confuse the matter with details." He smiled then left me alone to prepare dinner.

Edward returned about forty minutes later to find me asleep

on his sofa, a sleep I was just stirring from.

"Sorry, I didn't mean to wake you," he told me taking his seat in the leather, winged back chair that sat opposite the softly upholstered sofa I lounged on.

"That's okay. I didn't mean to fall asleep."

"About ten minutes for dinner and we can have a good chat."

I followed Edward through to his kitchen and took in my surroundings properly for the first time. It was a pretty house, well-appointed on the other side of the heath to Cy's. It seemed to have a homely feel to it with some classic English theme going on that did and didn't quite fit its owner.

I noticed Edward studying my curious gaze looking around. "I like your home."

"Thank you. It's not my childhood home, but it is the last family home I had, with my mother."

"Sorry," I replied with a sad smile.

"No need, El. She was happy here. We both were and I like the reminders that I have of her here."

"It must be a comfort," I suggested, not that I really understood gaining comfort from a house.

"Let's eat." Edward smiled as he passed me the cutlery while he grabbed two bowls piled high with a pasta dish. "Wine?" he asked reaching for glasses.

I was on the verge of compliantly accepting his offer when I remembered that I was Eloise Ross, my own woman and I didn't like wine. "No, thanks. I'm not a fan. Beer or water would be fine."

"Water it is. Unless you're a real ale fan?"

"Water's fine."

Tucking into yet another dinner with Edward seemed like the most natural thing to do, making me remember how he'd scared and intimidated me when we'd first met.

"I can't believe we've become friends," I blurted out, startling him.

"You can't? And why would that be?"

"Sorry, that sounded rude as if somehow I wouldn't want to be your friend. I meant that when I met you I was unsure who and what you were, and I was suspicious of your reappearance especially as you appear to have been part of Michael's inner circle and yet I had never heard of you."

"You never did ask Michael why that was though."

"No, I didn't. You could tell me." My suggestion made Edward laugh.

"I could, but sometimes it's best not to know everything. Michael and I were good friends for thirty odd years. We had fallings out. Our relationship altered over time and went through many stages but six years ago it changed. I needed him to be there for me, to be the one to lean on in my time of need; my mother was dying, my whole life was unravelling and he had met you."

"He chose me over you?" I asked, thinking that was obvious, although, maybe not.

"No, no. It's not that clear cut, El. Michael chose Michael over both of us," he replied, causing me to frown in confusion. "Look, he's my friend and he can be the most amazing man in the world, but he is also the biggest arsehole you could ever wish to meet too."

I laughed at his description; because nobody had ever described him in that way to me and also his use of arsehole that made me think of me and Cy. I almost falsely corrected him to asshole.

"You must know that about him, surely?" Edward asked with a disbelieving expression that I might not.

"I have only recently discovered that side to him."

"I see. Well, when I needed him, he let me down. Worse than that, he cast me aside, El. Dismissed my needs and I walked away, for self-preservation and I didn't come back until I was strong enough to face him and deal with him."

"I see." I repeated his words. "Well I don't, but I get the sentiment at least. May I ask you something, about Michael and me?"

"I might not answer, but ask away."

"Why has he given up so easily? Given me up so easily?"

Edward's eyes widened and although I wasn't upset at the ease with which Michael had given up, it had been a surprise and I wondered if there was a greater plan at play.

"Do you want him to fight for you? Refuse to let you move on?" Edward's tone was laced with concern and annoyance at my possible answer.

"No. He is so concerned with appearances, saving face and failure that I thought he might try to change my mind. He hasn't, which is fine. He plans to divorce me on the grounds of my adultery and Cy will be named. I can't really see him wanting to win me back. I just can't help being a little suspicious, that's all."

"He will save face by divorcing you on those grounds. You will be viewed as the adulteress whore who took advantage of him and he will play the innocent victim to perfection. I understand why he'd want to name Cy as a wronged husband, but I am surprised he'd do that to Elizabeth and Denny, but as I say, Michael always chooses Michael."

I nodded, inclined to agree with Edward's summing up.

"Do you think Elizabeth will react as badly as I think she will?"

"Worse probably." Edward laughed. I didn't. "But once she sees you and Cy together, how he smiles and how at ease he's become since the two of you came out things will be better. Let's watch some family viewing Saturday night TV." He smiled, already up on his feet preparing to leave the kitchen.

****

The sight of Balder bounding towards me across the heath literally had my heart swelling with love for the big dopey boy. I really had missed him, even the drool he was covering me in once he reached me, jumped up and literally knocked me on my behind, again.

"Someone's missed you," Edward observed looking down at my position beneath the dog.

"I missed him too," I replied which Balder took as an invitation to lick my face and slip his tongue into my mouth. "Eww, Baldy." I laughed as Edward reached down and helped me to my feet. "He looks well, happy." I briefly wondered how a sad dog should look.

"He is. Why wouldn't he be? He lives in a house where he

is rarely alone. He gets as many walks as he wants, with me or Michael. He eats the best food and his home life is settled again and now he gets to see you too. What more could he ask for?"

"Nothing I suppose. Is he settled again? Things between me and Michael became quite fraught towards the end and Balder always came to my rescue."

I figured I'd said enough without adding details Edward didn't really need.

"Yes, he is, and he and Michael have mended a few of the broken fences."

Balder was back at my side. Pushing his snout into my pockets as he searched for his ball that I happily threw for him, happy that he was living the life I had hoped for when I left him behind.

Chapter Thirty-Five

Although it had been almost a week since Cy had left, I was growing accustomed to his absence, not that I was enjoying it, but I was realising that I could do this, be alone, if I had to. My journey of self-discovery was being aided by Maya, Tia and Edward who between them were ensuring I was okay; eating regularly, not pining too much for Cy and also insisting that I shouldn't stay at home every night.

My dad had enjoyed a peaceful night's sleep following his meltdown and my bruised cheek and black eye that had come out fully the following day was now beginning to fade. He had been less agitated when I'd seen him on my usual Tuesday night but was very remote. I decided to visit more frequently for the time he had left and was unsure whose benefit that was for. Tia and Edward had been true to their promise of not telling Cy about the incident with my dad and as he had been calling less frequently, I wasn't going to inadvertently out the details myself.

My divorce was proceeding. I had received a call from Georgie who had explained that she'd confirmed with Michael's solicitor that he could divorce me and I wouldn't be contesting his accusation of adultery. Something stuck in my throat at that point of the conversation as I imagined Michael's triumphantly smug face. Georgie had broached the subject of the division of our marital assets and was taken aback when I explained that I wanted nothing else, unless official visitation with Balder was a possibility rather than the time Edward could facilitate. She told me to think about things. That as Michael's wife I was entitled to a share. I disagreed. He had more than covered my entitlements during our marriage and I didn't want anything else. Georgie was insistent that I should think it over and refused to accept my decision immediately.

****

"Do you fancy meeting later? I have agreed to take care of Balder this evening." Edward dangled a very tempting carrot in front of my nose as he entered the office after lunch.

"I thought I might visit my dad, but I could do later, after visiting."

"Perfect. That will give me time to have dinner and pick him up. What will you do for dinner?" He wore a thoughtful expression.

"I'll pick something up on the way, I promise," I added at his doubtful look.

He smiled and entered his office, Cy's office, reassured by my intention to eat. I left Edward in peace as I continued to work and only when it was afternoon tea time did I attempt to interrupt. I had his tea and biscuits on a tray, strangely the same biscuits I favoured, plain ones. No chocolate or fillings, always plain. I paused before I came into view at the open office door where I could hear voices, but knowing that Edward was alone I knew he had his telephone caller on speaker.

"So?" I heard Edward ask with some irritation.

"It's a mess," his caller replied, a voice I immediately recognised as Cy's. "I get it though. I am capable of running things in the U.S. easily and it was always the plan for Dad to run European things from the UK so it does make sense."

I felt sick and wasn't sure my legs weren't about to give way causing the tray and its contents to end up in a broken heap on the floor. I now knew that I could live and function alone, but that was when I thought I wouldn't have to, when I still believed in my happy ever after, but now?

"And El?" I heard Edward ask haughtily, making my heart swell for him a little as I thought that he might genuinely care about me.

"Edward," Cy snapped. "El doesn't need to know any of this. It may not even happen," he added as I felt the first of the tears slide down my cheek. How stupid could I actually have been to think that once he was back there, with his parents, that they wouldn't wangle a way to keep him away from me? I was more stupid for believing he wouldn't allow them to.

No voices followed for a few seconds and then Edward spoke again. "And of Christopher?"

"Fuck knows!" Cy sighed and suddenly sounded tired and dejected making me want to go to him, to hold him and make things better and then I remembered that he had plans to remain in The States. "He has literally disappeared. No sign of him anywhere. I've almost exhausted the possibilities," he expanded, but I didn't want to hear any more, even the sound of his voice now made me want to cry.

Quickly, I returned to the kitchen and allowed myself to expel some of the tears I'd been struggling to keep in then splashed my face with water and pulled myself together before returning Edward's tea to him. When I reached his door for the second time the room was silent.

He glanced up and smiled and then frowned, clearly I didn't look pulled together. "Are you okay?" he asked me, already walking towards me.

"Fine, fine." I brushed him off, already turning away.

"El, what's wrong?"

"Nothing," I insisted.

"Is it Cy?" Edward asked, and unsure exactly how to field such a loaded question, I shook my head and lied.

"I'm just a bit worried about my dad, that's all." I was worried about my dad, I was permanently worried about him, but this wasn't anything to do with the one person in my life I really could rely on.

"Why don't you get off then? Visit a little earlier than you'd planned and I'll call you when I have a time for playtime with Balder."

"Thank you," I managed between swallowed sobs.

I spent about an hour chatting with my dad before he called to Angela and asked to go to bed.

"Bye then, love," he called over his shoulder then turned to look at me, still sitting in the chair he'd been sitting next to until a minute before.

I watched him and hoped, prayed for some recognition from him, not that there had been any up until that point. Today I wasn't entirely sure who or what he thought I was, but it certainly wasn't his daughter.

"I hope you find some peace," he told me with a sad frown. "And him, whoever did that to your beautiful face, leave him, get as far away from him as you can, he doesn't deserve you."

For the second, maybe third time that day, I was crying. He thought I had been slapped around by a boyfriend or husband. He had no clue this was his own handy work, which I was glad of because I had never known my dad to be violent and the look of disgust on his face for the man who'd done this spoke volumes for how he would feel towards himself if he ever found out he'd done this to me. The truth was that I couldn't, wouldn't, walk away from the man who'd put these marks on me, never, and somehow I conveyed that in a look or something.

"Bloody hell," he muttered with a shake of his head. "You tell her," he said to Angela now. "Stell!" he stressed to Angela, mistaking her for my mother. "Maybe she'll listen to you because she certainly won't listen to me. Too pig headed, our Susan," he said with another shake of his head. I had wanted recognition, even if it meant being confused with my sister.

Angela nodded and attempted to lead him away, but clearly now that he had an injured Susan on his radar, he wasn't ready to leave.

"I love you Susie, but I can't believe it. This on top of everything else. Like that poncy, toffee nosed git wasn't bad enough. Mind you, I would have put money on him being a poofter." He frowned and shook his head as if remembering a very bad memory. "What will Elsa say? My poor Muffin, so innocent," he rambled. "I'll see you in the morning. Thank goodness it's my last night shift for six weeks," he muttered and then wandered down the corridor with Angela who he was still calling Stell!

I rejoined him in his room half an hour later once he was settled and laughed at the copy of Harry Potter on his bedside table.

"I thought you hated magic?" I asked his questioning gaze.

"I do, like trick magic, but not Harry, he's a wizard," he defended himself. "That woman who visits, she sometimes reads to me."

"Would you like me to read to you?" I asked, ready to accept a refusal as he didn't realise I was that woman that read to him.

"Go on then, if you've got time." He smiled.

I found the page he was up to and began, watching his eyes close and flicker just as Lulu's had when I'd read her a bedtime story. I really needed not to allow my mind to wander there or else I was likely to cry, again. I read the words on the page and choked as I read Dumbledore's words where he described death as the next great adventure to a well-organized mind. What did that mean for my dad? His mind could be described as many things, but well-organized, never. I closed my eyes briefly, then smiled at the image of my soundly sleeping father, looking like a normal man, at peace.

I wondered what he dreamed about. Did his addled mind fuck with dreams as well as memories and the present? No I decided. It gave me some comfort to believe that his dreams were lucid and real for him and that once he had to contend with death, he too would be able to embark on a new adventure, like I was going to, tonight with some Balder time and soon, alone when Cy relocated back to The States.

Chapter Thirty-Five and a Half (Cy's POV)

"Fuck," I hissed as I slammed the phone down with unnecessary force.

"Trouble?" my dad asked, walking across the hotel room to join me.

"Yes, trouble," I confirmed as I turned in the tub chair to face him. "Christopher is nowhere and until we find him Mom expects me to hang around."

My dad laughed, not that I saw anything funny in this whole shitty situation. I ran a hand through my hair roughly and immediately thought of El. Of the times her hands got tangled in my hair. God, I missed her. I was desperate to see her, smell her, touch her, taste her, and fuck her. I smiled as I imagined her telling me how I'd spoilt the sentiment with my use of those last two words.

I didn't think it was possible to miss another person as much as I missed her. I'd missed Chris when the depths of his treatment of Rhonda had emerged and I had essentially cut him loose, but I'd done that for Lulu as much as anyone. She was my baby and I needed it to remain that way, forever. I missed Lulu too. When she and Rhonda were in a different country to me, which they had been for about a year until we'd all moved to England, it had been tough, but that trip had led me to El, my other baby.

I thought about the night I'd met her. Could she have been any more beautiful, even in her office clothes that were a little creased from the work day and her make-up that had worn away? Those things only made her hotter, revealing the real her and when I watched her dancing, jeez. I didn't think I could have been any harder. I was wrong and had been several times since. She was sin on legs, a total and absolute mortal sin. I didn't doubt that she was the sort of woman who had got men killed. Made men kill and sent them insane with beauty like hers. I felt a smile curl my lips as I considered suggesting a little phone sex or even virtual sex. Fuck, I loved technology.

"Hey, what you thinking?" my dad asked.

I shook my head whilst wearing a huge grin thinking that if he knew what was going on in my head, he might just have a heart attack.

"You don't need to know," I told him smugly.

"Ah, El." He smiled back. "I never thought I'd see you this way over a girl."

I cocked my head at his admission. "Neither did I," I admitted. "But El, she is not just a girl, Dad. I have no idea how I'd wake up in the morning if she wasn't in my life. I love her, like real head over heels, marry her, have babies and a forever home love."

We both stared at my open, maybe too open confession.

"Oh son." My dad sighed, meaning he was about to burst my fucking bubble and I really wanted to stay there a while longer and aside from that there was every chance I was going to end up shouting and cursing at him if he did. "El is young, beautiful and bright…"

"But? Go on, we both know there's going to be one."

"Okay, but, she is already married…"

"Getting divorced."

"She and Michael…"

"No, don't you fucking dare!" I shouted, proving to myself that yes, I was going to shout and curse at him. "Do not finish that with anything resembling questions, doubts or accusations about her reasons or motivation for marrying him, please. Dad, I love her and she makes me happier than anyone deserves to be and I know how and why she came to be married to him and I also know she was in no way complicit in anything beyond loving her family and being innocent and manipulated."

"Your mother wants to go back to England, with Chris. Put

him into rehab over there, like we planned before."

"Okay, I get why she wants to, but she has to know that he will find drink and drugs anywhere if he wants to."

"I know."

"Plus, you are going to be a pain in her ass if you don't have work..." and then I understood. He'd said *like we planned before*, meaning he would be in my office and I would be... "No, not yet. I can't. El needs to sorts things at home. Her divorce and her family and then I will come back to run things this end, with her, my wife."

My dad's jaw dropped, but he continued, "Son, I don't think we can wait."

"I can wait." I pouted, feeling this slipping out of my grasp. Feeling El slipping away.

"Christopher..."

"Fuck Christopher! What makes him so special that we all have to drop everything and roll over? After all the things he's done, he's the god damn chosen one."

I stopped myself, somehow managing not to reveal my brother's drink and drug induced rape of Rhonda and the subsequent birth of her child, my child. I began to pace the floor, attempting to calm myself down, to gain control of my mouth before it ran away and cut my father in on the family's dirtiest laundry. Him and my mother I assumed.

The ringing of a phone that wasn't mine made me breathe a sigh of relief, knowing that he would answer it and leave me alone for a while.

"Hi, honey," he answered revealing his caller as my mother.

I watched him leave and then picked up the phone again and called Edward. He could be an ass but I trusted him with my business and El, not that I was sure why, but he seemed to genuinely care about her.

"How's El?" I asked without exchanging pleasantries.

"And hello to you too," he replied tartly.

"El, please, how is she?" I asked a little softer.

"She misses you. She's been seeing Balder with me and spending lots of time with her dad," he told me and suddenly I felt suspicious. Like there was something he wasn't telling me.

I'd had the same feeling when I last spoke to El and Tia. It seemed that I was becoming suspicious of everything involving El.

"How are things with you?" he asked.

I wasn't entirely sure really. "Dad and Mom have a plan for when we find Chris."

"Plan? What sort of plan?"

"Chris goes to rehab in England and Dad works the UK end of things while Mom flaps round and gives in to his every whim."

"And you?" Edward asked with a snap in his tone.

"It has been suggested that I could run things over here."

I had no idea why I was revealing this to Edward. Did I want Edward to do my dirty work and tell El, gauge her reaction to it?

"So?" I heard Edward ask with some irritation, partly at my news and also because I thought he was probably repeating himself.

"It's a mess," I replied, "I get it though. I am capable of running things in the U.S. easily and it was always the plan for Dad to run European things from the UK, so it does make sense."

"And El?" Edward asked with a very pissed off voice that told me I had been right to leave him at the office to take care of her.

"Edward." I almost snarled at him and the possible answers to his question. "El doesn't need to know any of this. It may not even happen," I told him, hoping it wouldn't, not yet.

"And of Christopher?"

"Fuck knows!" I said on an exhale. A tired and sad exhale wondering how I could make this situation right for us all, especially El. "He has literally disappeared. No sign of him anywhere, I've almost exhausted the possibilities."

"I'm unsure whether I want you to find him or not now. You're going to break her heart, Cy."

I nodded at the phone and the man at the other end of it, but still prayed that I wouldn't fulfil his prophecy. This needed to work out, especially as I'd promised her I wasn't leaving her. I wasn't, wouldn't.

Chapter Thirty-Six

Arriving for work the following morning, I found Edward already at his desk.

"Morning." He smiled as he looked up.

"Morning. How's Balder? Did you mention to Michael that he seemed a little off colour?" I asked, still worried about him.

"Yes, I told him. He was a little dismissive of it and then told me that he'd been a little bit out of sorts for a couple of days."

"Out of sorts, how?" I was becoming increasingly concerned for my dog's welfare.

"Loss of appetite, a bit restless, vomiting a couple of times. I'll call Michael later and check how he's doing if it will put your mind at rest. Yours and mine." He smiled as I went about my work.

****

I worked through the morning and considered the last twelve hours. I'd slept restlessly with thoughts of my dad and his conversation with me, or Susan as he thought I was. Then there was Balder's odd behaviour. At one point he'd almost seemed lame and looked off colour, if dogs did that. I had also allowed myself to think about my divorce and whether I should allow Georgie to negotiate a suitable settlement for me. And all of that before I even dared think about Cy and his relocation plans.

Honestly, I hadn't even considered when I'd entered into a relationship with him that he might return home, especially not as Lulu lived here unless she and Rhonda would up and leave too. Maybe that was another case of my naivety coming into play. Would someone more experienced have anticipated this or at least considered it as a possibility at some point in the future? My instinct was to think the worst of him. To believe he was conspiring behind my back, intent on breaking my heart. Then I remembered how many times he'd told me how much he loved me, the sincerity of his words and his expression. I also recalled the time when I had stormed out of the bath after he'd called me fair game. *We, you and I, we don't lie to each other.* I'd believed that when he'd said it and last night when sleep was proving elusive, I still believed it. Maybe I was being foolish, but I did trust him not to deliberately hurt me, not that I was expecting him to refuse to leave without me. I hoped for that, a little, well a lot, but I didn't dare expect it.

Cy called while I was on my lunch and he seemed strange. The conversation seemed strained and I was unsure why until I heard Elizabeth in the background, saying goodness knows what. I reminded myself that he wouldn't allow her to openly call me names or make disparaging remarks, certainly not when I was on the other end of the phone. I reminded myself again that we didn't lie to each other meaning that he really did love me.

"You sound tired," I told him, wishing I could go to him and lie down with him, make him sleep.

"Yeah, I am."

"Please take care of yourself."

"I am, baby. Dad and I have been on a few night flights lately and even in a bed I am restless. I miss you being next to me," he told me, and while part of my heart fell for him a little harder another part broke at how sad he sounded.

"God, I love you!" I declared dramatically, especially as I was sitting in a coffee shop with a potential audience close by.

"I love you too. I'm coming home real soon," he seemed to blurt out as if he hadn't actually planned on saying those words right then, or maybe he hadn't been planning on saying those words at all.

"It's okay. I understand that you have more important things to do at the moment."

I was aiming for reassuring and supportive but was unsure if I achieved it, even after Cy replied. "Nothing is more important than you and I feel shit that I am not there for you, but if you need me nothing and nobody could be more important than you El, never. You and Lulu, you're my world baby."

The sincerity in his voice was so much more than touching. I was moved to tears, literally it seemed as I began to sob down the phone.

"Please...do...not...be...nice...I...can't...handle...it..." I cried in a series of broken sobs that drew everyone around me into my drama.

"Don't cry. I need to hang up with you not crying."

"Sorry," I said on a deep sniff.

I attempted to stifle my tears over the next minute or so.

"You good?" he asked after a few seconds of silence.

"Mmm, fine. I'm sure you need to go."

"Yeah. I mean it, I'll be home before you know it, one way or another I am almost done here."

I heard voices in the background again, Elizabeth and Denny I assumed. Maybe that final affirmation was for them as much as me.

"Okay. I'll speak to you later. I love you," I replied and the lady nearest to me smiled. Everyone else seemed to have lost interest in me and my tears.

"You bet. I love you too."

In spite of my embarrassing crying in the coffee shop, I felt happier after speaking to Cy, further reassured that he wasn't leaving me, not like his parents wanted him to. Perhaps I was being unfair to Elizabeth and Denny if they felt it was in Christopher's best interests to do rehab in England. It was only reasonable that they'd want to be close and as Denny wasn't retired he would need someone to fulfil his role in America, and who better than Cy?

Maya and I were about to open a bottle of something claiming to be a ready mixed cocktail as we settled in front of a movie when my phone rang, Michael. I was tempted to ignore his call but I knew myself well enough to know that if I did, I would only wonder what he wanted and that would drive me mad, madder than having to speak to him.

"Michael," I replied causing Maya to raise an eyebrow. "At home," I answered instinctively wondering why he needed to know where I was.

His words were coming out quickly and I could hear that he was upset about something but it wasn't making sense, not really until he said, "Edward said I should call you. He's here too. I'm sorry, El." His earlier words filtered into my brain.

"How bad?" I asked with a full wobble infiltrating my voice.

"The worst. If you're coming you should come now, love. I could send Edward," he offered.

"No, I'm coming, just hold on, please," I pleaded, unbothered by his term of endearment. It actually sounded genuine, more genuine than it had for a long time.

Looking up I could see Maya already holding her car keys, even though she had no clue what was going on at that point.

****

The relatively short journey was took too long for my sanity and blood pressure, but as soon as Maya parked alongside Edward's car, I flew out of the passenger side and ran through the door before me.

"My dog, he's here," I breathlessly puffed as Edward appeared through a door off the main waiting area.

He hugged me, hard, too hard, meaning one thing, Balder was in big trouble.

"Where is he?"

"Through here." Edward released me from his embrace and took my hand to guide me into the consultation room.

"Oh Baldy," I cried, with tears freely running down my face at the sight of the big lad sprawled on a huge furry blanket on the floor.

"Look Balder, Mummy's here," Michael, who had also been crying said to the dog using a title I had on previous occasions refuted. Not today. He was my boy. The nearest I had to a child. The nearest Michael and I had to a child together.

"Hey, handsome boy," I said softly as I joined the dog on his blanket. "It's okay, I've got you." I leaned in to kiss him as I cradled his head that filled my lap.

"Mrs Stanton?"

I looked up to find the vet had joined us. I didn't even bother to correct his term of address for me. I supposed that in this situation, as Balder's mum, I was Mrs Stanton.

"Yes. What's happened?"

The vet looked at Michael and waited for him to speak and when he didn't the vet continued. "Your husband explained that Balder has been under the weather for a couple of days."

I nodded.

"Unfortunately, the cause seems to be related to his heart."

"I see," I replied with a nod, thinking I actually saw nothing at this point.

"When he was brought in Balder was struggling, but not too bad all things considered."

Again, I nodded.

"Unfortunately once he got here, he suffered a stroke, a major one. He's almost seven...a Great Dane's life expectancy is usually somewhere between six and eight, some get to ten, but they're the exception rather than the rule."

He was telling me that this was as much as we could have hoped for, as much as Balder could have hoped for, and that was wrong. How could somebody have less than seven years as a lifespan? And for me he was as much of a body as anybody else I knew and cared for. He'd been in my life as long as my husband had.

"But that's unfair. That can't be right," I protested, somehow thinking I could bargain for longer.

"I'm sorry. As I say, he's a good age."

"They never told us that on Scooby fucking Doo, did they? Here's Scooby, funny and a big tit despite his size, but Shaggy don't become too involved or attached because he is going to die before he reaches his tenth birthday!"

I was furious; with Michael, the vet, even Scooby bloody Doo, but not Balder. He whimpered, gaining my attention, distracting me from my fury and despair at the unfairness of this. I adjusted my position to place my head next to his and allowed him to make an attempt to lick my tears away.

"Honestly, I am surprised he survived it," the vet said grimly.

"He was waiting for you," Michael said and looking up I could see that he was crying again whilst Edward hugged him. That felt odd, over familiar, although they had known each other a very long time.

I looked down at the dog through a mist of tears. The dog could barely move and the furry blanket was wet at his tail end, wet and soiled.

"Is there nothing…" I began, but already knew the answer.

The vet shook his head again, making me cry harder still.

"El," Michael called before dropping into a crouch beside me. "We need to say goodbye."

The days immediately following Balder's death passed by in a blur. Edward had insisted on calling Cy who had been incredibly sweet and supportive, even going so far as to offer to get on the next flight home. I reassured him that I loved him for offering but I didn't need him to do that, although I did admit to myself that I wanted him to, but he didn't and that was fine because there might be a time when I really would need him. Little did I know that time was going to come sooner rather than later.

Chapter Thirty-Seven

Almost two more weeks had passed and Cy was still not back. He sounded as frantic as I was to return and give up on what seemed to be a futile mission to find Christopher and yet he couldn't, not yet. Both Elizabeth and Denny were becoming increasingly worried and fraught at their son's continued absence and due to that as much as anything, Cy felt obliged to stay a while longer.

Edward was being supportive of me. More than that. I wasn't entirely sure what I would have done without him. My relationship with Michael seemed less erratic. The unity of saying goodbye to Balder offered us some common ground that didn't involve arguing or being poles apart. I was unsure if Susan was still staying with him, but she hadn't made contact beyond a single text offering her condolences for Balder's loss, a gesture I really did appreciate. I'd met up with Tia a few times in between her quick flits back home to visit her distressed parents and I had also met up as many times with Rhonda and Lulu. I'd even had Lulu to stay overnight, at Cy's house when Rhonda had a meeting out of town. A meeting I suspected may have been a date kind of meeting.

It was Friday afternoon as I sat reflecting on my life when Edward called from the doorway. "I'm heading off in about ten minutes," he told me with a frown.

"You should be smiling. Early doors on a Friday."

"I'm away for the weekend," he told me, still wearing his frown that made me laugh now.

"You don't want to go away?"

"Yes, yes. I'm just worried, about you, with Cy still away."

"Ah," I smiled with affection now. "I am fine. Cy is a phone call away," I lied knowing that was only a half-truth as Cy was likely to be in the back of beyond for the next few days again. He'd told me that earlier that morning, but he was kind of a call away. "I have Tia and Rhonda and my brothers and sisters if I really get in a pickle and Maya, we're having a girly weekend with face masks and nail polish."

"You're sure?"

"Positive. Have a wonderful weekend with him or her, or whoever." I grinned watching the blush colour Edward's cheeks. Yes, he was having one of those weekends away.

He nodded before gathering his belongings and with a kiss for me, followed by a pep talk for me and Maya as he left, he was gone.

****

The sound of my phone ringing at one a.m. the next morning woke me with a start. It was probably Cy, either miscalculating the time difference or taking an opportunity that had presented itself to call. I didn't even check the display on my phone, partly because my eyes hadn't yet begun to focus.

"Hello," I answered husky from sleep, fully anticipating Cy's familiar voice replying.

"Ms Ross, Eloise Ross?" a female voice I didn't recognise at the other end of the line questioned.

"Yes, speaking."

"My name is Lisa. I'm one of the nurses at Garrison House, it's your father."

By this point I was out of bed and beginning to cast my pyjamas aside in order to dress quickly as Lisa continued to speak.

"Jeremy has been taken ill and we called the paramedics who are on their way to the hospital with him…"

Her words were blurring now. I got as far as which hospital they were taking him to and with a brusque thank you, I hung up. I finished dressing, grabbed my phone and a hair tie and quietly padded downstairs. With my handbag containing my keys and purse under my arm I was leaving. My mind was going crazy on the journey to the hospital, but somehow I managed to focus on the road ahead, just. I questioned whether I should call Cy, or Edward or Susan, but I decided I had nothing to tell anyone at this point.

My dad was in A&E when I arrived. The receptionist assured me he was in safe hands and that someone would be out to see me as soon as possible, but right now my dad needed them more than me. I sat, stood, tapped my feet and paced the floor for the next hour, an hour that seemed to last a lifetime. I swear I aged ten years in that waiting room. Every time a door opened or a doctor or a nurse appeared, I braced myself for them to call my name, but they didn't for over an hour and then a man of around thirty, dressed in scrubs appeared.

"Ms Ross?" he called to the few people that were in the waiting area.

I sprung to my feet as if I was announcing my confirmation.

"This way, please," he smiled and for a second, I was relieved that his smile was friendly rather than apologetic or consoling, but then I decided he would keep the consolatory smile and sad eyes for somewhere more private. Perhaps this friendly smile might be his professional, *please don't cry in reception and scare the patients* smile.

I obediently followed him through a security operated door until we reached a small office where he gestured for me to take a seat.

"I'm Doctor Adams," he told me and offered me a hand to shake. "Your father, he's stable," he began, allowing me to release the breath I'd been holding. "I believe he is a resident in a residential care home?"

I nodded.

"Their staff called an ambulance when he began complaining of discomfort of some sort. That, along with his confusion and agitation concerned them and they also noticed some drooping of his face."

"A stroke?" I asked.

It was the doctor's turn to nod now.

"How bad?" I asked and immediately thought of Balder.

"It's quite soon to say. However, I would have to say it is a significant one."

"You mentioned his confusion and agitation, he has dementia."

"The paramedics advised us of that, but he hasn't really been with us since he arrived and as we don't know him it's difficult to assess whether the stroke has exacerbated the dementia."

"Can I see him?" I was tearful as I wondered exactly what was going to be waiting for me.

"Of course. Are you alone?" Yet again I nodded. "Would you like to call someone, husband, partner, siblings, I believe your father is a widower?"

"Yes, my mum died about fifteen years ago. I'll call my siblings in the morning and my husband is about to become my ex-husband." I sniffed back tears, but not for Michael or my marriage. More for the fact that I was totally alone right now. Even Edward was out of town, but I wouldn't call anyone until I knew what was likely to happen with my dad. "My boyfriend is in America."

"If you're sure. Let's take you through to see him."

"Is he going to die?" I sniffed, attempting to stifle the flow of tears I held back.

"It really is too early to say and with his general state of health—"

We both walked in silence down the corridor before I was led into the resuscitation area where my dad remained on a trolley, attached to numerous machines that were making bleeps and pings that echoed around us. A nurse stood nearby and smiled as she saw us approaching.

"This is Mr Ross' daughter. She's going to sit with him for a while," the doctor explained to the nurse before turning to me. "We'll be close by, so if there are any problems call or buzz. We're hoping to get Jeremy up onto a ward soon."

It was three more hours before they found a bed on the ward and moved Jezza up there, where I was very quickly asked to leave. I supposed it was understandable that it wasn't really visiting time before seven a.m.

In the time I'd been there my dad had shown no signs of life beyond breathing and the bleeping of the machines confirmed that. I was scared as the ward doors closed behind me and knew that it was the inevitable that was scaring me. Whichever way I looked at it I was waiting for him to die, whether that was today, tomorrow, next week or next month and I was totally unprepared for it. I had no clue how I was going to cope with the loss. I accepted I was an adult and had missed out on my mother in so many ways, but now I was about to become an orphan. There was no way I could or would leave, not yet. Not until I was able to visit and check on him again.

I still wasn't quite ready to let anyone else know what was going on. Maybe that was selfish, but it had essentially been me and Jezza for the last six years and I needed a while longer. I did drop Maya a quick text to let her know where I was and what had happened. She didn't reply, but I didn't expect her to as it was the weekend and she liked to sleep in. I didn't contact anyone else, not even Cy. Especially not Cy.

The ward staff took pity on me and allowed me in just after ten. I received a few pitying looks and was unsure if it was for my dad or for the state I must have looked. After another couple of hours of sitting and watching, Jezza finally stirred and offered me a tiny lop-sided smile.

"Elsa." He grinned and dribbled a little making me cry the unshed tears I'd been fighting.

Taking his hand, we both cried until he fell asleep again. He'd remembered and recognised me. That would be the only positive in this horrible situation.

My belly was growling when I became aware of someone standing behind me. I turned to find Maya preparing to hug me.

"Come on, lunch," she said as my stomach let out a roar.

I offered no resistance to her suggestion and followed her to the ground floor canteen, but not before I'd made the staff aware of my whereabouts.

With a sandwich eaten and half a cup of coffee drunk, I called Susan who was still staying locally. How fucked up was our family that I didn't even know where she was? She told me that she would call the boys while I called Mary who would be at least a day away once she found a flight. Staring down at my phone, Maya spoke.

"Boss man will expect you to call."

"I know, but he has his own family stuff," I replied.

"Edward then, or Tia?"

"They'll call Cy."

"Somebody needs to call one of them. You need somebody El," she pointed out and I couldn't disagree with her.

"Maybe later," I conceded to her disputing expression. "I'm going back up to see my dad. To check on him and then I'll call Cy, happy now?" I asked tartly.

"Thrilled," Maya replied flatly.

I'd been sat at my dad's bedside again for another hour, a very long hour when he began to move around erratically, thrashing a little and then the machines began to sound loudly and alarmingly, causing a crowd of medical staff to appear. They pushed me out of the way so they could get to him. He was clearly in trouble. One staff member guided me away as the curtain was pulled around his bed. Maya was still there and attempted to talk me down, to calm me.

There was still no sign of my siblings when another doctor came and introduced himself. He explained that my dad had suffered a heart attack and was about to be moved to intensive care and that I should prepare myself for the worst. I only wished I knew how to do that. I nodded, a lot and hoped that Maya was taking it all in, just in case I needed to know any of it later.

It was a case of more waiting when Jezza was taken to intensive care. I sat outside in the corridor and pulled my phone from my bag. I selected Cy's name from my list of contacts. I was unsure what time it was where I was, never mind where Cy was. After just three rings my call connected.

"Hi baby, how you doing?" he asked and with five words spoken to me and not a single one uttered back, I began to cry. All attempts to speak, lost. "El, slow down, calm down, please. What's happened?"

I managed, just, to get enough words out to convey what was going on.

"Okay, I'm going to get the next flight out. I'll be there as soon as I can," he told me and I felt sure he was already looking up flights.

"You don't have to do that," I protested, but wasn't entirely sure of my commitment to that statement so I knew Cy wouldn't be.

"I told you before, if you need me, nothing and nobody could be more important than you El, never. You need me baby and I need to be there with you, so I'm coming home."

I thanked him between more tears. Once Cy had established I was with Maya he asked to speak to her. The conversation between them that I heard led me to believe that Cy was asking about Edward and my siblings.

****

Time passed slower in the hospital than anywhere I had ever known. Susan arrived late afternoon with my brothers and as the rule was a maximum of two visitors we took it in turns to sit with our dad who was clearly very, very sick. Our brothers left first, followed by Maya who promised to return with some things for me to freshen up after my refusal to leave the hospital. I had no idea what I was going to do when visiting time ended. I just knew I couldn't leave while my dad was still there, hanging on. Susan and I sat opposite each other, over the bed. We listened to the beeps and pings of the machinery that freed us both of the need and responsibility to speak for a while.

Eventually, Susan chose to speak. "Is your boyfriend not here?"

"No." My defensive reply assumed she was about to make a barbed comment or inference. "He's away," I added, but didn't explain further, nor did I tell her that he was coming home, to me, for me.

She was looking down at her own hands in her lap as she continued to speak. "I do love you El. Even when it doesn't seem that way. I always loved you, more than I ever thought was possible. Michael was the right choice."

Her eyes were raised now, looking at me. I believed her, or at least I believed that she believed her own words.

"I love you too, but Michael? He was never the right choice for me. Not as a husband. I thought he was, most of the time. I believed the rest of you when you told me he was and I know we needed help but it was too high a price to pay. Me. My life."

"You never said," she seemed to accuse. Maybe she felt guilty in some way.

"You never asked," I counter accused. "It's only now, years after that I understand how wrong and flawed the whole thing was. I love Cy and he loves me and that made me scrutinise and question everything I had with Michael," I admitted. "I did, still do care about him, but I never loved him like I should have."

"Like you love him? Cy?" she asked and although my boyfriend's name was more of a sneer than anything else, I let it go. She at least acknowledged that Cy existed and we were together.

"Like I love him. With everything I am. So much that it scares me, like I might not be able to take my next breath without him in my life."

I felt certain that my saccharine loaded words would turn Susan's stomach. They didn't. She smiled then laughed. "Hang onto it El, because if you both feel that way, this is it. Your one real chance at true happiness."

Her words were heartfelt and spoken from experience. Her pained expression and glossy eyes atoned to that.

"I am sorry, that I couldn't do this with Michael."

Susan shook her head frantically. "No, no, I'm sorry. I should never have allowed it, never mind orchestrated it. I was blinded by my love and infatuation with Michael. These last few weeks and Dad's words have resonated and I can't disagree with them, fool myself any longer. Even Michael has told me that we were both wrong to have allowed things to go as far as they did. He did love you though, in his own way."

I could feel my eyes drying out as I stared across at my sister.

"Why does it have to be *in his own way*? Cy tells me he loves me and never ever suggests that it's in his own way or that I'm his best chance at making it work, but Michael did and now you are."

"El, I can't answer that. Just know that you were his best chance and he did love you in his own way."

The nurse reappeared, ready to check obs, ending our conversation which had disturbed and reassured me in equal parts.

Susan left the hospital at the end of evening visiting whereas I chose to remain close by, just in case. Maya returned with Chad and some clothes and a toiletries bag as a nurse appeared and frowned at me before speaking.

"Please tell me you're going home," she said with a sad, but empathetic smile.

I shook my head. "No, I can't, just in case."

"We'll call you if he deteriorates," she reassured me with a gentle rub of my arm.

"But will he still be here, alive by the time I get here?" My blunt words caused the nurse to blanch slightly. "Sorry, I need to be here for him, at the end," I explained with a few hard swallows to keep me from crying, again. "I can wait in my car if it's not allowed, waiting here," I told her, gesturing to the seats around me.

"It's not encouraged, but it's not, not allowed. But maybe you should think about going home for a while…"

I sighed as I noticed Maya's expression agree with the nurse's suggestion while Chad slunk further back until he was almost in the lift.

"He can't be alone, not when he, you know, dies." I sobbed with the last word and my earlier plan not to cry was blown out of the water. "My brothers won't come here, one of my sisters lives in Australia and should be on her way at best. My other sister might, but sometimes she just gets Dad riled, most times. There's really only me, his favourite nurse from the home and my boyfriend, he likes him usually." I smiled weakly.

"He's away," Maya said to the nurse who was clearly looking around for the aforementioned boyfriend.

"He's on his way back from The States," I explained. "Look, the chances are when he arrives, I am going to be physically removed from this place at the end of visiting, but for now, please."

I sounded needy and desperate which seemed to seal the deal.

"I'll let the staff know where to find you if they need you."
She smiled. "I'm going to the canteen, can I get you something,
sandwich, drink?"

I shook my head and with a few words for Maya, including
sending her home I made my way to the nearest visitor toilet for
a quick freshen up before changing into clean clothes.

****

If I'd thought daytime hours went by slowly in a hospital
then the nighttime ones moved in reverse. I watched the clock
until three a.m. when I watched a crash team descend upon the
ward followed by them leaving and then a porter arriving with a
long black box. I sobbed silently as I watched the box and its
occupant leave the ward for the last time and selfishly thanked a
God I wasn't sure I believed in for sparing my own father, for
now.

I had no idea how long I remained crouched in the chair,
almost hugging myself with my arms wrapped around my own
body when I felt someone sit beside me and then an arm slid
around my shoulders. I knew it wasn't Cy, but I hoped it might
be right up to the point where I looked up and found Edward
pulling me into his side where I cried. Tears for the person
whose last minutes I'd been privy to in a strange and remote
way, for my dad who was barely hanging on, my mum who I'd
never really known, not like I wished I had and for myself. For
all of the errors and mistakes I'd made until Cy, and then I cried
for Cy because I missed him more than I thought was possible to
miss anyone and it had been weeks. Long, long weeks since I
had seen him and been held by him.

When I eventually came out from behind my veil of tears, I
hadn't expected to see anyone other than Edward and certainly
not Michael who was sitting opposite me looking incredibly
nervous and uncomfortable.

"Michael."

"Sorry if I'm intruding, Edward..." he blustered.

"El, I think we should take you home," Edward said before
I had chance to respond to Michael. Then looking at my startled
expression continued, "To Maya's or Cy's. He called to tell me
about your dad. He wants me to stay until he arrives, but he

doesn't know you've got a vigil going on and suggested you should stay at his, that both of us should."

"No," I snapped, shaking my head as I leapt to my feet before turning on Edward who didn't look quite as startled as Michael. "For fuck's sake! I am here waiting for my dad to die. I am shit scared that if I leave here, move more than two minutes away he will die without me. That he will be completely alone, like whoever the fuck they wheeled out of there earlier. He has spent so much time lost in his own mind that he can't be physically alone in his final moments. Maybe he won't know who is there, but I will. I need to do this last thing for him. I have to, and if you or Cy object then you can go now and tell him not to bother coming back, ever." My angry outburst had at least quashed my tears. "So, what's it to be Edward, are you staying or going? Because I am going nowhere."

"You need to curtail your language, young lady," he told me with a professor like scowl. "But if you're going nowhere then neither am I." Turning to Michael he said, "Maybe you could get us some horrendous tasting tea or coffee from one of those hideous vending machines."

Michael got to his feet immediately and disappeared, following Edward's suggestion, order, whatever it was. The Michael I had just seen was not one I had ever seen before.

"Cy should be back tomorrow, later," Edward corrected as we watched a new group of staff entering the ward, beginning their day's work.

I never did drink whatever Michael returned with. In fact I didn't see Michael before he left. Somehow I managed to fall asleep, being held by Edward and when I woke it was just after half-past eight, just an hour and a half before visiting began.

"Sorry, I think I may have been a little highly strung earlier," I said to Edward as I accepted the cup of tea and sausage sandwich he insisted I needed.

"You were upset," he corrected. "Eat your breakfast, you're wasting away before my eyes, and I don't need Cy accusing me of not looking after you." He smiled.

"Thank you. When we first met you scared me."

"I know, you're not that good an actress to hide your fear."

"I don't know why. I was suspicious of you and the reason for your sudden reappearance. Then there was the fact that you seemed to taunt me with Rhonda's presence at the hospital charity night. Did you know, then, about me and Cy?"

Edward shook his head. "Although I suspected. The tension between you was palpable and add to that Cy's scowl every time Michael looked at you or touched you and that's all before we think about your jealous lover pout and catty remarks aimed at Rhonda. So all indications were that you and he had more going on than employer and employee."

I nodded, unable to refute any of his claims. "Did you tell Elizabeth about us, about that night? She seemed to be suspicious of me from the get go."

"Elizabeth told me. You and Michael went for dinner or lunch and Cy and Tia gatecrashed I believe. That was enough for her to know."

"Really?" I asked, somewhat agog at Edward's revelation. "I had no idea she knew. Like I said, it was obvious that she had suspicions, but in some ways I always thought her suspicions were aimed at me as the married whore who liked rich men."

Edward shrugged without attempting to dispel my words. "I've told you before that Elizabeth loves her children. She's a wonderful mother and wife and she will see how much you mean to Cy and just how much he means to you, if you let her, and in my opinion you really should."

"What if she won't let me, show her?" I asked, relieved to be talking and thinking about something, anything that wasn't my dad and his impending death that was hanging over us like a big, black cloud.

"Cy won't allow her to exclude you without excluding him and Elizabeth would never do that, never. Look El, Elizabeth doesn't dislike you, she doesn't know you and if she did, she'd love you. There's not a single thing about you not to love," he told me sincerely and once more tears were filling my eyes, but happy, fond tears this time. "When Elizabeth met Denny it caused a scandal for her. Her family were old money and before Denny there was an Earl that had taken quite a shine. Her parents were from generations of social climbers so aristocracy was viewed as a real prize, but as soon as she met Denny, in a trendy bar with a rather suspect reputation she was smitten and she wasn't going to let him go, Earl or no Earl. Denny was viewed as crass and vulgar, from new money and lord help us, American," Edward said with a very over-exaggerated look of horror that made me smile. "Elizabeth has been where Cy is and Denny has been in your shoes which is how I know that you and Cy can do this. Win them over with a little patience and the obvious love you share."

"Thank you," I smiled, getting up to put my rubbish in the bin as Edward leapt to his feet.

"My phone," he apologised holding his silenced phone up.

With a brief kiss to my cheek, he scurried away to take his call, leaving me alone with just my thoughts and a slightly lighter load of worries to carry around.

Edward still hadn't returned when Susan arrived. Taking in my appearance she shook her head and frowned.

"You need to go home and sleep." Sensing my impending refusal she changed tack. "At least let me get you some food and a drink."

"I've had something. A friend came to stay a while, and Michael, but he left."

"Sure?" she asked before pulling me in for a hug that felt more than a simple hug about our father.

"Positive," I confirmed, still savouring her embrace that offered warmth and love.

"Shall we go in?"

"You go. I'll be in soon," I told Susan who had already released me and was about to enter the door to the ward.

Turning, I saw that Edward had returned and looked awful, like he was in need of medical attention himself. I rushed to his side and helped him to sit down.

"Are you okay? Are you unwell?" I asked, genuinely concerned for his health.

"Fine, fine," he said brushing me off. "I saw you, with that woman," he panted with a gesture to the door Susan had gone through.

"My sister, she seems to be mellowing or at least seeing

how wrong things were for me."

"Sister?" he asked in a high-pitched tone.

"Yes."

"Your sister is older than you?" he stated as much as asked.

"Yes."

"How much older?" he asked, which I did think was an odd question.

"Eighteen years, give or take a month…"

Edward looked aghast as he continued his questioning. "Your birthday, when is it? You said you and Tia were only a few months apart."

"Four weeks."

Edward was pacing, and although he didn't look ill now, he still looked like he might be sick at any second.

"Your sister," he began again.

"Susan," I clarified wondering what else to say.

"Susan?" he repeated, "Susan…" he repeated to himself and then began to trail off until he uttered one more word that sounded a lot like, "Sassy."

"Edward," I said, hoping to gain some insight into his harassed and agitated state. As I placed a hand on his arm he leapt back as if he'd been burnt by my touch and my use of his name.

"I have to go," he suddenly announced and leapt to his feet.

"Edward," I called, but he was already heading back towards the lift. "Edward!" I called again, this time with worry for the man I had become accustomed to and rather fond of, but he simply continued walking.

Chapter Thirty-Eight

My eyes fluttered open, allowing me to take in my surroundings. I was lying in Cy's bed with him and I could feel that he was already awake. Swallowing was tricky. My throat was sore, dry and my eyes hurt, then it all came back to me, how I'd got here, what had led to this. With the hard realisation registering in my mind I began to cry, silently until I felt Cy's arms that had been wrapped around me pull me closer, cradling me as my sobs became less and less controlled and louder.

It might have been minutes or hours that passed as I lay crying while Cy held me, making no attempt to comfort me beyond kissing my hair. I felt relief that he wasn't showering me with sympathetic words and sentiments because nothing was ever going to make this easier. I had been preparing for this reality for years, thought I had prepared for it sufficiently over the last few months and weeks, but the physical pain coursing through my body, the gut-wrenching sobs echoing around the room and the aching void in my heart suggested that I was anything but.

"Baby," he finally spoke. "Let me get you something to drink and maybe some breakfast, lunch?"

Clearly I'd been crying quite a while since waking to the reality that was this pain.

"I don't need anything," I replied in a very hoarse croak that proved me wrong.

I couldn't believe that it had only been twenty-four hours since I had been at the hospital having spent the night there. Edward had gone all weird and left and I'd joined Susan at our father's bedside where we'd chatted, friendly talk that had been alien and familiar at the same time. It took me back to a time when I was a little girl, about five-years-old and Susan and I had shared a room. I remembered her telling me stories and doing my hair. I remembered laughter, lots of it, my own and hers.

Our brothers had all arrived together after lunch and by late evening Cy and Mary had arrived, the latter looking exhausted after a day's flying.

It was as if my dad had waited for us all to be there because that's when he'd suffered another heart attack. The doctor had warned us at that point that he really was struggling and suggested that we should consider not resuscitating in the event of further cardiac arrest. The others had all agreed that there should be no further intervention and although I knew he wouldn't want to keep being brought back from the brink I wasn't quite ready to let him go. My siblings all wanted me to bend to their will, what we all knew would be our dad's will and it was a little overwhelming. With my dad in a side room Cy took me aside, out into a nearby waiting area where he said very little, not even opening the topic of my dad's future until I did.

"How can they just agree to let him die?" I'd asked.

"Is that what they're doing?" Cy asked in response.

"They don't want him to be resuscitated."

"Maybe, but why is that?" he'd asked, forcing me to reason this out.

"Because he wouldn't want to be brought back, to this, to an existence that will only prolong the inevitable."

"So?" was his simple prompt.

"I need to let him go, don't I?" I'd asked, but already knew the answer as I'd found myself encased in Cy's arms while I'd sadly sniffed back tears at the knowledge that my life was going to change forever very soon.

"El, come on, you need to drink and eat something," Cy said, already releasing me to get up from the bed.

I rolled over so that I was lying flat on my back and watched Cy pulling on some track pants meaning he was serious about getting up. I didn't want to get up and face this, any of it. If I got out of bed and went downstairs then I was going to have to deal with registering a death, planning a funeral, sorting through Jezza's belongings and I didn't want to. I knew that I'd have to, maybe not all at once but I wasn't ready, for any of it, just like I hadn't been ready to let my dad go the day before. As if to prove my lack of readiness I pulled Cy's pillow over my face and held it there, inhaling his scent and blocking out the world.

"Okay," I heard Cy mutter through the muffled hearing the pillow gave me. Then I felt weight on and over my hips, Cy's weight that was straddling me before the pillow was snatched from my grasp. "Baby, I can't tell you that I know how you feel because I don't, but you can't lie here and bury yourself in bed and pretend this hasn't happened. I do know Jezza wouldn't want that; he'd want you to remember the good times you and he shared and to be happy."

Tears were running down my face again, just because Cy's words refused to allow me to pretend that I still had my dad, even if he had been a shell of the man he'd once been for the last few years. Even that version of him was better than the one I had now, or more precisely the one I no longer had.

"Shit!" Cy cursed, at himself more than me as he began to brush the tears from my cheeks, with sadness and pain etched across his own face. "Baby, please, please stop. I know you're hurting and sad, but I need you to come and eat and try, even for just a few seconds not to cry, okay?" he asked as his forehead came to rest against mine. "I love you," he whispered against my lips before kissing me, gently, so gently that I thought I might have imagined it.

Suddenly, Cy was back on his feet and pulling me to mine to escort me downstairs where I intended to try not to cry, for a while at least.

****

Tia arrived as I was drinking tea that contained sugar, which was a shock to say the least as I didn't take any.

Seeing my face contort Cy explained, "For shock."

I considered refusing to drink it but decided that the look of dogged determination on his face meant that would have been pointless so I drank my tea, one grimaced swallow at a time.

"I was sorry to hear about your dad," Tia began as she sat next to me.

I made no reply. I attempted to acknowledge her comment, but also to stem her words of condolence that would almost certainly set off my tears again so gave her hand a squeeze. Cy put chocolate croissants before us and while Tia tucked in, I began to pick at mine, unable to remember when I had last eaten, possibly with Edward the previous day. Looking down at my phone I saw that it was after eleven in the morning and I had missed a call and a text from Susan.

<Call me when you're up and about, we need to make arrangements. Sx>

I gazed down and wondered when she had become less frosty in her dealings with me. Maybe I was questioning when she'd become frosty before her recent about turn. I suppose she had lost her father too so maybe she and I were discovering a horrible common ground that brought us together. I half smiled at the fact she'd text rather than relentlessly called, her single call having arrived a little after nine that morning.

"You okay?" Cy passed me a banana and a yoghurt.

"Cy," I began to protest at further food.

"Please, you've lost weight while I've been away and I have a feeling you're going to struggle to eat over the next few days, so try, for me," he pleaded gently, and the smile he offered me alone was enough for me to open the banana and break half off then I proceeded to eat it in tiny mouthfuls.

"I need to contact Susan. She text and called earlier," I explained as I found my yoghurt being opened for me.

"Eat first and then call her back," Cy suggested as Tia asked him a question I hadn't really been expecting.

"Have you heard anything from Edward?"

Cy shook his head and also gave his sister a disapproving frown when my own face morphed into one of concern.

"Why? Is he alright?" I asked them both.

Tia shrugged while Cy seemed to consider his response more carefully.

"He's gone AWOL. Nobody can reach him and despite us leaving messages, he's not responding. Did he say anything to you when you last saw him?" Cy reluctantly asked.

"No. He was just a bit weird. He came back and saw Susan who was just going to see our dad," I began with a wobble to my voice uttering the word dad. "He asked about Susan and then became a bit odd before turning to leave. I was worried he was unwell. I haven't seen him since."

A silent glance was exchanged between Cy and Tia that told me nothing. Just that this behaviour was out of character for Edward. Not that I'd given him any real thought since he'd left the hospital. Other things had taken over and filled my mind.

"What?" I asked both of them and neither of them in particular.

"Nothing," Cy replied quickly, too quickly.

"Cy, please, I am not a child."

I had aimed for my comment to strike a chord with him, to remind him that I didn't need protecting from whatever was going on and I think my words served their purpose. However, what they did primarily was remind me that I was not only not a child, but I was no longer anybody's child. I didn't have parents anymore. I was an orphan. A grown woman of twenty-eight, almost twenty-nine, and I felt totally alone and bereft.

"Hey." Cy spoke softly, calmly as he wrapped an arm around me and pulled me in tightly against his chest, stroking my hair. "I didn't mean to treat you like a child," he assured me which only served to make me cry more.

"I know," I stammered as I felt another hand on my back, rubbing, patting and stroking, Tia. "But I'm not anybody's child anymore, am I? I'm all alone," I cried and although I was hurting, I knew my words were melodramatic. But in that moment I felt alone, adrift. I belonged nowhere.

"Baby, you're not alone, you'll never be alone. You have me. You'll always have me."

I did feel comforted by his words and the strength of the conviction in them. We stayed together, holding onto each other for several minutes before I was calm once more and realised that Tia had left.

"Tia?"

"She has things to do," Cy replied, but I knew she'd left to give me some space.

"Where do you think Edward is?" I asked as we lay together on the sofa.

"Not a clue. This is very un-Edward like. I asked him to stay with you until I arrived and he assured me he would. I never doubted that and he didn't and now, nobody can find him."

"You could, or I could check with Michael," I suggested and then with a doubtful expression on Cy's face I retold him all of Edward's movements and comments over the weekend until his disappearance, but didn't mention Michael's appearance at the hospital.

"This makes no fucking sense." Cy rubbed his fingers through his hair, making me remember how many weeks it had been since I'd seen him. I hadn't even kissed him since he'd arrived the previous day, not really.

We were still lying together, facing one another, close enough that I could feel his breath on my face.

"Do you need to go to work? I assume Edward is a no show there too."

"Yeah. Maya is on alert to contact me as soon as he shows up and no, I don't need to go in. I need to be with you. Darius is on hand if need be and I am at the end of the phone."

"I'm glad you're here," I admitted landing a gentle kiss to Cy's lips.

Very quickly my gentle kiss had transposed into something deeper and more purposeful. I found myself lying beneath Cy as we attempted to devour each other, unsure who was most desperate for this. With only the t-shirt I was wearing separating skin to skin contact, I gasped when a hand slid beneath it. Cy's touch seared through me as it inched higher, ensuring that the only thoughts in my head were of me and Cy. Nothing and nobody else, just the two of us and a future we both wanted.

****

Freshly showered and dressed, I took in my appearance in the bathroom mirror and Cy was right, I had lost weight. Not a huge amount but enough to be noticeable. I also scrutinised the woman looking back at me and wondered if it was normal to shag your boyfriend on the sofa the day after you'd seen your father die. Especially when it had been on the back of the realisation that you were an adult orphan and some debate on Edward's location and sudden disappearance. It was at precisely that point that it occurred to me that I hadn't even asked Cy about his brother. Whether he'd been found or not.

Once I returned downstairs, I found Cy in the kitchen, chatting with Susan who had arrived a few minutes before.

"Sorry, I didn't hear you arrive," I apologised when she looked up at me and frowned, disapproval at everything I was in this house with Cy, I assumed. I was wrong I found when she began to address me.

"You look awful Eloise. Have you eaten anything?"

I nodded. "A little breakfast, Cy insisted."

"Good." She nodded with a small smile for Cy who said nothing. "You need to eat more though. I can't remember the last time you were so skinny," she accused and then guiltily added, "Yes I can, before you and Michael got married and when Mum died."

I could see tears welling in her eyes. Why had I never looked at our family circumstances from her point of view before? I had lost my mum after thirteen years, the last of those she had been ill and I hadn't truly had her during those times, but Susan, she had shared her life with our mother for thirty-one years and it must have hit her like my dad's death was hitting me now. She had also loved our father for her entire forty-seven years on earth compared to my almost twenty nine. Tears were burning my eyes and very quickly overflowing down my face.

"Sorry," I stammered as Susan hugged me. Cy continued to watch on, like he was seeing clearly for the first time.

"Don't be silly, you're allowed to be upset," Susan told me before Cy chipped in.

"Sure you are baby, but just try not to get overwhelmed."

Susan watched the exchange between us and rather than turning her nose up or sneering, she simply watched and when my eyes held hers, she smiled.

"El, the boys are happy to leave arrangements to us."

It was no surprise that the boys wouldn't want to take any responsibility or decision making for, well, anything. Although, I didn't doubt that they would be happy to take their share of any estate that might have been left.

"And Mary?" I asked with a sharpness I hadn't expected to hear or intended to infer. If anything I felt guilty to realise that I had actually forgotten about our other sister since I'd had the meltdown to end all meltdowns at my father's death bed.

"Baby, she's staying with Maya. Do you remember, last night? She didn't really know where to stay and I think she felt uncomfortable about staying here, so she is in your room at Maya's."

I didn't remember. I'd actually forgotten about Mary full stop so there wasn't much chance of me remembering where she was staying, even if she was sleeping in my bed.

"What about me? If she's staying in my room?" I was confused, because one, I had no idea how long she planned on staying, and two, where the hell was I going to sleep on my nights spent at Maya's.

"You're staying here, indefinitely," Cy told me firmly.

"I could speak to Michael—" Susan said but was quickly cut off by me and Cy saying NO in stereo.

"El stays here, with me," Cy told my sister with a polite firmness that she appeared to pick up on.

"Susan, please tell me that you're not planning and plotting for a future with Michael, for me," I pleaded. "I really thought we'd made ground, turned a few corners and that you were finally accepting my choices." I hoped I wasn't going to cry again. I was growing tired of the crying and because of the crying.

"I am, I do. I meant as a place to stay," Susan clarified and I truly believed her, so much so that I couldn't help but pursue it.

"What's changed Susan, beyond Dad?" I added with a waver. "Until this weekend we'd had little contact since you thought I needed to fix my marriage and make good on my vows, or yours, whichever," I added a little bitchily. "And then at the hospital you're meek and mild, telling me to hang onto

469

what I have with Cy and now, today, you're thinking of asking Michael to let me stay with him at my former marital home. So what's changed, or is this Susan, the reasonable one that wants me to be happy and to live my life, is she all a façade?"

Susan looked hurt at my words, but I meant them. I had no clue what I was dealing with here, with her. When I remembered the big sister who read stories and plaited my hair it was this Susan, the one I'd described as meek and mild. Yet when she made suggestions involving Michael, I mistrusted her motives. After all, I had been used as bait, currency, a gift, whatever the fuck I had been at twenty-three and it confused me.

"Michael has changed El. Well maybe not, but I understand him better and I can see how wrong the two of you were. I am so sorry, sorrier than you could ever know about every decision I have ever made where you're concerned. I want you to be happy, to have and to be everything you want and deserve."

I believed her and when I looked across at Cy who was leaning against the kitchen counter, his coffee cup frozen in mid-air between his waist and mouth, his expression one of amazement, but nodding he seemed to believe what she was saying too.

Chapter Thirty-Nine

I had no idea just how many choices and decisions were involved in a funeral and was grateful for Susan's presence along with Mary and Cy, who hadn't returned to work until he'd chauffeured us around and everything was organised. He refused to allow me to go back to work, insisting I needed some time. I was grateful in some ways that I could remain at home and finalise arrangements. I also spent some time with Mary who I hadn't seen since I'd married Michael, Susan too, although there still appeared to be an atmosphere hanging between them.

I had begun to sort through my dad's belongings until there were only his personal effects which were now in one of Cy's guest rooms. He hadn't really left much of value in his will, but had left some specific items to each of us; my brothers had each been left a watch and Susan and Mary had been left a ring of my mother's. I had been left a pearl necklace that had apparently belonged to my great-grandmother who had left it to her granddaughter, my mother, and now it was mine.

****

"You almost ready?" Cy asked, his reflection appearing behind me in the mirror.

"I don't really know," I replied with total honesty. "Any news on Christopher?" I added, thinking that I still hadn't asked about Cy's brother in a few days.

"Nope. Dad is still trying to track him down. It's like he has literally dropped off the face of the earth." He sighed, taking my inherited necklace from me and fastening it around my neck. "But he will turn up, Chris always does."

"What about Edward? Has anyone heard from him? I can't deny that I am a little concerned."

"Baby, today is going to be hard enough for you to get through without you getting stressed out about Edward and Christopher," Cy seemed to warn as his hands moved from my neck and snaked around my middle.

"I just hope there's no fighting," I sighed.

"Fighting?" Cy queried, pulling me tightly into his body.

"Yeah, my brothers and cousins sometimes get a little lairy when they've had a drink and that usually results in fists flying."

I had never been overly embarrassed by my brothers before, but suddenly, explaining to Cy how they usually behaved when alcohol was involved, I couldn't deny that I did feel a little uncomfortable and abashed by and for them.

"Any fists come flying in your direction and I might just be joining them," Cy replied a little too seriously. "Will Michael be there today?" he asked with a slight bristle.

"I don't know for sure. Susan said he had spoken about attending, maybe out of duty as my," I paused when I saw a thunderous look spread across Cy's face at what he anticipated I was about to say. "My dad's son-in-law or maybe as moral support for Susan. I suppose we'll see."

"Mmm. I know this may not be appropriate, but you look beautiful." He smiled and kissed my neck gently making me feel confident that the black shift dress and matching jacket was the right outfit. "My mom called and sends her condolences," Cy told me with a smile that said he was relieved Elizabeth was extending an olive branch in my direction and I couldn't deny that at least something positive was coming from this. "I'll give you a couple of minutes. I'll wait downstairs," he said with a final peck to my cheek.

I nodded and with a sad smile watched Cy walk away and gave myself a final once over knowing that I just needed to get through the day. I adjusted the clip that was holding my hair up and slipped on my black court shoes leaving me as ready as I was ever going to be.

****

Since my dad had no home of his own, his funeral

procession was leaving from my brother's house. Wayne's house was only a couple of streets from our old family home. It seemed appropriate and something our dad would have approved of. I was fairly certain that Cy had never been on an estate like ours. I was unsure if he was prepared for it as we turned off the main road. We passed the parade of shops whose only purpose seemed to be to provide shelter for local youths, the resident homeless drunk and the customary drug dealer who seemed to be doing something illegal judging by how quickly he disappeared after spying Cy's black car that I knew was the sort often favoured by the police for their unmarked vehicles and they could regularly be found around here, although usually at night.

My brother's house was a fairly typical semi-detached and was almost identical to the properties that neighboured it. The red bricks looked old, the windows and doors tarnished, generally tired and in need of a lift, like many of the residents. As the car came to a stop at the roadside, I became aware of curtains twitching and a hive of activity around Wayne's home. I briefly wondered if he had volunteered his home for the starting point of my father's final journey or if he'd been bamboozled into it.

"This is where you're from?" Cy asked as he opened the passenger door and offered me a hand.

"Yes, well, two streets away," I replied with a warm smile as I realised that there had been no judgement or criticism in his question. "You've never been anywhere like this I'm guessing?"

Cy shook his head as I came to stand next to him.

"It's not the best neighbourhood," I conceded a little awkwardly.

"You came from here, it has a lot going for it as far as I am concerned," Cy replied making me melt a little at the sincerity in his voice and then laugh as I watched him cringing at his own words. All sad thoughts and apprehension about the day ahead gone for the moment.

"Jeez, how lame was that? I'm just glad nobody was here to hear it."

"I'm here, I heard it." I grinned. "In fact, I don't think I will ever forget it."

"Which means you won't let me forget it either." He gripped my hand more firmly, allowing me to lead him through the gate to see flowers beginning to gather on the small lawned area of the garden as the door opened revealing Wayne who welcomed us.

It was another twenty minutes before anyone else arrived and then there was a steady succession of people in and around the house, most of whom I knew and a few I either didn't recognise or didn't remember. I seemed to be under the scrutiny of a lot of people, maybe because I was with Cy, the man who wasn't my husband. Not that the majority of people outside of my family would have recognised Michael if he'd stood before them.

I spent a good amount of time introducing Cy before I looked up and saw my niece, Lois, enter the room with her father, Neil. As soon as our eyes met, she made her way over to me.

"El, how are you?" she asked as she pulled me in for a hug. "I can't believe, well everything." She frowned before looking behind me where Cy stood with one hand resting on my hip, a little possessively, but mainly comfortingly.

"I know. I'm okay, well not okay with Grandad," I said rubbing her arm when I saw her lip begin to wobble as she thought about her grandad, my dad. "You haven't met Cy, this is Cy, my boyfriend. Cy this is Lois, my niece, although we kind of grew up together," I explained as I concluded their introduction.

"Good to meet you. I've seen photographs of the two of you," Cy replied as he offered Lois an open hand to shake.

Fortunately, she accepted Cy's greeting as she queried, "Photographs?"

"Yeah, in El's room, next to that Belle doll," he explained making me and Lois smile.

"You still have that!" she exclaimed loudly judging by how many heads turned in our direction. I nodded. "Well I still have my Cinderella," she admitted.

"Long story," I told a confused looking Cy. "But I always

fancied myself being Belle from Beauty and the Beast, with the dark hair and all that, and Lois as a blonde thought she was Cinderella. Speaking of which, where is Prince Charming?"

"Meeting me at the crematorium. Miles needed to work this morning, something that couldn't wait, but he has the afternoon off."

"Hey?" Cy whispered. "If you're Belle, does that make me The Beast?"

"I dunno, I suppose..."

"El, El," Mary called before coming up beside me. "Susan's here, with Michael," she whispered crossly.

"It's fine, really," I reassured her and I was mostly okay with the fact that they had arrived together and that Michael was here, with my family. At my father's funeral. About to be in the same room as Cy. "I just need some air," I hurriedly said before pushing through the people around me. Cy followed closely behind.

I took in several deep breaths as I stood in the garden looking over the floral tributes that were accumulating. Cy was just behind me. I could feel him, but he said nothing. He didn't need to. I wasn't upset that Michael was here, that he was offering Susan some much needed support, like Cy was doing for me. It was just a bit weird that my first time being in the same place as Michael whilst with Cy was here, at my father's funeral. Part of me also felt slightly pissed off with Michael that when my father was alive and he was my husband, although technically he still was, that he had shown less than no interest in my father.

"Who's that?" Cy asked causing me to glance in the direction of a near identical car to his pulling up.

"No idea," I replied instinctively, but as the two uniformed officers got out of the car it fell into place, especially when one officer went straight to Cy's car and the other went to stand near Michael's. "Really?" I asked with a shake of my head as I approached the unmarked police car.

"Can I help?" I asked shortly.

"I don't know, can you miss?" the older of the two asked with suspicion as the other one came to join his colleague.

"The cars," I began.

"Yes?" the first officer asked with a glance at his colleague.

I laughed. I couldn't help it but it was funny that the sight of two expensive, shiny, top of the range cars immediately led the police to think the worst of anyone associated with them.

"This is my boyfriend's car," I began as the second officer spoke.

"El? Eloise Ross?"

"Yes," I replied turning my full attention to the younger officer. "Toby? Toby Warner," I exclaimed with a smile. "Wow, how long has it been, twelve years?"

"At least," he grinned back before leaning in to hug me. "I always think of you when I come onto the estate."

"Yeah, well I am not convinced that you're really paying me a compliment." I laughed as I stepped out of his embrace. "Deprivation, drugs, drink and the odd bit of theft and prostitution and you think of me."

"Not what I meant." Toby blushed as his colleague coughed at the same time that Cy placed a possessive arm around my middle, allowing his fingers to settle at my hip a little too firmly.

"Miss, the cars…" the first officer prompted.

"Mine," replied Cy already handing over his licence.

"My boyfriend," I clarified.

"And this one?" Toby asked, pointing at Michael's car.

"My husband's," I replied with no thought for how it sounded.

Both officers exchanged a surprised look while Cy's fingers dug into my hip so firmly it pinched.

"Ex-ish husband." I added the ish in case I found myself being accused of lying to the police.

"I heard you'd got married," Toby said.

"Yeah and now you've heard she's getting divorced and has a boyfriend," Cy snapped, clearly unable to stand by silently any longer.

"Yours, Sir," the other police officer smiled as he handed Cy his driving licence and took a couple of steps back to speak into his radio, presumably checking out the cars that had caught their attention.

"Your brother?" Toby asked as he pointed to the flowers behind us.

"My brother's house, my father's funeral," I explained with a hard swallow to prevent my tears from falling so soon into the day.

"I'm sorry. Your dad was always nice to me," Toby smiled.

"He was just nice," I replied as I saw a blur from the corner of my eye, a moving blur of something black. A hearse. The one carrying my father.

My sisters, brothers and I travelled together to the crematorium in the lead car behind the hearse that was followed by another couple of official cars carrying my father's grandchildren and my sibling's spouses. Cy was meeting me there, as was Michael, although he was meeting Susan rather than me.

The journey was a short one but when you're travelling at the slow pace of a funeral procession even short distances seem to take forever. I was sat between my sisters who were both looking out of their own windows and quietly sniffing while I sat with my eyes cast down looking at my own hands wringing in my lap. The silence around us was deafening, none of us daring to speak. Scared that words would lead to thoughts and emotions that once unleashed would be uncontainable.

The car was noticeably slowing, even with the speeds we'd been travelling and as I looked up I could see that the hearse in front was coming to a stop under the canopy at the entrance to the crematorium. We were halting behind it and then the doors were opening.

This was real and this was happening, it really was time for us to say our final goodbyes.

Chapter Forty

Shaking the hand of the vicar as we left the crematorium saw me breathing a huge sigh of relief that I had got through the service relatively unscathed. I had no idea that I had so many tears left to cry nor that the physical pain I had felt could get any worse, but I had been wrong on both counts. Cy's presence had been the only thing that had kept me together at all. His physical and emotional support as he held me throughout the service. He continued to hold my hand, keeping me close as we made our way out into the sunny sky we now stood beneath.

Michael approached me a little awkwardly, making me feel sorry for his discomfort so I offered him a weak smile that was enough to encourage him to continue walking towards me.

"El," he whispered as he leaned in and placed a chaste kiss on my cheek.

I put an arm forward to reciprocate his affection with a short hug and realised that those gestures felt far more natural than any others we had ever shared.

"Cy," Michael said a little more shortly, clearly he still felt animosity towards my lover if not me, his adulteress wife. "Your solicitor has contacted mine," he told me after a few seconds. Maybe he was struggling to know what to say now that he had joined us.

I nodded, unsure what I should say in response. The things I had hoped to secure from my divorce were now gone; Balder was dead so I would never gain any access to him and my dad's care home fees would no longer need paying so any incentive for financial reward was now gone. I just needed a divorce, plain and simple.

"Maybe we should meet up and discuss things," Michael suggested.

Before I could respond Cy interrupted. "I really don't think now is the time or place and El is not in the right frame of mind to make significant decisions, which I think you know," he accused.

"I was talking to my wife," Michael sneered.

"You were talking to a woman who is grieving and struggling to get through one day to the next. You were talking to my girlfriend," Cy responded defensively, defending me and somehow attempting to put Michael in his place.

"Really, your girlfriend?" Michael laughed. "I think her husband might have a little more sway than her boyfriend." He openly scoffed at the last word which was enough for me. They were both pissing me off with their display of machismo whilst speaking about me as if I wasn't even there.

"Stop it!" I snarled on a whisper, refusing to draw attention to myself and unwilling to make my father's funeral a circus. Moreover there was no way I was going to allow Michael and Cy to force the deterioration of this solemn occasion into an episode of high drama, maybe not of Greek tragedy proportions, but we were well on the way. "You both need to stop it. I am here you know, not that either of you seem to realise that fact."

They were both staring at me a little unnerved by the stony quality to my voice as well as the fact that I was now standing away from them both, having taken several steps from Michael and shaken myself free of Cy.

"I get that you two feel you have something to prove, but not here, not now. This is my dad's funeral, not a fucking bar for you to brawl in. So, you want to continue with your *who can piss the highest competition*, find another wall."

With that as my parting shot, I flounced away and I actually did flounce. Like I didn't think I was even capable of, well not since my teenage years.

I only got as far as Angela who I hadn't seen until I was mid flounce. She stood with a couple of her colleagues who seemed more shocked to be viewing my juvenile strop than Angela herself did.

"El." She smiled as she enveloped me in a long, warm hug. "How are you?"

"Honestly? I'm not entirely sure," I told her frankly. "I swing from hysterical crying to forgetting everything that has happened, kind of."

Angela nodded before introducing me to her colleagues who were very sweet in their lovely comments about the time they'd spent with my dad. One of them was telling me about an occasion where he had told her all about his relationship with my mum when they'd first met. How much they'd loved each other and how he knew from day one that he would never meet anyone like her again, never love like her again. I smiled as I heard the story I had heard before, years ago when I was a little girl and wondered how I could have forgotten that love like that was real. That it was what everyone should strive for. That I hadn't found it in my marriage but had found it with Cy, maybe from the connection we'd both felt on that very first night. As cross as I had been with Michael and Cy I could feel some of it dissipate as a body drew up at my side and an arm slid around my waist.

"Hey baby," Cy said before leaning in to kiss my cheek gently. "Sorry," he whispered before turning to Angela who was smiling broadly and the other two who worryingly looked as though they were about to faint. My second of concern disappeared when I realised they were swooning, over Cy.

Angela and I exchanged a smile before she spoke. "Nice to see you," she said to Cy. "Jezza missed you while you were away. I know he probably never said but he really did enjoy your visits, just you boys. I think when he was lucid it made him feel better knowing that El had you and that you'd take care of her."

I looked between the two of them, momentarily confused and then realised that Cy must have visited without me.

"And you didn't think to tell me?" I asked feeling a little anger resurfacing.

Angela quickly figured out that this *just the boys* thing was news to me and continued to speak, but to me this time. "How are you now, El?" she asked and I had no clue what the now actually meant. Fortunately, or unfortunately for me she continued. "Jeremy had no idea what he was doing. He was very agitated and confused that day he hit you, but it really wasn't him and for him you weren't you," she told me.

I didn't need to look up at Cy to know that he was taking in all of this information. Information I'd managed to keep from him up until this point and as Angela began to speak again it became apparent that she hadn't finished inadvertently revealing more secrets. I also didn't need to see his face to know he was pissed off with me. I could feel it rolling off him in waves and washing over me.

"I know your friends were concerned. The gentleman was especially worried, but I assured him that nothing like that had ever happened before."

I nodded, hoping to offer some reassurance to Angela that it was fine, that my friends were fine even if my angry boyfriend was anything but.

"I really am very sorry for your loss," she added. "He really was a one off, our Jezza. If there's anything we can do, please get in touch." With her excuses made Angela and her colleagues moved away.

Still I said nothing and made no effort to make eye contact with Cy. After all, I had nothing to say that would be anywhere near a reasonable excuse for keeping that incident from him.

"And you didn't think to tell me," he accused, recycling my own words.

"Cy," I began, but was interrupted by Mary appearing.

"El, we need to go."

"I'll go back with Cy," I explained.

"No, you go with your family," Cy interjected brusquely. He sounded angry, as though us being in the confined space of his car was more than he could stomach. Mary had already linked an arm through mine and prepared to lead me away when Cy called after me. "El, I'll see you there baby."

I smiled. He was mad as hell but he didn't want me to be worried or concerned by that. He was tempering his own feelings to reassure me. With a few quick blinks I pushed my tears away and allowed Mary to lead me back to the car.

****

Watching Cy standing at the bar of the pub where my brothers had chosen to hold our dad's wake, I smiled. He didn't look too out of place, even if the clothes and shoes he wore probably cost more than the whole place was worth. That might have been an exaggeration, but he seemed to have the knack for blending in effortlessly. I was still enjoying the view of my boyfriend when I became aware of Michael sitting down next to me, looking less than impressed at being in such a dive, which The White Hart was. There was no denying it.

"El, can we talk?" he asked with a very worried expression on his face.

"Wayne and Gary have made sure that your car will be safe," I told him thinking his worry was for his car on the car park that was almost like a forecourt for the local car thieves and joyriders.

"What? No, no, it's not that," he replied. "It's Edward."

"Edward? Is he okay?" I asked, worried too now. "Michael he literally disappeared, the day after you both came to the hospital," I said as Cy appeared, standing over Michael, clearly unhappy to find my husband sitting next to me.

"I thought we'd agreed Michael, this is not the time or the place," Cy began before I interrupted.

"Sit down, please," I urged him. "We were talking about Edward."

"Have you heard from him?" Cy asked Michael who shook his head sadly.

"No, nothing. El was just saying she saw him the day after we went to her at the hospital."

I watched as Cy's eyes widened and he shook his head at me and mouthed my own words that I was beginning to regret uttering with every reuse of them aimed at me, *and you didn't think to tell me.*

"You see El, Edward does this. It's how he is. He gets involved and he pushes and pushes…"

"Sounds familiar," Cy chipped in and we both knew he meant me and my pushing rather than Edward.

"Anyway," a confused Michael continued. "He pushes for

more and more and the more you give the more he wants until you can give no more and then he runs, sulks and licks his wounds because he feels he's been betrayed or let down by you."

I wasn't sure I actually understood what Michael was saying, although I remembered Edward's accusations that Michael only ever put his own needs first and would only give so much, but I nodded anyway.

"I've called him, text him. I even went round to his house a couple of times," I told Michael who raised his eyebrows.

"His house? He took you there?"

I nodded again. "I stayed there a few weeks ago, when Cy was away and I'd had a bit of an accident." I wondered why going to Edward's house was such a big thing. I also risked an apologetic glance in Cy's direction for my *accident*.

"He was happy though," Michael sighed. "I know you and he were getting on and he had Tia here too. What could have happened? He did text me to say he needed some time, the same day you last saw him and nothing since."

"You're worried, really worried, aren't you?" I already knew the answer. I knew my husband well enough to read his emotions and understand his feelings from his expression alone.

"Yes." He got to his feet. "If you hear from him…"

"Of course, and if you do?"

"Of course, love." He smiled and bent down to land a single kiss on my cheek. "Call me and we'll meet, sort out the divorce," he said, straightening and then with a curt nod for Cy Michael walked away leaving me, Cy and a dark cloud hanging over us.

****

I followed Cy through his house until we finally arrived in the kitchen where he was flicking the lid off a bottle of beer then offered it to me. After refusing it he took a long, slow swallow of it. Watching him I could see that he was tense, angry still and yet the movement of him swallowing the liquid, its journey from his mouth, along his neck and beyond was strangely erotic. I was sure I had some serious issues when the movement of his Adam's apple had me releasing a single, quiet moan, especially as I was fairly certain we were about to embark on a huge row.

"You should have told me," he informed me with a large dose of accusation.

"Which bit?" I asked and regretted it before the second word was out. *Which bit?* That is what I'd actually asked as if inferring that some of my secrets were acceptable to keep.

The slamming of the beer bottle hitting the counter top made me physically jump but it did give Cy my total, undivided attention. My eyes were fixed on his that were boring into me with intensity and real honest to goodness cold fury.

"Which bit? Are you fucking serious?" he asked but required no answer as he continued his rant. "All of it, everything. Your dad hit you, badly enough that Edward was called—Angela said the man, which would indicate he wasn't alone, that there was a woma—Tia! Fuck! Not content with lying to me, you what? Coerced them both to lie to me too? The man I trusted to take care of you and my business and my sister! Why would you keep that from me?"

"Cy," I began, hoping he'd let me explain something, anything now that there was a pause for me to speak.

"What?" he snapped. "I thought we didn't lie to each other, and every time I think that you somehow manage to prove me wrong." He sighed, sadness and disappointment taking over from anger now. "Do you love me? Do you want to be with me, only me? Or do you want Michael? Do you regret us and want to go back?"

I was thrown by his questions, especially when he attempted to move past me.

"I love you, more than anything. I thought you knew that, believed that. I can't imagine being with anyone else, ever. I could never regret us Cy, never. As for Michael, I don't want to go back. I never really wanted to go there in the first place."

"Then why didn't you tell me that he came to you at the hospital?"

"I don't know, but he kind of just turned up with Edward," I explained to his very reasonable question. "I didn't want you to think that I had reverted to type, allowed Michael to take care of things," I admitted. I felt shame for my marriage and former relationship with my husband. "I should have told you about

Michael and if you hadn't been so far away and hung up with Christopher and your parents, I would have told you about my dad," I explained and allowed a few more tears to escape.

"So this is my fault? That I wasn't here?" he queried.

"No, no!" I insisted. "That's not what I meant, but your parents needed you and you needed to be there for them and I needed them not to hate me by summoning you back. Edward and Tia wanted to contact you, to tell you what had happened but I made them promise."

"I get that," Cy admitted a little reluctantly, stepping closer to me. "But you needed me. I needed to know and to come and take care of you," he told me as he lowered his forehead so that it rested against my own. "You do not get to circumvent me, baby, not with stuff like this. Agreed?"

"Agreed," I whispered before Cy's head tilted slightly so that his lips were almost touching mine.

"There's me and you, and then there is everyone else. Together we stand strong and face whatever is going to be thrown at us, okay?"

"Okay," I agreed as a tiny, gentle kiss landed on my lips. The sensation of Cy's lips barely grazing mine was akin to how I imagined it felt for the petals of a flower when a butterfly landed.

My own lips were responding in kind, although I could feel that my desire was for something harsher than the timid touches I was receiving. He also realised that when I bit into his bottom lip as he teased me by preventing my attempts to capture his mouth and move things forward.

Had I known the reaction my nip of teeth would have garnered I would have done it sooner, much sooner. I felt disorientated slightly as I felt myself floating backwards until I was firmly pressed against the wall. Cy's mouth had shifted from my lips to my ear as he crushed me with his body.

"You are so fucking impatient," he whispered as I realised he had literally picked me up and found the nearest flat surface to hold me against.

My legs had spread themselves around Cy's hips, the action forcing my dress up so that my stockinged thighs were exposed.

With my fingers pushing their way into his hair I tried to pull Cy's head up, his lips back to mine.

"You pushing?" he asked against my ear as he refused to allow me to pull him anywhere.

"Yes." I whined without any shame or embarrassment for my desperation. I needed this, we both did. I needed Cy to believe how important he was to me and why my lying had never been anything other than me doing what I thought was best. "Oh God," I cried when I felt a finger grazing my exposed inner thigh.

"I think we could make this a religion baby," he told me with a short laugh before his finger was pulling and teasing the lace of my pants.

"Please," I pleaded, unable to imagine coping with this being a drawn-out affair.

Clearly we were both feeling in the mood for some instant gratification judging by how quickly Cy breached my underwear and without any warning he was pushing a finger inside me. With a moan I sunk my teeth into my own lip as a second finger entered me causing a wonderfully exquisite burn. Neither of us spoke, instead we both used a combination of breathing, panting and groaning, but no words. Cy continued to pump his fingers in and out, encouraging my body to accept him freely. Quickly, there was no longer any resistance. My body was softening, moistening as he coaxed it into preparation. In a matter of seconds my body was unoccupied so that Cy could unfasten his trousers and push his underwear down and then I could feel him, probing my entrance. One of his hands gathered my wrists together before pushing them above my head where they were held against the wall while his other hand cupped my behind and then he thrust inside me. The pace was as far from leisurely as I'd ever known. Hard and fast thrusts pushed me towards climax quickly, somehow the physical act and the emotional exchange we were sharing were responsible for it. I tried pulling my hands free from Cy's grip. I wanted to touch him or hold him, but the more I fought for control of them the more he fought to prevent it which frustrated me mentally as much as it excited me physically and sexually.

"Mine baby, all mine," Cy said. "Who do you love?"

Without hesitation I replied immediately, "You."

"And who is the only one who gets to fuck you, forever?"

"You, only you."

"You better fucking believe it." He almost snarled as my body began to clench and tense around him, inside and out until I was coming undone a split second before he did.

Chapter Forty-One

Over the next few weeks things began to return to normal. I was back at work and was glad of the distraction it provided from my own grief. Mary was still in the country and showed no signs of leaving Maya's which I apologised for on a daily basis, but Maya was enjoying my sister's company it seemed, especially since she had split up with Chad. Cy seemed to be enjoying my sister's current living arrangements as it meant I was a permanent fixture in his bed and his house with most of my belongings having made their way there too. Susan had also remained local, staying with Michael still. I occasionally allowed my mind to wander to how they might fill their nights but quickly pushed those thoughts away. Michael and I had met to discuss our divorce which he'd agreed not to contest or been insistent on him divorcing me on the grounds of my adultery. I was unsure whether he was doing it for me or Denny and Elizabeth who were becoming less vocal in their objections to me, but either way I was relieved and grateful.

Christopher was still AWOL and Elizabeth was making regular calls to Cy in order to discuss her concerns, and I suspected trying to entice him back home, but he was showing no signs of wanting to or being prepared to leave me again and for that I was thankful. Edward still hadn't returned or responded to any of my attempts to contact him and I was becoming more concerned, unlike Michael who kept repeating that this is what he did, but was also desperate for some confirmation of his wellbeing. I didn't know Edward well enough to refute that claim, but something was nagging in my mind, something telling me that he hadn't simply stropped off to lick wounds. Hell, the last time I saw him he didn't have any wounds.

****

Cy had just come into the bedroom and was studying me carefully as I lay in bed waiting for him to join me.

"What?" I asked a little suspicious of his scrutiny.

"Just wondering, are you excited?" he asked making me smirk a slightly rude smile.

"Not yet, but if you could get your arse in bed." I giggled before squealing when Cy propelled himself onto the bed to hover over me.

"It's ass, and I was thinking about your birthday tomorrow." He grinned back before leaning down to kiss me, a hard and deep kiss that surprised me as I had been expecting something a little gentler following his reference to my birthday. Pulling back into a sitting position hovering over my hips he continued. "But I reckon I can get you excited between the sheets too."

I laughed at his cocky expression but couldn't deny what he was saying. I had never met anyone who could excite me like he did, between the sheets or not.

"I don't know that I'm excited about tomorrow, it's a bit weird. I know my dad hadn't remembered my birthday for years, but it's weird that he won't be here," I whispered slowly in an attempt to control my tears and emotions.

"I know, baby," he told me brushing a thumb across my cheek. "But I promise we're going to make it the best birthday you've ever had," he pledged, sending my emotions haywire for good reasons now.

"Who's we?"

"Me and Lulu, but she's not coming til after breakfast," he explained before kissing the tip of my nose and then he was standing up and striding towards the bathroom leaving me wearing a huge smile for the birthday I had been dreading. He was already making it the best I'd ever had.

I woke alone, which was pretty unusual unless Lulu was staying. Cy and I had fallen into an easy pattern whereby we usually woke together or once one of us was awake the other one became aware of the other moving, but not this morning. I was alone in bed. I glanced at my phone and saw that it was after nine and prepared to get out of bed when Cy appeared in the doorway singing happy birthday to me. The smile plastered to my face was broadening with each word and that was before he revealed a tray carrying tea, pastries, orange juice and a single red tulip in a vase.

"Thank you." I smiled and shuffled into a sitting position, tugging the sheets up to cover my naked body before tucking them under my arms.

"You're welcome." Cy leaned in and placed a delicate kiss to my cheek.

"Are you joining me?"

"For breakfast?"

"Mmm, and back in bed." I figured I could negotiate for both as it was my birthday, not that I usually needed to negotiate for time in bed together.

"Breakfast, yes." He grinned grabbing a pastry that immediately began to drop crumbs onto the bed. "Bed no."

"No?" I asked, then it turned into an exclamation. "No!"

"No," Cy repeated. "Not yet," he added, softening the blow to my ego as well as my libido. "Later, we'll make a date," he told me as he offered me a bite of his pastry. "But we have a busy morning."

I made no reply as I heard a noise from downstairs, nothing specific or anything I could name, just an odd noise.

"What was that?" I asked preparing to rise from the bed.

"Nothing, I'm sure." Cy replied quickly and maybe a little nervously. "But I'll go check. You eat and drink and shower and dress and then come down to open your gifts before Lulu arrives."

Before I could respond Cy was up on his feet and retreating downstairs leaving me in no doubt that he was up to something, but nothing bad, of that I was sure.

I followed his instructions and once showered and dressed in leggings and a t-shirt I made my way downstairs barefoot.

Entering the lounge I was taken aback to find balloons, banners and huge arrangements of flowers, all of them tulips with the exception of one that was a large vase containing gardenia and daffodils.

"We have flowers," I stated. "Lots and lots of flowers."

"Mmm, although we don't, you do."

"Thank you," I smiled as I sniffed back some happy tears that they were all for me. That he had gone to so much trouble.

"You don't need to thank me," he told me brushing away my gratitude. "You have presents to open so sit down."

He had clearly gone to a lot of trouble and considerable expense in his choice of gifts. I opened a beautiful hand-crafted diary, a pen that must have cost a month's wages, then there were bangles, another handbag, my favourite perfume and chocolates.

"You really have gone all out," I accused.

"Wait til next year," Cy almost threatened, making me laugh until I saw his serious expression but the moment was broken when I heard a noise from the kitchen, that same noise I'd heard earlier, in bed.

"What the bloody hell?" I was already moving the numerous gifts from around me.

"You stay. That's your surprise." Cy took my gifts and placed them on the table nearby before pressing me back into a sitting position.

I watched him leave and wondered what on earth my surprise entailed. Cy's voice was whispering a little too quietly for me to hear what he was saying in the kitchen, but he was talking, maybe to himself or more likely cussing me under his breath. In only a minute or so he returned carrying a box. A beautiful gold box that had a removable lid. The same lid that Cy almost knocked off as he carried the box to me and placed it next to me on the sofa.

I paused and teased the edge of the lid as a very impatient Cy said, "Just open the box, please."

I wondered what his sense of urgency was, but complied anyway and then the reason for his haste became apparent.

"No way," I whispered in excitement and wonderment. "For me."

"I was kind of hoping for us." Cy crouched down on the

floor between me and the box.

"Aww, Cy, I don't know what to say," I told him as a beautiful bundle of black and white fur came bounding into my lap, dragging the box with him part of the way. "Hello," I laughed as he leapt up at my face that he proceeded to kiss. "Does it have a name? Is it a boy or a girl?" I asked between spells of avoiding a puppy's tongue in my mouth.

"Boy and he is awaiting his name."

I realised that this was who had been making all the noise. "Has he been in the box all that time?"

"Yes baby. I got up at six this morning to collect him and have kept him in the box." Cy frowned whilst still smiling. "No, he hasn't. He's been in a crate in the garage while I came upstairs or cosying in his new bed in the kitchen the rest of the time, between running around the garden like a crazy thing, speaking of which he probably needs to pee. He does that a lot." Cy reached down to pick the puppy up before taking my hand and pulling me to my feet.

Excitedly I virtually skipped into the kitchen and the garden beyond to watch the puppy running around the garden like a crazy thing, which he did for about ten minutes and chasing the string toy Cy and I took turns to throw for him. He also had about seven toilet trips before following us back inside where he collapsed in his bed.

"I think we broke the puppy." I laughed as I smiled down at him in his comatose state flat on his back.

"I think we did, baby," Cy agreed leaning in to kiss my temple. "Happy birthday." A little hesitantly he asked, "You're not mad at me are you, for the dog, after Balder?"

"No, no, never. He's beautiful and he's ours." I wrapped my arms around Cy to hold him close. "What sort of dog is he?"

"An English springer spaniel. I thought about a Great Dane but then I remembered you were a little pissy about their life expectancy," he teased a little.

"Edward told you that?"

"Mmm."

My introduction of Edward hung between us a little but a strange little yelp from the dog alerted us to his dreamy state.

"He needs a name," I suddenly said.

"He does, so you go and think about naming him and I'll get us some coffee."

"What about Hector?" I asked, wondering why every name I liked Cy didn't.

"No."

"Milton?"

"Milton Miller, really?" Cy asked.

"Milton Ross," I corrected.

"No chance, he has my name," Cy replied defiantly.

"Really?"

"Yes, fucking really. Our dog has my name."

"My dog," I corrected.

"You are such a bitch," he snapped.

"And you're an arse."

"Ass," he corrected with a small sulk.

"It's arse! What about Buddy?"

"Miller?"

"Yes, bloody Miller, Buddy Miller," I conceded to see a complacent smile shaping Cy's face that was facing my own from our position lying on the sofa together.

"Pleasure doing business with you, Miss Ross," he said, proceeding to kiss me until the sound of yapping from the floor nearby interrupted. "Buddy, we need a conversation."

I laughed as I watched Cy calling the dog out to the garden once more.

****

Nervousness was oozing from Cy when he returned carrying the dog who looked a little uncomfortable himself.

"You two okay?" I asked.

Cy placed the dog in my lap and then dropped to the space at my feet. "There's something else for you."

"You are spoiling me," I accused, and although I didn't need gifts lavishing on me, I couldn't deny that I loved having Cy's undivided attention.

"Buddy has it, on his collar."

I looked at the puppy who was conveniently staring up at me with his tail wagging frantically. His position offered me a perfect view of his neck that was adorned by a simple red, leather collar that had a small velvet pouch attached.

With a frown I removed the package and began to open it by pulling the drawstrings loose. With my first two fingers inside the bag I pulled out a square package that was concealed by a piece of paper that was wrapped around what felt like a box. Cy's earlier nervousness was verging on panic now as I pulled the paper into one hand whilst attempting to stop the dog eating it. I now had a navy blue, square, leather box in my hand and a paint colour chart in the other.

As my gaze flitted between the two items, I was unsure which one to proceed with first. I had seen a pair of simple stud earrings a few weeks before with what I imagined was a tear drop shaped diamante detail but upon seeing the price I'd realised they were real diamonds and although Cy had offered to buy them for me I had vehemently refused. Clearly, he'd waited for a moment that I couldn't object to. That only left the paint chart that I was already holding up between us until Buddy jumped up and attempted to take it from my grip, a move that was intercepted by Cy.

"My hallway that you object to. I told you I was thinking of getting it decorated. I thought you might like a say in that." He smiled offering the colour chart back to me before placing the dog on the floor.

With a little yap we both turned to look at Buddy before laughing at the dog who was scurrying off into the kitchen.

"You really want me to help you choose a colour?"

It dawned on me that I had never been involved in decorating choices before, not unless you counted the posters on my bedroom wall as a teenager.

"Nobody I'd rather choose colours with," he replied with sincerity that I immediately believed.

"Okay," I agreed with a stifled giggle. "You shouldn't have, you know," I told him as I turned my attention to the box in my hand.

"We'll see," Cy replied mysteriously as I began to open the box expecting to see my diamond earrings glittering back at me.

"What the fuck?" I exclaimed, unsure if I was asking a

question at all.

No questions were required when I looked across at Cy who had adjusted his position so that he was now kneeling on just one knee and taking the diamond solitaire engagement ring from the box that was shaking in my grasp.

"Now, a very wise woman, a bit of a bitch though, told me that when I did this if there was any chance of being declined I should lead with this, so here goes. Eloise Ross I can't bear to be without you. I can think of nothing else, day or night but you and the idea of you ever being with anyone else drives me to the verge of insanity. I need to make you totally and utterly mine. Without you at my side for the rest of my life would mean my life will be less fulfilling and more painful than anything I can imagine, and as a man I personally love the idea of you taking everything I am, especially my name. Will you marry me?"

Chapter Forty-Two

My mouth was dry, unlike the palms of my hands that were damp, clammy and sweaty. I was unsure if my breathing was more laboured but it certainly felt as though my respiratory function was compromised. I had allowed myself to imagine a life and a future with Cy, being his wife and having children together, but I had never allowed myself to think in such detail as this, his proposal and I was actually still married.

Cy was still on one knee, looking at me, waiting for a response.

"They're not earrings," was my response, clearly not the one Cy was expecting, but he was at least still smiling, for now.

"No, baby, they're not."

"It's an engagement ring."

"Mmm."

"I'm married," I clumsily stammered.

"You're getting divorced," he corrected, his smile looking a little forced now. "So?" he asked after a deep breath that seemed to calm and centre him.

I wondered what the so meant but quickly realised that he was using that word as a prompt for me to respond to his proposal. The next single word I was about to utter was going to change my life forever, whichever word I said. Did I want to marry Cy, to be married again after divorcing Michael? Did I see any future that Cy wasn't part of?

"Yes."

"What?" a rather startled looking Cy asked making me laugh as I held out my ring finger.

"Yes, yes I will marry you. Would love to. I can think of nothing I want more," I told him before the feel of the platinum band was slipping along my finger and then Cy was leaning in.

"Thank fuck," he whispered a split second before his lips closed over mine to kiss me with love, reverence and possibly a little relief.

****

Rhonda had arrived with Lulu about an hour after Cy's proposal and had clearly noticed the large engagement ring on my finger. Despite her attempts at discretion there was no mistaking the way her eyes kept flitting to my hand.

"Mommy, can we have a puppy too?" Lulu called as Buddy collapsed in a heap at my feet.

"No, honey. Puppies need lots of attention and Mommy has to go to work and you go to school," Rhonda explained.

With a sad pout and tears welling in the little girl's eyes I felt sorry for her.

"You can share Buddy if you want to."

"Really?" the little girl squealed as she confirmed what that meant. "Do you mean like he'll be my dog too, for real?"

"Yes, you and me and your daddy."

"Yay, Mommy did you hear? Buddy is my dog too."

"I heard that," Rhonda smiled before making her excuses to leave.

Maya and Tia, who arrived just as Rhonda was leaving were less tactful in their pursuit of information on my marital status of the future when they cornered me in the kitchen, out of Lulu's hearing.

"Did you know?" I asked Tia who immediately shook her head.

"No. I knew how serious he was, and I imagined it would happen, but I guess I thought he'd wait until you were divorced."

I nodded, her assumptions were fair. Although, I did feel a little uncomfortable that other people would think this was weird, being engaged to be married before I'd even got divorced.

"I'm guessing I won't be seeing boss man's tattoos any time

soon," Maya pouted making us all laugh.

"I think you're guessing right," I agreed with another laugh. "Is it still okay, Mary staying with you?" I asked thinking that I needed to speak to my sister soon to establish her plans.

We were all interrupted by the sound of Buddy barking as Lulu chased him through the house before coming to a standstill in the kitchen.

"Buddy likes me to chase him," Lulu squealed excitedly.

"He does, but I think we need him to calm down a little now," I told her as I opened the door for the dog to have a slightly calmer run around without the chasing.

"And we shouldn't really be running inside the house," Cy added as he came to a standstill behind me. "Hey baby," he whispered as he kissed my neck.

Lulu followed Buddy outside while I wondered just how long that one word, *baby* and the simple action of a single kiss would have my whole body driving headlong into sensory overload; every inch of my skin came to life, goosebumps covered me as my breathing increased, and I didn't doubt my pupils had dilated as if I'd just had the biggest hit of my life, which I had because Cy was my drug, the only one I had tried and needed.

"Why all the red tulips?" I asked as I watched the dog chasing himself as much as Lulu before glancing through to the hall where one of the many bunches and arrangements of red tulips sat.

"Because red tulips carry meaning, perfect love," Cy explained.

I was already pulling his face to mine, preparing to kiss him for loving me, considering our love perfect and for asking me to marry him. "Could you be any more perfect?"

"And I really need to be getting back to work," Maya said awkwardly, but was already preparing to leave. "Bye Buddy, bye Lulu," she called outside before hugging me and rushing for the front door.

"So why the mixed ones, the flowers?" I asked Cy as we returned to the lounge where the only none tulip arrangement was.

"Not a clue, they're not from me. They came before you came down."

With a curious frown I pulled the card from the arrangement and was startled by the words before me.

My Dearest Eloise,
Happy birthday.
I'm sorry...for everything.
Edward xx

"They're from Edward." I handed the card to Cy.

"What does he mean, he's sorry for everything?"

I shook my head as Tia took the card from Cy and read it for herself. "I guess he means for leaving you and your dad."

I nodded my agreement.

"And maybe for disappearing and ignoring your attempts to make contact with him," Cy added.

"Daddy, El, are we having cake? Buddy's asleep again," Lulu cried as she came rushing into the lounge to join us, breaking my thoughts of Edward, worrying thoughts of where and how he was and why he had disappeared at all.

****

"This is not how I expected to be celebrating our engagement," Cy told me as he appeared in the bedroom doorway with Lulu's sheets bundled in his arms.

"I wasn't expecting to be engaged so I guess we've both had surprising days."

"My belly hurts," Lulu cried from her position in the middle of Cy's bed.

I climbed onto the bed and with one arm around her I pulled her closer before using my other hand to rub her tummy.

"Baby, I'm going to go and put these in the laundry," Cy said lifting the sick covered sheets. "And then I'll be back."

"Okay," Lulu and I replied together, although the little girl was half asleep already.

"Check on Buddy, please," I said knowing that I'd already heard him whimpering and crying.

"Sure thing." He smiled before leaving me and Lulu alone.

I was in exactly the same position as when he'd left me and Lulu was snoring gently when Cy returned.

"Diamonds suit you," Cy smirked as his eyes fixed on my left hand stroking Lulu's tummy.

"Mmm, about that," I began as Cy joined us on the bed.

"What about that?" he asked, propping himself up on his pillows before pulling me and Lulu a little closer.

His face was expressionless but somehow I knew I was about to change that with my next words.

"I feel a little awkward, wearing it."

"What? Why?" he snapped loud enough that Lulu jumped, forcing Cy to calm himself a little.

"You don't want to marry me?" he asked with sadness and disappointment.

"Of course I do, it's just that this seems weird. An engagement when I'm still married…it makes me feel odd. My sisters seemed freaked out by it, and Tia…shit, what about your parents, do they know?" I felt nervous myself now. I didn't want to spoil this moment in our lives or make Cy feel that I was anything other than committed to him and our future, but I also didn't want to alienate his parents any further, not when so recently they'd, Elizabeth, had softened towards me.

"My dad knew I intended to propose and I spoke to him earlier so he knows that you've accepted. I haven't spoken to my mom, but not for any reason beyond her already dealing with Chris still being MIA. But whether they or anyone else likes it or not I want to marry you, period."

My thoughts of removing my ring, of waiting until my divorce was final, and worst still of what other people might think dissolved with Cy's renewed declaration of wanting to marry me.

"Okay." I smiled, leaned over Lulu's head and landed a single close lipped kiss on Cy's lips. "I love you."

"I love you too, even if you're on my bed in pyjamas!" he grimaced with an arched brow that made me laugh.

"Hey, little people do not need to see me naked."

"Maybe not, baby, but I sure as hell do, but tomorrow. Tomorrow we'll celebrate our engagement properly."

"Was Buddy alright?"

"Mmm, he was kind of hoping to come to bed too, but once he'd been outside and we'd played a little he got inside his bed in the crate and he's safely settled in the kitchen now."

A moan left Lulu as she woke up startled. "I feel sick again."

Cy scooped her up and rushed off to the bathroom where I heard the poor little girl expelling more of the contents of her stomach.

"Daddy, is this really too much cake?" she asked tearfully, referencing Cy's comment when she'd first complained of tummy ache.

"No baby, it's not."

The little girl's reply was another heave.

Chapter Forty-Three

Three weeks passed and still nobody had heard from Edward except for a *you're welcome* text he'd sent in response to me texting him a simple thank you message for my birthday flowers.

Mary had returned to Australia but with thoughts of relocating back to England. My room at Maya's remained unoccupied after Cy had refused point blank to me moving out of his, even using Buddy and his needs to persuade me, not that much persuasion was required.

Susan and I had continued to rebuild our relationship and she had been supportive of my intention to marry Cy.

The details of my divorce had been finalised and I had eventually accepted a very small cash settlement that even Michael had insisted on. Cy was less than thrilled with me bringing Michael's money into my marriage to him, but it was agreed.

Buddy had quickly become a real member of our family, mine and Cy's, and after leaving him alone for only one day we had enrolled him in doggy day care that we dropped him off at each morning on the way to work and then collected him on the way home. That was exactly what we'd done tonight and after a detour to collect something for dinner we were home. I had run straight upstairs to change and was preparing Buddy's dinner before putting ours onto plates when Cy came up behind me and snaked an arm around my middle, holding me so that he could perfectly place his lips on my neck to nuzzle.

"Dinner is going to be cold," I warned him.

"Eating is overrated," he whispered against my neck making me feel inclined to agree with him.

His other arm was stretching along mine until his hand was covering mine, his fingers gently toying with my ring. I smiled as I remembered how my wedding ring had caused him physical and emotional pain when he looked at it or touched it and now, this ring. His ring, he couldn't stop touching it; when we held hands, danced, like this, and when we had sex, he always made a point of touching my ring at least once now when we had sex.

"What are you thinking?" he asked as his tongue found the shell of my ear.

"About sex," I blurted out, which was the truth but maybe not quite what I meant.

Cy laughed at my honesty. "I fucking love you baby, you and your one track mind. I hadn't realised just how much I'd missed sex during office hours until you returned to work."

"I thought it was me with the one track mind," I laughed.

"Same track, same mind," he told me as the hand wrapped around my middle slipped beneath my loosely fitting yoga top and found my naked breast.

With care he began to caress the globe in his hand, weighing it almost before honing in on my hard and sensitive tip that was being stroked and circled, driving me crazy with desire.

A low moan was my response until the sound of the intercom sounded making Buddy bark and Cy move away.

"Bollocks," I muttered, returning my attention to dinner.

Cy laughed as he made his way to see who was calling.

****

"But why?" I asked as we ate dinner and another arrangement, virtually identical to the one I'd received for my birthday sat nearby, plaguing me.

"I don't know El. Not a clue, baby," Cy replied as he glared across at the offending flowers.

"It's so fucking cryptic," I hissed as I turned the card over in my hand and reread the message.

My Dearest Eloise,
Apologies for not contacting you sooner.

I will see you very soon…we'll talk.
Edward xx

"Edward does have a flair for the dramatic," Cy muttered. "But if he doesn't show up soon, I am going to put him on his ass when he does show."

"Arse," I corrected.

"Pushing?" Cy asked with a slightly raised eye brow.

"I dunno." I pouted. "I still feel pissed off."

Cy frowned as he moved his empty plate away. "Baby, I have no issue fucking your anger out of you if it's aimed at me, but do not bring anybody else into it or you won't be the only pissed off one here."

"Sorry. Maybe I just need to stop thinking about this. I mean why would he only contact me? Is he fucking with my head?" I asked and for the first time I wondered if my first impression of Edward had been an accurate one. Was he dangerous and my fear had been well placed?

"I dunno, he does sometimes yank people's chains but I honestly have no clue what the hell is going on with him right now. Oh, and you're not thinking, you're overthinking and you need to stop."

"I might just go and play with Buddy for a while, switch my mind off a little."

"Good girl, and then we can take a bath and have an early night, maybe try a little pushing," Cy said and whilst his face had a smile on it I could tell he was unhappy, with Edward, not me.

****

The following morning I was irritated, agitated, maybe both with a side order of restlessness thrown in. I had barely slept all night; once I had finished playing with Buddy I was still wound up and even after a shared bath with Cy I was still antsy, sufficiently so that the sex that had followed had ended up being a little like going to war. A battle that Cy ultimately won, but the ache in my limbs and the throb of possible bruising seemed fitting as war wounds this morning.

"Hey, you okay?" Cy asked as he entered my office space

from his own.

"Yes, thank you. Sorry, about last night," I began but was waved away.

"Baby, we've covered this already. Now, please, stop overthinking."

I nodded.

"Look, I have to go and see some people on the tenth floor, but later, maybe we can cut out early and take Buddy for a walk, grab some dinner and chill."

"I'd like that." I smiled, my agitation lifting, being replaced with love for Cy and some guilt that I had allowed my annoyance with Edward to linger. Clearly, I hadn't mastered the overthinking yet.

Cy had been gone for about an hour and I had calmed myself, even managing not to think about Edward when I felt someone approach. I looked up knowing someone was there but nothing could have prepared me to find Edward looking at me with something akin to sorrow.

"Eloise," he stated simply.

"Where the bloody hell have you been?" I shouted as I got to my feet. "Do you have any idea just how worried everyone has been? You disappeared, for weeks and then you sent flowers for my birthday and then nothing until yesterday when more flowers arrived and then you turn up here. How dare you, you selfish bastard," I screeched now.

"Mind your language," he chastened, almost ignoring the real content of my questions and comments. "I needed time to think, to straighten things out and I have."

"What? What the fuck does that even mean?" I asked earning myself a reproachful frown.

"Eloise, please. I want to explain, properly, but I need you to stop shouting and swearing."

I wanted to swear at him just to spite him, but I didn't, I nodded.

"Cy will be back soon and I'm sure he'll want to see you so will you have some tea or coffee while you wait?"

"Thank you," a relieved looking Edward replied.

Getting to my feet I heard my text alert sound so quickly

checked to find that I had a PPI claim worth £7000 that I had no knowledge of.

"Tea or coffee?" I asked a little less curt and turning towards the kitchen expected Edward to follow.

"Erm, would you mind if I wait here, in case Cy returns?"

"Whatever," I replied with a wave of my hand that was intended to be dismissive but came across as sulky.

I stomped and banged around the kitchen only to find I was still annoyed when I returned to my desk where Edward sat. Placing the tray down I sat and watched him, waited, but there was nothing, we simply stared at each other until the silence was killing me.

"Come on then. You said you wanted to explain to me. Michael has been worried about you, and Cy and Tia, everyone," I snapped impatiently, wanting to punch Edward and hug him at the same time.

"I needed to get away, things were getting out of hand. I have called Michael, we're meeting up soon. I wanted to see you first. I felt bad about how I left. It wasn't your fault and I know I let you down."

"So explain, please," I pleaded, gently, not wanting to add to Edward's expression that was already one of pain.

"Will you meet me, tonight, at my house? You and Cy, please?"

It was his turn to plead now and despite myself I wanted to agree to meet him.

"What the fuck are you doing here?" Cy's voice echoed around the room, startling both me and Edward. "Scratch that. Where the fuck have you been?"

"Eloise, think about tonight. Oh, I was sorry to hear about your father," Edward said already on his feet and turning to face Cy. "Shall we?" he asked with a hand gesturing towards Cy's office.

They walked away together and once at the threshold Cy turned and smiled at me.

"You okay, baby?"

"Yes, fine," I replied, although the truth was I had no clue how I was at that point.

****

"Do you have any clue why we're here?" I asked as Cy and I stood at Edward's door waiting for it to be opened. I had a strong suspicion he knew something of why we were here and why Edward had run away when he had. His behaviour since they'd met at the office and his random questions indicated something wasn't right.

"Yes, a wild goose chase I think, although, I should have said…" the door flew open to reveal Michael, not Edward was the interruption that threw both me and Cy.

"What are you doing here?" we asked in stereo.

"Not a clue," he replied as he gestured for us to walk in. "I don't know where Edward is either. I was invited and he left about five minutes after I arrived with the assurance he'd be back."

We sat in discomfort in Edward's lounge, awaiting his return in an ominous silence for about ten minutes.

"Sorry, I'm back," Edward called as he entered the lounge where we all sat. "Right, have we all got drinks?" he asked like the perfect host before sitting down in his armchair once he was happy we were all comfortable. "Eloise, I am unsure where to begin with what I have to say," he began as Cy interrupted.

"Edward, is there a reason Michael is here? I must admit I'm confused."

"I want to be honest with Eloise, about everything, including Michael."

"Edward, what are you doing?" Michael snapped angrily. No, not angrily, scared and nervous.

"Would somebody please tell me what is going on here?" I felt as scared and nervous as Michael appeared to be, especially as he had begun to pace the floor.

We all seemed to be watching my husband's pacing, but nothing was said for a couple of minutes until Edward seemed to tire of Michael's actions.

"For goodness sake Michael, sit down! This is your fault that we're in this position, sort of." He softened towards the end.

I watched as Michael did as he was told and sat in the same seat he'd occupied previously as Edward continued to speak,

"Thank you. She deserved better than she's had and all of you have done this to her, one way or another and it ends now."

I was becoming more clueless with every passing second, my glance moved between Edward and Michael and then as far as Cy who frowned.

"Edward, what is this, really?" Cy asked. He took my hand and pulled it into his.

"Sorry. Eloise, this is all a bit of a mess really love, but you deserve the truth. Starting with me."

I said nothing.

"Do you remember when you asked me whether I'd ever been in love?"

"Yes, one man, one woman."

"Exactly. I went to a bar. I was young and curious, plus a little confused. I had found women to be beautiful, but I had never found one attractive to me, sexually."

I still had no idea why he was telling me this, but I allowed him to continue.

"A man approached me. Older than me by a few years and he scared the hell out of me, but he awoke things in me, feelings."

"Edward," I began with confusion.

"No, no, please let me continue, it's important, you'll see. There was a club, frequented by younger people of all persuasions. I went there and I met a young man of the same age. He was as scared and confused as I was in so many ways, but together we found our way. He was my first male lover and the only man I have ever loved."

I nodded, he'd told me some of this before but the details seemed so important for him now.

"I quickly told my mother that I was in a relationship with another man and she was totally accepting of it, had been expecting it I think." Edward smiled with an arched brow. "I wish she was here. She'd do this properly. Anyway we fell in love and I was quite open about who and what I was, my lover not so much so. He was ashamed and embarrassed by us so pretended he was *normal*." Edward sneered as I glanced up at Cy who nervously twirled my engagement ring, something that didn't go unnoticed by Michael, although he said nothing. Cy looked as though he knew what was unfolding here. "I wanted him, all of him and I wanted the world to know but he got scared. What would people think? How would it look? We plodded on for another few months before I gave him an ultimatum. He chose appearances and we split.

"I don't understand," I told Edward who smiled.

"You will. We met again, a few years later and he was married and I was involved with someone, a woman, you remember my one woman? We decided that we would make up, be friends."

"Right."

"Anyway, more of her later. That's what happened we remained friends, but because he couldn't resolve what he was, his marriage failed and we had an affair. As soon as things became too serious for him, when he was at risk of his dirty secret being discovered he panicked and would push me away and take a new wife. We danced the same dance for years until my mother was dying and then I realised that I needed someone who would put my needs first, someone who wouldn't be embarrassed by me so I gave him the usual ultimatum and he chose decency and respectability, but he didn't have a wife to fall back on, so he procured one, didn't you, Michael?"

Chapter Forty-Four

"What? I don't understand," I cried, staring at Michael. "Michael," I prompted him hoping he'd say something, anything really.

"Tell her," Edward told Michael who was still staring at my engagement ring.

"You're engaged," he finally said.

"For fuck's sake!" Cy muttered beside me causing me to turn to him and on him.

"You knew?"

"No, no, not about this, of course not. At least not until Edward began his trip down memory lane."

"Michael," I called again, but he just sat in his chair looking between his own lap and my ring.

"We're not divorced yet…"

"Michael," I squealed. "Cut the crap! What the fuck is going on? What does Edward mean? You and him and us?" I cried.

"Eloise, please," Edward chipped in.

"Back off Edward," Cy warned as Michael began to speak.

"I'm sorry."

I glared at the man I had married and he was totally unrecognisable now. He was red with shame and embarrassment, but shame for himself and what he was, not for me or what he'd done. He was simpering and yielding as he looked across at Edward from under lowered eyes so I turned to the puppet master in this.

"What have I ever done to you for you to treat me this way,

huh? Or is it simple jealousy that six years ago he cast you aside, again?"

"No, not at all. I care about you, Eloise," Edward replied with only hurt detectable in his voice. "They've lied to you, all of them and I wanted you to know the truth, all of it."

"So you thought you'd tell me the truth did you?"

"I suppose I did. I wanted you to know, to believe that this," he gestured between me and Michael. "That it was flawed from day one, before you were even involved. You should never feel that you bear any responsibility for the mess it was or became."

"Does this make any sense to you?" I asked Cy who shrugged initially.

"Kind of, the sentiment."

I nodded and then turning to Edward I conceded that he had meant me no ill in this revelation. The revelation that what though, that my husband was gay or bi-sexual, that his lack of interest in me was down to my gender?

"Shit!" I leapt to my feet. "It wasn't me. Your lack of interest in me, it really was you," I shouted in Michael's face.

"El, love, I didn't know what to do. I needed to gain some balance in my life after Edward…"

"Are you two having an affair, again? Oh my good lord, it was you. The lover. That's why you were in and out of Michael's life and why we never met until…" I turned back to Edward as all the pieces began to fall into place. "Cy, let's go," I cried, already heading to the door where I waited for Cy to catch up with me.

"Baby, you might want to wait," Cy said as I reached for the door handle.

"For what?" I asked feeling all of my mixed emotions about to be turned on Cy as I threw the door open.

"El, what on earth is going on?"

I looked at the space the door had occupied until a split second before and was more than a little startled to find Susan standing there.

"Susan?" I enquired with a confused frown.

I heard Cy hiss out an increasingly common, "For fuck's sake!"

"As requested," Susan replied, ignoring Cy's curse.

"Requested?"

She looked as confused as me, maybe more so. "You text earlier, this address and the need to meet," she replied.

Clearly I hadn't, but how?

"You," I accused turning to Edward. "In the office, you sent the message to Susan, but why?"

I was becoming dizzy with all of these twists and turns the evening was taking.

"You need to hear the rest Eloise, about my lady love," Edward said, his voice now joining us in the hall with a silent Michael skulking further behind. "And here she is, Sassy."

Looking at Edward I wondered what the hell he was talking about, but when I looked back at Susan she was as white as a sheet. Ashen, as though she was about to pass out.

"Edward!" Cy warned angrily. "Do not do this, not like this. Please, think of El," he added with some kind of appeal in his voice that appeared to reach the other man as he addressed me and then Cy.

"Eloise, please forgive me. I should never have done this, not like this. I'm sorry." He stepped closer and reached in to give me a gentle kiss on the cheek that I stiffened beneath. "Cy, take her home."

"I don't understand," I protested as Cy wrapped an arm around me and prepared to guide me around my sister who looked as though she was about to vomit. She was shaking like a leaf, as if she was in actual, medical shock.

"Edward," Susan whispered softly, with loving familiarity I'd barely seen before and never outside of our family. As if nobody else was there, like she couldn't see anyone else in the crowded hallway. She continued to speak. "I don't understand. How do you, why, what?" She began to stammer aimlessly and then her face hardened as she fixed Edward with a colder stare. "No, no! You can't, she doesn't even…this is between us."

"As you wish," Edward responded. "For now."

****

Cy bundled me out and we got all the way home before we spoke.

"What do you know about that whole fucked up mess back there?" I asked once Buddy was settled after the excitement of us returning home.

"He told me there were things he'd found out, about you and I didn't know about Michael and him, although I'd suspected a couple of times over the years and then brushed it off when it seemed I was wrong."

"What were you going to tell me when we got to Edward's house?" I asked thinking he'd looked guilty and had appeared to be about to confess to something.

"Shit, baby. This is awkward and I don't want to hurt you."

"Tell me, please."

"This afternoon he told me that he'd known Susan, he called her Sassy. He knew her years ago, he loved her."

"She was the only woman he's ever known?"

Cy nodded. "He loved her, El. She broke his heart and he never saw her again until he caught sight of her at the hospital that day."

"Which is what freaked him out," I stated rather than asked. "Shit, after all those years. Did he know about her and Michael, their connection, if not mine to Susan?"

"No, not a clue. Michael seems to have kept his relationships in very separate compartments, except for his family and closest friends who most likely never suspected anything else about them."

I nodded. This was why people had told me that Michael was never happy, that he'd loved me as much as he could, in his own way. All of those words and phrases were swimming around my head as I tried to make sense of everything.

"I had no idea Susan would be there tonight," Cy said. "Look, there's more."

"More?"

"Mmm. Edward. Shit, I have no clue how to tell you this. He thinks he's your father."

I stared wildly at Cy's words. The wild outrageousness of them.

"He can't be, just because he knew Susan. My mum wouldn't...she loved my dad... they were devoted. No, he's wrong," I protested. Edward was actually deluded if he thought there was any possibility of him being, well, anything biological to me.

"Baby, that's not what he was saying. Shit, look I am just going to say it. He thinks, is certain he's your father and that Susan is your mother."

I allowed Cy's words, Edward's thoughts to resonate and register in my mind. He was wrong, he had to be. I was Eloise Ross, youngest daughter of Jeremy and Stella Ross. I was an accidental baby, a happy accident, a mistake, whichever phrase you wanted to use, but there was no disputing my parentage, there couldn't be.

Edward was deluded, mentally ill maybe. He had known Susan, loved her and then when it had ended, he had managed to make it something else, something more. I hadn't even begun to process my gay husband having a lover who believed he was my father. That wasn't a priority right now, especially as I had no clue how to deal with that one.

My vision was beginning to blur and my hearing was muffled. Cy was talking to me, he was crouching before me. Nausea and fatigue washed over me, this was shock, had to be and who wouldn't be shocked when faced with such ridiculous claims.

"Baby, please," Cy's voice was getting farther and farther away like he was travelling in the opposite direction, in a tunnel.

I couldn't speak, words wouldn't form, and actual thoughts were struggling to make sense in my mind so actual words leaving my mouth were unlikely. Pushing up, I attempted to get to my feet only to find the world going black and then nothing, darkness, silence and emptiness.

****

Light began to infiltrate my eyes as I slowly opened them and took in my surroundings, Cy's lounge. Specifically the sofa, my head propped up on his lap and Buddy lying at me feet as I came to.

"Hey," Cy whispered as he gently stroked my hair.

Instinctively, I tried to leap up but was prevented from moving too quickly by Cy who was pulling me back down a little.

"Take it easy. You had a panic attack or something and fainted I think, which is not that surprising."

"Sorry." I sat up so that my legs that I was hugging were pulled in tight to my body. "It can't be true, can it?" I asked and for the first time considered the possibility even though it made no sense.

One look at Cy's face told me that he and I were on very different pages on the topic because he very clearly believed Edward could be and probably was my father.

"I called my parents. I asked them about Edward around the time you would have been conceived. My mother met Susan, a couple of times. Only in passing but didn't doubt that they were serious."

"You mean shagging when you say serious?" I asked feeling only anger now.

"No, not really, but serious as in love and planning a future at some point I think."

"Go on."

"With hindsight my mom could see the strong resemblance you have to Susan and Eloise, Edward's mother. Your sist... moth...Susan, she broke Edward's heart. Mom said he was a different man after she left him, broken."

"She lied about her age," I told Cy, suddenly replacing the image I'd created for Edward's lost love with one of Susan and acknowledged we were physically similar, very.

"Mom said she was young."

"She lied to him. He told me, her dad," the words caught in my throat. Her dad, my dad, except all indications were that he was hers, not mine. "He confronted Edward about her age and when he in turn confronted her, she admitted it. He was angry and hurt that she'd lied to him."

"Dad said he'd always suspected that there was something more between Edward and Michael, but it was only ever a suspicion."

I nodded, still not ready to look too closely at Michael and Edward. Susan and Edward were enough to be going on with at the moment.

Cy went to let Buddy out into the garden a short time later and that is when I seized the opportunity to go upstairs to one of Cy's spare rooms where my dad's, Jezza's things were being stored, his papers. Surely there'd be something there.

I'd barely opened the first box of things when a breathless Cy came up behind me in my position sitting on the floor cross legged sifting through papers.

"You scared the shit out of me!"

"Sorry." I smiled weakly as I turned to him. "I just thought there'd be something in here."

"Okay," he said as he took a place next to me and began to work through some papers too.

We worked meticulously for about half an hour when Cy said, "Baby Ross."

I turned to see him holding up the tag off my hospital cot when I was born. Taking it from him I was disappointed that the mother's name was simply S. Ross, but was that Susan or Stella? I put it to one side and added the matching wrist tag and a few baby photos, some with Susan who did look tired enough that she might have just given birth and some with my mum, with Stella who didn't look as though she'd had a baby for some time. There were no photos of me with my siblings or my dad.

"Where's your birth certificate?" Cy asked as he emptied another box.

"I don't know." I shrugged. "If I needed it for anything Dad sorted it and then Susan, she even sent off my passport so I've never needed it."

The look of suspicion on Cy's face was matched by my own feelings when I heard those words out loud. Why hadn't that ever seemed suspicious to me? Because I had trusted them, both of them, all of them.

"Would Michael have known?"

"I don't think so. Susan had been sorting his stuff out for so long he wouldn't have thought anything of it I don't think," I replied thinking that of all the things Michael had been complicit in this wasn't one of them, of that I was sure. "I don't even know what I'm looking for here." I sighed as I chanced upon a few more photographs and in the middle of them was a little white notelet with a hospital logo on the front. I opened it and smiled at the grainy image of me in the womb.

"Baby's first photo." I smiled as I moved closer to Cy so that he could see it.

"You?" he asked.

"Mmm, judging by the date," I confirmed and that is when I saw it, in the top corner, the patient's name. "Fuck, it's her, Susan Ross," I cried. "Susan is my mother which means…"

"Edward is your father."

****

For the next three weeks I managed to avoid Susan and Edward. I refused to speak to them or see them. They were on the banned list at the office so they couldn't get past security meaning I was safe. Cy kept me safe. I knew that he would rather I had faced them and somehow dealt with it but I had no clue how to even begin that, so I avoided. They had both resorted to texting me a couple of times a day, really just reaching out and keeping the door open for me. I knew that's what they were doing with their actions and yet in my bitterly confused state I chose to view it as simply fucking with my head and trying to manipulate me.

Michael had been in touch and I had actually seen him. I kind of understood his position, the need for perfection and being perceived in the required way, which was his way, the way he'd been brought up. He had tried to do the right thing, all of his life and had been sad, alone, often unloved and lonely. Now, having been outed to me by Edward, he seemed happier, as if he no longer cared, or maybe he just realised that nobody else cared whether he was gay or straight, if he was married or divorced and for that I was thankful, to Edward I supposed. Thankful that Michael might experience real love as it should be felt. I had avoided discussing him and Edward, or Susan, however he had intimated that he and Edward had found some sort of resolution to things and that Susan was in both of their lives, but I didn't pursue what that meant. He even went so far as to wish me well, me and Cy and expressed a desire to be friends, eventually. It turned out I had been correct in my assumption that he hadn't known or even suspected of any connection between Edward and Susan, never mind my true parentage. Their common connection to him was simply a coincidence. I chose to draw that conversation to a close when I realised that my soon to be ex-husband had slept with both my mother and my father.

Christopher was someone else who had eventually made contact, with Cy, pleading for help, help that Cy had provided in the form of finding a rehab facility in England. One Christopher wanted to go to, one of his choosing. I had actually loved Cy a little more when he had bent over backwards to help his brother, despite everything he'd done. That action along with his handling of their parents, Elizabeth more than Denny, calming them, helping them to accept Chris' decision, accept and respect it. Elizabeth seemed to have gotten over her objections to my relationship with Cy. I had no clue why, but when she'd visited, to see Chris, she had been warm and kind. She'd even gone as far as to thank me for making Cy happy. Maybe Edward had been right that she would come round when she saw how much we loved each other. She even invited me for next Thanksgiving.

When I didn't think about the messed up heritage I had yet to accept, I was happy, happier than I had dared to dream of. I had never understood soul mates but now I got it; Cy was my other half, together we were one and with Buddy we had our own family unit that made my life worth living, and when Lulu joined us it made me dare to picture an actual future with babies, a happily ever after with my Prince Charming, just like when I was a little girl.

Epilogue

Three Years Later

My parents, that still felt and sounded weird after having one set of parents for so long only to get a second set, the real set I supposed, Edward and Susan who were sitting in the lounge, my lounge. Something I hadn't always believed was a possibility. But once I'd given them the opportunity, they'd explained what had happened.

Susan had lied about her age to Edward and when she'd come home pregnant my dad, Jezza, had flipped. He'd found out who Edward was and sought him out to confront him. He told Edward Susan's true age and then put him on his arse. He never even hinted at a baby, me. As Edward had once told me, he had seen Susan and confronted her about her lies, something he'd found unforgivable. Believing that Edward would and could never want her, not really, not long term, Susan, pregnant and alone had agreed that she would give me up to her own parents and she could then continue with her own life and make something of herself. I couldn't fault their motives, any of them, but I remained resolute that they should have been honest, with me if not with Edward.

So many of Jezza's rants and comments made sense now. He had been confused and as such I had assumed his words were incoherent mutterings when in truth they were lucid memories and feelings from a time I had never known.

I took in the scene before me and it was odd to say the least. Along with Susan and Edward there was Michael who sat cradling my baby while Buddy lay at his feet, keeping guard. We had been through so much to get to this point, but here we were, all of us.

The sound of breaking pottery made me jump and my daughter who had been contentedly sleeping in Michael's arms cry.

"Mommy," cried my son who at almost two and a half was rushing towards me with a horrified expression. "Daddy broke it," he told me as I scooped him up into my arms and kissed him as Lulu appeared behind him.

"He kind of did," Lulu confirmed. "Daddy wants Sam to play baseball," she explained with an arch of her brow that made me smile.

"Baby, we might need a new planter outside, it kind of broke," Cy said as he appeared behind the children.

I had intended to chastise my husband but as I turned to look at him I began to fully appreciate him in a plain white t-shirt and khaki shorts and decided a broken planter was a small price to pay, for this, for my life.

"Baseball?" I asked him.

"Maybe," he replied looking at Lulu and then across at Sam who was yawning and rubbing his eyes. "We really need to work on team spirit with Daddy," he told them as he moved across to Michael where he retrieved a crying Elsa from Michael's arms.

"We should probably put these two down for an hour," I told our guests.

"Of course, carry on," Edward smiled as he called to Lulu who he was asking about school.

Closing the nursery door behind us I turned to see a smiling Cy watching me as I carefully put Sam into his bed while he nursed our daughter who was already falling back to sleep. God he was gorgeous anytime, but when he was being the gentle father that he was to our children he made gorgeous a totally inadequate adjective. The sight of my husband, the living image of masculinity and virility cradling a baby, the representation of innocence and vulnerability really did do strange things to me, hormonal things. I'd been permanently one word short of suggesting adding another baby to our family since our daughter had arrived only three months before. I knew that I'd be pregnant again in the next six months. We'd begun trying to conceive Elsa just after Sam's first birthday but now we had two, three counting Lulu, another one would be a doddle.

He placed Elsa in her cot before we exited the room and took a break from our guests by going into our own bedroom via the light and brightly decorated landing area that had once been a standing joke between us.

"Missing the old interior, Mrs Miller?" Cy asked as our door closed softly.

I loved being Mrs Miller. I had never embraced my previous married name the way I had Cy's. Sometimes I actually forgot that this wasn't my first marriage, my only marriage.

"Not really. That wall and carpet were unforgiving on my arse and knees."

"Ass," he corrected making me smile at that thing we'd shared from the beginning.

"How weird is this? Our, my family? Can you imagine having to explain this to our kids? Lulu is already beginning to question how Edward can be my dad when I had another dad, and then she also wants to know just how my sister can be my mum. She hasn't yet figured that my parents are in a polyamorous relationship with my ex-husband, but I am sure that's going to come eventually."

I was venting slightly, I knew that, but this was still slightly chaotic. I hadn't actually seen Edward or Susan until my divorce had become final and Cy and I had set a wedding date, so whilst the relationships were established the situation was still quite new.

I was at risk of ranting rather than venting as I continued, "And when I return to work again, both of the kids will be with Susan for a couple of days a week." I gasped as I considered her offer to provide some help with childcare. "And they'll pick up on it. How will we explain it to them? That the people I call mum and dad are dead, yet their grandparents are alive and kicking and living happily with Uncle Michael who used to be my husband like Daddy is?"

"Ssh, we've got this," Cy soothed as he pulled me closer,

against his chest that was now naked. I'd been so wrapped up in my own ramblings that I'd missed him removing his t-shirt, revealing the tattoo I loved so much. The extended tattoo that now had two more eyes woven into it, Sam's and Elsa's and the date of our wedding. I smiled as I thought of Lulu's comment when we'd first spent time together about *Daddy having a tattoo for me*, which he had. "You're overthinking, baby," he told me as he stroked my hair and then took a step back to look down at me. "We'll make the kids understand, everything, including the fact that Uncle Michael was never ever Mommy's husband like Daddy is," he said with slight frown before smiling again as he continued. "It's unconventional, but it's okay. It works for them. This is our life, all of us together, our family and it's perfect."

I nodded, he was right. It worked for them and so long as we were okay with their choices there was no reason to think that our children wouldn't be and yes, this was our family. The family I had craved, dreamt of but rarely dared to believe I might have, but I did. I had everything I could ever want because of Cy, my husband.

"Thank you," I whispered.

"Hey, I don't need your gratitude. I made a deal with Jezza," he revealed, startling me slightly.

"What?" I asked as he gazed down at me with nothing but love and care.

"We struck a deal. That I would do nothing but make you happy, keep you safe and love you like you always deserved to be," he told me, causing a mist of happy tears to cloud my eyes.

Maybe my life was a movie now, a fairytale and this, well, this really was my happily ever after.

THE END

Keep reading for a sneak peek at Elle M Thomas' latest release, Revealing His Prize.

About Elle M Thomas

Elle M Thomas was born in the north of England and raised near Birmingham, UK where she still lives with her family. She works in local education and writes in her spare time with dreams of becoming a full-time writer.

Whilst still at school, and with a love of writing slightly risqué tales of love and romance one of her teachers told her she could be the next Harrold Robins. Elle didn't act on those words for many years. In February 2017, with her first book completed and a dozen others unfinished, she finally took the plunge and self-published the steamy romance, Disaster-in-Waiting as an e-book.

Elle describes her books as stories filled with chemistry, sensuality, love and sex that she always wanted to read and her characters as three dimensional and flawed.

You can keep up to date with all things Elle M Thomas on social media here:

Twitter – Elle M Thomas Author - @ellemthomas24

Facebook – Elle M Thomas and Elle's Belles

Instagram – @authorellemthomas

Goodreads – Elle M. Thomas

Have you read Revealing His Prize by Elle M Thomas?

Chapter One

"Reece," screamed Frankie. "Come and help me choose what the hell I am going to wear tonight."

"That is a little stereotypical of you, relying on your gorgeously stylish gay best friend to choose your outfit!" Reece grinned, totally ignoring Frankie standing in just a pair of nude satin pants. "Right, are we going for professional, artistic or smoking hot?" asked Reece with a cheeky grin that was obscured by the nylon sleeve of the kaftan he stood behind in Frankie's wardrobe.

"You really are a dick, but I love you and you dress me far better than I could ever dress myself, but all of the above. I need to appear professional and artistic if I am being viewed as the woman to bring this building to life and smoking hot is good, just in case." She giggled nervously. "But not too hot, I don't want to draw attention to myself."

"You are beautiful and would look great in a refuse sack, but I thought you had sworn off men?" Reece began flicking through the dozens of dresses Frankie had, most of them cast offs from Anna.

"I am, but a little teasing could be fun, or maybe not," sighed Frankie feeling anxious and doubtful again at the thought of the opposite sex, especially teasing them.

"Hey, don't get yourself down, not about that arse, Nate. He really isn't worth it and was never good enough for you. You need to see that and get back on the horse."

"Or not! Maybe you could just find me a pair of sweats and a sweatshirt and we could eat ice-cream and drink cheap wine."

"No chance. You have to go tonight and meet with the important man who has commissioned you to sell his new building to the world." Reece threw the dress of his choosing towards her. "You have fabulous boobs babe so don't even consider a bra or tape tonight."

"Come with me," Frankie pleaded, suddenly nervous again.

"I thought Anna was going with you," sighed Reece, desperate to say no.

"She said she'd meet me there, but she is flaky at the best of times, especially if Shawn miraculously becomes available to shag her. Please, Reece, for me, I'll love you forever," she begged with a smile at his melting resolve.

"God, I hate how weak you make me. It's a good job we both like dicks or we would be a couple and I would be seriously fucking whipped. If this thing tonight is dull, I am going to kick your arse all over the mats at krav maga tomorrow!"

Laughing, Frankie looked down at the cocktail dress Reece had selected and frowned, wondering how to accessorise. "Reece," she called just as his back disappeared from her view, indicating he was going to change into something suitable to be her plus one.

"Silver, strappy, T-bar sandals and silver dangly earrings only," he called back, making her laugh louder.

"You're that predictable, Nolan," she told her own reflection as she slipped the dress over her head and smoothed it down.

****

Reece really did have a great eye for what suited her, Frankie thought as she looked at the turquoise chiffon dress. It revealed her neck and shoulders courtesy of the silver, metal ring that held the fabric around her neck before the gathered, ruched fabric encased her breasts while an embroidered silver band pulled the dress in, emphasising her more than ample chest, then finally the loose fabric fell flatteringly in a full skirt finishing just above her knee.

Grabbing the silver shoes Reece had recommended she slipped them on and was glad of her pedicure the previous day. Her bright red nails illuminated the twisted, leather robe design across her toes before the same design made up the T-bar style and then continued around her ankle to where the buckle fastened on her ankle.

Finally, the dangly, shiny earrings were added, her natural loose curls were teased and her look was complete. Next to no make-up was required, courtesy of her flawless skin. Just a little natural gloss, a hint of bluey-green eye shadow and mascara was enough to emphasise her high cheekbones, deep brown eyes and rich chocolate brown hair. She found a silver clutch and threw her phone, purse and keys in.

"Done," she called as she exited her bedroom to find Reece wearing a black dinner jacket, dress trousers and the whitest shirt she had ever seen.

He really was one of the most handsome men she had ever known, and he was right that they would have been a couple, a wonderful couple, had he not been gay. With her heels on, she was almost the same height as Reece's six feet and her legs looked like they went on forever.

"If you can't pull looking like that, then there is something horribly wrong with the heterosexual men of this world," smiled Reece leaning in to place a single kiss on Frankie's cheek. "Invitation?" he asked as she took his arm.

"Oh bollocks!" she cried, running back towards her room for the essential invitation that would act as their entrance.

"You really do have a foul mouth, Frankie."

"I'd have preferred filthy to foul but hey ho," she grinned mischievously as she returned a second later with the exquisite cream card with black writing.

"Definitely time for you to get back on the horse!" he grinned, tugging her arm through his.

****

The cab was crawling in traffic just a couple of streets away from their destination when Frankie looked down at the invitation that she was nervously fingering in her lap.

"You okay?" asked Reece.

"Mmm, nervous I suppose, this is huge for me. I have deliberately stuck to small, less prominent projects, then I entered this stupid fucking competition to promote Mallory fucking Ivory Tower to the world! Come and have an office in one of the most expensive office blocks in the world, photos and paintings by Francesca stupid Nolan. What have I done Reece? What if someone recognises me? This is huge in business circles, this building. God, I feel sick!" announced Frankie as she leapt from the cab that had stopped at traffic lights just before the building.

She was on the verge of hyperventilating by the time Reece's reassuring arm made its way around her shoulders.

"And breathe babe," he told her, pulling her against his firm body.

A tall, dark man pushed past them with a token, 'sorry' but when he looked back Frankie felt her whole body shudder as he stared at her for a split second. His nearly black hair was in complete contrast to his bright blue eyes that seemed to look through her, penetrating her soul. She was sure that he had somehow seen her for who and what she was, and despite her state of panic, he'd managed to arouse her and calm her in just one look. Maybe Reece was right and she did need to get back on the horse, or at least find a suitable mount.

"I'm okay," Frankie announced, suddenly pulling back from her friend. "Let's walk the last bit." Taking Reece's hand in hers, they then strode on towards Mallory fucking Ivory Tower as she'd called it in the cab, knowing it was actually called Mallory City Scene.

The degree of security at the door shocked her despite knowing how prestigious and expensive this building and its office space was. Her bag was checked, a security detector was run across her body, and at one point she thought they were going to frisk her. The I.D. she and Reece provided was scrutinised, their names were radioed through to the top floor, and just as they thought they'd jumped through all of the hoops necessary, Anna arrived; so they had to go through the same scrutiny again after Frankie lied about her other housemate, introducing her as her assistant to secure her own entry with two plus ones.

Exiting the lift on the fortieth floor, Frankie grabbed a glass of champagne as a waitress passed by.

"Can I be of assistance?" came a well-spoken voice from behind her, making her jump.

"I don't think so," replied Frankie, confused, as she faced the willowy blonde woman before her with a clip board.

"You are?" she asked with a red lipped pout rather than a smile.

"Sorry, Frankie Nolan," she replied realising there was still more security to get through.

"The artist, competition winner," she suddenly smiled. "This way please, your friends can enter the bar and you'll re-join them shortly. Sorry to bamboozle you as soon as you've arrived, but it's very busy tonight and the schedule is tight," she told Frankie before rushing her through to a smaller room where a couple of dozen other people were gathered.

The blonde woman exited, but not before speaking to a group of suited men then gesturing towards Frankie made her feel even worse than she had at the roadside.

A deep voice that sounded how she imagined the richest and smoothest chocolate might sound, asked her, "Are you okay?"

Preparing to turn, she smiled, hoping that the image wouldn't be a let-down, but imagined that it probably would be. She prepared herself to come face to face with a stocky businessman in his mid to late fifties, possibly perspiring due to the sweltering heat of this building, or maybe that was just her.

"Fine, thank you," she said with her best sincere smile

painted on. She turned and gasped. Yes, she actually gasped at the sight of the man before her, well his chest at least. The man who was obviously laughing at her gasp.

"You look a little the worse for wear," he grinned as he gestured down at her empty glass.

"What? No, I am not drunk, it's my first one in months. I have a tendency to be melancholy in drink at the moment, so I'm avoiding it. Well, my friends are banning me really," she told him, blabbering on, making him smile wryly with an arched brow. God, it was him, the tall, dark man with the eyes and the look from around the corner. "You saw me earlier, you looked at me," she said with an almost accusatory tone.

"I did?" he asked. His nonchalance disappointing her that he'd forgotten, or not remembered, that he hadn't felt what she'd felt. "Are you okay? You look a little flustered, the terrace is open," he said, gesturing towards the open door.

"Yeah, that might be for the best. If this whole thing is as bad an idea as I think it might be, I can always throw myself off the side of the building," she said seriously, already striding outdoors followed by her companion.

****

Once outside in the cold air, Frankie took a deep calming breath, but as her companion reached her side, the heat from indoors was back, meaning it was him. He was making her hot, and wet, she suddenly realised, forcing her to clench her thighs together tightly. What was it with this man? He was handsome, beautiful and had a wonderful physique, big and muscular and those eyes, she could get lost in those with very little encouragement. Maybe as she ran her fingers through his hair, pulling it gently, then harder to bring his lips to hers.

"Fuck!" she cried at her thoughts, and only when he appeared to choke on his water did she realise she'd said it out loud.

"Maybe we should trade names first," he laughed.

Embarrassed and flustered she turned to face him again, immediately regretting it when his eyes flashed to her breasts, where her nipples had pulled into tight points, and her lack of a bra did nothing to conceal them.

"It's, erm cold isn't it?" she asked and flushed further as his smile suggested that he knew she was not cold, that her nipples had nothing to do with her temperature and everything to do with him and how he made her feel.

"Here," he said slipping his jacket off to put it around her shoulders. His body warmth still resonated from the fabric and his smell lingered. The smell was woody, citrus and him, God he smelt good, better than good and his aroma being so close was doing nothing to calm her.

"So, I assume you have a name." He had little expression as he studied her.

"Frankie, Frankie Nolan."

"Frankie Nolan?" he asked, but not of her she didn't think, he seemed to be musing over it.

"Is that a problem?"

"What? No, I just wasn't expecting a man's name for someone so beautiful and so obviously a woman." He frowned at himself, seemingly annoyed.

Her colour deepened several shades at his words.

"Francesca," she told him, desperate to gain his approval, even if it was only for her name.

"That's much better." He smiled. "You're the artist?" he asked, but again his question was self-assured enough that she knew he knew she was.

"Unfortunately," she replied, making him frown again. It was a look that didn't suit him and one she wanted to replace with a happier one, the amused look that made her melt. The one that made him look younger and carefree, although she suspected he was probably not much over thirty, but that might put him ten years older than her.

"You didn't want to win the competition?" he asked, obviously irritated and confused. A twitching muscle in his cheek confirmed his annoyance.

With a sigh, she attempted to explain. "I entered it on a whim. I have a friend, Anna, and she is very encouraging; and it's hard to succeed within art circles without some luck or money, and I'm usually short on both. She, Anna, was seeing a guy who ran a small, exclusive gallery who liked some of my work, but wouldn't exhibit me unless I could offset the costs if it went tits up. He told Anna about the competition to put together the portfolio using various media for this place and she told me. I filled out the application and while I poured another glass of wine and decided I wouldn't submit it, Anna and Reece sent it online and here I am."

"I see, well congratulations," he said with a smile, then allowed his tongue to leave his mouth to lick his bottom lip, almost causing another gasp to escape her lips.

Her eyes were glued to his tongue and lips, desperate to feel them, taste them, to have them running all over her body. She really needed to find someone soon if she was going to keep having these thoughts, these unusual and unwelcome thoughts. Either that or get a new vibrator, one that wasn't so noisy that it kept Anna and Reece up.

"Who's Reece?" he suddenly asked.

"We live together." Her response seemed to cause a further frown along with the twitching muscle thing again. He might be gorgeous, but was a bit of a moody sod she decided.

"What about you? Do you have a name?" she asked, thinking that he hadn't reciprocated with a name.

"Of course, Adam, but you can call me anything you like," he said sounding far cheesier than a man who looked this gorgeous should, with his perfect dark hair pushed into a waxed messy style, those eyes framed by the dark lashes, the high cheek bones, the strong square jaw and those straight lips that just begged to be kissed.

They both laughed at his line and her heart lurched at just how much more gorgeous this man managed to look.

"Pleased to meet you, Adam." She smiled. "Do you know Mallory? His people called me and said he'd be here to meet me."

"I do know him, but you don't seem so keen on meeting him."

"I hate business men. They're notoriously boring. Well, the ones I've met are and I imagine he has no artistic interest in this project, it's probably something he got roped into. I can see him now, fifty- five, balding, middle-age spread with an overindulged wife and kids at home while he uses his position and money to address his erectile dysfunction with a combination of little blue pills and high-class hookers. Am I close?" she asked, wondering why she had allowed all of those preconceived, prejudiced images of a very rich and influential business man to spill out, especially as Adam had admitted to knowing him. Shit! What if he was a friend, his son? He was obviously influential himself or he wouldn't be in this smaller group of people.

"Adam," called a voice from behind him. "We're ready."

"Cool," he called to the voice before turning back to Frankie. "Francesca, I have a couple of things to do, but we should pick this up later. In fact, let me leave you with a question to ponder."

Frankie removed Adam's jacket from around her and felt saddened to be losing his heat and smell but nodded at his suggestion. He leaned in as he accepted his jacket, so close that his mouth almost touched her ear, his breath making every nerve ending in her body tingle, and when he placed a hand on her bare shoulder, she shuddered as her heart rate quickened and her chest heaved.

The words that followed made her gasp, again, more breathlessly though, because of their shock value, but also because she was desperate to know the answer.

"Think about it. Catch ya later." He left her standing alone, open mouthed, breathless, aroused and scared shitless as she realised that he may be the horse she should get on, but she had never met anyone like him before, anyone to have made her feel like he just had. At that moment, she knew if she climbed on board that particular mount, she might never get off, not in one piece anyway.

****

She returned inside and found Adam had disappeared so chatted politely to a couple of other people before everyone was escorted back into the main reception for dinner, where speeches and publicity shots would be taken, and the willowy blonde lady had assured Frankie that she would meet Mr Mallory.

It only took a couple of minutes to find Anna and Reece

enjoying the free bar and judging by their merry state, she'd been gone quite some time. Taking her seat for dinner with her friends, Frankie suddenly wished she'd come alone, alone enough that she could think about Adam's question and possibly even answer it.

Dinner came and went in the huge space that was going to be an open office with views to die for across the city and possibly one of the most expensive office spaces in the world. Everyone's attention was called as a small, temporary stage became central to proceedings. Some kind of M.C. began rambling about the vision, the building, the future, the mind and genius of the head of Mallory, the name, the brand, the man, Adam Mallory.

Frankie's eyes were glued to the stage as Mr Mallory, the 'man with no artistic interest in this project, fifty-five, balding, middle-age spread with an overindulged wife and kids at home while he used his position and money to address his erectile dysfunction with a combination of little blue pills and high-class hookers' took centre stage and filled it beautifully. It was Adam, Mr Mallory was Adam, her Adam!